REMEDY
By
Margaret Afseth

ISBN: 978-09921638-0-8

This book is dedicated to my brother Ron, my technical support; and to my daughter Kathy, my ever-present helper, and encouragement. Thanks both of you for always being there for me.

TABLE OF CONTENTS

Prologue:

The meteor shower broke into Earth's atmosphere against a midnight sky. Few on the planet even saw it. The unit was small...only consisting of twenty-one streaks of light, and...all landed at the same location.

****

"What are your plans?" asked the female, leaning in to view the blueprints on the small stone table.

"I thought, since we are presently expanding three single units to house new pairs, we might as well add a second passage just behind the single female quarters. The two hallways would converge at a fork, here." The mason pointed to a spot on the diagram in front of them. "The logistics should be simple. I can annex each single female unit, and those in pair housing also, for those appointed to them, then create a huge dorm for the extra humans. It would resemble the male single quarters."

"How many compartments will be in it? We should have no need for fourteen, as with our males."

"I agree; we need no more than six."

"Would we have room to make a recreational common area for the humans, one much like our own, without the feature wall of course?"

"I can do it, if you wish it?"

She agreed, then sat back to consider. "What of the 'Keepers'?"

A second male answered. "The barriers 'Keepers' are programmed to hold the humans within the compound boundaries, so that none may inadvertently wander out of our safety zone."

"Good. Remember, human needs will differ from ours. Need I remind you, they possess no powers…much as when we were dormant? I fear we may have forgotten what that is like."

"I have prepared for that also. A 'Keeper' will be assigned to each human, programmed specifically to the individual, much like those we use in our quarters in sleep time, only these will be with them at all times. They will not be aware of their presence…at least at first, as the units will be on invisible mode unless called upon. Oh yes, and certain familiar foods and necessities will be readily available."

"We will still keep appointed guardians on our own single females, will we not?" questioned the third male present.

"Of course, that is a given…for our safety," she agreed. "We must all use exceptional restraint while these humans live among us. Their privacy is of utmost importance. That means you are not to monitor their inner thoughts, unless I choose otherwise. At all times, our minds remain closed to their memories. No probing! That will handicap us some, but I believe it is necessary."

"Is there a punishment for breaking this rule?" queried one male.

"I will take each separate incident into consideration."

He nodded in agreement.

"I believe it will also be easier for the humans if we spoke aloud, unless of course circumstances deem other wise. When you think of it, it is rather rude to be carrying on a silent communication in their presence when they can not hear...similar to someone speaking a different language, and conversing in it, when one among them failed to understand. See that all our people are aware of this new ruling."

One of the men frowned, then his face deadpan, he jokingly commented, "I believe I have forgotten how to speak verbally."

Even the Lady chuckled at that.

"Need I remind you gentlemen?" the female cautioned quietly. "There is to be no sexual contact."

The males nodded soberly.

"Now," asked the Lady. "What of the banquet?"

"That should be no problem," a fourth male declared. "The tables were made for partner places. The humans will simply occupy the extra settings."

"Very well." She turned again to the mason. "How soon until we are ready?"

"Give me another week, and I should have enough set up to begin."

"Then we are agreed? We will proceed in two weeks time?"

Approval was unanimous.

CHAPTER 1

It was pouring rain; the roads were slippery. Chantel could not distinguish the sky from the pavement in this pitch-blackness; the sheets of water were that dense.

Where is the horizon? Where am I supposed to turn?

And the streetlights were no help. They blinded her reflecting off the wet asphalt like that.

Suddenly, the truck appeared from nowhere. The resounding tearing impact drove her back to consciousness, trembling and screaming.

It was only a dream!

****

Her hand still shaking, Chantel reached for the switch on the bedside lamp, flooding the sparse room with light.

My accident was over twenty-five years ago. Why are my nightmares back again?

Throwing off the covers, Chantel moved her atrophied legs over the edge of the bed, and sat up. Reaching for her wheelchair, she pulled it closer, shifted and lifted using her arms, transferring to the conveyance, then buckled herself in.

She rolled to the window. The night sky was as dark as it had been that night. The rain had let up, but static lightning ripped at the far away blackness time after time. The thunder was distant. That meant the storm was retreating.

Why is the crash back in my dreams? I thought I had conquered that a long time ago.

She had been only twenty-five at the time, with a promising career ahead, as a chef in the military. When the collision had taken place, she'd had her whole life to look forward to, but instead she had lost everything that night.

Because the mishap had happened while she was on leave, not work related, there was no compensation. They had just cut her loose.

For three years, first in hospital, then in rehab, Chantel had been alone to recover. With both parents dead and no living relatives, her friends all military out in the theatre of war, there had been no one to lean on.

Then when she had finally made it back to the real world, her training was useless. Back then, who wanted a handicapped commissionaire or a disabled chef. Why, public washrooms weren't even wheelchair accessible, leave alone a restaurant kitchen handicap friendly.

It had taken a lot of fighting to obtain a disability pension, and the battle for a wheel-chair accessible housing unit was even more difficult. She had struggled long and hard to get both!

Where am I going to go now that the landlady is dead? My monthly allowance will never cover rent somewhere else, not at the cost of housing these days.

It was hard to be sympathetic to the family of the deceased, when they were leaving her in dire straights by selling the units as condos.

Where am I to get the money to eat, let alone buy a suite?

Somehow, though she was now fifty, life didn't seem much better than after her release from rehab at twenty-five.

Chantel wished she could go back to a time when she could walk, and start life over.

****

Morning finally came. The sun was brightly shining, but Chantel was at the computer surfing the want adds oblivious to its warmth. She had three weeks to vacate, and this could not wait any longer.

I have to find a job!

What is this; a live-in nanny? They are accepting handicapped applicants?

Can I take care of kids? Why not?

I can sure try! Anything for a place to live and food in my belly!

It is the only prospect out there!

"Let's see," Chantel wondered aloud. "How do I apply?"

'Required: companions for younger and elder family members of visiting sovereign...'

"Oh man! Royalty yet? They'll never take me."

She read on: 'Income unlimited with possible life time benefits...'

"I could live with that...if I could get it."

'Needed age range 25 to 85.'

"You're kidding! Well, I certainly fit right smack in the middle."

'Must be female, American or Canadian raised…'

"Somebody's bound to say this is discriminatory."

'…Of any ethnic origin. Those presently of criminal intent need not apply, but any who are pardoned, have a criminal past, or handicaps will not be disqualified for such.'

"Do they really mean they'd take someone like me?"

'Other professional training would be an asset."

"Okay?"

'Must be prepared to leave this world behind…'

"Wouldn't I ever love to do that! What ever do they mean by that statement?"

'And enter exclusively into another society which will be unfamiliar.'

"Guess they mean a different culture…well, I'd do whatever it takes."

'Those without family ties would be preferable.'

"What on earth is this? Maybe this is one of those joke ads?"

'Utmost secrecy will be expected of all applicants.'

"This is weird! But…my situation surely can't get any worse. I can keep a secret, if that's what they want… If I don't try this, I'll always wonder if I could have gotten it… The worst they can do is say no."

'If interested contact 'Aopato Auto'@ international.com. just check box below.'

Chantel put a check mark in the box, and pressed send.

"Wonder what 'Aopato Auto' means?"

****

An hour later Chantel had an answer. The e-mail received gave a place and time to apply.

At least now I have an interview.

CHAPTER 2

The city had received an unusual amount of rainfall these past three months, and the tributary was dangerously high and swift as it flowed past the concrete wall on which Chrystal was perched. Heedless to her dangerous position, arms wrapped around her chest, her legs suspended over the edge of the barrier, the twenty-five year old rocked back and forth in agitation. The tears blinded her eyes, flowing in rapid succession down her cheeks.

"You going to jump?" a male voice bluntly asked.

Starting violently, Chrystal lost her balance and would certainly have fallen were it not for the strong arm of her inquisitor, as he hastily reached out and circled her slim waist wrenching her to safety.

He plunked her down unceremoniously, on the opposite side of the barricade, with her back to the cement, then sat down next to her.

While she caught her breath, Chrystal took note of the man. He was not much more than a year or two older than she, with copper-blond hair that was straight and fell to his shoulders ending with a slight curl at the ends. His body was strong and fit; the eyes blue.

"Whatever possessed you to sit like that?" he asked annoyed. "You trying to off yourself?"

Chrystal was trembling. "No," she admitted sheepishly. "I...forgot where I was."

"You're disking me!" he retorted with amazement. "What's got you so bothered you forgot you're on a barricade hanging over a fast-flowing, deadly river?"

The doll-like face turned to a mask of despondency; the blue eyes flooded, and the sunshine head dropped into her delicate hands. Chrystal gave way again to shuddering sobs.

"Ah...come on...don't cry," he pleaded awkwardly. "It can't be that bad..."

He sat quietly, not attempting to touch or comfort her further, just giving her time.

After a while when she was calmer, she drew in a steeling breath, wiped her cheeks with the sleeve of her sweatshirt, and sheepishly looked up.

"I'm sorry."

Her chin still quivered, the eyes threatened to spill moisture again, and her voice had gone hoarse, but Chrystal made a staunch effort to steady her grief.

"I...I guess I should say...thank you."

"You don't have to, if you don't want to." He held out his hand. "I'm Shawn."

She clasp it without much enthusiasm, limply, revealing her own name, then dropped his hand abruptly.

"You must think the worst of me..."

"Naw," he laughed. "I've got a sister. I know how emotional females can get."

That almost made her cry again.

"Ah, I'm sorry. I'm good at saying the wrong thing...still learning to be a nice guy..."

"No...no. It's me. It's not one of my better days."

He let her sit silent for a time, just waiting her out.

Man, he is patient! she thought. *That is rare in a guy.*

"Care to talk about it?" asked Shawn.

Chrystal shook her head.

"Sometimes, it helps to talk to someone. I find strangers listen pretty good, and they don't judge because they know nothing about your past behaviour; most never see you again."

She smiled dejectedly, but still said nothing.

"Maybe I could actually help?" he offered.

"Not unless you know where I can find work," she allowed finally. "And...a place to live...and give me a new family," Chrystal added, as an after thought.

He grinned at that. "That's a tall order. What kind of work do you do?"

"Until today, I was a teacher," she declared with venom. "That was until they decided I was too...intimate with the kids."

"You mean...like listening to their problems, touching hands, hugging them to comfort?"

"You got it! Apparently, that's no longer permitted!"

"Ummm...I always say, a teacher's no good when they're not genuine; can't keep the kid's attention."

"My thoughts exactly!" Encouraged by his apparent empathy, Chrystal found bravery. "I got fired at work, and I guess that old adage was on my back today...'bad luck happens in threes'. When I got home, I was locked out of my basement suite. The landlady tells me, my cheque bounced, and she already has a renter to replace me…"

"Whoa!" Shawn declared in sympathy. "You said, three?"

"Yes…it is the third strike." Her voice dipped, trembling on the verge of tears again. Her eyes lowered to take in her hands. "Last month, my mom suffered a heart attack and died instantly."

"Ah…I'm soo sorry. What about your dad…your siblings, can't you go to them?"

"It's been just me and my mom since before I turned twelve. Dad died in an industrial accident."

"Sorry to hear that…"

"I don't know what I'm going to do…now…"

Shawn sat thinking. "Well," he said after a time. "I can't bring back your mom, but…I might know a possibility of work…"

"You do? Where? Oh, but…likely they won't be any different. They'll look at my record, and never consider me for a teaching position…I'm also a pretty fair artist…"

He smiled at her hope, the unconscious boast; let it pass. Suddenly she was embarrassed again.

"Sorry…what kind of a job? I kinda jumped to conclusions."

"I know where there is a need for a companion-nanny, teacher type, and I have an in with those hiring…I could put in a good word for you."

"You would do that?"

"Sure."

"Where do I apply?"

"Where are you staying for the night?"

Sheepishly she looked at her shoes again. "I guess at a women's shelter...the landlady seized all my stuff as payment for the missed rent."

"Do you have money to buy a newspaper? Or can you get to a computer and go on line?"

Chrystal looked at her watch. "The library closes in an hour, but if I hurry I can use a computer there. They let you use the Internet for free."

"Okay...here's what you do. At the very end of the classifieds: work available is an add. It will begin like this: 'Required: Companions for younger and elder family members of visiting sovereign...' Just follow the instructions at the bottom. They'll answer back, and tell you where to go for an interview, but...you'll have to wait at that terminal until they E-mail back the location and time of your appointment. If you miss it, it won't come again."

"Then, I'd better get a move on, or I won't have enough time."

"I'll tell them to rush the answer."

He rose to his feet, offered her a hand and helped her to rise. They stood uncomfortable for a second.

"I suggest you wash your face before you go into a public place like that," he offered hesitantly. "Maybe, you can find a service station on the way..."

She lifted her hands to her face, chagrined.

"Oh...yeah. Guess I must look a mess..."

"You look beautiful…just a little wet." He moved to pass behind her. "I'll see you around…after you get the job."

It dawned on her then, he did not know her last name, but when she turned, he had already disappeared.

All that lingered was a faint scent of ginger.

How odd. He smells of ginger, Chrystal thought. *I did not notice that before. And man! He must be able to walk fast to disappear that quickly!*

CHAPTER 3

Darla sat on a stone bench watching, as small children played in the triple spouts of the spray-park. A curly carrot-topped boy of about seven played exuberantly, running about from shoot to shoot, his skinny body in shorts, naked to the waist. Heedless of the other juveniles, intent in his own world, he suddenly collided with a miniature four year old. The tiny black girl hit the concrete violently, and started to wail, while the boy carried on passed, only to slam into another bathing suit clad, very pale, white girl, not much older than the first. Scolding caregivers and consoling parents flooded the scene, to rescue and reprimand as warranted.

They always pamper the dumb little creatures, thought the buxom, sixty-plus observer. *Serves them right, not watching where they're going. Kids were all stupid. A nuisance! Pests!*

Darla had wiped too many runny noses; changed enough dirty, crapped bottoms for a lifetime. It had turned off the attraction to the soft, cuddly, helpless beings. Her empathy died in her teen years; the sympathy even before that. The fatherless, the abandoned, those scarred mentally and emotionally, these had been her companions since she had been orphaned at age eight.

Having been too old for adoption when placed in the residence, the matron had seen fit to commandeer Darla as slave labour. Every howling, inconsolable infant; each lost and insecure foundling; and the stubbed toes, scraped knees and bloody noses had all been handed over to the 'older girl'. Darla had endured until she turned eighteen; then she lit out of there one night through the bathroom window, and never looked back.

Through misfortune or luck, call it what you wish, she had landed a job cleaning the offices of a private investigator. The hunger for under cover work, and her talent for the con, had taken her the rest of the way. She had ridden the wave, right to where she was now. With no family ties, she made the perfect operative.

An attractive, full-figured woman in her mid-sixties dropped to the bench beside Darla. Though her hair showed white at the temples, the blue-black waves and the unruly errant stray curls, gave an appearance of stunning beauty, and off set by the darker than usual hue of her skin, the lady would have turned any man's head.

Darla felt jealous.

Compared to her own hair, cut short, thinning and standing on end, the peaks dyed in raspberry streaks against the black---she had always tried to encouraged the feel of Goth-like rebellion---but with her over-weight figure, Darla realized here was no comparison. This new wench would give her a run for her money. All though Darla might display the attitude of the 'cougar', beside her present companion, she would loose out every time.

"You Ziva?" Darla asked.

The other woman nodded slightly, but seemed more intent on the raucous children playing at the spray park, then in speaking with her. That annoyed Darla.

She preferred the complete attention of those around her. This woman would not be allowed to give her less. Should she continue to do so, she would pay the price.

"I hear you're up for retirement next year," Darla observed bluntly. "You game for a little field trip before they put you out to pasture?"

The stunning woman turned her head, and looked unenthusiastically at Darla. "I suppose. What does it involve?"

That's much better! Now, at least I have her attention.

But still the new comer seemed less than thrilled.

I'll have to light this fire, if we are going to work together. Mind you, I could call the shots more easily with her like this.

"There's this add in the newspaper, see... They suspect its been placed by a terrorist organization. Not that there's anything in it that says that, mind you. But, they are recruiting women of all ages, and that's suspicious. They say they're needing companions for the family of a visiting foreign diplomat...except there's no such person."

"And...we're supposed to do what?"

"They expect us to infiltrate, dummy," Darla retorted sarcastically. "You never been in the field before?"

"No. I've always worked in communications. I was told, if I did this, I'd get a better severance package."

"Well, you better get more into it if you want that to be fact, girl," Darla reprimanded. She waited a second to let her words sink in, then went on. "Okay," she decided. "I'll do the prep, tell you what's to be done. I'll keep you on track. That means I'm heading up this operation; you answer to me, hear?"

Ziva nodded. "Guess, you know the field better than I do."

That's more like it!

"Neil's our handler. If you say you've worked computers, they should put you in communications. When they do, you send Neil the co-ordinates, and we're away.

"I've already answered the add for both of us. Your job is to get the message out, as soon as you can. And leave the rest to me."

Darla pulled a medal on a chain from her pocket. "I want you to wear this. It's got a homing device inside."

Ziva took the chain gingerly, handling the St. Christopher medal as if it were hot.

"I'm Jewish!" she protested hotly. "This is a Catholic icon!"

Darla shrugged. "So…if they notice, tell them you've converted."

Ziva grunted, disgusted, but still placed the chain about her neck with no farther objection.

I have a second bug in my watch, just in case they discover that one."

"So…when does all this go down?"

"Happening in about an hour," Darla stated. "Soon as we drive there. When we get there, just let me do the talking."

CHAPTER 4

At fifty-five Angel needed a break. Most of her working life since university had been spent as a computer programmer, but her real love had always been writing. She had been dreaming of a career in journalism as long as she could remember. What had stopped her was the financial side of things.

For years she had been sending in submissions to major newspapers across the country, and some had even brought her substantial monetary gain, but because her hobby was only part time and freelance, she had never made it big.

Nearing the age where her longings would soon be futile, Angel had finally made the plunge, took early retirement, and decided to pursue her dream. It was while perusing the newspaper for ideas for a larger story, perhaps even a book, that she had discovered the add, and on a whim, had answered it.

Angel was excited. There was a real prospect here. Maybe if there was enough human interest in this, she could even place a book in the hands of a publisher.

She researched the strange name on the Internet, but mostly came up blank. All she could determine was the words were in Greek, meaning 'Invisible Ones'. It was an unusual moniker for a nation...if that's what it was.

Maybe this is a scam? But even if that is the case, I will have a story. I will know soon enough.

Angel entered a large room filled with chairs all down the centre; the aisles were at the sides along the walls. The room was basically empty, except way down near the front on the left, about five rows from the front, second seat in from the wall, an elderly woman sat, cane between her legs.

Well, they said the acceptable age was twenty-five to eighty-five, but I never thought someone that age would actually apply.

Angel made her way down the aisle toward the senior.

Might as well sit with her, she reasoned. *I can start by pumping her for information.*

"Is it okay if I sit here?" Angel asked, pointing at the empty chair beside the woman.

"By all means, join me," she agreed.

Well, at least she is affable.

Angel dropped into the seat. "I'm Angel." She offered her hand as she introduced herself.

"I am Sonia." When they clasp hands, the returned grip was firm.

In Angel's analytical mind that meant confident, attentive; she had always been one who evaluated people by their reactions and attitudes.

"Are you answering the add?"

Sonia turned to look at Angel. She wore sunglasses, even inside.

Strange, thought Angel.

"Are you?"

The older woman had answered with a question of her own.

Evasive answer, Angel noted. *Either she has something to hide, or...she wants to avoid the correct answer.*

"Yes," Angel admitted aloud. "I'm actually hoping to find a story. But a few bucks on the side won't hurt. See, I've always wanted to write full time, and I thought this might give me a good angle for a book. You never know what could come out of this."

Sonia just smiled, but made no comment. It seemed she was a woman of few words...or she chose them carefully, when she did speak.

The lady appeared to be in her late seventies, dressed well, and she smelled clean. In fact a vanilla/cinnamon scent lightly perfumed the area around her.

Must be the soap she uses, Angel decided. *At least she doesn't smell as bad as some of the elderly I've encountered.*

This senior did not appear to be hard up, but then many of the aging population were adept at hiding poverty.

A wheel chair pulled up beside Angel, and stopped. The woman in it was maybe five years her junior, but it was difficult to be certain considering her twisted body. A blanket covered her legs, and a small satchel sat in her lap; half–gloves protected her hands against injury and calluses. The conveyance she rode was not motorized.

Angel wondered how long she had been trapped in that chair.

"I'm Angel." This time she did not offer her hand, out of fear she might do injury to the invalid.

"Chantel," the woman offered.

They did say, handicapped could apply, Angel reasoned to herself. *I sure hope for her sake, they meant what they said.*

The room behind the three began to fill up. Soon only the seats at the front were empty, and these too were quickly taken, except for the three seats directly ahead of them.

Finally, a young girl in her mid-twenties approached, slid expertly past Chantel's wheel chair, and dropped into the seat directly in front of Angel. She was slim, blond with blue eyes, and the cutest little doll-like face.

Angel leaned forward to introduce herself.

"Hi." The newcomer turned sideways. "I'm Angel. This is Sonia on my right, and Chantel in the wheeled conveyance."

"I'm Chrystal."

"A lot of women answered this add. Do you think it's for real?" Angel asked.

"Oh, I sure hope so," Chrystal exclaimed worriedly. "I really need a job right now. This guy Shawn told me about this add."

Before Angel could question farther, a heavyset woman came up behind Chantel and rudely tried to move the locked wheelchair forward.

"The least you could do is move to the back! You're blocking the way!" she complained, giving up at last and moving around the vehicle. With great difficulty, she squeezed past Chrystal as well, plopped down next to her, unconcerned by the fact that the woman with her was forced to move past her knees to get to the last empty chair.

The pair were both at least over sixty. They were as unalike as a rat and a bird: the first being decidedly over weight, with hair dyed black, spiked with raspberry red; the second, with a figure of pleasant proportions and long wavy blue-black hair that fell to her waist.

Boy! Aren't they beauty and the beast? thought Angel. *I wonder if they are a set pair?*

Beside Angel, Sonia hid a slight smile behind her hand, chuckling softly, almost as if she had heard the thought…or perhaps, came to the same conclusion.

Angel had the weirdest sensation of someone standing over her, and simultaneously she thought she heard someone whisper, I want that one!

Angel scanned the people about her, wondering who had spoken. The voice had sounded male, but there was not a man in the entire room.

Sonia doubled over.

"Are you okay?" Angel asked, concerned.

"Oh." Sonia pulled back, straightening. "I'll be fine." But her voiced sounded strained, as if she was in a fit of laughter, and was making a valiant attempt to suppress it. "Don't worry about me."

"You're sure?"

Sonia nodded.

Dismissing the incident quickly, Angel's attention was drawn back to the new arrivals. She decided she might as well introduce herself. Reaching forward, she tapped the ugly, abrasive one on the shoulder.

"I'm Angel"

The woman half turned. "Darla," she growled, with the voice of a bulldog, that matched her personality perfectly.

And the beauty responded, in a pleasant mellow tone, "Ziva."

"That's a Jewish name, isn't it?" Angel observed. But the beast gave Ziva a vicious warning jab in the ribs, and the other woman decided not to comment in return.

At that moment, another white haired individual stood behind Chantel in her chair, moved past her and hesitated, gazing about uncertainly, searching for a seat. Darla had seen her slip around the chair, and her annoyance resurfaced.

"Make her move to the back," she ordered inconsiderately. "Stupid cripple's dreaming anyway, if she thinks she'll get hired."

Chantel began to unlock her chair, but Sonia was on her feet immediately. "Stay, Chantel," she suggested softly. Then to the new arrival, she added, "Why don't you take my seat? I need a bathroom break, anyway."

"But where will you sit when you come back?" asked the disconcerted new comer. "I don't want to put you out."

"I'll be okay," reassured Sonia, slipping past Angel's knees, and quickly escaping to stand beside the wheelchair.

She's unusually agile for her age, Angel observed.

"Why don't you move, you stupid cripple?" hissed Darla.

Chantel looked as if she had reached her limit. She unlocked the second brake, but the space was too narrow, and she tried unsuccessfully to turn about, finally choosing instead to back down the aisle to the back.

Sonia had turned toward Darla, annoyance visible on her face. It appeared she would debate with the woman, but then seemed to think better, moving away to follow after Chantel, her cane keeping step with her indignation.

The new arrival took Sonia's seat, somewhat ill at ease. To allay the situation, Angel introduced herself as usual.

"I'm Angel."

"Karine," the other returned in a clear Irish brogue.

CHAPTER 5

The back door of the room suddenly closed with a resounding slam. All heads turned toward the rear entrance. A man in his early fifties stood in front of it. His stance was relaxed, but clearly military in posture.

All heads returned to the empty space at the front, as a second man came quietly through another door on the left side. He was taller than the first, and thinner, but there was a definite resemblance between the two.

The man at the front cleared his throat.

"All applicants have arrived; interviews will now begin," he announced in a quiet but clearly audible voice. "Please proceed through the side door one at a time, beginning with the back row. Please wait until the previous party is finished before you take your turn."

He then returned to the side door, to stand in a posture similar to the man at the back, and stood waiting.

Heads again turned to the rear. The man at that door made a gesture with his head toward the woman seated at the left end of the back row. She rose to her feet, walked the aisle to the front, and the second man opened the side door for her, closing it again when she had passed through.

Then the waiting began.

****

It was hours later when Angel finally got her turn. Upon entering, she was shocked to find Sonia behind the interview desk, but before she could comment, the older woman grinned and explained.

"I found it enlightening to sit among the applicants while they waited," she admitted, amusement in her tone. "Their real motives and personalities came out from under cover."

Angel immediately thought of herself. *Did I say anything that will jeopardize my chances?*

"Well," Sonia suggested. "How about you tell me about yourself. I already know you like to write stories. We could use someone like that for the young ones of the future."

Is she really thinking that long term?

"How lengthy is this employment?"

Sonia smiled. "It can be a lifetime endeavour."

"Oh my, I never realized..."

"Do you wish to withdraw, or are you prepared to leave all behind and take a risk?"

Angel thought about it. *It isn't like I have anyone waiting for me...*

"Do you have any living relatives?"

Now, that is a weird question?

"No, actually, I don't."

"How about friends who will miss you?"

What an odd line of questioning.

And then Angel was suddenly facing a blunt reality.

She sighed. "Actually, now that I think of it," Angel admitted. "I think I've let life slip by me..."

"You've never married?"

Angel shook her head. *What does that have to do with the job?*

"How about a boyfriend?"

"The one guy I liked died of an aneurysm when we were eighteen…we were engaged at the time."

"And you've never found another compatible sole mate?"

Angel shook her head. "I guess in my anger at what happened, I buried myself in my training, and after that my job."

"And what was that exactly?"

Man! This woman is good at drawing you out. She gets to the root and guides the interview well, thought Angel in appreciation. *Can't believe she got me to be so free with my personal memories like this. I never meant to bare my soul.*

"I was a computer programmer. They were even experimenting with artificial intelligence when I left…but I wasn't allowed to be a part of that."

"That is why you left?"

"Not exactly. I took early retirement to pursue my life long dream to be a writer. Not sure that was so smart now…"

"Did you not like the work you were doing?"

"Oh, I loved it…especially when they started with the robots, but they shifted me to another department. Twenty-five years I worked in the same area. It was like they thought I wasn't trustworthy, or something. Guess…I'm too outgoing…too open. I talked too much."

Sonia smiled sympathetically. "Would you consider that field again, if you had the chance?"

"I'd jump at it!"

"Good. We have such an opening available."

"But I thought you were looking for companions."

"Ummm...we have other needs, as well."

"Do you need my degrees, diplomas, records? I don't even have my references. I never expected this, so I'm unprepared."

"That's okay. We will take your word, and we will judge by your work ability."

How unusual. It's refreshing to be accepted as truthful for a change, but...is this for real? There must be a catch.

"I've got a job with you, then?" Angel asked in disbelief.

"If you are willing..."

Angel nodded.

"To leave all behind?"

Oh, that! "If that is what you require."

"Well, you may return to the outer room, and we will give you some time to think more on it. A list of those chosen will be announced in a little while. Should you change your mind by then, you may still say no."

CHAPTER 6

Chantel had hidden herself away in the far right back corner while the other women each took their turn ahead of her. She had decided this was all a mistake, and would have left right away, except that the man at the back door stood blocking her way, and he had not been inclined to let others pass, leave alone allow her to leave. She had seen a few try, only to be turned back.

It was hours later when Darla and Ziva decided to leave their places, walking to the rear by way of the right wall aisle, and heading right toward her. Chantel realized there was nothing she could do; if they saw her, there would be an encounter…again.

Darla caught sight of her first. "Are you still here, freak?" she hissed venomously. "Haven't you realized yet this is for able bodies. There's nothing here for you? Besides they're looking for people with a brain."

Chantel had encountered others of this mentality. She knew this bully saw her only as a deformed shell, and assumed her mental capabilities and feelings had been stripped away as well. Whether she chose to defended herself or remain silent, the attitude of others would not change. She had learned that long ago. There were two personalities in the approach to her: they were either condescending or overly attentive. She did not like either. Her main desire was to be treated as if she counted.

Backing away, Chantel made an attempt at escape, but unlocking the wheel chair was a mistake. Darla caught the nearest handle grip, and began to spin the chair. That put her behind Chantel, who was now completely at her mercy.

Ziva stood to the side, apparently disconcerted, but not enough to make an effort to help either way. The backs of the crowd hid all three from the view of others.

Darla spun the chair a full circle. If she kept at this, Chantel knew what it would do to her. She cringed, but that only encouraged the beastly woman. The chair spun again, more rapidly this time. Tensing in reaction, Chantel felt her equilibrium tip.

The abusive woman half laughed under her breath, realizing her callous actions were actually causing discomfort. She spun the chair faster then next time.

Every muscle in Chantel's upper body tensed.

"You going to leave? Or do I have to tip you out of this contraption?"

Ziva was growing concerned, but her effort at objection was weak at best. "Darla, I don't think this is really necessary…"

Darla turned a scathing look her way. "So, what? You think you're my conscience now, do you? This is for her own good. And I don't want to hear another word from you, or I'll deal with you later."

Ziva backed down.

Darla spun the chair rapidly, twice. It made Chantel extremely dizzy, and now nausea rose up in her throat.

"Going home yet?"

Chantel had reached the place where speech was impossible. If she tried, what came out, would be nothing but stutters, merely enforcing Darla's idea, the wheelchair bound woman was an idiot.

The chair spun rapidly, again and again, and again.

"Time to tip over," Darla laughed at a whisper.

The chair spun just another half circle before a powerful hand suddenly stopped it. A male voice, seeming far away, spoke.

"Why are you two out of your seats? Return to your places or forfeit your chance at a position."

Darla's voice came across condescending, dripping with pleasantry. "We just needed a bathroom break; she was in the way. We were helping her move…"

The man scowled at her.

"You were doing much more than moving her," he declared with suppressed anger. "Return to your seats…now!"

"You don't even have a weapon," Darla countered sweetly. "How are you going to make me?"

His eyes narrowed. "Just keep testing me," he challenged.

Darla was obviously ready to go farther, but Ziva pulled at her sleeve, then started away on her own, up the aisle. With no audience, for the first time, Darla seemed to deflate, weighing the consequences, deciding she wanted the job more than to buck this new authority. Chantel could hear her retreat, but as the area was behind her, she could not watch.

The man moved around to the front of her chair, knelt down on one knee. "You okay?" he asked gently, taking one of her hands in his.

No, I am not okay! It is already too late. I am going to embarrass myself before all these people.

The room was already fading at the edge of her sight. The nausea was too close too make an effort to speak.

If I could only tell him!

Chantel closed her eyes. Seconds later she felt a cold water bottle near her lips.

"Drink," he whispered quietly.

She swallowed a sip without opening her eyes, then another, all the while wondering why the convulsions were delayed.

Beginning to feel better, she opened her eyes.

She thought his blue eyes changed. At first, they had a vertical black slit at the centre, like the eyes of a cat. Then his eyes returned to normal again.

Am I hallucinating now too? That never happened before. What was in the drink he gave me?

Her vision was clearing; the room had stopped spinning.

My seizures never stopped abruptly like this before!

"Just rest for a moment longer," he cautioned. "Suck on this." He slipped something like a small square of chocolate into her mouth.

"Now." He stood up and went behind the chair, out of her line of sight. "I'm going to wheel you to the front…"

"But…" she objected. "What about the door you were guarding?"

"I've sealed it. No one can get out. Besides it's time you went to see Sonia."

Sonia? wondered Chantel. *Why her?*

****

The guard from the rear entrance backed into the room just as Angel's interview ended. He slowly turned, pushing Chantel in the wheelchair, forward.

"Mom," he interrupted. "This one is acceptable. No need for the screening."

Both Chantel and Angel looked surprised.

Sonia looked up at him. For long moments their eyes locked, as silent communication went between them.

"Zane," she said, an obvious warning in her tone. "You invaded her privacy!"

"Opps!" His face went from confident to shame. "I forgot!"

Sonia frowned. "And why did that happen?"

Sheepishly, he came around, and stood beside the chair.

"Aw, circumstances got a bit…unsettled; needed corrective measures."

"How far did you go?"

He sighed. "Just balanced."

"Let me see." He reached out his hand palm up; she placed hers over it for just a second, then both dropped their hands.

What ever is that about? Angel wondered. *Are they telepaths or something?*

"You realize what you have just done?"

He dropped his head slightly, as if he had done something wrong. "She's a female ...I understand, mom," he replied, quite contrite. "But, I couldn't just leave her like that ...I accept the bonding."

"We agreed to certain rules, for this very reason, " Sonia pointed out gravely. "You know the consequences...to us all, if this goes wrong."

He looked up, his face eager. "I am willing!"

"You know it takes two...if...by chance, you are refused," Sonia cautioned, barely above a whisper. "My son, you will forfeit your life! I can not...do not, want to lose another!"

He looked at her, pleading for understanding. "I choose. I accept responsibility, and...any results."

Angel had never seen anyone so eager for punishment. *Is he a masochist?*

"Did you consider the whole when you did this?"

He dropped his head in shame, then he quickly raised it again, meeting her gaze solidly. "Mother, you have always taught us every life is of value. If the cost for this is my life...separate me, so it will go no farther."

"No." Tears sprang to her eyes. "Zane...you are too much like me..."

He grinned. "It will work out."

"Young ones! Ever the optimists." A smile played with the corner of her lips. Then she sobered again.

"And what of this tendency to invade privacy?"

"It will not happen a second time; I promise." Zane turned to Chantel. "Forgive me. I am sorry…"

Chantel had sat through the entire conversation, puzzlement evident on her face. She frowned now. "For what?" she asked baffled. "You helped me!"

"Understanding will come to you later…"

Zane stepped back, returning to a stance of rigid attention. He was once more soldier-like.

"Will any of this go against her?" he asked pointedly.

"No. I agree with your choice…and we will accept the result."

He sighed in relief. "Thank you, my Lady."

"Shush! Not here!" Sonia reproved. "What am I going to do with you?"

Zane laughed impishly, then quickly steeled his features.

"I would understand if you didn't want me," Chantel interjected, referring to her placement. "If I'm really not suitable, I can just go. I don't expect special treatment."

Sonia smiled, as if what she said had pleased her. "Zane has found you…will fit quite nicely," she declared pleasantly. "His will is acceptable, as far as we are concerned."

Why is it, I get the impression they are talking about something entirely different than appears on the surface? Angel wondered.

"Return Chantel to the outer room, Zane, and …out of harms way," Sonia added.

Again with the veiled implication, have I missed something here? Angel mused.

"And you may go, as well, Angel."

Angel escaped quickly through the door, with Zane pushing Chantel directly behind, like children breaking free after being disciplined by the principal.

****

Zane sobered immediately upon entry into the larger area, becoming once more the stoic custodian. He wheeled the chair to the front row of seats, blocking the left aisle completely. He stood protectively beside Chantel, giving her the feeling of being treasured, something that was so very rare in her life it brought tears to her eyes.

As Karine went for her interview, and after her Chrystal, he still remained by her side.

Did his mother somehow give him new orders?

But when Darla and Ziva attempted to pass by her chair, Chantel was shocked at his reaction. Zane turned to Darla, his attitude one of cold fury. He spoke harshly, something Chantel had never expected of him.

"Go around. This way is closed! The right side will suffice from now on."

He is like a bear defending its cub.

The two women were forced by this action to back track along the seats, and come up the right aisle, track across the front in full view of everyone, making it apparent they were in ill favour, and then enter the interrogation room.

And when Darla came out immediately, obviously angry, as if she had been taken to task, all eyes followed her disgraced condition, all the way back to her seat, with wonderment.

Zane stood quietly, unconcerned by the obvious amazement of those behind him; standing sentry to the end.

Only when Ziva returned, and Darla entered the interview room a second time, did Zane relax, slip away down the left aisle, and return to his post at the rear door.

Chantel felt a regret, when he no longer stood beside her.

CHAPTER 7

Karine was already nervous when she entered the smaller room, and her discomfort was exacerbated by the fact her interrogator turned out to be none other than the old lady who had given up her seat to her.

Their ages were relatively about the same, but that was not a comfort. No doubt this woman had an education and had lead a life of interaction with a higher class of people than Karine was used to. It was another reason to feel ill at ease.

Karine had not reached her present age safely by being unobservant. Her life occupation had taught her quickly not to trust people. A few steps behind Darla and Ziva, but remaining at the rear of the chair, no one had noticed her. Karine had noted this woman's reaction to the pair, the way Angel and the senior seemed to share amusement at Darla's weird appearance. She was also aware Darla's behaviour caused annoyance to this important woman.

What will the woman think of me? Obviously, she is judgemental...what if they really did not mean what was said in the add? She is their go between.

Maybe I should fudge the facts a bit?

With trepidation, Karine took a seat in front of the desk.

"I am Sonia…"

Karine looked up, then quickly dropped her eyes feeling exposed.

Why does the woman wear sunglasses? And...she doesn't even have a note pad. Is this being recorded?

"Your name please? The first name will suffice..."

Karine felt relief; still she kept her eyes lowered.

"Karine."

Sonia waited. Karine grew uncomfortable.

"You have beautiful hair, Karine," Sonia complimented, in what was obviously an attempt to relax her applicant. "What colour was it when you were younger?"

Karine reached up to touch the soft white waves. "I was...auburn; I used to wear it longer...down to my...ah, hips."

The men liked the way it fanned out about my naked body like a cape.

"It must have been pretty then. Did you like it that way?"

Karine raised her eyes. *What kind of questions are these? They are personal, have nothing to do with a job.*

"That's better. I prefer you look at me."

Well, I wouldn't mind to see your eyes, too. thought Karine.

Sonia grinned, almost as if she had heard what Karine had been thinking.

"Shall we get on with the interview?" Karine nodded. "What is your exact age?"

"I'm seventy-eight."

"And why would you want to work again at your time of life?"

Well, obviously, you are still working! Why can't I do the same? Karine thought defensively, before she caught herself.

She sighed. Guess I'd better be honest with this one. I have nothing more to lose.

"I have no senior benefits…I live on the streets."

Wouldn't mind a bed to sleep in like you have either.

"Why have you no benefits?" Sonia asked softly. "Is it because you lack an address?"

Karine swallowed back her shame. *Is that sympathy in her tone?*

"When I came to this country, I never had the chance to…become legal. And… my job wasn't…"

"Covered by benefits," Sonia finished for her. "I understand."

Karine doubted she could.

"Where were you born, originally?"

"Ireland."

"Before we go farther, Karine," Sonia interjected. "I need to warn you. Our head of security has just joined the monitoring of this interview, and…we do check into background if we need to."

Oh well, that is the end of it then, Karine decided. *Might as well get up, and leave right now.*

She prepared to rise from her seat.

"Don't give up just yet, Karine…please give us a chance," Sonia pleaded. "You have not been disqualified. In fact, there is an interest…"

Is she wearing some sort of wire so they can tell her? Maybe that's what the glasses are for?

Karine pulled her seat back in.

"How were you employed…until you could no longer work?"

"Ah…" Karine knew there was no way to get around this. "I was in the…ah, in the pleasure trade,' she finished uncomfortably at a mere whisper.

"And your function in it?"

Man! Do I have to spell it out for her?

"I was a stripper…"

"And…"

"The show girls weren't allowed to do tricks on the side!"

Even though she could not see pass the glasses, Karine felt Sonia's eyes drill her. "You are telling me you were never sexually active?"

Karine dropped her eyes to her hands.

"I warn you, your placement depends on your honesty."

Karine looked up, fighting moisture she could not hide. Her cheeks burned with the hot shame of embarrassment.

"What does this have to do with the job?"

"Honesty means everything to those involved. You are not being judged for past behaviour, we simply...require ultimate truthfulness. It is extremely important to the interested party."

"You won't hire me...if I..."

"I would hire you in an instant, Karine. But I wish you to be completely honest here."

Karine dropped her eyes once more, not able to face head on the rejection she expected.

"I was...a prostitute."

"Okay. Please look at me," Sonia requested, not missing a beat. "That's much better. Any sexually transmitted diseases?"

Her obvious lack of concern caught Karine by surprise. Maybe I've misjudged her?

"I was just checked for AIDs... it was negative, and none others that I am aware of."

"You were not very active?"

"I was mostly on the floor...they liked my looks, but...I had a rep...they knew I wouldn't sleep with them. They called me...'the tease'."

Sonia nodded in a preoccupied way, as if listening to another conversation not audible to others. Karine assumed she had lost her interest.

But Sonia came alert suddenly. "Our head of security has just accepted you," she admitted with surprise. "Please go to the outer room to await the announcement of final selections. "Please...do not leave!"

"Are you sure? I know I'm not good material, but I...I think I can be a good companion."

"I know you will be," Sonia reassured softly. "Go to the other room now, dear."

Karine almost jumped for joy as she left Sonia's presence.

I have a job! A real job, for the first time in my life!

CHAPTER 8

Chrystal laughed outright, when she entered the room and saw that Sonia was her interviewer.

"Oh, I've used that trick on my kids," she giggled, taking a seat at the table. "It's the best way to get to know them!"

Sonia smiled indulgently.

"You have come highly recommended," Sonia admitted. "There is no need for me to spy on you."

"Ah, yah, about that." Chrystal wrinkled her nose at the memory. "That wasn't one of my better days...the day I found out about your add. I'd just been...ah, let go, and ...I'd lost my apartment...and all."

Sonia made no comment.

Uncomfortable now, Chrystal realized she'd spilled more than was needed. She went quiet, placing her hands in her lap to ease her tension.

"Have you ever worked with older children?" Sonia asked.

"Yes. Actually, I've got the qualifications to teach up to grade twelve, and I have taught a class of nine and ten year olds."

"The position is as a teacher/companion for a highly advanced five year old. Do you think you could keep up with someone with a thirst for knowledge, who absorbs adult subjects voraciously?"

"Sounds very bright," Chrystal agreed "I think I could, if I had the right material available to me, but I have none of my own."

"She will be challenging, but if you have trouble controlling her enthusiasm..."

"I'll be certain to ask for help."

"Excellent. We will make sure what you need is accessible."

"Do you need my..."

"No need," Sonia reassured, before Chrystal could say her documentation was lost. "At the risk of appearing rude, our interviews have gone on longer than expected, and we still have others to go. Since you were already acceptable, and we need to complete on schedule before dark, would you mind very much if your interview is cut short? I am certain there will be plenty of time for us to establish a relationship once you are settled."

"Oh no, I fully understand. It must have been an exhausting day for you. I know just waiting has been..."

Chrystal realized she was rambling again.

"Well, okay then." She pushed away her chair, and bounded to her feet all in one motion. "I guess, I wait in the next room?"

"Please do."

****

Darla and Ziva entered the room together.

Sonia looked up annoyed. "Were you not told the interviews are separate?"

Shock registered on the faces of both women at finding the old lady that had been sitting with Angel when they arrived. Darla was quick to recover however.

"We're together. Can't you interview us as a pair?"

"Definitely not," Sonia stated bluntly. "I will take Ziva first."

"But I was next in line," Darla objected.

"Because you seem unable to obey set orders," Sonia declared. "I think it will do you good to wait a little longer." Sonia regarded Darla without smiling. "I will take Ziva first, thank you."

"Who the hell put you in charge?"

"Shall I call for one of the men?" asked Sonia evenly. "Or perhaps you are not interested in this position after all."

Darla definitely did not like this old biddy. However, neither was she enthused at a second confrontation with the man outside.

"It's okay." Ziva broke into the uncomfortable silence. "I'm sure I can handle this on my own."

Darla rather doubted that, but now she had no choice.

"Please, go back outside and wait, Darla," Sonia ordered firmly.

Darla turned about, looking toward the door, still quite unwilling.

"And," Sonia added, seeming to deliberately place insult after injury. "We have no need of a paired couple."

Darla made a rude noise. "We ain't...a couple. Just met."

"Very well then," Sonia decided. "You should not find it difficult to wait while I interview your new found friend first."

Darla shrugged, and left the room steaming.

****

Ziva dropped into the empty chair, as the door behind her closed with a slam. She was almost relieved she was the first to be examined. And at least with Darla in the other room, she would not have to be so careful with what she said.

Sonia went right into the interview without missing a beat.

"Age please?"

"Sixty-four."

"And where were you raised?"

"I grew up in Israel."

"Tell me some of your personal history. Are your parents still living?"

"My parents died in an suicide bombing when I was sixteen. I have no siblings." Ziva knew the interviewer's drill, so she simply rattled off her history. "No other relatives. At twenty, I came to America as an exchange student, four years later became a citizen. I am trained in computer repair and office management; I'm familiar with most software..."

Sonia showed sudden interest. "In what capacity have you been employed to date?"

"I taught a class in basic computer for five years, and I've been working in a communications position for the last thirty-five years."

"Why would you seek employment with us?" asked Sonia astounded.

Ziva did not miss a beat, simply shrugged. "Need a change. Do you need the name of my former employer?"

"That's not important. Would you consider work relating to your field of expertise?"

"I guess...I merely wanted a change of scenery. Sure, why not?"

Ziva's nonchalant attitude did not seem to impress Sonia. She studied Ziva for many moments.

None of what I said was a lie, reasoned Ziva.

She hoped she was coming across confident, and willing as Darla had suggested.

"When did you first meet Darla?"

Now where did that come from?

"Just this morning, before we entered the hall."

"You are not friends?"

Ziva shrugged. "I'm not even sure I like the woman." Ziva had suddenly realized, knowing Darla was a hindrance here. It was time to distance herself from her. "If I have to work with her, I guess I can live with it, but it's not my preference."

"She can be caustic," Sonia agreed.

Ziva laughed at the image that brought to mind. "Guess, she got to you too, eh?"

Sonia nodded solemnly. "Don't worry. If she is chosen, we are quite capable of handling her type."

Then Sonia came back with another shift in focus that caught Ziva off guard. "Have you any military training?"

But Ziva recovered quickly. This was not her first time with an adept inquisitor.

"I did a two year term in the army. It is compulsory for all young adults in Israel."

"Are you a devout Jew, then?"

"Not really. Since I left my homeland I've kind of adjusted my beliefs."

"How are you at taking orders?"

"I usually do what I'm told, but I don't like being forced or tricked into situations."

"Did Darla do that?"

Once again, that caught Ziva by surprise.

Man! This lady picks up on things. I'll have to watch myself better.

"Ah, Darla and I just met. How could she matter?"

Sonia switched thought trains again.

"Would you say you are stubborn?"

By now Ziva wasn't surprised by anything she was asked.

"Yah. I can get my back up. I'll stand my ground when I think it's needed."

"Do you have a boy friend?"

Ziva didn't even blink. "No time for one. Say, just what does this all have to do with being a companion?"

"It is just background. And I doubt you will be placed as a companion to a female. Should you be acceptable, it would be in another capacity. We have other positions available."

For a moment, Sonia simply studied Ziva. The Jewish woman had the impression she was listening, but for what Ziva could not imagine.

"You have good qualifications," Sonia finally said. "But we are undecided..."

Who is the we she is talking about? There's no one else here.

"Perhaps, if you could tell me more about your personal preferences? Your life."

Ziva shrugged. "I don't really have much outside of work. Since I came to this country...I've mostly kept to myself."

"Do you like to read?"

"Well, yes, and I also like music...and movies."

"What genre?"

Ziva thought a moment. It was so rare she had spare time.

"I like murder, mystery, romance...a little SiFi..."

Sonia smiled, amused. "You like Science Fiction? Would you know an alien if you met one?"

Ziva laughed, self-consciously. "Don't really believe such things exist. I live in the real world...just read the wild imaginings of some authors. It's amusing; takes my mind off reality when it gets too mundane."

Ziva thought she heard a chuckle, but when she looked at Sonia's face it was a mask of passivity.

Ziva frowned. *Is there someone else in this room?*

She turned her chair to view the door behind her, then rotated full circle back the other way.

Nope! All alone, door closed. I must have imagined it.

"I believe we have everything we need," Sonia decided. "When you return to your seat, send Darla in to me."

Ziva arose, wondering if she had simply been brushed off, or if she had a chance.

CHAPTER 9

The man from the side door walked to the centre shortly after Darla returned from her interview. Her meeting had seemed short, and strangely, she could remember little about it. Usually, she was noted for her memory skills.

The room grew quiet, as the man stood waiting. At last, when all eyes were on him, he spoke.

"We regret we have inconvenienced you for so long, but the wait will soon be over. All positions have now been filled; however, many of you were unsuitable. Those who were not chosen, please remain after I have revealed the selected names. The entrance will continue to be sealed while our appraiser takes a short break. She then wishes to address all of you. It should not be more then another half hour."

Indignant words and moans followed. The annoyed complaints were ignored. The man continued.

"Only ten women were chosen. As I call your names, please proceed to the front and wait on the left side, as a group. Those acceptable are: Angel…Carmen…Chantel. The last may remain where she is positioned…"

The woman in the wheelchair visibly relaxed.

"They picked the cripple?" Darla spat in disgust.

"Please, come forward," the man encouraged again.

Angel and another woman, a little older, moved out into the aisle.

"Chrystal, and…Darla."

"I got in!" Darla hissed under her breath to Ziva. "Wish me luck." She made for the aisle.

Actually, Darla felt a little surprised she had gotten in.

Maybe something I said in the interview changed the old biddy's mind.

"Jenna…Karine…May Lin…"

A very elderly Asian woman was the last to enter the aisle. She shuffled in small steps across the front to the group standing beside Chantel's chair.

"What good could she possibly be?" Darla remarked indignantly, as she moved to stand beside Angel. "She's got to be at least eighty!"

"I think she's probably going to be placed with another older person," suggested Angel. "That was the reason for such an age range."

Darla harrumphed. "They'll both sit and sleep away the day," she objected sarcastically.

"I guess that's their prerogative, isn't it?"

Darla didn't much like this woman either.

"Morgan…Ziva."

Well! thought Darla. *We both got in. Didn't think she had it in her.*

Addressing those in the remaining seats, the man reassured, "Please be patient; the rest of you will soon be permitted to go home."

Then he returned to his post by the side door, leaving the group he had called standing there.

Is he testing our stamina, or what?

****

The room behind them buzzed with annoyance. Darla leaned in to speak in Ziva's ear. Her breath smelled sour, causing the Jewish woman to draw back to prevent a gag reflex.

"That big hunk by the side door?" she whispered. "It might be worth your while to cultivate him a bit. I think he's the one who's really in charge."

Ziva looked at her, frowning. "Just what do you suggest I do?" she asked indignantly.

"Do I have to spell it out to you, dim wit?" Darla hissed back. "You sleep with him! Get him between the sheets, and I'll bet you'd hear all his secrets."

Disgusted, Ziva turned away; silently wishing the woman had been rejected.

"Personally, I'd prefer..." Darla grinned maliciously. "To lie with one of the younger women...if the ones we companion look as good as he does."

Ziva made no comment.

I guess, even if I don't agree with her personal choices, I still have to work with her.

Finally, Ziva decided to speak her mind.

"I really don't agree, that these guys are terrorists..." she confided in a low voice.

"Shut your guff!" Darla hissed. "You want to give us away? And...you're not paid to think. I'm the brain here!"

"They didn't pick me as a companion, you know," Ziva persisted. "I don't know what they want me for."

"How do you know that?"

"Sonia said, I wouldn't be suitable as a companion."

"What did you tell her, you dim nit?"

"I gave her my work history…"

"Did you give her the name of the firm?"

"No. She didn't want that. For all I know, I'll just be kitchen help…"

"Don't matter where you are. You still got eyes, and you can find their… equipment. What matters is I got inside; you're just along for the ride. You're expendable."

Well, thanks a lot! thought Ziva. *If I were so unimportant, why'd they even send me? I could have worked another half year, and not have had to put up with this oddball!*

CHAPTER 10

Exactly one half hour later, and seemingly without communicating with each other, both men in the room moved into action. The one from the interview doorway walked to the centre front, placing a chair in the direct middle of the open space, while the second, simultaneously, rapidly moved down the right aisle, crossed in front of the empty row of seats, and joined him.

Sonia came from the side entrance, walked carefully in sync with her cane across the front, and sat down on the lone chair. The two men took up positions on either side, like sentry bookends there to guard her, their posture relaxed but attentive.

The crowd went expectantly silent.

"Those who were chosen, please be seated in the front row," the man who had been at the side door requested.

Ten women scrambled to find placement among the unoccupied chairs, relieved to at last be off their feet. They were now seated directly before Sonia.

When all was still again, Sonia began speaking, her voice soft and gentle, yet easily heard by all.

"By now, most of you know me. For those who were missed when I interviewed, I am Sonia. The men beside me are my two sons: Lance on my right; Zane on the left."

She waited quietly, as if debating her next words.

"We are of a species different from that of humankind…"

Once more she paused, waiting to see their reaction. But most seemed slow to comprehend, either simply rejecting the thought as being improbable, or a joke. When no response was forthcoming, Sonia continued.

"I was truly saddened by what I found here today. Out of fifty plus women, I found few who showed empathy and proper respect toward senior authority. This was especially so among the younger women. I was under the impression you were seeking employment."

The women began to fidget, their discomfort evident; many dropped their gaze to their hands, or looked at each other with mild amusement.

"I was assumed to be just an employee by many I interviewed. In their opinion, I deserved no consideration. Others were judgemental, deciding because of my age, I could not possibly possess wisdom, and had lost the power to reason. Some, at this very moment, are still thinking this. I suggest you adjust your attitude before you seek another placement."

Sonia paused again for emphasis.

"This is why most of you were rejected by us."

Someone from the far back yelled, "You have no right to judge us by attitude. That's discrimination! It has nothing to do with the job."

"Oh, but it had everything to do with this position! If you treat me in such a manner, how will you attend to those I place in your charge?"

A quiet murmur of acknowledgement, coupled with regret, ran through the crowd.

"I have observed your kind. You are an example of how your own elderly are treated. It is a sad commentary to your race. You see what you think is a stupid, powerless individual, and you treat them with distain. You considered me beneath you…"

Again she paused. When she spoke again, there was menace in her voice.

"Trust me. I am far from what you assumed!"

Someone near the front made a rude sound.

"I trust that those we have chosen will remember, and consider the lesson learned here today, and never underestimate me in the future."

Sonia's gaze went to Darla and Ziva, as if this warning was meant personally for them.

"Who does that old biddy think she is?" hissed Darla under her breath.

"I have power enough to destroy your universe," Sonia stated bluntly, as if in answer to her words. "But…fortunately for you, I would never do that…at least not on purpose."

A ripple of laughter broke over the crowd, then quickly turned to embarrassed uncertainty, when neither Sonia nor the men with her, seemed to view her comments as anything but serious.

"She's just a senile old woman," someone chided. "I for one have had enough of this. I'm out of here!" Rising from her seat, she turned to leave.

"You will stay where you are," Sonia returned quietly.

"You sure think you're somebody, don't you?" the woman challenged.

Zane stepped forward. "You will obey! Sit down!"

Whether out of fear, or simply because she realized it was safer not to argue, the woman dropped into her seat.

He turned to the crowd, his eyes narrowing.

"Sonia is our leader," he stated with more calm than expected. "And from now on we expect you will treat her with the dignity she deserves."

Dead silence. He stepped back again.

Suddenly, Sonia reached up and quietly removed her dark glasses.

A unified gasp of shock came from the crowd. Sonia's eyes were much like those of a cat, a purple hue with a vertical black slit down the centre.

"Crap!" whispered Darla, backing against her seat in fear. The realization had finally dawned that Sonia might indeed be Alien, and capable of what she claimed. "What have we gotten into?"

Someone in the crowd behind whispered, "She's wearing contacts. It's all just to scare us into submission. This is one of those Trecky Cults."

Darla relaxed visibly. She reasoned *that could well be true. This woman has done nothing unusual to show the abilities she claims. She has not proven herself.*

Darla felt embarrassed she had shown weakness. Now, she would need to save face.

Whatever got into me? I'm harder than that!

****

Chantel, on the other hand, was not surprised at all. She knew now what she had seen was not hallucination. Zane had similar eyes.

He must be in disguise!

****

Sonia was speaking again. "I could easily correct your attitudes," she stated candidly. "But as someone previously stated, 'enough of this'. I will leave that chore to your own kind. Those who were not chosen will simply find yourselves back where you belong…with no memory of this encounter."

A murmur of sudden fear passed through those behind. Then abruptly, the room was empty, except for the chosen ten, and the three in front.

Some of those remaining looked back to make certain of what had happened, then every woman tensed, their eyes riveted on Sonia.

Mass hypnotic suggestion? wondered Darla.

Sonia allowed the resulting silence to drag on.

Darla began to feel uneasy again.

"I notice things," Sonia said quietly. "I see…and know, when you do not." She was looking directly at Darla and Ziva now. Her eyes narrowed as if in warning. "Do not under estimate me!"

****

Ziva's heart was in her throat.

What have I gotten into?

"Well." Sonia's demeanour changed to the pleasant elder lady they had seen at the interviews. "Enough of that! I tire of being the ogre. Let's get down to the business at hand."

Her audience relaxed a bit.

"My people were listening and watching through my eyes as I interviewed each of you. Together we saw your willingness to leave the conditions of your life. Each of you were individually selected specifically because of other talents and attributes. Not a one of us finds you unsuitable for the purpose for which you were selected."

Ziva wondered, *what is my purpose here?*

"Before we go into duties, I will tell you of our species. Ancient Greeks called our people the 'Aopato Auto'; loosely translated it means 'Invisible Ones'. We are telepathic, our minds in union. Our communication would be inaudible to you normally, unless we chose for you to hear us. We are emotionally and physically separate, but are over all one unit. An example is the human body with arms and legs, yet only one being. That is why we seemed to operate in tandem without obvious orders. Each completes the other, freely sharing memories, thoughts and experiences, as we did during the interview process. Thus, there are rarely secrets between us. We are able to see into you...but before hand, each has agreed, today would be the only time we invade your privacy in that fashion. For your own comfort, from this moment, we will refrain from following your every thought. This might prove a difficult task for some of our younger members, but they have agreed to do their best. Please forgive them, should they accidentally fail at this. They are used to openness..."

When the women realized the implications of what had been disclosed, uneasy looks passed among some. They were wondering, what was expected of them?

"My people promise, from this point, to try to refrain from the reading of minds," Sonia clarified. "In fact, we have decided to make it possible for you to share in our communications with each other. They promise to speak verbally while in your presence, so as to keep as few secrets from you as possible."

Those listening sat as if stunned, too dumbfounded to voice what they were feeling: confusion, astonishment, some trepidation, even terror.

Sonia looked to the man on her right. "Are you prepared, Lance?" He nodded solemnly. "Please watch as my sons take their true form."

Sonia was suddenly alone at the front.

Fear entered the room, near palpable. Heads turned searching, each woman obviously wondering where the men had gone.

"I failed to mention one important factor: we can not be seen by the naked human eye." Sonia grinned. "Hence the name 'Invisible Ones'. But...we have developed a device which will not only allow our thought communications to be audible to you, but will also permit our image to be seen."

Ziva shivered. *Maybe, there was another one of them in the interview room?*

"Lance...Zane. Please turn on the bands."

"Ho...oly Crap!" Darla exclaimed beside Ziva. The woman pulled back against her seat, as if trying to escape through the back of it. "I was messing with that!"

Ziva heard Chantel giggle.

Why she's not afraid at all!

Both men had just appeared out of thin air. They still were standing at the front where they had been before, but they had decreased in age by half, were now in their early twenties, and had gone to over seven feet tall. They were strongly built, muscular, blond, with cat-like eyes. Sonia's eyes; only blue with a vertical black slit. Mirrored in them was amusement at the reaction they were receiving, but otherwise, they stood stoic, unmoving, with arms folded across their chests.

Now, Ziva was certain one of them, or one like them had been in that room during her interview. The prospect filled her with dread.

"Each of us has been fitted with a similar headband." Ziva noticed the plain yellow-gold band across the forehead of each man. "When turned on, without conscious effort, it will keep us visible and audible to you. We thought it unfair of us to converse soundlessly while in your presence. However, we will continue to withhold our inner memories and private thoughts from you...until we know you can be trusted. We promise we will not turn off these bands for any reason."

But can their word be trusted? Ziva wondered.

CHAPTER 11

"I wonder what she looks like?" Chrystal whispered to Karine. "Maybe she's younger, too?"

On the other side of the Irish woman, wheelchair bound Chantel observed Sonia frown.

"My human age would be no different, Chrystal," Sonia stated, causing the young woman's eyes to go round with embarrassment at being overheard. "And my hearing is quite good for that age." She smiled. "Two Earth years equal to one of ours; makes my actual age thirty-eight according to our reckoning. However, the manifestation I have chosen would be correct were I human. As to what I really look like...I think, I will delay that visual until we are in a safer environment. It is sufficient that you have seen a male."

Chantel looked at the other nine women. Her chair was turned sideways, so she had a full view of their faces. Tension was apparent on every one. It seemed the more facts Sonia revealed the greater their apprehension.

What is the big deal? Chantel wondered annoyed. *So what if these men are giants. They are protective, gentle, and kind...at least that is my experience with Zane.*

Mind you, Darla and Ziva might have cause to worry.

Chantel had the feeling Zane did not much like Darla.

"Zane! Behave yourself!" Sonia warned without turning her head, and Chantel started at the suddenness of the curt command. "I am aware of what you are doing."

Lance turned away to hide a smile of amusement.

"You boys!" Sonia reprimanded, though a small smile played at the corner of her lips as well. "So you figure this has become too formal, do you?"

Both men grinned, and said in unison, "Yes, my Lady."

Surprise registered on the face of every human present.

"Zane?"

"Yes, mother?" he returned, feigning innocence.

Sonia frowned. "Remove it!"

The other women turned as one toward Chantel. She was suddenly aware, felt the wreath of flowers in her hair, but it was gone again before she could reach up to touch it.

In some way she felt special he had singled her out, but on the other, with all the attention, it was disconcerting. Chantel knew heat was rising in her cheeks.

"Are we about ready to return to the gravity of the situation now?" Sonia pointedly asked. "I promise not to bore you much longer."

Zane's gaze went to the ceiling above him, like an errant student reprimanded in class, and every woman, except for Darla, laughed.

Sonia turned to her youngest son. "Do you want me to banish you from the room?"

Giggles ran through the women. The picture of small Sonia chasing the giant Zane, finally brought a snort from Darla.

"No...but could we hurry. I'm getting muscle cramps."

Lance too, looked at the ceiling, having difficulty keeping a straight face. Sonia's eyes narrowed.

Both men attempted a show of mock fear. "We'll be good!" they exploded in unison.

Sonia turned back to the seats, waiting a moment until the laughter subsided.

"You see," she stated placidly. "They can be civilized with the right incentive."

Both men went stoic.

By this time every human present was highly amused...and relaxed.

Sonia smiled indulgently. "We are usually quite fun loving, but if we get too serious, Zane can always be counted on to liven things up. Now, where were we before you cut up? Oh, yes, those head thingies."

Lance grinned; his brother remained sober faced.

"Now Zane's the good boy," Sonia marvelled with mock sarcasm.

Zane burst out laughing, and the women unable to help themselves, fell to giggling like schoolgirls.

"Mom," Lance scolded. "Now, you've got the bug. May I remind you, we are nearing darkness?"

"Sorry," Sonia apologized. "I must be getting giddy. It's been a long day. Enough!" she proclaimed. "I believe they are relaxed enough now."

Suddenly, Chantel realized, it had all been an act for their benefit.

Is this what it will be like living among them?

It was beginning to sound like the encounter would be fun.

****

As gravity returned, a dark haired woman in her mid-fifties spoke up.

"May we ask questions?"

"Yes Morgan, you may," agreed Sonia. "I would be surprised if you did not question, considering your law enforcement background."

Ziva tensed. She is a cop? Wonderful! Why on earth does she need a job?

"I was wondering," Morgan queried. "Is it possible for something to interfere with your band devices or could someone, say without your knowledge, turn them off?"

Sonia chuckled. "You fear the men might be walking about unseen by you. If they did that purposely, they would have me to deal with."

"As reassuring as your words are, you haven't actually answered my question."

"True. The only way the bands will cease to function is if they are short circuited by a powerful energy drain, or an emotional overload causing the wearer's life force to become too weak to support it. It is maintained by our own energy force. A companion may shut it off if they deem it necessary, but none of you will be told how this may be accomplished…for our own safety. Also, the band shuts on and off automatically when we jump."

The words were out of her mouth before Ziva realized she had spoken aloud. "You mean teleport? You can do that?"

"We can do many things, Ziva," Sonia admitted evenly. "And it's nice to see your SiFi knowledge is not wasted."

Ziva's face grew hot. *She's mocking me, because I said I didn't believe in aliens. Man! I sure blew that one.*

Darla turned toward Ziva, her eyes inquiring but angry.

Oh man! Am I in trouble now. She thinks I spilled my guts in that interview.

"I only told her, I like certain movies…" Ziva whispered, defensively. "Nothing more."

Darla glared. "You better not be undermining me," she hissed.

****

"Before we go any farther," Sonia decided. "This has been a long day for you, and I am certain you are all hungry. Please partake as we continue."

Angel, like everyone else, found bottled water in one hand and a sandwich of choice in the other. She felt famished. Ham on rye being her favourite, she was not about to look a gift horse in the face, nor question how it had come to be there.

Sonia did not eat. Nor did her two sons. They still stood on either side, unmoving, like sentries bent on remaining attentive no matter the discomfort.

Angel wondered now, whether Zane had just been funning around when he complained of the muscle cramp.

"And now that we have finally come to your duties," Sonia declared. "Lance will carry on."

She sat back quietly, as if resting.

She must be so tired, thought Angel sympathetically.

Lance took a step forward. "There remain only twenty-one to our species: six females and fifteen males. We have an enemy who has…decimated our kind in the past. Because we are so few, we need help. In order to free up our men, we need to know our females are not left alone when we are on guard. That is why we have chosen a companion for each…"

"Ah." Morgan raised her hand slightly. "May I ask a question?"

"Of course."

"If you have only six females, why would you need almost double of our women?"

The man hesitated for a second before answering. "There are other duties…some in the kitchen. We had hoped for more choice…but, because so few qualified, the other positions…"

"Some will pull double duty," Sonia interrupted, clarifying. "Do not worry; we will co-ordinate your work schedules. I will continue Lance."

Her son stepped back obediently.

"Morgan, your mind is quick to spot discrepancy. I am pleased by your concern. It gives me a chance to present some added facts, and…the rules."

She paused, taking in the entire ten with her glance.

"We do not require any of your women to provide sexual favours, a thought that has entered the minds of some. The male sleep chambers are off limits at all times, and the men will not be allowed into your private areas. We are a 'one pair for life' species. Our individuals are celibate; they retain abstinence until paired. This is something that is essential to our emotional balance, especially so for the males."

Morgan frowned, and seemed about to ask another question, but Sonia quickly changed the subject.

"There is one more thing that needs addressing. I am sure that as you meet the rest of us, you will encounter difficulty telling us apart. I will give you one major key that should hold you in good stead. I sincerely hope it will help you.

"Each of us has a personal scent exclusive from any other. If you learn to recognize the fragrance of the person to whom you are appointed, you should have no difficulty. We ourselves, identify each other in this fashion, even when we are in disguise or before we are visible. An example: Angel, what is my scent?"

Astounded that Sonia should call upon her, Angel had to think for a moment. Then she recalled her first impression of Sonia.

"Why, it's a mixture of vanilla and cinnamon!" she exclaimed excitedly.

"Correct. Even though I am disguised or may go invisible, my scent can not be masked. This also will give any unseen male away...should our enemy have knowledge of his essence.

"Most of us have only a single scent. I have a double because I am 'Leader Female' as well as 'Ultimate Healer Female'."

"The female 'Ultimate Healer' scent is vanilla," Zane supplied. "The 'Ultimate Healer' male scent would be almond, plus a second scent. And a pair couple's scents will change when they are together, as well..."

"We will overload their memories son," Sonia cautioned. "There will be plenty of time for other instruction later. And as Lance warned earlier, darkness comes quickly."

Are they afraid of the dark? wondered Angel.

"It is time to prepare," Sonia stated quietly.

Lance took over again. "Your luggage has already gone ahead of you. You will find it in your appointed sleep quarters when you arrive. And yes, we even have what you left in the entry and your cars...

"By coming here, we consider that you have agreed to our terms. From now on, we are your sole providers and advisors. Your consent was in your mind at your interviews, and the time for backing out has past. For your own safety, you must follow our rules from now on."

Zane moved forward, continuing the instructions where his brother left off. "We have taken the liberty of removing all undesired articles from among your possessions. You will have no farther need of drugs, medications, alcohol or cigarettes. If any should be needed we will supply what is necessary.

"Also, for security purposes, all electronic equipment has been confiscated: no laptops, cameras, watches, radios or cell phones. They will not work where you are going."

****

"Ziva," hissed Darla. "Hide your medallion."

Ziva quickly slipped the Saint Christopher medal inside her blouse.

****

"Lance?" asked Zane.

"It is done," agreed the other.

The watch on the wrist of each woman had abruptly vanished.

"May I remind you," Lance reiterated. "Anything electronic or battery powered will not work once we transport."

****

"What of the medal?" Zane asked silently, nodding toward Darla and Ziva.

"Let her keep it," returned Lance with the same method of communication. "It will be useless when we enter Sanctuary, and they won't be able to trace fast enough as we jump."

****

Sonia again took over. "Chantel, Zane will carry you. The wheelchair goes no farther. You will no longer need it."

The old woman rose to her feet. "Gentlemen, I will see you on the other end."

Both men nodded slightly. Sonia abruptly vanished from the room.

CHAPTER 12

As soon as Sonia was gone, the women seemed to tense in fear or anticipation of what was to come next.

Zane moved toward Chantel. When he stood before her, he dropped first to one knee, and to the surprise of everyone, asked a question.

"May I touch you?"

Chantel's jaw dropped. *No one has ever been this courteous to me in my life.*

Just a bit rattled, she answered: "Of…of course."

He slipped one arm beneath her legs, the other around her back, lifted and stood.

The sensation made her giddy; she quickly wrapped her arms around his neck for support, fearful of the added height.

"I will be carefully not to drop you," he reassured softly.

His scent was very evident, now that he was in his true form, and at close proximity. Chantel liked his fragrance; it reminded her of thyme.

Zane moved quickly across the floor, stood at the very centre of the open space. Sonia's chair had vanished.

"Please ladies," Lance ordered. "Form a circle about them."

As they were instructed, the others hurried to shuffle into position.

"Join hands," Lance commanded, and as the women complied, added, "Ready Zane?"

"When you are…"

Lance stood at the upper centre, just beyond the circle of human women, reached out with a hand spread to either side.

"If you close your eyes, it will not be so disorienting."

He did so himself. Chantel closed her eyes, dropping her head against Zane's chest.

"You may open your eyes."

****

A collective gasp went out from the women. The room had changed around them, but they had felt no movement. They were now in an enormous cavern of black granite, the walls and ceiling luminescent with some sort of hidden lighting. An empty door frame stood gaping across the floor to their left, and another closed door to the right.

"Please be seated," offered Lance.

Chairs appeared behind the women, and they each took a seat.

"Eric?" Lance seemed to speak to the empty air. "We are ready for the 'Keepers'."

A table appeared behind him, and Lance gave farther instructions. "When your name is called, please come forward. As the 'Keeper' rises, you must touch it for it to personalize to you specifically. From then on it will supply your needs, guide you where you need to go, and tell you when and where to report to duty, hence the name 'Keeper'. Eric is in another room. He will activate each unit; sometimes it may take up to five or ten minutes for your 'Keeper' to activate. Please be patient.

"Once your 'Keeper' has adjusted to you, it will move above your head. Do not be alarmed by it; it is actually programmed to protect you, never to hurt you. Follow it through the exit door; it will lead you to your sleep quarters. You are given two days to assimilate to your surroundings, then your duties will begin."

He turned to Zane. "Jade is ready."

****

Zane moved away from the other women carrying Chantel. Uncomfortable with the fact she was being carried, Chantel attempted to engage him in conversation.

"Ah, so how did you like Earth?"

She felt him chuckle, deep down in his chest.

"We are still on Earth," he said gently. "Actually, I grew up here, spent twenty-five years in your military."

Chantel was astounded. "Did no one realize what you were?"

He laughed again. "I was in dormant form then. Someday I will explain better."

She pondered what he had said, then asked another question.

"Can you use what you learned from us to defend against your enemy?"

"Maybe we could use it against humans," he stated jokingly. "But our methods of battle are quite different from human involvement…however, I am now 'Leader Warrior' for our own defence."

He had reached the closed door; it opened silently to him.

****

A small glowing sphere appeared just above and beside Lance. He looked up.

"Don't be frightened," he reassured. "This is just the 'Keeper Sentry'."

"It's robotic, isn't it?" Angel exclaimed excitedly, thrilled at seeing an actually working model in operation.

"I am an artificial intelligence," agreed the miniature object.

Angel clapped her hands in utter delight. "Oh, I knew that was possible!"

Lance grinned at her uninhibited enchantment, and Angel made a valiant attempt to be more dignified.

Lance returned to the task at hand. "Are you ready 'Keeper'?"

"Indeed, sir."

"Then I will turn them over to you."

Lance proceeded to the empty hallway doorframe, taking a position of relaxed vigilance, much the way he had done at the interview hall. Zane appeared again outside the closed door across the way, and took up sentry there. Once more they were obviously kept within boundaries.

Where is Chantel? Angel wondered.

But the 'Keeper' was of more interest, and she soon forgot the handicapped woman.

Angel noted, the 'Keeper' was both globular yet stellate: a rotating, multi-pointed, rainbow coloured tiny star with beams of ever changing hues flashing from it in pulses. Angel curbed the desire to get close to and analyze it.

What a marvel of advancement! she thought. *Will I actually get to work with these things?*

"Ziva will come forward, please," intoned the 'Keeper Sentry".

****

Ziva had not expected to be called first. Obviously, they were starting in reverse this time.

Rising to her feet, she approached the table cautiously. One of the small silver globes lifted from among the others in the box on top, hovering just inches above and directly in front of her. Her trepidation increased her heart rate.

"Place both hands on your 'Keeper'," the sentry ordered.

Ziva reached out in uncertainty, enclosing the small, round shape. Nothing happened.

"That will do," sentry intoned. "Step back and wait."

Ziva obediently did what she was told.

Five minutes past, then ten.

What is wrong with the thing? she thought impatiently.

Suddenly the object activated, and Ziva jumped. The lights flashed all directions.

It looked just like the 'Sentry Keeper' now. Rising in the air, it spoke.

"Ziva is to follow me," it ordered.

Ziva laughed. "I just follow it now?"

"That is correct," agreed the 'Sentry Keeper'.

Her 'Keeper' moved slowly toward Lance at the exit door. He stepped aside, and as her 'Keeper' zoomed through Ziva hurried to follow.

The Jewish woman was so glad to be out of there, it felt like she finally was free.

What a day!

****

It was an hour and a half later, and only three women were left. Morgan had followed Ziva; May Lin after that. Then Karine and Jenna. Just after Darla had gone, the door behind Zane opened, and he stepped aside. Chantel emerged.

In unison, the remaining three women gasped in shock. Chantel was walking, her body straight, the limbs strong.

Chantel seemed in a state of shock however, sitting down beside Angel in an almost mechanical motion.

"Chrystal will come forward, please," intoned the sentry.

But Chrystal was too distracted by Chantel's changed condition to even hear her name.

Zane moved to her side, and bent to whisper in her ear. "Chrystal," he quietly rebuked. "Please take your turn. Tomorrow comes too soon, and we are all weary."

"Oh, sorry."

****

In the interval between, after Chrystal had left the room, Angel leaned over to Chantel.

"What did they do in there?" she quizzed.

But the answer that came back made no sense at all.

"Zane has a sister…their women are so beautiful! Jade was once a cripple like me." Tears formed in Chantel's eyes, slipping down her cheeks. "She took my ugly twisted legs, and…mine turned whole…but it hurt her so. It hurts them when they heal, but…but she did it for me anyway…"

Angel wondered whether Chantel had gone addled in the process. *Whatever is she talking about?*

"Chantel will come forward, please," interrupted to sentry.

Chantel wiped at the moisture on her cheeks, rose to her feet and like a sleepwalker, approached the table.

****

Angel was now the only one left. Lance still stood beside the outer door, but Zane had vanished from the room shortly after Chantel had left. One other woman by the name of Carmen had gone up just after Chantel.

Angel was bone weary. She felt numb.

The things I have seen today seem…unreal. Will I wake up in the morning and find it was all a dream?

"Angel will come forward, please," sentry called.

In a near trance, Angel went through the motions. At last, the time came to follow her 'Keeper' down the hall. The entry doorway was empty. Lance too was gone.

Through black granite halls, the machine led her, until at last they entered a huge chamber with bedrooms on both sides of the hall leading in.

"The shower facilities are at the end…"

Angel looked down to an empty doorway far away, but she had no desire to wash up. She was too weary.

All I need is a bathroom break. Then I think I'll sleep for a week.

The 'Keeper' stopped at a room with walls made of pink quartz.

"This will be your home," it stated quietly.

Home sounds so welcoming. All I want to do is crash.

The couch in the corner looks so inviting.

The 'Keeper' vanished.

Angel went to the washroom, then dropped onto the soft comforter of mauve. It took only seconds before she had left the last twelve hours, for oblivion.

CHAPTER 13

It was the last place she had expected to find a Navajo Indian, especially one over seven feet tall. He was just standing there in the black granite hallway, lost in thought.

Jenna had been so famished, she had gone looking for the kitchen, but it seemed there were miles and miles of hallways but nothing resembling a place to eat.

Don't these creatures need nourishment?

The laughter of children made the Navajo turn toward her. His dark hair was woven into two braids, and he appeared to be in his early forties. Unlike the two other males she had seen, whose eyes were blue with a black slit, this man had eyes of deep turquoise with a rust-brown slit. They were penetrating, yet somehow appeared gentle, giving comfort.

A sudden rush of air from behind caused Jenna to turn just in time to side step a young female of about five. She was no more than four foot tall with blond curls and distinctive purple eyes like those of Sonia. At her back, obviously chasing her, was a pre-teen boy.

"Kara! Ram!" Both children came to an abrupt stop, turning to face the elder, the girl still giggling, the boy suddenly awkward and uncomfortable, as if caught at a deed for which he was embarrassed.

The boy had darker skin than that of the other two, his hair straight and jet black. He was at least two foot taller than the girl, with eyes of chocolate brown.

If I didn't know better, I'd think he had been India born, mused Jenna.

"Are you suppose to be running where there are others in your way?" asked the Navajo sternly.

"Sorry, Sky," the boy, who had been addressed as Ram, apologized. "It was my fault. I was chasing her...we were playing tag."

"Kara?"

"I forgot, great-gramps. Are we allowed to play in the gardens?"

"As long as you stay within the barrier. But first, there is something that needs doing. You almost knocked this human off her feet."

Jenna was suddenly self-conscious. "Oh, that's okay..."

"It is not okay."

The boy and girl turned to Jenna, and in unison whispered apologetically. "We are sorry for being so inconsiderate."

Truly embarrassed now, Jenna could only nod.

"Can we go now, great-gramps?" the girl pleaded.

Great-gramps? Did I hear right? How old is this guy?

Sky must have agreed, but Jenna had heard nothing. The children vanished.

"No jumping from in here either," warned the older man.

"Aw, great-gramps…" The protest came from mid air, then the two reappeared once again.

"You are to walk. It is too easy to be injured when you are excited. Ram, you are a guardian. Your actions should be in keeping with that."

"Sorry, sir."

The girl reached for the boy's hand, as they walked away down the passage, careful not to be caught running. But as soon as they rounded the corner, they both giggled, and Jenna heard Kara say, "Sorry. Didn't mean to get you in trouble."

The boy's answer was lost to the distance.

Sky shook his head at their antics, and with a few quick steps was beside Jenna.

"You seem to be lost?"

Jenna laughed self-consciously. "I've been looking for the kitchen for at least fifteen minutes."

"Come. Follow me; I am going that direction."

He matched his steps to hers, slowing to a pace easier for her, walking easily beside her yet guiding in the right direction.

His scent was almond.

Didn't Zane say something of this last night? Almond is supposed to be the male healer scent.

But this man also had a subtle second scent.

Is it sage?

Considering he looked native, it didn't surprise her.

But didn't they also say, only the 'Healer Ultimate' had two scents?

Before Jenna could question him, they arrived at their destination.

They first walked through a huge room containing multiple tables and benches. It was large enough to accommodate at least fifty. Both the tables and the benches were of grey marble, but the walls of the chamber were again in black granite, with lighting some how coming from inside the stone.

Sky led her behind a counter at the far end. Here she saw a large grill and refrigerator against the back wall. Cupboards, containing dishes, lined one side of this space, and pots hung from the ceiling above.

"What would you like?" asked Sky.

"Oh, I can make it myself, if you just show me where things are."

"And what specifically do you seek?"

"Do you have makings for a sandwich? That would tided me over."

"Bread then?"

"Yes."

"Just speak what you require. It will appear before you. Your 'Keeper' is always present to provide for your needs, even though you can not see it. I will remain, to make certain yours is not faulty."

"Oh…okay. Ah…bread."

A loaf of bread appeared on the counter.

"If you specify a type you prefer, it can do that also."

"Oh…rye bread."

The loaf changed from white to rye.

"I will leave you then. You seem to have the hang of it."

After the man left the room, Jenna tried other requests. "Lettuce…ham…"

Each appeared when she spoke the words aloud.

This is fun…and easy.

But where are the utensils?

"You looking for a knife?"

Jenna started, and spun to face a table nearby, where the sound seemed to come from.

He slowly became solid, a teenage boy sitting at the table eating a sandwich of his own. He was gangling and blond, his eyes more silver than blue.

Now she realized it, the aroma of cloves had hung in the air from the first…his scent?

He dropped his hand from the band around his forehead, and excused himself.

"Sorry, there was no one else in here when I came, so I turned the dumb thing off. I know we're not suppose to do that, but sometimes a guy needs a little privacy."

Jenna laughed good-naturedly. "You've been watching me all this time?"

He shrugged. "Yeah. Don't sweat it. My name's Tyler."

"You hiding from someone, Tyler? You do something wrong too?"

His eyes narrowed, reproving her. "Sky knew I was here. And don't talk down to me like I'm a kid. In human, I'm older than you are."

Jenna was surprised. "Sorry. How old are you then?"

"In human, twenty-nine; our reckoning, not quite fifteen."

"You mean…in your years I'd only be…"

"You wouldn't even be fourteen."

"Wow! It might be fun to be a teen again. I wasn't so lucky the first time around. So…can you tell me where the utensils are?"

"Just ask for it…like you did with the other things."

He did it for her before she could speak aloud.

"'Keeper', give Jenna a table knife."

The knife appeared in her hand.

"How do you know my name?"

"Common mind connection."

Jenna frowned. *What does he mean by that?*

"We all watched the interviews."

"Oh, oh! You watched me?"

"Like I said, don't sweat it. Better make your sandwich."

As she went about making her own snack, he continued eating. When he finished, he sat watching her.

"You do realize," he broke in after a time. "Who you were ordering around before?"

"His name was Sky. That's all I know. Oh yeah, and he's great grandfather to Kara."

He laughed.

"What's so funny?"

"Well, first off, Kara's my niece. When did you see her?"

"Just before...in the hall...with Sky."

He snickered again.

"What's so all fired funny?" Jenna demanded annoyed by his impudence.

"The way you call him Sky...so familiar...as if he's just another guy."

"Well, isn't he?"

"Not really. Sky is Sonia's pair. You were giving orders to...well, the equivalent, in human, would be...he's like...the King."

Shocked, Jenna let her jaw drop most unbecomingly.

His grin spread across his features. He was enjoying every bit of her discomfort.

"Don't let it bother you," he finally excused. "They are both very approachable... interact like we're all one big family, which we actually are. More than half of us are related."

Somehow that did not ease her feelings of embarrassment and guilt.

Obviously, I've been very presumptuous and rude to Sonia's partner. That could mean trouble...if they are the kind to take insult. Great way to start out girl!

But Sky did not seem to take offence. Wonder if Sonia is the protective kind?

Tyler rose to his feet.

"Next time, ask your 'Keeper' for directions. It's assigned to serve you."

"I gathered that from what, ah…he said."

He grinned mischievously again. "You can call him Sky, same as we all do. Just remember who he is." Then he added as an after thought, "I was only teasing you…"

Jenna wrinkled her nose in annoyance. "You're a rascal, you know that?"

"Nah, that's not me; that's my brother Shawn. If you think I'm bad, just wait 'till you meet him."

Jenna shook her head in disbelief at his audacity.

"So, how do I get directions from my 'Keeper'?"

He grinned mischievously.

"Just ask out loud…or think it. It reads thoughts, too."

Jenna turned hot, realizing he could do the same. *Has he been listening to my thoughts?*

He chuckled. "Well, I got to get back. See you around."

Then, he just vanished.

It seems so natural to them to just pop in and out like that. What I wouldn't give to be able to do that too.

CHAPTER 14

It had been difficult reintegrating after being on the street, but once Karine realized her 'Keeper' was always with her, and operated when she spoke aloud, it had made the transition smoother from then on.

At first the 'Keeper' service happened by accident. In her senior moments, Karine had developed the bad habit of talking out loud when she was frustrated or missing something. She had not meant to grumble; she had simply been too cold in the night. Like an unseen leprechaun, the 'Keeper' had fulfilled her wish.

She learned quickly the value of her helper. Not only did it give her an extra blanket, it helped her to find her comrades, the lunchroom, and the small common room set aside for recreation. The 'Keeper' had even produced a copy of her favourite book, which she was reading at the moment in that very room.

At seventy-eight Karine had found the interviews and the arrival at this place , which she now knew was called Sanctuary, to be taxing both to body and mind. She needed those two days to recuperate.

Though she had a room of her own, away from the others, she still had met some of them. It seemed she was one of the two oldest chosen, the other being a Chinese lady by the name of May Lin.

At present, May Lin sat across from her reading her own book. The fact the woman could still read was surprising enough, but even more remarkable was that her book was in Mandarin. The beings of this facility had thought of everything.

May Lin looked to be about eighty. She was short, stooped and walked with very short steps. Her appearance was wizened; a small oriental lady in drab tan slacks, smock and black flat shoes. She wore her grey hair in one long pigtail down her back.

A small 'Keeper' floated through the gaping common room doorway.

"May Lin and Karine will please follow. It is time to report for duty."

Karine marked her page, setting her book and reading glasses aside. She watched as May Lin shuffled across the space between them, then joined her.

The 'Keeper' did not take them far, only to a fork in the passage, then down a second hallway a short distance. After bidding them to proceed into the room opposite, it vanished.

As soon as Karine entered, she realized it was a second common room, but its beauty was breathtaking.

It was huge, the ceiling at least twenty feet above them. The walls were of mint green marble, three of which were inset with floor to ceiling ledges holding thousands of books. In the corner nearest the door a large chess set of black and white onyx sat on a stone board of rust and cream squares. All about the room, under the volumes of reading material, were tables and benches of black granite interspaced with comfortable forest green easy chairs.

But it was the far wall that first caught your eye and held you spell bound. Cascading over the vertical obstacle was an actual, honest to goodness, very real waterfall. It sent sprays of moisture out into the air around it, causing multi-coloured rainbows to form at the ceiling and in the corners nearest it. Though the cataract was gentle and slow, it seemed muted as if an unseen barrier kept moisture and sound at bay. It never came near the numerous tomes.

So this is the library, Karine marvelled in wonder. *How did they create a waterfall inside this room?*

"Isn't it beautiful? It's natural. Our mason incorporated it into the room."

The voice she heard was that of Sonia, yet when Karine turned to look, she saw a much younger woman then the lady from her interview.

Even though Sonia was now over six feet tall, and in her late thirties, she was petite, her skin a cream-pink, her cheeks held the rosy flush of health, and her gold-blond hair shone as the waves came to unruly curls around ears and neck. But the Amethyst eyes would always give her away.

"Sonia?" Karine queried in surprise. "Well now, you do have the look of a right Irish beauty."

Sonia laughed, pleased by the compliment, and patted a nearby chair. "Come sit. If you are to be my companion, we might as well relax."

****

Out of shyness, May Lin had stayed hidden, directly behind the big boned Irish woman. As Karine moved to approach Sonia, the smaller Asian woman came into her employer's line of sight.

"And what have we here?" asked Sonia. "May Lin?"

"I too was told to come, honourable lady." May Lin dropped her head, lowering her eyes in respect. Timidly, she asked, "Have I displeased you?"

"Oh, no! Oh, no!" Sonia reassured quickly. "I am not offended by you. I am simply caught unprepared. I was under the impression I would only have one companion. My overseer guardian has made an error." She patted the seat on the opposite side from Karine. "Come...sit...both of you. I will set this right immediately."

Hesitantly, May Lin sat down on the very edge of the large seat offered to her, while Karine dropped heavily into the other.

Sonia's voice took on a note of annoyance. "Chi Cho!"

His voice preceded his visual. "Yes, my Lady?"

As the male became slowly solid before them, May Lin was shocked to find he was an oriental like herself. Though he towered over them, more than seven feet tall, and appeared half her age, she had the impression of aged wisdom. The burnt umber skin was smooth, the dark pigtail at his back jet black, and the pointed goatee beneath the flat nose was equally so. He appeared young, yet May Lin could not shake the feeling he was older than she.

In trepidation, she rose to her feet, and the brown slit eyes noticed her immediately. She dropped her head, lowering her gaze in a gesture of honour to him.

"May Lin." She raised her eyes to her new mistress. "You may remain seated."

Again, May Lin sat down on the very edge of the seat, utterly uncomfortable, her eyes downcast.

Sonia turned to address her overseer.

"Why have I two appointed companions?"

May Lin looked up. The man's eyes had turned to Sonia.

Chi Cho frowned.

"My Lady? It appears…both Djura and I chose for you…"

"Without checking with the other?"

"Apparently so," he observed.

"Well, I see no need to have two," Sonia declared pointedly.

Chi appeared uncomfortable.

"Does my Lady wish me to send one back to her former life?"

"Which one would you sacrifice?"

Chi sighed. "My Lady, I am truly sorry. We both meant well…"

"I know…too eager. Or am I mistaken?"

Chi looked away, which greatly surprised May Lin.

"No, my Lady." He hesitated, returning his eyes to Sonia. "What would you have us do?"

"It is your mistake?"

He closed his eyes for a second. "Yes, my Lady."

"Then you must rectify it."

He frowned.

"May Lin is for you…remember?" Sonia pointed out softly.

He looked at her in shock. "My Lady!" he protested indignantly. "We were to be …discreet."

"Yes. But you have brought this on yourself. You avoid your responsibility under the guise of placing her with me."

He closed his eyes a moment, saying nothing.

"She will serve you," Sonia declared. "May Lin?" She spoke without turning. "This one has a tendency to ignore his own needs. You are to see he eats regularly and actually rests at his sleep times."

A flush rose to the cheeks of the male.

May Lin was trembling. *Is he also no more than a servant? And how am I to persuade a big man such as he to rest if he does not wish to?*

But May Lin knew what her answer must be. "Yes, honourable lady," she whispered.

"My Lady," Chi pleaded. "Have mercy…all will see…"

"No argument, " Sonia said firmly.

Their eyes locked and held for a second longer then necessary. He was the first to drop his. "Yes, my Lady," he meekly agreed. "Will that be all?"

Sonia nodded. Chi moved as if to leave, but quickly turned back.

"If anyone needs an attendant it is Djura!" he declared hotly.

May Lin gasped audibly at this daring audacity. She thought, *He will be punished now for certain!*

As if reading her thought, Sonia quickly hid a half-smile.

"I know," she agreed softly. "You are two of a kind. That is why this mess came about in the first place. Both of you are equally guilty of avoiding the inevitable."

"I admit, we each hoped to put off responsibility. I regret my action now, my Lady. And you are right to force it public. Then we...I must be honourable. I deserve this..."

May Lin was so astounded her jaw dropped. Never had she known a man of this ethnic origin to speak his mind or act in this manner toward those he served. To argue with his employers, as if on equal footing...and to admit fault...it was beyond her understanding.

"Chi, this is not meant as punishment..."

"I know that," he said quietly. "I have...how do you say it? Put the wrong foot first..."

Sonia chuckled. "Indeed. Some day you will have to apologise...to her," she added quietly.

Does she mean to me? Why would he need to apologise?

The man's image faded for a second then came back into focus.

He's embarrassed? Is he reading my thoughts?

Sonia closed her eyes, as if deeply thinking on the problem. "I will compromise ...so this will be less uncomfortable for you both."

Sonia opened her eyes again; the male's eyes held eager hope.

What kind of relationship is this? wondered May Lin. *They treat each other with familiarity, like friends, like family.*

"You are my guardian on duty presently? asked Sonia.

"Yes, my Lady. Djura is on sleep break."

"This is what we will do. And Djura is to do the same as regards to Karine." Chi nodded his agreement. "See that he understands there is no negotiation on this…"

Once more Chi nodded.

"I will keep both women on as my companions. They will serve alternately as the two of you do. When the guardian is on duty, the female will serve me, as well. When you go off today, take May Lin with you and accommodate her in the annexed apartment behind your quarters. Our law of celibate still applies to you unless your circumstances change…am I understood?"

Relief flooded his face. "Yes, my Lady."

"See that she understands your intentions."

His cheeks turned a shade darker. "Yes, my Lady."

****

"Karine will be Djura's helper. Again annexed chamber, and the same rules apply with her."

Sonia turned to the Irish woman. "You will also see that Djura takes time to eat and rests on his off times. He tends to believe he is invincible."

Karine watched the Asian male's eyes light with amusement.

What sort of man is this Djura, anyway? Karine wondered.

"And Karine…" Karine turned her full attention to Sonia. "He will resist you. And so as you understand, he will not require sexual favours."

"Ah…yes, my lady."

A small smile of amusement played at Sonia's lips at the use of the address her men used for her.

"My Lady…" interrupted Chi. "For now…am I to stand watch…outside?"

"Yes. Leave both women with me until Djura awakes, then you can take care of these matters."

"He will not like this," Chi warned with gravity.

"I know. But he will obey," Sonia observed. "He always does."

The Oriental looked searchingly at Sonia, as if probing for deeper meaning.

"You may go now, Chi. And next time…do not under estimate me," Sonia cautioned quietly.

"I do know better," he admitted.

"Yet, you both must always try."

The normally reticent Asian grinned, as if he had enjoyed the challenge. He then abruptly vanished.

****

When Chi was gone, Sonia turned smiling, her eyes filled with mischief.

"Sometimes, with some men, a woman must be quicker and more shrewd than they are." She winked. "These two are my best, but they are both too proud to let you see their true feelings…you have to slip it out of them. I suggest that if you each ease their vulnerability, your male will treasure you. And…they will then guard you with their lives. Remember that in your dealings with them."

Did Sonia know all along? Did she allow this to happen on purpose? wondered Karine. *What sort of man is this Djura, that it is necessary to do that?*

****

This woman has wisdom of Confucius, May Lin observed amazed. *Perhaps, honourable sir is not in such a bad place as I first thought.*

CHAPTER 15

Though Jenna was actually twenty-seven, she was known to act more like a teenager. As she had told Tyler, she had been deprived of that carefree time, and deeply regretted it. She had never experienced girl talk with a sister, nor gone shopping, or done like activities with friends. That was why now, at every opportunity, she lived life to the fullest, and for the moment.

When her parents died in a boating accident her grandmother had taken her in, and having a fortune at her disposal, the lady decided to live out her fantasies vicariously through her granddaughter. It was hoped Jenna would become the virtuoso the old woman had always wanted to be. And the matriarch had spent her entire fortune to that end.

Even from kindergarten, there had been lessons in flute, piano, the harp, violin, and any other instruments meant to be mastered by a prodigy. Always, there was the practice, practice, practice. Grandma had said, if you worked hard enough, you would become perfect at whatever you were doing. Yet this pupil had been master of none.

Jenna had never wanted to be that good. She just wanted to be an average teenager; go to parties; visit with other girls her age; have a boy friend. But her grandmother would allow none of that. In her eyes, Jenna was destined for better things!

Most of her life from high school on had been spent at music boarding school. At that place you lived music: it was classical, jazz, western, even rock and roll. Jenna had endured it all. Here she felt inferior, not jealous mind you, but out of place. She found no kindred spirit among her classmates. Their goals were to be the best, to someday be famous. Hers was not.

Jenna had never been the competitive type. She knew from the first, she was not concert material, and an audience terrified her. She shook with dread at every performance.

Then just recently, her grandmother had died. At the reading of the will, Jenna had been set free. However, not only was she now alone in the world, Jenna discovered, she was also a penniless pauper.

Her job hunt had been vicious. Who out in the real world wanted, or needed, an unfinished music teacher, or a mediocre musician terrified of crowds? At last, in desperation, Jenna had decided to change occupations. She had answered that add, only to find they actually needed a music teacher.

She realized she had been hired because of her experience, but Jenna wished it had been for anything but that. She had been appointed to Nadia, though as yet, she had not yet met the girl. Today had come her summons, and she had no idea what to expect.

How old is this child? Is she like Kara?

As Jenna followed her 'Keeper' through the stone hallways, she was filled with trepidation.

I don't know how to teach! How do you instruct an alien in music? Did they reason in the same fashion as a human, or was there some other way they learned? What if she was tone deaf?

Arriving at the suite, Jenna found an open doorway.

Why don't these guys use doors, like normal beings? Am I just supposed to walk in?

She was too polite to do that, so Jenna rapped on the wall outside.

A girl of about eleven popped into the opening, a creature of such stunning beauty it took Jenna's breath away.

"Oh, no need to knock," the girl exclaimed pleasantly. "Just call out."

Jenna had never laid eyes on someone so lovely. Brown eyes with a gold slit were the first thing you noticed, then the smooth caramel skin, and the long black spiral curls.

Wow! What a showstopper! This child doesn't need to play music; she is the music...if music were a picture...or a person.

"Well, don't just stand there with your mouth all agape. Come in!"

Nadia stepped aside, and as Jenna moved inside, continued talking.

"Oh, I think you are so pretty!" Nadia enthused. "And you're only five years older than I am. We'll have such fun together."

Jenna frowned. Did she just say, only five?

"I'm a little older then that...I think."

Mind you, Tyler did say I'd be only fourteen in their world.

"In human I'd be...twenty-two!" Nadia proclaimed indignantly.

"No kidding! Girlfriend, you look too young." Jenna suddenly realized she was being too familiar. "I'm sorry, ah…what should I call you?"

"I like girlfriend," Nadia decided. "Sounds like we're pals. And I'd love that."

She is a kindred spirit. Wow!

"How old are you…really…in your years?"

Nadia wrinkled her nose. "Eleven. Just divide by two. But, I actually have two years of university."

"Ah…is that what you call school?"

Nadia laughed outright. "No silly. I went to your university."

"Really?"

Nadia grinned. "Come sit down."

Jenna dropped into a nearby seat, and Nadia did like wise.

"Oh, I just love your hair. I used to wish for fair hair…and blue eyes," she added wistfully. "Of course, now I could look any way I want, but…Chad likes me like this. We match when I stay normal."

"Is Chad your boy friend?"

For a second Nadia's image dimmed.

I wonder, is that how they blush?

When she returned to focus, Nadia went on to another subject without answering Jenna's query.

"I don't think the guys are quite ready yet…"

"What guys? For what?"

"Oh! It's the most exciting thing," Nadia exclaimed exuberantly. "We are going out!"

"Out?"

"Out of Sanctuary. My gran has given me permission to go to the biggest conservatory on Earth…"

Jenna frowned. "Why?"

"She says I may copy all the available song books and sheet music, and all their manuals on techniques, and everything else pertaining to music we find there. Do you realize how much knowledge that will make available to us?"

Jenna was puzzled. "I would have thought your species would be far more advanced in musical knowledge then our race."

"No," Nadia admitted sadly. "I am our only 'musical receptive', and I have no musical training…hardly any, accept what I learned in grade school. I only know the flute."

"So you want me to teach you. Is that correct?"

Nadia nodded.

"What happened to the other musicians among your people?"

"The 'Opposites' hated music…"

"And?"

"Grandma says our music records were lost in the ethnic cleansing of our world…"

"These 'Opposite' guys, they killed all those that liked music, I presume?"

"Yes. All those with the music gene…actually, they slaughtered all of our side of the species…except for a few babies. There are only two 'Pure' left now."

Jenna assumed she spoke of herself. "Oh, is that why your skin tone is so different from the others?"

Nadia laughed at her errant presumption. "Oh no, I'm not a 'Pure'. Gran is the only 'Pure' female remaining. I'm part Eritrean."

Jenna blinked. "Isn't that…human?"

"Yes." Nadia agreed with candour. "Most of us are part human. Chad is Ethiopian…"

Again, with this Chad. Who is he?

"And Ram is from India…"

"I've seen Ram."

"We are not all the same. Humans are not all the same."

"But," interrupted Jenna. "I thought your mother was Jade? Chantel mentioned her. Chantel's the one who was in a wheelchair when we came."

"My mother is Jade," Nadia agreed. "But she is part human also."

"That means you're what…a quarter Eritrean…black?"

"Multi-racial…yes."

Jenna was quiet, not quite certain what to say next.

How long have these guys been on Earth?

"Do you have something against the blacks of the human race?"

"Oh…oh, no! No! I'm just…a bit puzzled. I'm having a hard time trying to figure this out. How long have your people been on this planet?"

Nadia grinned mischievously. "This time…or before?"

Jenna frowned.

And Nadia laughed, amused by her perplexity. "Actually, we were all born on Earth…"

"Really?"

"Yes. Grandma's father and mother were two of the original babies saved, hidden dormant on this planet."

Before Jenna could pry farther, a disembodied voice interrupted their conversation. "Nadia, are you coming?"

"Yes! Yes, we will be right there."

"What would you like me to do while you are gone?" Jenna wanted to know.

"Oh, you are coming with us!"

"Ah…and just how are we going to get half across the world?"

"The way we always do," Nadia proclaimed frankly. "We jump. But two females may never go alone. Chad always accompanies me as my guardian, and gran has appointed my cousin Tyler to escort us. He is a 'Warrior Guardian', so he will be good protection."

"I know Tyler…we just met…"

Nadia grinned impishly, as if she knew a secret Jenna was not privy to "I know," she declared pointedly. Then she reached for Jenna's hand. "First we must jump to the outer meeting room," she added.

CHAPTER 16

When they materialized at the conservatory, it was night and the floor they were on was empty of people. The space held a monstrous, vast library.

Tyler let go of Jenna's hand, and turned to the other two young people.

"Okay guys. Go for it. Have fun."

Chad chuckled, as Nadia moved off quickly into the first set of shelves. "She'll soon forget where she is with the joy of this find."

"Keep a close watch on her, Chad," Tyler warned. "The machines of the 'Opposites' can pick us up in here."

Chad nodded solemnly, moving away to follow Nadia.

The boy was about fourteen, though Jenna knew from previous conversations with Nadia and Tyler, his human age would be twice that. That would put both Chad and Tyler in their late twenties, the same as Jenna herself. Except for Nadia, they were all about the same age.

Jenna easily saw Chad was of Ethiopian heritage. Unlike Nadia, with her fine, loose, spiral curls; the boy had the nappy, tight, dry hair of the race. He stood at least six foot five, with skin so black he disappeared in the shadows. He held himself erect, walking with the straight-backed posture evident to the culture. He exhibited a tendency to be excessively enamoured by Nadia, with a resulting over protectiveness, and alertness to her welfare. Jenna found it endearing.

There was one other difference between the boy and girl. Though his eyes were also brown, the slit in the centre of his was black. If Chad narrowed his eyes, he vanished completely in darkness.

As she watched the two disappear, Jenna thought to herself, she would give just about anything to look as young as these kids.

I sure don't like appearing the grown up here, when most of them are really in my age group!

Tyler stood, seeming preoccupied, watching as the other guardian disappeared. Jenna decided, now was a good time to ask questions.

"Are 'Opposites' of a different race, or are you all of the same species?"

He turned and stared at her, as if not following her train of thought. Then he frowned.

"They once were...the same, but...they turned 'Opposite'."

"Okay? What does that mean? Do they look like you?"

He shook his head. "No, not any more."

"So what do they look like?"

"Much like a giant lizard. They smell bad, are very mean and evil. Deadly! Trust me, you don't want to come face to face with one."

Jenna laughed, not sure to take him seriously. "Maybe your ancestors have boogyfied them? I mean, come on, that's really opposite from you. Have you ever actually seen one?"

For a moment, he just stared at her in astonished disbelief.

"You think our adults would scare us with stories?"

"Well, you've got to admit, it does sound a little far fetched."

His eyes narrow in anger. "I'll have you know, I've done battle with them. And believe me, they are worse than any horror movie you've ever seen."

For a second she forgot they were equal in age. "You've done battle! At your age!"

Disgusted, Tyler turned away at the insult. Choosing to ignore her, rather then return with an unpleasantness of his own, he studied the rows of shelves in the shadows.

It dawned on Jenna; she'd been very insensitive. "I'm sorry...I just...find all this...hard to believe. Both what Nadia has told me, and now...you. It seems like a tall tale."

Boy! I'm just turning the knife deeper here. Better shut my mouth before I choke on my own words.

Tyler did not turn back as he defended. "Our side of the species is not able to lie..."

Again disbelief was there in her thoughts, though this time she held it down.

Can I put my foot in it any worse with this guy?

Abruptly, he chose to be pleasant again. He turned back with a condescending word. "I keep forgetting you are only human." Then with graciousness, he added: "I too have a suspicious nature. It's not a bad thing. Keeps you from swallowing everything without question. Actually, that's a good protection measure I admire in you."

Jenna was amazed. *Is he praising or insulting me? He's acting so superior. How dare he?*

Once more she forgot his human age.

Tyler grinned, as if he were listening to her thoughts. Jenna dropped her eyes, certain her face had gone a darker shade of pink.

"So…any other questions you would like to ask?" he said amicably.

Jenna turned to look at the darkening shelves beyond, just to snub him. A sudden idea struck her.

"Aren't you guys kinda stealing from us?" she challenged, turning back around. "We put centuries into developing this music, and you just take it without asking!"

"Actually, you are quite right," Tyler admitted. "Grandma Sonia feels the same way. That's why she had Chi set up an anonymous foundation offering a grant to the under privileged. It works automatically without being monitored. The system searches for promising musicians who have no means to pay for a musical education, then sends them funds, sets up the board and room, with meal tickets, etc, all without human awareness, or need for us to track the progress."

"And where does all this cash come from? You steal that too?"

This time she could see the indignation; he had to make an effort to not take offence.

"Chi has billions invested in your markets. He holds innumerable holdings in real estate all across the planet."

"This Chi is a pretty rich alien…"

"Chi was born here! We all were! He spent eighty-six years dormant on this planet. He grew up an orphan, on the streets of Taipei. He worked hard for every penny he has. None of his riches came by dishonesty! And, he generously shares it."

Silence filled the air. Jenna knew she had overstepped. She felt foolish now, yet she could not let him win the argument. She would not let it go...not just yet.

"What do you guys mean...dormant?" she returned with sarcasm.

He made a rude sound.

"Before we changed, we lived human-like."

"And no one noticed you?"

Tyler sighed, as if forced to deal with an errant child.

"We didn't even know what we were...until the 'Opposite' came hunting us. It seems it wasn't enough to kill our ancestors...our grandparents."

Jenna dropped her eyes at the anger in his. *His isn't kidding about these things.*

Then a thought struck her.

"How come we've never seen these "Opposites'? They've never been reported on Earth."

"Want to bet? You're always doubting what I say." His voice had quieted somewhat; his anger cooled. "But, I'd like to ask you this, did you know we existed before this?" he asked quietly. "Did you not see how well we can hide?"

She had to think about that for a moment.

"The human race tends to think it knows about everything, but there is much that escapes them. Our ancestors have come and gone from here for centuries. They have found your race to be naïve...also, arrogant and aggressive. Because of this attitude, the mind set that you always assume you are right, we considered you as deadly to our species as the 'Opposites'."

Jenna's jaw dropped. "You think we could harm you?"

"Oh, yes!" Tyler declared vehemently. "Your race has done us a great deal of harm in the past!"

Then, he abruptly switched topics, as if he realized he had revealed too much. It was as if this subject was forbidden, and he had just crossed a line; as though someone had just reprimanded him for it.

"I am afraid we will have to forego any farther discussion. I must get to my appointed tasks."

Jenna was a debater; combative by nature, she would have liked to continue to defend her race, but Tyler closed away that prospect.

"Come," he ordered, taking her by the hand. "Two females together in this room at this time of night is unsafe. We don't want to lose Nadia. After all, she is our only 'Music Ultimate'."

Jenna had no idea what that was, but she immediately caught on to the fact that Tyler considered her a handicap, and that brought her hackles back up again.

"You think I'm a liability? Why did you bring me at all?"

At long last Tyler realized how deeply he was offending her. He quickly made a direct effort to correct his mistake.

"I am sorry," he whispered contritely. "You are not unwanted...but...you will attract undesired attention..."

Jenna pulled her hand from his. "How? Why just me?"

Tyler sighed, frustrated. "This room should be empty. If the 'Opposites'' scanner passes over us, they will see the heat signatures. Chad can hide his own and Nadia's, but you, because you are a human, and your signature is different...a lone human female is sport for them. Then they will also quickly realize we are here. If they come, they will find Nadia...they go after our females...they torture them. We must leave...now!"

Is he frightened for just Nadia? Or for me too?

Impatiently, forcefully, Tyler grabbed her hand. He jumped abruptly. Suddenly they were in the glass domed concert auditorium with the night stars above them. But in her mind, she went back even further.

Jenna had not been in a recital theatre since her grandmother had died. She felt unexpectedly fragile, disconcerted and vulnerable. Past fears crowded in on her, brought tremors.

And Tyler misread her reaction.

"I am so sorry I offended you," he apologized profusely. "I know better, but sometimes, I speak without thinking. I never meant to put down the human race. They are part of me, too. I got carried away. I've never been good with a girl..."

Tears in her eyes, Jenna's heart melted. Maybe he isn't so bad after all.

"Aw, I forgive you," she quickly responded. "And I know, you were right about my race. We are rather egotistic, pompous, sadistic, and obtuse sometimes, but we can also be loving, and…"

He laughed. "I know that," he admitted, embarrassed. "But, I get frustrated by circumstances sometimes, and forget to see the best of human nature. I'm still learning at my grandmother's knee. Which reminds me…at the risk of offending you once again, I really must do the tasks I was sent perform…"

"Oh, I thought that was just an excuse."

He shook his head, exasperation returning to his features.

Oh, brother. There I've doubted his truthfulness again.

"Is there anything I can do?" she asked to cover the uncomfortable silence.

He chose to let it go. "Just be watchful, and warn me should anyone come." Then he added, " Oh…and I need you…ah, to be quiet, please?"

****

Jenna finally took a seat on a stool. Tyler stayed motionless with his eyes closed for what seemed like hours, and she not only was tired of the lack of interaction, but exceedingly bored.

How can he do that without getting cramped? What is he doing? And why did he bother taking me along at all? He sure didn't need my company!

It was then she heard the footsteps approaching.

"Tyler," she hissed urgently, reaching out to shake him.

Before her hand brushed his arm, he came instantly alert. "Don't ever touch one of us when we are in watch mode," he warned gently. "What is it?"

"I think someone is coming."

"Yes," he agreed. "The security guard is making his rounds. Do not fear. He will not see or hear anything. Just remain still."

The man entered from the stage door, carrying a lit flash light. Walking casually by them where they stood on stage, he shone his light over the darkened seats, listened a moment, then wandered away again out through the opposite door.

When he was gone, Jenna turned to Tyler in amazement. "How come he couldn't see us?" she whispered.

Tyler answered her in a normal voice. "I have a shield up over the room. It blocks sight and sound. He could have touched us, but never would have known. When we first came, I put his mind in...hypnotic sequence. It's easy to do to a human, but doesn't work as well with 'Opposites'."

Jenna frowned. "You can do that to all humans?" The thought went through her mind, Did he do it to me?

"I would never do that to you, Jenna. Believe me, we have not done it to the women we've brought to Sanctuary. We prefer you with your will intact. Please don't fear me, Jenna."

Jenna looked away, disconcerted.

When she thought about it, maybe these guys were as deadly as the 'Opposite' they feared.

"We would never harm you women. We picked you…because, we knew we could trust you."

"Okay," she agreed, to prevent another argument. "I believe you."

"Please Jenna, believe me when I tell you this. Our species is not capable of lying. We would say nothing, rather than speak an untruth."

"O…kay?"

Tyler sighed. Though he knew she was unconvinced, he let it go. Trust took time.

"I must return to what I was doing. Thank you for the warning. You did exactly as I asked."

"If he comes again, ah…should I call you?"

"He will not…but yes, should something or someone enter this room, warn me."

He returned to his motionless stance, his eyes closed.

****

Chad and Nadia appeared beside them. Tyler came alert, and turned toward them.

"That was quick."

"Oh, Tyler," Nadia cried enthusiastically. "It was all so interesting, I couldn't help absorb it as rapidly as possible. I didn't want to leave anything behind."

"You got everything?"

"Oh yes!" Nadia exclaimed happily. "It will be such a benefit!"

"Then we should get going. I too am finished."

"How is the home planet?" asked Chad.

"Safe...for the present."

Can he somehow observe their home world from this distance? wondered Jenna. *Maybe up this high it is closer?*

She was about to ask, when Nadia suddenly distracted both males.

With a sigh, the young female's lids slid shut, and she unexpectedly went limp in a dead faint. She would have fallen had not Chad quickly reached out to catch her.

"Whatever's wrong with her?" exclaimed Jenna in alarm. "She was fine only moments ago. What happened?"

However, neither Tyler nor Chad seemed unduly concerned. They acted as if this were a common occurrence.

"She did too much too fast," stated Tyler matter-of-factly. Then added to Chad, "You'd better carry her; you are her 'pair compatible'."

Chad swept the unconscious girl into his arms. Tyler grabbed Jenna's hand, placed his other on Chad's shoulder, and the glass domed concert hall disappeared.

They reappeared directly in Nadia's chambers.

Chad placed Nadia gently on the bed.

"Take up guard outside the suite as long as she is down," ordered Tyler.

Chad vanished.

Tyler turned to Jenna. "Now, it is time for you to do your job. You were hired to watch over her in just this sort of situation. Stay right beside her until she awakens... understand? If something unusual is happening with her call out to Chad. He's right outside."

"Like what?"

"If she shows signs of...fading, or anything like that."

"Okay." Jenna took a seat in a comfortable chair next to the bed. "Is this some sort of seizure?"

Tyler looked at her without expression, then chose to ignore the question.

Looks like he can't trust me with that answer, Jenna realized. *What is he hiding this time?*

"When you do get to rest yourself, your room is directly through there." Tyler pointed at an inner doorway to the right she had not noticed before. "Your rooms connect."

"Now, you tell me!" she complained in annoyance. "I walked all around by the corridor when I came earlier."

Tyler grinned sheepishly. "Oh, well. You got to see the scenic route."

"Oh, thanks heaps!"

He laughed impishly. "Well, anyway...for next time...you will know. I've got to go report to my gran. And males aren't to stay with a female when she sleeps...unless they're pairs. Good night."

Then Jenna was completely alone, watching over the beautiful sleeper on the bed.

Where did Nadia put the copies of the music? wondered Jenna. *She came away with nothing. And why did replicating the works place such strain on the girl? What really had happened to Nadia?*

These beings are so very strange!

CHAPTER 17

It was May Lin's time to serve Sonia. She had just entered the leader's sleep chambers.

"Come sit with me," Sonia suggested softly, patting the seat beside her.

Obediently May Lin lowered her aching frame to the small divan against the wall.

Sonia took her tiny hands in her own. "Show me your memories, May Lin," she entreated. "Tell me of your life. I wish to know you."

May Lin found it impossible to resist, obeying without reserve. All her cultural restraints seemed to have vanished. The words as she complied were inside both their minds.

"As a young girl, my marriage was prearranged," she remembered. "At thirteen I was given to an older man…"

The mauve onyx walls of the room disappeared, to be replaced by the paper shack walls of the past.

"My mother had already gone to be with the ancestors, and my father joined her shortly after I went to live with my new family. My original family would cease to exist except in my memory, as I entered this man's household. I now belonged to him alone. There, I became… least."

May Lin pursed her lips with the unpleasantness of recall. "My mother-in-law was harsh; I could not please her. Then I had a girl child, and I was in dishonour."

May Lin gazed at the walls with unseeing eyes. "My girl child was taken from me at birth, put in an orphan home. I learned many years later she died there...of neglect. I would have made a good mother." She moaned with the agony of regret.

Steeling herself against the pained thoughts, the oriental went on. "When I became with child a second time, and the family discovered it too was female, they caused me to miscarry, and by that, I was made unable to...have another child."

May Lin gave way to soft weeping. Sonia caressed her hands gently, soothing away the hurt. "Please, go on," she pleaded sympathetically.

May Lin swallowed back the tears.

"My life became one of shame and distain. My husband was not a gentle man, and now he had no need of me. His relatives were most unforgiving. When my mother-in –law died I became property of the sisters."

Like it had been yesterday, May Lin's recollection of that time was vivid. "I was as nothing in the home, a rat in the corner. I was for cleaning and cooking, while my sisters- in-law enjoyed privilege...because they had boy children. They had continued the family name as was their purpose. I had not fulfilled mine."

"When my husband died," May Lin declared with shame. "I was cast out on my own."

"And what was your age when this was done?" probed Sonia.

"I was sixty-five."

Sonia shook her head with annoyance. "How have you survived since then?"

"For the past fifteen years I have begged on the streets. Then one day I saw a newspaper blow by me. I caught it, to use for insulation in my clothing. But I saw the add, so I read it. I thought it would be impossible for me to be chosen, but I try anyway. Then, they did not even interview me. I was accepted because I am Chinese."

Sonia smiled. "Perhaps that is so, but other factors might be in play as well. Tell me, when did you learn English, and come to the Americas?"

"My husband saw better opportunity across the water. We came with his family when I was fifty."

"You were cast out while in this free country?"

May Lin nodded. "Is easy to be lost in a….'China Town'."

Sonia was puzzled. "How did you learn to read and write, if you were on the streets?"

"I sneak into school after hours, for warmth. Mission school was on. I hide each night while they teach from Mandarin to English."

Sonia grinned. "You are one resourceful lady," she complimented with approval. "Because of that you could read our add. I think you deserve a better life.

"Close your eyes, May Lin…"

May Lin felt suddenly very weary. She fought the drowsiness flooding over her, conditioning causing her to the resist.

I must not sleep now. This is rude.

"Do not fight me, May Lin," Sonia pleaded softly.

It was the last thing May Lin heard.

****

When she opened her eyes next, Sonia had released her hands, and her male, Sky, was standing over them. The Navajo shook his head in disapproval, his attitude one of rebuke, yet not of condemnation.

"You have been naughty again, dear one," he reproved. His voice held affection; no judgement. "You know you should not heal alone."

When she looked back at Sonia, May Lin was shocked. She had unmistakeably aged. There were wrinkles at the corners of her eyes, and her cheeks were severely lined. One side of her mouth sagged as if she'd had a stroke; even her hair had gone white next to the temple.

Sonia smiled weakly, but said nothing.

May Lin looked down at her own hands. They were soft, young and smooth again. She touched her face, realizing it too had changed. And her energy level had returned. She felt more like a younger woman, then the age she was.

Did Sonia do this?

Sky had followed her actions. "You are looking twenty years younger, May Lin. My Pair has given you a new lease on life. As you can see, when she heals she takes on what needs healing. Use this new life well. Sonia also has removed your curse." The approval was there in his tone, even though he had scolded his partner. "It is possible now for you to have children," he added.

Tears sprang to the Asian's eyes. "Oh, but master," May Lin whispered. "What good will it do now? I am still an old woman. Who would even have me?"

"I happen to know of someone," Sky reassured, "who would greatly cherish you ...given half the chance."

May Lin blushed, knowing full well to whom he referred.

Sky slipped his arm beneath and around his female, lifting Sonia carefully, and carrying her to the bed. He laid her gently against the pillows, then took a seat at the edge beside her.

May Lin had followed.

The Lady does not look good, May Lin decided. *What has she done to herself? And because of me.* May Lin wanted to weep in gratitude, yet felt apprehension for her benefactress.

Sonia's eyes closed wearily.

Sky sighed. "My pair is too soft hearted. She can not bear to see unalleviated suffering. Time and again she will risk her own welfare for the sake of others. That is what makes my heart ever fond of her...no one can ever keep her from healing. But...I am not so sure this was the wisest move just now."

May Lin felt guilty, as if she should somehow have prevented her.

Sky turned to her, as if sensing what she was feeling. "Do not blame yourself," he reassured. "Our females have this need to heal. The cost if they do not would be much greater. Some day, you also, will understand..."

Sky stood to his feet. "It will take her time to heal back. I must leave; I have perimeter duty. We cannot leave our safety only in the care of 'Keepers'. I need you to stay with Sonia during the few hours it will take her to recover…"

"Will she be…okay?" May Lin asked in a low whisper.

"As okay as is possible during this time. Do not fear," he reassured. "But I do require a promise from you…please, tell no one of this weakness in our females."

May Lin thought he referred to the matter that Sonia had healed her. Her eyes opened wide with astonishment.

"Oh, Master, I would never betray this secret."

He followed her train of thought easily, dismissing his own request because she failed to understand.

Sky chuckled when he realized the embarrassment public knowledge of her affliction, and the healing of it, would cause. "Of course…you would not. What was I thinking. I have nothing to worry about…"

Then Sky let it go, and stood, gazing down on his loved one. "She will be my beautiful Sonia once again in only a few hours. And even should she not heal back right, I would love her this way. It is the heart inside that is my treasure."

Turning to May Lin, he stood towering over her. But May Lin feared no longer. She had learned: here was a gentle giant.

"I will be going," he declared. "Should she not return to normal in the next few hours…should she begin to fade, call out for me. I will hear you wherever I am, and another will take my place, so I can come to help her. In the mean time, do not touch her until she again opens her eyes."

He looked back at his pair one last time, fondly smiling; then he vanished.

CHAPTER 18

May Lin had been with Sonia until late. When Sky did return, he had said his female was repairing fine, and today May Lin was to take free time. But May Lin knew on her off days she was to care for Chi Cho.

May Lin entered the lunch room the next day to prepare the morning rice, but much to her consternation, Chi Cho was already present and eating. Disconcerted, she took her place just behind him, to his right, awaiting instructions.

I do not think I sleep in. I sleep little; mostly I worry about mistress. How come this man get here before I do?

Chi Cho turned to look at her, but said nothing, so she waited, ashamed that she had failed to serve him properly.

Chi Cho pushed his bowl away. "Have you eaten female?"

"No, honourable sir. But I need not..." May Lin kept her eyes downcast.

"Eat." A small bowl of rice appeared opposite him at the table.

Uncertain what to do, May Lin looked about the room. It was still empty, as it was very early, too early, apparently, for those who were not early risers.

"May Lin, be seated," he ordered quietly.

He want me to sit in his presence...and eat in front of him?

"Yes. I do," he declared bluntly. May Lin's eyes went wide with shock.

As she obeyed, he was apologizing. "Forgive my intrusion into your thoughts…"

May Lin looked at him astonished.

This man like no oriental I have ever known. Any other would not apologize.

"Please. Eat."

May Lin descended to the very edge of the seat, moved the bowl toward her, and as there were neither chop sticks nor other utensils beside the dish, she began to eat carefully with her fingers, feeling uncomfortable because he watched her every move. Chi waited patiently until she was at the last morsel.

"You are whole, female," he observed quietly.

May Lin looked up in amazement, the rice half way to her mouth, her jaw open. Understanding made her cheeks grow warm. She swallowed the food, almost choking.

He switched to Mandarin.

"And you look much younger."

"How do you know?" she whispered in the same tongue. "I was to keep it secret." A sudden flood of fear past over her. "Oh, the honourable lady, and the Sky male will not be pleased with me…I have misgiven confidence."

His eyes showed amusement, but it did not reach his stoic features.

"I know our 'Leader Pair' well. They are not easily angered. Especially Sonia. Should you ever see her temper flare, the situation will be dire indeed. As for my knowing your condition; though thought probes are disallowed, our capability to sense inner feelings can not be turned off."

May Lin felt over warm again. "Honourable sir, I still am...old lady," she protested. "And you are much younger..."

"I am older than you...in human."

Again she was taken off guard.

"Were we to blood heal you and make you like us, you would be only forty," he pointed out. "You would than be three years my junior."

Suddenly May Lin's view of the male was altered considerably.

****

A very young alien woman materialized beside their table. She appeared no more than sixteen, with long straight blond hair and the most unusual eyes: one was blue; the other amethyst like Sonia's.

"'Morning Chi."

Chi turned his eyes to the younger female. "It is good, lady Jessica," he agreed.

"And you look lovely, May Lin," Jessica observed.

May Lin's eyes went wide again. As Jessica moved behind the counter, the elderly Chinese whispered in Mandarin. "She can tell also?"

"Our people are in union; we have no secrets between us. The fact Sonia has healed is apparent to us all."

"But I thought I was to keep secret?"

135

"It is human kind that is the danger. They need not know our leader is weakened. They do not need to hear details."

May Lin finally understood.

These beings do not trust the other women. Maybe, she thought. *The women will not even notice I am different. To most I am merely inconspicuous anyway, though some have been unkind...*

"Darla and Ziva are not nice to you?" Chi interrupted brusquely

Is he doing that mind thing again?

"I am sorry," Chi said contritely. "It is a hard habit to break. I am used to being observant. Humans are too easy to read..."

Is he talking of hearing my thought? How do I keep distance from this man? This is not proper. I am exposed...naked before him. My every reflection is there for him to see. How do I fight this?

"I promise, I will do it no more," Chi assured. His eyes narrowed. "You did not answer me."

May Lin knew she could not ignore him. "Darla no worse than others in past. Ziva only follow example given."

He seemed to accept her assessment, even if he might not agree.

"You are to speak English so humans understand when they are present," instructed Chi. "Mandarin for when we are private."

He stood to his feet. "Come we go now. The humans do not need to see you just yet. That Darla creature comes."

May Lin wiped her mouth hurriedly, rising also. Their bowls had disappeared from the table.

Chi reached out, took her elbow, and they were suddenly down in a valley, among small rice paddies.

****

"Today is free day," Chi stated tersely. "For you also. We spend it together as Lady request."

May Lin did not think he was asking, so she said nothing. Gazing about, she realized they were in a small Chinese vegetable garden.

"But first, we pick what we need."

"I pick?" May Lin suggested, daring to correct him.

"No," he bluntly disagreed. "You carry. I pick."

A woven bag appeared slung over his one shoulder, as the man gazed about. He walked to one of the canals, and crouched.

Chi dug in the murky water bringing up a handful of Suey Choy. Standing again, he placed it in the pouch as he looked about. He moved on, repeating the process, this time finding small bamboo shoots. Once more they were dropped into his bag.

Chi moved on with May Lin shuffling behind, until they came to a drier area. Here he found Shiitake. They too went in the pouch.

But he seemed reluctant to pass his burden to his companion.

May Lin waited patiently. She was good at that.

Finally, he turned, took her elbow, and suddenly they were in a more western style garden.

He moved away from her again, searching. Chi crouched between the rows, dug in the dirt coming up with green spring onions. He moved down another row where he picked peppers, a red, one green and lastly a handful of hot chilli peppers. All went into his sack.

He seemed to have forgotten May Lin.

Chi moved along the edge of the garden, and as he passed a squat orange tree, he picked two and placed them in his bag.

"For dessert," he declared.

"I carry?" queried May Lin.

Chi frowned as if reluctant, but finally passed the bag to her. He took her arm again, and once more they were in a different place.

Here he found ginger root, and garlic cloves. Chi passed them to May Lin, who placed them obediently into the pouch.

It was beginning to feel heavy.

At last he stood looking about. "Good enough," he declared in a satisfied manner. "Now, we find place for picnic."

May Lin raised her eyebrows, but she did not voice her question.

"Sonia say, good ice-breaker."

May Lin frowned.

He closed his eyes and just stood there.

"Ah! Yes!" Chi exclaimed, as if he discovered something inside his mind.

Opening his eyes, he took her arm once again, and suddenly they were by the bank of a small lake.

May Lin was beginning to feel dizzy with all their moving from place to place.

She turned to look left where she heard and now saw a waterfall dropping down from forty feet off the mountain, only half the actual elevation of the monstrous peak.

Her lips formed a silent oh, but no sound escaped her.

Never had she seen something this beautiful in reality.

A blanket made an appearance at her feet, spreading out on the sand. Chi motioned to it.

"Sit please," he directed, and May Lin obediently sank to her knees at its edge.

She watched as a four by ten foot flat rectangle of stone formed between blanket and the water's edge.

Chi also went to his knees upon the platform, as a small braiser made an appearance. The satchel she had carried abruptly disappeared from her side, reappearing in his hand. Chi began unloading his cache. When the wok appeared at his side, he set it on top the hot coals.

May Lin wondered at his actions, yet hesitated to ask.

He looked up, as if once more he had seen into her mind. "You may speak, when you have questions."

Hesitantly, May Lin voiced the puzzlement that plagued her.

"Honourable sir. How do you do that? I hear no order to 'Keeper'?"

"We need no 'Keeper'," Chi informed her. "I think what I want; it become so. My mind do work. The 'Keepers' made to give humans power similar to us. Make things easier for them."

Her eyes went round in astonishment, and she said no more.

Chi returned to what he was doing. She watched in fascination as crushed garlic and ginger transferred into the hot oil without being thrown in, the green and red peppers suddenly in slices, following; after that the green onions, all without the touch of his hand. Next he added strips of chicken. Where that had come from, she had no idea.

She marvelled, and then wondered, *is he making Kung-Pao Chicken?*

Finally, she could hold her peace no longer.

"Lady say I serve you," May Lin objected.

"Not today," he returned determinedly. "I cook. You watch…and rest."

May Lin did not like that. *Man no serve woman!* she thought indignantly.

She knew her place; years of conditioning would not disappear over night. Her culture had taught her well: man's place was the superior, and women were the servile. May Lin had no idea what to do when not allowed this safety net, and she was not used to being idle.

She watched, her body taunt with disagreement and frustration, as Chi Cho continued to prepare the meal himself. Soon she was bored by the process, and turned her thoughts, away for her own peace of mind.

Her gaze wandered beyond the miniature lake to the valley in the distance: fields and fields of grain as far as the eye could see: wheat and barley; corn and oats. Farther out there were growing crops she could not identify surrounded by fruit trees of every kind, fields of flowers and honey bee hives. Far beyond were barns for cattle, pigs and chickens, and all about were the huge connecting mountains that surrounded everything. May Lin found it breathtaking.

****

Chi was used to caring for himself. He liked to cook, even this manual way. But he knew something was not right in this endeavour.

Why has the female gone so tense? I promised not to invade the privacy of her mind, but that limits me. What other way is there to connect?

This one is so withdrawn...so silent.

Finished preparing the meal, he set aside his Wok, caused the braiser to vanish. Chi set out the small serving bowls, the chopsticks and the finger bowls of water, a lemon slice floating on top of each.

Still the female did not speak. He had lost her attention; that was obvious.

Help Sonia, he cried out mentally. *I do not do well with this female. What do I do wrong? What causes me to fail?*

The voice thought answered. *You do fine. Remember what your old world was like. She is still caught in it. Her old habits need fixing, as did some of yours. Recall the first time you had tea with me? She is uncomfortable, as you once were. It takes time to make new the old...and not easy for her.*

But, what am I to do, my Lady? pleaded Chi. *I am not female. You are. Help me, please.*

You must help her to express what she feels out loud. And you...be honest and open...gentle.

Chi sighed with resignation and frustration.

****

"Speak to me, female," Chi ordered in annoyance.

May Lin started at his harshness.

"I grow tired of this silence. If I had wanted such quiet, I would have come alone."

May Lin dropped her eyes in shame.

He seemed to realize he had hurt her, and made an effort to rectify the mistake.

"You may give your thoughts and feelings freely to me," he pleaded softly. "I would count it a privilege to share them and would cherish your words."

She said nothing, only gazed back with puzzlement and uncertainty in her eyes.

Chi sighed. "I too am learning new," he offered. "If you do not wish me to invade your thoughts, you must learn to help me. I am no longer used to silence. I will fail at my attempt to be non-intrusive unless you learn to share your musings aloud. Our species shares intimately each idea." He took a deeper breath, making a valiant attempt to express words he was not used to sharing in anything but instant thought. "I am lost without my ability to read you…your silence handicaps me…"

He dropped his head in sudden dejection. It seemed pointless to go on.

May Lin felt disconcerted. *I am hurting him? He wants me to speak aloud, to share things no one has ever heard from my lips before. Can I do this?*

Finally May Lin spoke aloud, but wisely, she chose a subject safe for both, by her own reasoning.

"Your world is beautiful," she ventured carefully.

His eyes lifted to hers, and he nodded.

"This is not our world. We remain on Earth."

His eyes took in the bushes around them, the waterfall beyond.

"This valley was created by us to give us protection while we are here. Yes, this is spectacular, but we do now have another world. It lies beyond your view, out in the stars …I would like to share it someday with you…"

Did he imply more by that statement…a future together? I am an old lady…my time is past.

Daringly, he went on. "I would have you as my pair," Chi clarified boldly. "But, for now…" He dropped his eyes, to ease her alarm. "We get to know each other…first."

May Lin felt her cheeks flush, but she did not voice what she was thinking.

When he knows me, he will change his mind.

He raised his eyes again; she felt his gaze pass over her, though her own were pondering her folded hands in her lap.

"As the females have suggested, 'I must court you first'."

May Lin's head shot up in astonishment. That is a western custom!

"This is not our way, honourable sir," she protested softly.

He shook his head. "I am no longer Oriental," Chi returned gently. "I am 'Aopato' now. We have learned a better way."

His eyes held a sense of longing. "Soon you too will see...and, you will like this way..."

"If it mean you cook," she fired rebelliously. "May Lin not like you court!"

Quietly, he thought on that a moment, while she trembled, fearing she had been too bold. Chi raised one eyebrow.

"We cook together?" he offered. "Com...pro...mise..."

May Lin almost did not say it out loud, but remembered just on time, it would be safer to speak her mind.

She shrugged.

"Maybe...that be good."

The meal appeared between them, hot and steaming.

"Now we eat?" he pleaded.

"I serve!"

"Yes," Chi agreed.

He had prepared Stir Fried Rice, Moo Shu Pork rolled in Mandarin pancakes, Kung Pao Chicken on a bed of noodles, and Dim Sum complete with three sauces for dipping: a mild plum sauce, sweet and sour, and one of lime ginger.

May Lin filled his small bowl with each in turn, handed him his chop sticks, and sat back to wait for him to finish before replacing each with the next dish. At the third filling he stopped.

"I will not eat another morsel unless you partake at the same time," Chi declared staunchly. "Compromise…"

So May Lin finally gave in, joining him. And she was content to stop her own repast when his bowl needed refilling.

They ate in silence, as was Oriental custom.

At the end he offered her an orange.

And then came tea. She poured, and together they raised the tiny cups to their lips. Each placed thumb under the bottom of the handless cup, the index finger on the rim as they drank.

****

The afternoon had fled away when they were finished. The remnants of their meal had vanished, and they rose to their feet.

"Let us go walking," he suggested softly. "May I touch you?"

She nodded, suddenly no longer uncomfortable, though wary still.

Chi took her hand, and for the first time May Lin became aware of his scent, the mild aroma of liquorice.

It suits him.

The scent brought back memories of a time long past when as a child May Lin had walked with cherished father…Chi reminded her of him.

Maybe…to court is not so bad after all.

CHAPTER 19

A small 'Keeper' appeared in the woman's common room doorway. Ziva and Darla had been talking in whispers, while Angel was reading in a corner, and Morgan and Carmen were playing cards across the room.

"Ziva and Angel will please to follow."

Angel put her book down, and Ziva reluctantly rose to her feet.

"I'll just come along," Darla decided, getting to her feet as well. "See what this thing wants with you."

"Darla is not to come!" the 'Keeper' warned. "You will be prevented."

Darla harrumphed. "Oh, as if you could stop me, you stupid thing."

Morgan and Carmen looked up, suddenly interested in what would happen.

Ziva went first, followed by Darla. Angel sidestepped her to fall into step with Ziva. The minute Angel moved past, a visible light barrier formed between the front pair and the chunkier woman, effectively separating them.

Unprepared, Darla slammed against the obstacle, cursing. Amused, both Morgan and Carmen laughed instinctively, which caused Darla to send them a scathing look that would have fried an egg. The two women quickly returned to their card game.

Darla returned to her seat, her mood livid with anger.

I'll fix that thing. I'll just wait until it drops the barrier.

But more than an hour later, the light shield was still up. When finally it did drop, it was too late to retrace their steps, leave alone find the two women.

****

Ziva felt no regret that Darla was prevented from following. The woman was like a dark cloud constantly with her.

"Have you noticed," Angel observed, as they walked side by side down the granite hallways following the 'Keeper'. "Even though the outer entrances have no doors, the males never enter where we human women are suppose to have privacy? I bet even if you asked one in, they wouldn't accept. It's like they have a certain code of conduct..."

"Actually, I prefer it that way," Ziva admitted. "At least I have an alone place."

They arrived at a doorway sealed by a light barrier, much like the 'Keeper' had raised back in the common room.

"Enter please," they were instructed, and their escort abruptly vanished.

"That's the same kind of force field that stopped Darla," Angel whispered. "I'm not so anxious to try. You want to go first?"

Why is it people always expect more of me than I want to give? Ziva wondered in frustration. *Coward!*

Reaching out tentatively, she moved her hand to the shielding. It passed through.

"Come in ladies," a male voice called from beyond. "It's programmed to allow you two in."

Ziva stepped into the light curtain, passed through, coming out into a massive dimly lit room filled with electronic equipment. One wall was covered from waist high to ceiling with dozens of viewing screens. A counter situated horizontally beneath these, came just even with the chests of the two men in rolling chairs watching the monitors. The biggest man she had ever seen swivelled his seat to face them.

"I am Joel," he stated. "This is Eric."

The smaller man turned also. Though he had the strange slit eyes of the species, he looked every inch a bookish professor without the usual spectacles. Eric was slight of build, looking small beside Joel, yet he must have been over seven feet himself. His short cropped auburn curls were askew and the brown eyes shown with delight.

Angel had just entered through the barrier behind Ziva. Always the extrovert, Angel offered her hand to Eric.

"I'm Angel."

Eric caught her hand enthusiastically in both of his, held it just a second too long, then dropped it abruptly, and turned back to the monitors.

"Sorry," he excused over his shoulder. "Don't mean to appear rude, but need to keep my eyes on things."

"I understand," Angel agreed pleasantly, not the least bit offended. "Wow! What a room!"

"Joel, will you brief them?" Eric queried.

"Sure."

The first man stood up, and both women took a step back, intimidated by his size. Joel towered over them, at least seven foot five. He was far heavier than Eric, perhaps near to four hundred fifty pounds, though he carried the weight well, proportioned in the upper body, the deltoid, pectoral and triceps, rather than his legs. These also were twice the size of any normal human man. His hair was a light brown, and the eyes an unusual silver in colour with a rust vertical slit.

What extraordinary eyes he has, Ziva marvelled. *Haven't seen any that colour among the others.*

His scent was also more evident to her than that of his partner.

I'd say his fragrance resembles Chilli Powder. But I kind of like the aroma of cooking chilli, anyway.

The other guy smelled of mint.

"You are Ziva," Joel prompted, bringing her back to the moment.

She nodded, but didn't speak, too overwhelmed by his size.

To put them at ease, Joel sat again, and went right into the instructions. "We will man this centre in shifts. Your 'Keepers' should see you report on time when it's your turn. One human with each of us. Ziva, you are with me; Angel with Eric."

He turned back to the man at the monitors.

"Can you handle for the rest?"

"Yep!" Eric agreed without looking back.

"I'll go on sleep break then," Joel decided. "And I'll walk Ziva back to her quarters."

"Pleasant dreams," Eric wished him. "Don't forget to leave me my worker.'

Joel chuckled, as if some joke had passed between them. "I guess he means you can stay here with him, Angel. Don't let him ignore you. He tends to get submerged in his duties. Don't let it bother you if he's a little preoccupied. When something catches his interest, you have to bring him back to reality every so often."

"Oh, thanks 'Pure'!" Eric playfully reproved, still not looking away. "Listen to who's talking, eh?"

"I'll see you…Fin," Joel returned, grinning.

This time Eric also laughed. "Get out of here man! You need sleep."

Joel turned to Ziva. "Come."

Again with the orders. Well…guess he is my boss here.

****

Once out in the hallway, Joel started walking. Two steps of hers, equalled one of his.

"If you want me to keep up to you," complained Ziva. "You'd better take smaller steps."

"Sorry." Joel slowed his pace to match hers.

Ziva had never been a small woman. Over six feet herself, she was also big boned, but next to this man she felt like a midget. Not to mention, he made her feel old. He looked half her age, though they'd said something about that difference at the first briefing.

"So, how old are you…really?" Ziva brazenly asked.

He chuckled, amused. "In human? Two years older than you."

"Ya, right! I'm sixty-four, I'll have you know."

"I am aware of that."

Is he really older than I am?

They walked silently for a time. Finally, Ziva broached another question.

"Just what is it we are doing in that room?"

"Monitoring the planet, the space around it, Sanctuary and beyond its perimeter."

"Why? You expect to be attacked or something?"

He turned to look at her, his eyes narrowing slightly.

"Do humans ever consider danger might come from space?"

"I suppose some fanatics do…"

"At this moment, your planet has intruders right in its back yard that are quite deadly to your race."

"Yeah! I know. You guys!"

"I don't mean us…"

He let his statement hang in the air, choosing not to elaborate, simply turned and began walking again.

Ziva had made one mistake, not taking Sonia seriously. She was not about to repeat her error. If Joel said there was another deadly enemy nearby on Earth, she was inclined to believe him…until she proved it differently. After all, they had said, they could not lie…also, if that statement could be trusted.

They had arrived at the outer door to the woman's dorms.

"I suggest you get some rest…even if you do not feel tired," Joel suggested. "We have the night shift. And I'd advise you…do not speak of what I have just told you, nor of what you have seen. We will know if you do."

Is he threatening me?

Abruptly, Joel vanished.

Ziva began to wonder why they had summoned her at all, only to return her immediately right back to her quarters. They could have simply ordered her to rest.

She was almost certain; it had been to separate her from Darla.

Do they suspect what we are up to?

One thing Ziva did understand. If she wanted to gain their trust, she could not tell Darla what she had just heard and seen.

CHAPTER 20

"You are very quiet, female," Eric observed softly. "I know you are usually very out going. Silence is not your forte."

What was there about this guy's voice that made it so familiar?

"I know you from somewhere," Angel mused in puzzlement.

He chuckled. "You have a good memory for voice tone. I was monitoring this station when you first met Sonia. I made an error, had the sound on, and unwisely spoke aloud. Sonia had all she could do to keep from laughing."

"At you?"

"No." Eric laughed again, a chuckled that was infectious. Turning toward her, his eyes had filled with amusement. "She had read what you were thinking, about Darla and Ziva. That's when I knew we were compatible."

Angel remembered it now. "I heard your voice!" she exclaimed in trepidation. "You said, 'I want that one.' What did you mean?"

He turned back to his view screens, leaving the silence hang in the room for long moments.

"What did you want me for, Eric?" Angel asked firmly. "You'd better be up front with me, mister!"

He finally turned to look at her suddenly seriously. "There are not enough women in our species..."

"I figured that out a long time ago. What are you saying? You picked me as… what is it you guys call it?"

He said nothing, just returned his eyes to his work.

"Do I get a say in this?" asked Angel indignantly.

"If ever you are unhappy here, I will personally return you to your life." He turned pleading eyes toward her. "But, I would find letting you go extremely hard."

Angel dropped her eyes, and her cheeks turned warm.

He went back to his monitors.

Doesn't seem like such a bad guy…

"I'm too old for you," she finally ventured.

He turned, grinning from ear to ear. "You humans! Can't seem to get past that age variance, can you? I'm fifty-seven in human, and…" he added. "You'd be twenty-seven in our counting."

Angel frowned. "You're confusing me. How old are we in…both."

He laughed. "Let's see." He thought a moment. "In human, you are fifty-five; I am fifty-seven. In our years, I am twenty-eight and a half; you are…"

"I know!" she said annoyed. "So basically, we are the same age. I get it! So, who cares about age, anyway?"

"I don't." He chuckled.

"Men!"

He laughed again, and turned to the monitor.

"So what's so interesting, anyway?" she asked after a time.

Eric tapped a nearby screen. "See here."

Angel moved closer to see where he was pointing.

"A group of 'Opposites' have set up a base camp about two miles outside Sanctuary's perimeter."

"Here? Outside this place?"

"Yep."

"These are the enemy Sonia spoke of?"

He nodded. "They are stragglers who were never involved in the battle a year ago. They must have slipped into Earth's atmosphere after we migrated to our new planet. We never expected they'd have reason to go after humans once we were gone."

"They are harmful to humans?"

"Extremely. They enjoy torture of any species, but especially humans. You scream a lot."

"Are you protecting us?" Angel asked in amazement.

"That is part of the purpose for watching them."

"What is the rest of your purpose?"

"Our own safety," Eric admitted blandly. "But, when Sonia says it is time, we will simply put a stop to their activities."

"Why do you wait?"

"They target our females, and because we still have too few, our strength is unbalanced. We need the females to balance the warriors."

"So they keep you from fighting by attacking your women."

"That's a simple way of putting it, yes. But it is much more complicated."

"So that's why you men want…"

"To pair. Yes, but that too is a bit more complicated."

"How big are these characters, anyway?" Angel peered closer at the monitor. "Geesh, but they're ugly! Is this real size?"

"No. They are just under eight feet tall…pretty foul smelling also…and vicious."

"Don't think I want to see one up close."

Angel sat back in Joel's extremely large chair.

"Do you think you can keep an eye on the screens by yourself for me? Just watch for changes anywhere."

"On all of them?"

"As many as you can. If you see either a human or an 'Opposite' enter any other screen give me a shout. Oh, and if a ship shows up near the planet, as well."

"'Kay."

Eric moved behind Angel to another bench against a side wall, and sat down to work.

"What you doing over there?" Angel asked without looking away.

"I'm trying to programme a band similar to ours for humans, only this should work opposite from ours. I'd like to separate functions. Right now the

'Keepers' are over taxed; they do all the work. We need to free some of them for defence..."

His words disappeared in thought as he was concentrating. A moment later, he came back again, continuing the explanation as if there had been no interruption. "At present the 'Keepers' supply your needs, and are there for protection, but if you wore headbands that gave you abilities similar to our own...so you could supply your own needs as we do ..."

Again he lost his train of thought, as he worked over his project. Angel waited patiently, all the while watching her screens.

Abruptly, Eric continued.

"It would make things so much simpler. You would still be 'Keeper' defended, of course. And maybe even then, it would be safe to take you beyond the boarders of Sanctuary. Earth has many beautiful sights..."

She laughed. "Do we ever get free time so this could be done? I mean...go sight seeing?"

"Oh, yes. Actually, we could put the whole Tech centre on 'Keeper' monitor. I think that's what we'll do for the banquet."

"What banquet?"

"Oh, I guess you humans don't know why we are here. Sonia's two daughters are being paired together in a grand ceremony..."

"Why would you pair two women, when your men out number the women? They can't reproduce together, can they?"

Eric exploded with laughter that had Angel turning in indignation.

What did I say that was so funny? It seems a fair question; why is he laughing at me?

When finally he could speak again, Eric explained.

"I guess, when you can not follow my thoughts, my words out loud can be misconstrued. Let's see if I can rephrase better."

He was silent a second.

"Each daughter will be paired to the male of her choice. But…they will do it… ah, one after the other, in the same ceremony."

Angel felt her face suddenly go hot with embarrassment. She had jumped to conclusions.

"We have decided," he continued. "To have the ceremony here on Earth, because it seemed fitting. Each of us was born here…and the couples met each other here…and courted at Sanctuary."

"Well…" Angel found sensible words escaped her at the moment. "That… ah, sounds better…when put that way." Her rising chagrin simply would not pass.

"Better watch the monitors," he suggested, his grin wide.

Will I ever live that one down? I'm sure he'll use that one to tease me.

But Eric did not use his advantage to belittle. He set to his task once again, and Angel turned round to survey the screens. After a time she dared to break the silence.

"This double wedding sounds like fun…"

"Oh, yes!" he agreed with enthusiasm. "We are all looking forward to it. It is our first pairing ceremony…ah, but, it will be quite different from what you have experienced."

"Do we get to see it?"

"Yes…actually… Will you be my…ah, what are the best words in English? Would you do me the honour of being my companion for the meal?"

"I'd be delighted. I suppose, we dress formal for this occasion?"

"Most certainly."

"Now, where am I going to get a fancy dress? I wasn't expecting to use one."

"Try 'Keeper' power," suggested Eric.

"So, when will this happen?"

"When we are ready."

Angel chuckled. "You guys aren't on a schedule?"

"Nope. Sonia will tell us when the time is right."

"Sonia's considered pretty special in your eyes."

"She is our life…litterly. We are all connected."

CHAPTER 21

Ziva had not seen Darla in days. Actually, that had been a bonus. And getting to know the big man she worked with was not half bad either.

Joel was really a jolly, gentle giant, but she would never tell him that she was growing to like him...not to his face. Nor could she admit it to anyone else.

She knew she must keep her distance, if she was to fulfill this assignment. At the moment, her retirement settlement superseded any personal involvement. She needed that to survive in the future.

Darla came from somewhere behind her, startling Ziva, as she was heading for the sleep area.

"Where you been all this time?" Darla demanded. " Almost 'pears like you're avoiding me."

"I wasn't. I'm on shift work; have to sleep days."

"So they placed you. What's your job?"

"Like you thought. I'm in their..."

"Communication centre?"

"I guess, you could call it that."

Darla slowed her pace. "They got ships out beyond our satellites?"

"Not that I know of."

"They don't communicate with the rest?"

"Rest of what?"

"Their fleet, dummy," Darla reproved with indignation. "You think I'm stupid? They must come from somewhere."

"They told us this is the lot of them."

"Ya right! You believe that, then you're stupider than I thought."

Ziva knew better than to contradict this know-it-all woman.

"Anyways, you got access to the internet? A computer?"

"They have an old one in there. It's connected."

"Did you try to get through?"

"I'm not left alone much...only if Joel goes to check with the others on something."

"Joo...el is it? Don't you get side tracked, ya hear. We can't afford that."

Ziva's hackles went up at the way she said Joel's name. She almost defended the huge man, but thought better before she voiced the thought aloud.

"So did you even try?"

Ziva sighed. *Man! This woman has a one track little mind.*

"Yes, I tried. I sent the message a couple times. Don't think I'm getting through. At least, I don't get any answer back."

"You sure you're sending it to the right E-mail address?"

"I know where to send it. I've been on the receiving end more times then I can count."

"Well, you better try a little harder, or you can kiss that severance package you're hoping for goodbye. I can nix it with one word. Hear me?"

"Why would you do that?"

"'Cause I can; that's why," Darla hissed, just as Karine came up even with them and passed on by.

When the older woman had moved out of earshot, Darla changed subjects abruptly.

"Where is that broad sleeping, anyway? It sure ain't in our dorm."

Ziva wondered if she dare tell her. *Maybe it'll take the heat off of me.*

"I've heard some of the women are housed behind the male suites. They have access so they can serve the men they're assigned to. May Lin serves some Chinese guy, and Karine is behind a guy named Djura. Big Arab fellow."

"Never seen him! But I hear he's head of security. That just might be worth lookin' into."

Ziva turned to look at her companion questioningly, wondering just what she was hatching now.

"Never you mind. I got me something cookin' up here." Darla tapped her temple with one black polished nail, and laughed lasciviously. "Just leave it to me."

She was silent for some minutes, walking rapidly, deep in thought.

"Haven't found a way yet," she said suddenly. "But I learned we're inside this here mountain, see?

And I got out this door…there's a valley down below. Got to check it out more…"

Ziva wondered if Joel knew Darla had been outside.

"Anyway, at least they haven't put me to work yet. Gives me more time to look around."

"They could be watching you, you know."

Darla snorted in derision. "They can't sneak up on me. I got a good smeller."

Ziva almost laughed. "They've got 'Keepers' everywhere."

"So? They're here to serve us! And that can be used to our advantage."

Ziva wasn't going to correct her. Seems, she knew everything.

CHAPTER 22

Karine knew she was supposed to see to the needs of the man, Djura, but as yet she had not even met him. Today May Lin served Sonia, and that meant Karine had a free day. And finally, just a moment ago, the 'Keeper' had warned her to get ready to meet the man.

This time, the 'Keeper' lead her in the opposite direction from the norm, to a beautiful sunken garden. As Karine entered, the robotic escort vanished, leaving her alone to find the one she sought on her own.

She stepped down on to one of three paths. At the convergence was a black marble statue of a young African boy, and as Karine passed, noticing the inscription beneath, she stopped to read it.

'In loving memory of Asa,
Twin to Chad.
Missed by all.
He died a valiant warrior.'
How old was this kid?

And isn't Chad the name of the one who hangs around with Nadia, the black female?

She had seen the two together when the young girl came to visit Sonia.

How sad...to lose his twin at such a young age.

Karine moved away, taking the path to the left, following it around the exquisitely landscaped hide-away, finally coming up behind the man on the bench.

She drew in her breath in dread at sight of this being. Even seated, he appeared colossal, near eight feet tall, solid with strong well-developed musculature. Was he employer, her owner, or…master?

What will I be in his eyes?

She was only five foot four even with her big boned structure. If he ever turned ugly, Karine realized she wouldn't have a chance.

The man turned when he heard her, his face a mask of suppressed rage, and Karine trembled inside. He appeared to be Arabic, with a beak like nose, light molasses skin tone, short dark tight curly hair, and brown slit eyes, though the slit was near invisible. He would have easily pass for human, were it not for his size.

"I…I was told to come to you." Karine found herself stammering with nervousness. "You are…Djura?"

"I sent for you," he acknowledged, an icy tone to his voice. His eyes drifted again to the short wall just a few feet in front of him, as if mesmerized by it. Karine turned, following his gaze, and her eyes went wide at what she read from the plaque in the middle of the wall.

'In Memory of the Warrior Myron
Brother to Sonia and Joel
A loss great to their souls.'

She spoke aloud without thinking. "Sonia had two brothers? What happened to him?"

His face changed, the voice tone devoid of all feeling, as if he'd shut down, so she would no longer see evidence of his emotion. He did not turn to look at her, when he answered.

"He committed suicide; took a ship full of 'Opposites' with him; nearly destroyed our species, and this planet in the process."

Her jaw dropped.

When did that happen? Are the authorities of earth aware?

Then the full import of his statement hit her. Karine objected verbally. "But...it says, a great loss..."

"To your mistress, it was. Sonia nearly died of the grief."

"Oh...oh," Karine whispered in sympathy. Then her thoughts went to the statue behind her. She turned to him. "Back there...there is a statue..."

It was as if she had struck him; he litterly jerked back with the recoil.

"Asa." Djura moaned the name as if it tortured him. "He was our first casualty. He died before...because of Myron. The man could not follow...as he should."

Djura shook his head, as if annoyed to have to face these memories head on.

"Enough!" he thundered. "The past can not be changed. I came here to have this meeting at a neutral setting, but...I have never liked this place. The memorial garden is depressing...a place of supposed might-have-been. Foolishness! Stupidity!"

"But..." Karine objected in a hesitant tone. "It's beautiful here."

His eyes narrowed. "To you maybe. For me it is ugly, a reminder of failings... my own...his. Enough said!"

She stood there waiting, chastised and silent. He continued to stare at the wall, in a world of regret.

Finally, he came to the present with an effort, and spoke again, his voice low and harsh.

"You will cover yourself when you are with me. You reveal too much," he hissed.

Karine's jaw again dropped with the shock of his brutal assessment.

"I am an old woman...sir! With no sex appeal left."

"And I am an old man...who has been alone far too long."

This is old! He has the appearance of a middle-aged man.

"In human I am eighty plus one. Older than you!"

Did he just read what I was thinking?

"Yes!"

"Yes, you read me!"

"Indeed."

"You stop that!" she ordered, her Irish temper flaring, the brogue very evident in her voice. "Sonia says, you're not to do that! It's forbidden!"

His eyes narrowed. "True." He seemed to study her in a new light. "And Sonia is right," he conceded. "But you are too easy to read."

Karine dropped her eyes.

Silence reigned.

"Tell me something woman." The venom was back in his tone. "How did you remain in the pleasure trade so long without being intimate?"

He thinks I lied, Karine realized in shock. Sonia believes me, but he doesn't.

She looked up, meeting wrathful eyes. His narrowed in warning.

Is it wise to tell him the truth?

"You had better," he stated menacingly.

This time Karine knew better than to point out his transgression.

"I learned how to turn a man off abruptly," she whispered, humiliated. "The money was always already paid up front, and…the trick was then too embarrassed to say anything. He usually thought it his fault.…most never used me again."

"And your handler did not detect this?"

"He found out…eventually."

"And?"

"He punished me, but…he couldn't beat me. That would make me unsuitable for exhibition, so he…used another method."

For the first time, Djura's eyes softened.

"You do not like me because of what I used to be?" Karine observed miserably. "I can not change what I was…"

"I do not reject you for that, but…you are human."

"And you hate humans?"

"No. Sonia has taught me forgiveness. But humans can not be trusted."

"Humans are your enemy, then?"

"They are not friends. They have been very cruel…to some of us. However, I am half human myself…the weaker side of me. I am not proud of that fact."

That caught her by surprise.

He returned to the original topic.

"I can not judge you for behaviour in your past. Were I to show you what I did, you would find it is much worse than your offences."

Once more, she was surprised by his words.

"I was not a good man," he admitted. "But…Sonia has been gentle with me."

He always refers back to Sonia, like she has the ultimate wisdom for everything.

"She does."

He's done it again! Maybe I should just tell Sonia he's breaking the rules.

"She already knows. I am security; I am to watch the minds of others."

"You stop reading my mind!" Karine shouted angrily.

He actually winced. Then Djura turned his eyes to the wall once more. The silence carried on for some minutes.

"You are to cover your shoulders with a shawl," he finally said, his voice more subdued. "Wear clothing less revealing, not so tight…a longer dress perhaps. I will permit your hair uncovered…but it is not to be loose…"

Who the devil does this guy think he is? Karine thought rebelliously. *Is he Muslim or something?*

If he had read the thought, this time he chose to ignore it.

"These practices…you used to turn the men off?"

Karine looked up, uncomfortable, as their eyes met.

"You are to use them on me, if I get too…familiar."

Never in her life had a man asked for that! And there had always been men who lusted after her.

Karine's eyes filled with moisture; all the fight went out of her. "Yes sir," she agreed quietly, shame colouring her tone.

"You are a good woman in your heart," Djura allowed. "But when I see your body… I become most physical."

Her temper hit the surface again, and flared hotly. "Well," she retorted bitingly. "That makes you no different than every other man I've known!"

His features went from shock to hurt.

"Obviously," she continued venomously. "You've never had a relationship with a woman other than sexual…"

Karine turned away so angry she could spit. Disappointed, feeling rejected and dirty, for some reason expecting better of him, her understanding of her own behaviour, a mystery she was at a loss to explain.

Why am I always expecting to find something different, when no such man exists?

"You are mistaken," he said quietly. "I have loved deeply...a long time ago. I loved my Seema...beyond measure."

Karine whirled back angrily, not ready to give clemency. "Did you treat her like this?" she demanded.

Djura looked away, rather than meet her eyes directly. "I treated her...much worse," he admitted with remorse. "I was given the task to torture her to gain information..."

"Your people do that?" Karine exclaimed in outrage. "I thought your species was supposed to be non-violent!"

He widened his eyes in shocked consternation. "No. Oh! Never! Sonia would never permit...even one unkindness! That took place when I was still dormant. I was then in Arabian interrogation...Sonia has set me free of such brutal tendencies."

Karine was not so sure he was over his brutishness.

What kind of man are you?

His eyes narrowed again, as if she had deeply offended him.

"'Keeper'!" Djura thundered. "Cover this female in looser, more modest, clothing!"

Karine shivered, feeling suddenly exposed.

Abruptly her slacks and blouse changed to a long flowing dress with an over-the- shoulder contrasting scarf.

"Change her hair. Braid it in a loose braid behind her back."

The space around them felt pregnant with the intensity of desire, and Karine realized that somehow he was showing her what he was feeling.

The revelation swept her breath away.

How does he do that?

Just as rapidly, the sensation changed. The garden seemed a depressing place. Karine wanted to weep, and as she felt the connection break, he shut himself away again.

"Sonia has given the order; you are to remain with me as I work today," he declared reluctantly. "But, for the moment, I need...to be away from you."

And then, he simply vanished.

As if there had been an actual battle, the faint smell of gunpowder lingered in the air. She had not been aware of his scent until he was gone.

Fire and brimstone very much suites him, she thought.

When she was certain he was really gone, Karine dropped heavily to the caste-iron bench he had vacated. Covering her face in her hands, she gave way to body shaking, hear wrenching sobs. Not since the days of her youth had a man brought her to tears.

****

Fifteen minutes later when he came visible behind her, Djura did not expect to find her crying.

Females are too soft. I did not mean to batter her so.

It filled him with remorse. He had expected this one to be hardened, yet her soul was so bruised it bled at his touch.

She is too fragile, Sonia, he mourned. *I will only cut her to pieces. See, what I have already done. There is no gentleness in me.*

The thought voice that answered reassured. *You promised to try Djura. She needs you more than any other. And it is not good for you to be alone. Your life will be forfeited.*

My life is nothing. You know I would give it any day.

But that is unnecessary. Do not be like Myron. Please. Try. You will find the way. Do not give up.

Djura sighed.

Karine started violently, and turned, her eyes still swimming with moisture. The sight ripped his spirit.

How do I do this? he moaned in thought.

Sonia's answer came back equally non-verbal.

Do not give up...never! Keep trying until your last breath is gone.

****

She had felt him standing behind her, but when she turned, he was suddenly gone again. He became solid seconds later, this time in front of the bench. For a moment, he stood looking down at her almost tenderly, then lowered himself to one knee. Though he did not touch her, she saw that he wished to, but was holding back, being careful.

"Forgive me, female. I am sorry," Djura pleaded softly. "I have hurt you. I am coarse at times; rough around the edges. I forget…you have feelings also…"

Karine wiped at the tears on her cheeks, surprised at his apology, and extremely embarrassed that he had caught her crying.

"Our females say, I take my duties too seriously," he went on. "I forget to take off my mantel of defence…to relax; be gentle. I need help to do that."

Moisture again threaten at the corner of her eyes, and she quickly brushed at her lashes.

"I wish to tell you something. You are not to blame for what men have done to you, and I do not want to be another like them. You fought back the best way you knew how. I am very proud to know you…of the woman you have become…"

A tear slipped down her cheek without her permission. Karine could not clear her thoughts; he was befuddling them. No man had given her praise before.

"Please, do not cry…it makes me want to comfort, and… I must not touch you. I do not trust myself."

Karine brushed at her tears, steeling herself.

Is he for real? Is this when I'm supposed to turn him off?

She did not want to…not this time.

"Be yourself with me, Karine," he said softly. "It is I who must self-discipline."

He rose to his feet, so gigantic, towering over her, yet somehow, her fear had dissipated.

"Will you come with me now? I must see to my duties."

Before she could answer, or stand up, he had disappeared again.

Now what?

Wherever he had gone, she had no idea how to follow.

This man was an enigma, obviously a proud individual who would hold himself aloof for the sake of image, but she had found his gentle side...

And she liked it.

A few minutes later, so as not to startle her a second time, Djura reappeared just in front of the bench.

"So sorry," he exclaimed almost breathlessly. "I forgot you can not teleport. Please, will you take my hand?"

I've knocked him off balance! He's absolutely rattled.

Karine stood and reached for him, keeping a straight face, hiding the smile she knew she shouldn't give way to, dropping her eyes shyly. When their hands touched, they were instantly in Technical Centre with Angel and Eric.

"Aww...he didn't forget you this time," laughed Angel.

Karine felt the warmth spread down her cheeks to her throat.

A chair appeared beside Eric's console. Ignoring the females present, Djura took the seat.

"So, what do you have to show me?"

Karine stood gazing at the wall of screens.

Wow! They have cameras everywhere!

Djura turned suddenly realizing Karine was still standing. Another chair appeared between his chair and Angel's.

"Be comfortable," he ordered, once again fully the male in control. Then he turned back to Eric.

Karine took the seat.

"The 'Opposites' are developing some sort of weapon." Eric confided, pointing at a screen.

Djura leaned in for a closer look.

"We can not see enough to determine its use."

"I doubt it's to use against humans," Djura surmised. "They don't consider them a challenge. Probably, it's something else to use against us."

"That's my thinking as well."

Angel leaned into Karine. "I like the dress you have on," she whispered. "Looks good on you."

Djura turned to meet Karine's eyes, amusement evident in his own.

He heard!

Djura winked at Karine, and she quickly dropped her head, her cheeks burning.

The big guardian turned back to Eric.

"Could this be an anti-energy beam?"

Eric thought a moment. "Possibly…but if that's the case, it's meant to drain…."

"It would be deadly," Djura observed ominously. "they have found a large scale way to drain our energy!"

Outspoken Angel had been listening, and interrupted as if she was used to being a part of the discussion.

"Eric wouldn't something like that be as dangerous to humans as to you?" she asked.

He seemed quite willing to include her, as if she were trusted, and it was a matter of habit to explain things to her.

"Our energy is different from yours. This wouldn't affect a human even should you be standing right next to us."

"Of course, that is what they plan!" Djura hit the table with his palm in his certainty. Both women to start violently, but in his concentration he did not notice. "They perfect that and we will have no defence, especially if they catch us off guard. They have discovered we have humans with us, and are distracted by females. They believe they have found our weakness."

"Well, they are right about that!" Eric's eyes narrowed with consternation. "We need to know more." He shook his head. "If I had a copy of their schematics, maybe I could find a way to deflect this weapon."

Djura leaned back in his chair, deep in thought. "We could destroy it if we knew what it was composed of. I can send in a pair of guardians to take a closer look. Maybe they have made a smaller prototype. Could you work with that?"

"Certainly try."

Djura suddenly remembered the women.

"You two are not to mention this to anyone," he cautioned.

Eric quickly jumped to Angel's defence. "She's confidential. You are fortunate Ziva isn't the one present…"

Djura nodded agreement to that statement, then stood up.

"Be careful, guardian," Eric warned. "We are too few to lose anyone."

Djura turned to Karine. "Come," he ordered, reaching to take her hand.

"You can't take her to guardian sleep quarters, Djura," interrupted Eric. "This can wait until tonight. Then I will go with you."

Djura accepted the correction without resentment. Turning again to Karine, he asked, "Would you like to see the gardens? I can always inspect the 'Keepers' while there."

"Sure," Eric remarked, tongue-in-cheek. "Those 'Keepers' really need to be checked."

Karine saw Eric grin and wink at Angel. Djura, as if he had eyes in the back of his head, turned on Eric. "I saw! You have a female with you at all times," he objected. "Surely I am permitted a break!"

Eric laughed outright, and held up his hands, as if to ward off a coming blow. "First time I've ever heard of Djura wanting a break."

Djura sent him a scathing look at his teasing.

Karine could not explain what possessed her, for without thinking, she jumped in to the giant male's defence.

"Sonia said he needs to take breaks."

It was obvious both Eric and Angel found that funny, but Eric kept his features schooled. "Did she now?"

Karine was about to come back with a smart remark, ready to do battle, but Djura took her elbow, and the room with its two chuckling occupants abruptly disappeared.

****

When they materialized in the gardens, Djura had only one thing to say.

"You are like a little street fighter, female." His voice was low with approval and pride. "But you must choose your battleground better. My brothers are not the enemy, remember that."

Then he took her hand, and they went walking.

CHAPTER 23

Carmen needed this job. It wasn't easy to get employment when you were sixty, and had been out of circulation for months.

She had always been an observer, and she had noted Ziva was a follower as well. But that did not mean she wanted to cosy up to her either. Neither had Ziva wanted camaraderie. But Darla had somehow centred in on Carmen, and Ziva followed whatever the other woman suggested.

Darla had picked up the fact Carmen had something to hide: she kept to herself a lot of the time; she was not a people person, especially since her breakdown. And since they had arrived here, Carmen had been off her anti-depressants, making it really hard to function. Most of the time she would hide away; just wanting to cry...or sleep away her life.

To be a companion had sounded so good, easy, but Jade seldom wanted her with her. She and Ryan were always off somewhere together, which gave Carmen too much free time, leaving her at loose ends.

Darla saw an opportunity in this, a chance to torment. And she did so with a vengeance. However, Morgan, on the other hand, read Carmen's insecurities as a wounded soul, coming to her defence, befriending or at least trying to.

Carmen felt unprepared to handle real life with out the meds, leave alone being integrated into an alien culture. She did not dare to admit her problem was depression, that she needed medication to balance, and Darla's harsh attention only exacerbated the situation. But for Morgan's protection, Carmen would not have survived it this long.

Today Morgan was gone, serving Rhea; Ziva was away at work also, and mercifully Darla had taken off somewhere on her own. Carmen knew she was not benefiting herself remaining in her room. She had steeled herself, and stepped out to do some much needed laundry, going in search of the washing facilities, but as so often happened when things got too much, Carmen could not find what she sought, and panicked, was presently lost in the marble corridors.

A scent near that of rosemary filled the corridor ahead, and Carmen cringed.

One of those alien males is coming. I can smell him, and there is nowhere to hide.

The burly giant came whistling around the corner. He stopped short upon seeing her.

Whew! He needs a shower. That's got to be why his scent is so strong.

The male had the bulky build of a labourer, muscular arms and legs in proportionate to his seven-foot height. The pleasant grin below those penetrating brown slit eyes, and his dark curls all askew, made Carmen feel suddenly, disconcertingly, like she wanted to laugh.

It was unreasonable; she always was more for crying nowadays, then feeling pleasure. Why would his person evoke this reaction in her?

Soberly, he addressed her, not scolding exactly, merely pointing out a fact.

"I don't think you should be down this way, female," he observed candidly. "This is the end of the line...the men's dorm."

"I'm sorry." Carmen dropped her eyes, pondering the floor. "I was looking for the washing machines."

"Whoops!" He slapped his forehead with a massive hand. "I guess that's one thing we forgot. No laundry room."

"Oh..." Carmen was really uncomfortable now. "I...I...maybe, I should wash them in my tub?"

"Actually, no." Then seeming to speak to the air, he called out. "Hey, Chi..."

Carmen shivered. *I'll never get used to the way they can talk to each other wherever they are.*

"Where's Ryan? I'm going to need him for a time."

A disembodied voice answered. "He and Jade are by the waterfall pool."

Carmen recognized the voice as the one the women called 'May Lin's fella'.

"Perhaps, Wade can help you. He has been taking up the slack to give them space."

"Okay. Tell him, I need him for an hour to do some water work."

The man in front of her turned back to Carmen. "My name is Marcel. If you will give us an hour or so, I'll make you your laundry room."

Carmen automatically disbelieved him.

No way can he do it that quick. If he does, he's a miracle worker.

Curious she asked. "How do your people do laundry?"

"We don't. If we wear something we like twice we just wish it refreshed."

Carmen looked down at his grubby jeans.

Following her gaze, he laughed good-naturedly. "Looks like I need to do some wishing, eh?"

Carmen kept the smile she was feeling from her face. *I'll say,* she thought.

"Tell you what. I'll send a 'Keeper' to tell you when we're finished, and it will guide you when you want to go there. Okay?"

"I guess, that'll be alright."

"Your quarters are back that way." He pointed the way she had come.

Carmen started away, then as a thought struck her, she turned to him again.

He had been watching her still.

"Ah, how do you know where they put me?"

"You are Jade's companion, right? Carmen?"

"Yes."

"Good. I made your rooms, so that's the way you go." Once more, he pointed, and stood there as if determined to bar her way from going any other direction. "You aren't allowed at the men's dorm," he added pointedly.

I know that! Carmen thought suddenly indignant. *Why would I even want to go there, anyway?*

Arriving at her bedroom minutes later, Carmen toyed with the thought.

Wouldn't it be nice to just wish my clothes clean? Then I wouldn't have to go out at all.

CHAPTER 24

Karine was weary, almost falling asleep where she sat. She had forgotten to bring a book.

Sonia often sat with her eyes closed in silence. Karine understood what she was doing, because Djura had explained: Sonia monitored everyone and everything with her mind. She was constantly aware. When the female sat like this she was sometimes giving counsel to others, or watching and protecting. She heard everything. The world of these beings was not a private one, as was the human world; their minds were communal.

It was hard to understand how they gave each other privacy, but Djura had disclosed, the others could be shut out when they wished to create a surprise, or delay answering. He had said, Sonia was the most gifted at this, that in her wisdom, she sometimes kept private hurtful details hidden.

But at times, as now, while Sonia was thus occupied, it was boring for her companion to be watching from the outside, and Karine was wishing the 'Leader Female' would share some of what was going on. This communal race, these wonderful collective relationships, caused Karine to long to be a part of them. Yet Sonia remained reserved.

Another puzzlement to Karine was what her purpose was here. No one had explained why she had to stay with the female; all they had said was, 'in case'.

In case of what? Why would such a powerful mental being need her?

Sonia opened her eyes. "Djura." she called aloud. "Please, enter my chambers."

Karine was aware, Djura served at the same time she did, standing watch invisible just outside the doorway. And that was another thing Karine failed to understand.

Why did they guard Sonia so possessively, as if their very lives depended upon her?

She could understand why they never left one of their females alone, there were so few of them, but with Sonia it was almost obsessive.

Djura came visible between the women.

Karine knew not to draw his attention while he was on duty. She must not be a distraction; he needed to be heedful of Sonia alone, and Karine understood.

"Karine needs a break," Sonia stated. "Jessica has been experimenting with ice-cream flavours. Why don't you take your female down to the lunch room and be samplers?"

"That leaves you unattended, my Lady."

"I will be safe. Go."

"We will bring you some, when we return," he suggested.

Karine stood; obediently Djura took her hand, and they were immediately in the kitchens.

****

She felt rather hyper from the many sweet samples she had accepted, but Karine knew Djura had indulged even more. Jessica was hard to refuse, and obviously the Arabian had a sweet tooth.

187

She smiled to herself. *I'll have to remember that for the future,* she told herself.

Usually, when Djura was with Karine, and not serving Sonia, he tended to pay exclusive attention to her. That was why, now as they sat at a table just relaxing, she noticed when his concentration abruptly wandered.

She was used to his looking away occasionally with a frown; Karine was learning to read the outward signs of disapproval or annoyance. Like Sonia, as head of security, Djura was on constant alert, and at any point in the conversation, he might receive a query or summons from one of the others. This time it was different. His back suddenly straightened jarringly, as if he'd become aware of a threat.

"What's wrong?"

"Sonia has gone outside," he answered in a worried tone. "Are you ready to go? We should join her."

Another factor Karine was learning to accept was the mode of their transportation, moving rapidly by teleportation. Compliantly, she stood and offered her hand.

****

Sonia had taken a seat on a log bench high above the waterfall. It was the first time Karine had seen the valley from up this high. The scenery was breathtaking: fields of golden grain stretched for miles in the distance; flowers and vegetable patches, interspaced with barns and pasture, all with the ribbon of the river running down the centre.

"Come Karine, sit!" Sonia ordered pleasantly. "I agree, it has been rather boring inside."

I guess, I shouldn't be surprised Sonia has been in my thoughts.

She didn't mind really. If her mistress couldn't be trusted, no one else here was safe either.

Karine dropped gratefully to the vacant seat beside the female.

"So where is that ice-cream you promised me, Djura?"

He chuckled. Instantly, a bowl filled with the creamy frozen treat topped with caramel sauce, and a spoon appeared in Sonia's hands.

"Ummmm; my favourite." At once, the lady dug in with gusto.

Karine giggled. Sometimes, the 'Leader Female' seemed more like a young girl, then what she really was.

While they waited, Karine raised the shawl from her shoulders to cover her hair. The sun seemed extremely hot up here.

"Is the heat too much for you?" Djura asked with concern.

"I'm fine…now."

As Sonia finished, the bowl abruptly vanished from her hand, and she sat quietly content, enjoying the scenery.

"You are watching that stupid human?" Djura observed in annoyance.

Karine couldn't see anything. Are they doing it in their minds?

"Yes," Sonia admitted, in a quiet voice. "But, do not refer to her in such a derogatory manner, Djura," she reprimanded. "Her life has not been easy."

"Neither has it been easy for any of the others, nor any of us either. We do not go about attempting to deliberately harm another..."

"Be careful Djura. Your future crosses paths with this one, and not in a pleasant way. I cannot yet see it clearly but know there is trouble coming your way."

"I am forewarned, my lady," the Assyrian acknowledged. "What is she up to now?"

"She seeks a way out of Sanctuary."

Djura shook his head. "Perhaps...to allow her here was a mistake?"

"She will not be here much longer," stated Sonia emphatically. "I truly had hoped she would learn the error of her ways."

Are they speaking of Darla or Ziva?

"We speak of Darla," Djura admitted, answering her thought.

You still find it hard not to do that, Karine thought answered.

"You are not giving Karine her privacy, Djura," warned Sonia.

Karine looked up at him standing beside her, and tried not to smile. His face showed no emotion, pretending unconcern just for her benefit.

"But, I like it in her mind," he admitted unabashed, his voice low and sensual.

"And did she give you permission," Sonia queried, her face expressionless.

"Aw…I never thought of it in such a way."

Karine could not bear to see his discomfort, nor hear him reprimanded.

"It's okay," she broke in. "It's actually easier that way. But…sometimes, I wish I could see what he thinks."

Sonia chuckled. "To be honest, he does not even let me into his deepest thoughts."

To ease their scrutiny, Djura shifted the topic.

"So where is the rebellious female?"

"At the base of the falls, just below us. She's trying to climb the sheer cliff."

"Foolish!" Djura muttered.

"Won't she see or hear us up here?" whispered Karine.

Sonia shook her head. "I have blinded and deafened her where we are concerned. Because you are between us, she will not even be aware of you Karine."

"Can you do that with the rest of us women; to other humans? I mean…cause us not to see or hear what's really there?"

"I do it only to those who mean us harm."

"What harm does Darla intend against you?" Karine asked in surprise.

"It is best that remain her secret," Sonia stated. "For now."

Djura seemed to feel the need to deflect attention from the subject at hand.

"You should not have come out here alone, my Lady," he dared to scold. "The 'Opposites' monitor us as easily as we them. They could quickly destroy a 'Keeper' and get through to you. It is not safe to be out here without guardian protection."

Sonia wrinkled her nose. "I was not alone," she declared quietly.

Lance's voice came from the other side of the bench, and Karine gave a start.

"Do not make me come visible warrior overseer. They can not detect me in this state."

Djura winced. "Well done guardian! I am getting lax. I did not even pick up your scent. Must be too much ice-cream."

Lance laughed. "More like, someone distracting you."

Karine felt her cheeks go hot.

Sonia interrupted. "And when will you approach your female choice, Lance?"

For a full long beat, an uncomfortable silence hung in the air.

"Soon," Lance finally agreed.

"It is not wise to procrastinate son."

Lance sighed.

Djura seemed to feel the need to come to his rescue.

"So," he asked. "How do you like duty out here in the fresh air?"

Lance grabbed the lifeline willingly, and again turned the subject to Darla.

"I've found it very refreshing fishing in the pond…until that human showed up, and invaded the peace. She reminds me of my prison tormentors: no heart, and the mind to go with it."

"Guardians!" Sonia reproved softly.

The men went silent. A few seconds later Sonia let them down gently by changing the topic once again.

"How was your foray into enemy territory, Djura?"

Karine's heart jumped to her throat.

"We did not dare go too far in," Djura revealed. "They had detection sensors everywhere, and to deactivate even one would have put them on to us. I deemed it too dangerous to proceed. We will have to wait for them to make a move."

A thoughtful silence reigned, then Karine suddenly realized they had deliberately gone to silent communication, shutting her out.

Why do they do that? Is there something they still do not trust me with?

Sonia and Djura suddenly both went tense.

"That stupid female is going to break her neck!" Djura hissed. "If she slips again, she will fall to her death."

I thought they didn't like her? They must have seen her in their mind's eye, 'cause I sure can't see anything.

"Aw, Lance," Sonia pleaded. "Will you see to her?"

"What do you suggest?" her son asked, unconcerned.

"Make a pathway up this side of the cliff. See she finds it quickly. And…get her back inside."

"That defaces the view," he objected. "And also makes this spot accessible to others. It's your favourite hide away, mother!"

"Do you want to see a life lost?"

"No," reluctantly admitted.

"You can always put it back the way it was, once she's away safe. Go! Now!"

For a second Lance went visible, his face showing annoyance, then he disappeared once more.

"I think it is time to go inside," Sonia decided.

She had jumped before Djura could take Karine's hand and follow.

"Stupid human!" Djura hissed under his breath. "She spoiled Sonia's outing, and she gets out so rarely now as it is."

CHAPTER 25

Marcel dropped down to sit against the wall outside Carmen's quarters. She had been sleeping ever since she had finished washing her clothing. The woman had not eaten either.

What can I do? I am male. But I don't dare leave her in this condition.

Obviously, Jade had not picked up on the woman's perchance to melancholy, no doubt because they had spent little time together, and Jade was presently preoccupied with her up coming pairing ceremony. Jade was too excited over future expectations to realize the danger to her human companion.

Has Jade even seen her human?

This worried Marcel. The females were suppose to see to this side of things. He did not blame Jade, even as he realized the extent of Carmen's unbalance.

Is my 'Leader Female' aware?

Sonia, may I deal with this? Marcel pleaded urgently. *She is my selected female. I picked her. If I am unable to separate, I lose less than if I leave her this way.*

If you are willing...and able. Sonia returned. *I will permit it this time. Be careful guardian.*

Marcel had skipped his rest period, only showered, changed and eaten after they had completed the laundry area, which as he had promised had taken but an hour. After his encounter with Carmen in the hallway, he had been plagued by the situation. In his mind, a little sleep deprivation never hurt anyone.

That Darla human has harmed my chosen female. Because of her my Carmen has totally retreated, and I wouldn't have even known had I not met her in the hallway.

Marcel was steaming, so angry he could spit.

Leave her alone already! Just because she is weak emotionally doesn't mean she has no value.

Steady guardian, Sonia cautioned. *That one will be dealt with shortly.*

Marcel took a deep breath, calming immediately.

****

"Get up, female!"

Carmen rolled over, moaning. Her 'Keeper' was hovering just inches above the blanket.

"Go away!"

She rolled away, facing against the wall. It followed.

"You have a visitor waiting in the hall."

Carmen moaned again.

"Get up!"

"You're not real. None of this is real."

Outside, Marcel winced. *She is that bad! It is worse than I realized, and my control of her 'Keeper' is limited.*

"I am very real, female," her helper declared. "Sit up!"

Reluctantly, Carmen rolled to her back and stretched out.

What will it take to get rid of this thing?

Her blanket vanished.

"Hey! I thought you obeyed me!"

Outside, Marcel grinned. *Good, she is fighting back.*

"When your welfare is at stake, I revert to the first rule," the machine answered.

She pulled her knees forward and sat up.

"And that first rule is?"

"No harm must come to my assigned charge. Said creature will not be aloud to harm itself."

Carmen grimaced.

"Guess that's good to know." She shifted until her feet hung over the side of the cot. "So, how do I get rid of you?"

"Sorry, I am not programmed with that answer."

"Fine!" Carmen returned indignantly. "So, who's outside waiting? Darla?"

"No. Subject is male."

"What!! What would a male want with me?"

The pesty little thing ignored the question. "First clothing, then food!"

"One track mind, haven't you?"

Again she was ignored. Jeans and a sweatshirt appeared on her body. Her straight white hair smoothed against her head like a cap.

"Go relieve yourself," ordered the machine. "Your bladder is uncomfortable."

"Not even that is private here!" Carmen rose in annoyance to comply.

Listening outside, Marcel grinned. *This one has a feisty side. I like that.*

When Carmen returned from the lavatory, there was a tray of food waiting on the bedside table: toast, scrambled eggs and an orange.

I'm not hungry, she thought petulantly.

"I don't want that!"

"Eat or I will be forced to feed you as well."

The image of a fork filled with eggs chasing her around the room made her cringe and decide it was best not to fight this. She needed to pick her battles wisely.

"You can do that?" she question, as she sat down beside the tray. "You are just a machine."

"Eat!"

She dined in silence. When she was finished, the tray vanished.

"Come," ordered her caretaker.

"Who is he? Maybe he's gone by now?" When she approached the doorway, her 'Keeper' vanished.

Maybe, I can just go back to bed?

****

"Carmen," Marcel called from outside. "Would you come out here, please? I need to talk to you."

Oh, man! It's the guy from the other day.

Coming to the opening reluctantly, Carmen asked, "What do you want?"

He rose from the floor where he had been sitting against the wall.

Had he been listening to what had gone on in the last half hour?

Marcel moved to stand in front of her. Too close...in her personal space! Carmen moved back a step, threatened by his nearness.

"Oh, please! Don't go back in," Marcel pleaded. "I've been waiting for hours...a guy could fall asleep sitting out here."

"So, why didn't you go to bed?"

"Well..." He shifted uncomfortably. "I kinda wanted your help..."

Sounded like a lame excuse to her. "I don't think I can be of much help to you." Carmen turned her back to re-enter the room.

"Pleease..."

"What good could I possibly be to you?" She kept her back to him, hiding the sudden tears that sprang to her eyes. Her mood had abruptly plummeted.

Marcel reached out and gently touched her back, soothingly running his hand across her shoulders in comfort, as if her understood her very thoughts. Carmen shivered.

"Please come out," he pleaded again. "I mean you no harm."

Carmen steeled herself, turned and stepped outside.

"Come." Buoyed by her effort, he eagerly started down the hall. "I want to show you something."

She followed obediently, down the short hall to what at first glance looked like a huge banquet hall.

"So, what is your first thought when you enter this room," he challenged, turning to face her.

Tiny star-like lights had come on in the ceiling when they entered, and the walls glowed with an inner light, but still it seemed dark to Carmen.

"Why is the whole room done in blue-black? Doesn't it depress you?"

He chuckled. "Somehow I knew that would be the human reaction. Recall the headbands we wear?"

Carmen nodded, stepping farther into the room.

"We made them so you can see us, right?"

Once again, she nodded.

"Well, at night we can be seen…without them."

"So?"

"Our enemy hunts us that way, so…it isn't safe for us to be out in the dark…"

It suddenly dawned on Carmen. The room looked like the midnight sky.

"Oh, I get it! So you simulate where you can't go."

"It gives us the feeling of…like a barbecue at night."

"I can understand that…"

Carmen swivelled to her left to take in what looked like pictures painted along the walls. The first one by the door caught her attention. She drew in a sharp breath.

"Oh! That is just an awful picture. Why would anyone want that in here?"

The circle was about five feet high, with a red border: a picture depicting a battle scene above a planet with enemy space ships hovering over the surface, shooting streaks of blue, white and red toward adults fleeing with babes in their arms. It was a night scene, and the fear on the faces was near palpable.

"It is so horrible! Look at the terror in their faces. It looks so real," Carmen marvelled. "It makes me want to cry."

"That depicts the destruction of our progenitors," Marcel revealed quietly. "Sonia's parents are the babes in their arms."

That put a whole new light on the matter. Tears sprang to her eyes, and abrupt contrition flooded her heart. "I'm so sorry," Carmen said in remorse. "Me and my big mouth. I didn't mean to offend. Who painted this? It's very good. So realistic."

"I did. Let me show you some of the others."

She followed him to another picture. All were painted directly on the bare stone.

"This hall serves as our memory wall as well. See this one?"

This one was of a tiny girl of about two years old. She was climbing a ladder up to a shingled rooftop, the space between it and the lower floor empty as if they had raised the roof to create a second floor between. The child seemed suspended in space between earth and sky.

"That is Sonia as an infant."

Carmen peered closer, then gasped. "Why, she looks...human!"

"She was a dormant. We were all born here...as dormants."

"What do you mean by...dormant?" Carmen turned to him frowning.

"We have lived most of our lives right here on Earth in a human-like condition, until Sonia was able to change on her own."

"Why? I mean, how come?"

Our ancestors hid their children here among humans to save them, and...the 'Opposites' hunted the young ones killing all of them in time. We are their children, and when our parents died we were left on our own not knowing what we were."

Marcel turned away as if the memories were hurtful.

"Now, the enemy still seeks us...to annihilate the species."

"Oh, I am so sorry," Carmen whispered.

"Look at the rest of the pictures," he offered. "I'll just wait here."

She wandered about the quiet room for some time; all the while he remained silent.

Carmen found a picture of a woman in a wheelchair.

"This is Jade!" she exclaimed.

"Yes. Her first husband Nadia's father was killed in a car accident. Jade was a cripple for many years."

"Oh! Oh! Oh!" Carmen moaned with sympathy.

She no longer considered these pictures ugly. The story they told rent her heart.

The last oval a black circle edged in red seemed empty...until she looked closer. At the very centre was an inscription.

Carmen read it aloud:

'Remember our failing that we may do it no more.'

"What does that refer to?" she asked in a puzzled tone.

Marcel sighed deeply. " Once many of us rebelled against Sonia's control." His voice lowered to hoarse regret. "We paid a dreadful price...she especially."

"What sort of price?"

But he would say no more.

****

"Come," Marcel suggested. "Over here."

She moved to him where he was standing near the larger table. Lifting her, he sat her upon the black granite surface so her face was level with his.

"I want to tell you of my childhood."

Again, he stood in her personal space but somehow it no longer felt threatening.

"I grew up on the streets of Athens, Greece. I was actually a brick layer." He chuckled, and took a seat beside her on the table. "Sonia gave me the duty of building Sanctuary; from mere labourer I became a master designer and artist. She has been very good to me...

"But enough, my plan was to tell you of my past. From my earliest memories my mother used to tell this story of how my father died. She said this gigantic dinosaur came out of nowhere and caught the two of them; that it tortured my dad until he went mad.

"Nobody believed her. See my mom was bi-polar. Everyone just thought she was a fabulous story teller, though they thought it peculiar she would make up one about such a topic...my dad was reported to have been killed by a freak lightning strike."

He looked down at his big hands in his lap. Marcel sighed with regret and shame. "I've since found out she was telling the truth. She described an encounter with the 'Opposites'. I wish I could tell her now how sorry I am for not believing her."

Why is he telling me all this?

Marcel met her gaze. "My mom didn't raise me. I kinda raised her. The mood swings were spectacular. When she was up she did everything from sky diving to track racing, but the lows..." He shook his head. "She really went down on the lows. It was like taking care of a self-destructive hypochondriac. Some days she just lay there in her own excrement...I was five first time I had to clean her..."

Now, Carmen knew why he was telling her this!

"I know the tell tale signs of depression. My mother used to hide it well…but in the end, I still didn't see in time…she took her own life."

The silence that followed could be cut with a knife.

Her tears were already blinding her as she tried to jump down from the table, escape him, but somehow he was faster. He was standing in front of her, blocking her way, wrapping strong arms around her, when she started to sob.

****

Sonia jerked rigid.

"Djura!" screamed Karine in panic to the guardian beyond the doorway. "Something is wrong with Sonia!"

His mental thought voice came back strained and pain filled.

She helps to heal Carmen. Do not panic so.

Is he involved also? wondered Karine. *He sounds like he's hurting.*

If her image dims, Djura warned. *Call out for Sky…*

"Why not you?"

We are all connected, but…Sky is Sonia's pair. He must balance her. Just watch… His voice sounded weaker. It is difficult to communicate just now…do not worry. We will be all right.

But Karine could not help but wonder. *What is wrong with Carmen? Seemed they were always keeping details from her. When will they trust me completely?*

Karine had seen so little of Carmen. She had always remained apart from the others.

Maybe like Chantel she has some illness she hid from the rest.

****

As Marcel held Carmen the memories she had kept at bay for so long flooded back: the home invasion; her son's kidnapping; the doubting law enforcement officers; the province wide search, then the battered infant body...

Carmen howled in agony trying to fight Marcel's hold.

"No," he reassured softly, holding so tight she could barely get her breath. "Let it come. Face it! It must be dealt with to recede."

The visions flooded over her: the false accusations, the charges...and the trial.

Sure it ended in acquittal, but so many still think I'm guilty. I did not kill my husband...and I'd never kill my own baby!

And then came the breakdown...there had been no way to live with the loss.

Carmen at last went limp in surrender; the weeping finally softened. Marcel gently placed his hand behind her head, brought it forward against his shoulder.

His arms are sooo comfortable.

****

The world seemed a brighter place to Carmen when Marcel at last released her. He did not discuss what had just happened; he turned to the present.

"Now," he said, stepping away. "You were once an interior decorator; what can I do to improve this room, make it more inviting to a human?"

Carmen laughed self-consciously, brushing at the moisture on her cheeks.

"Well...you could change the wall behind the larger table," she suggested. "Put a setting sun near the bottom, and...lighten the merging strips of blue down to meet it...or the sun could be red-orange and the graduating colours in yellows and blue-greens until the top is your blue-black."

'Aw...my Carmen is back! I like that last idea best."

She found herself blushing, giggling self-consciously. *He is infectious!*

But then he surprised her even more. The wall at the back of the room changed. The sunset appeared just as she had envisioned it.

"How...how did you do that?"

He grinned mischievously. "The way I do all my work."

"No wonder you could make a laundry room in an hour."

"So, what else?"

"Well...the side walls...make a flower garden along each side."

"Excellent," he breathed in awe. And it was so.

The plants appeared so real; it looked like they grew from the stone. And the sun touched each petal with just the right illumination: ambers, mauves, tangerine and multi shades of greens.

"Man! Does that ever make the room!" Marcel marvelled. "We make a good partnership. I think I'll have you help me with the new pair quarters. You have talent lady."

"I have talent? Wish I could do what you can do."

"Someday," he grinned. "You never know…"

****

"Well, look who's come to join us," sneered Darla as Carmen walked into the lunchroom. "I was beginning to think she didn't need to eat…like a robot or something."

Jenna looked up, raised her hand, and pointed to the empty seat opposite at her table. Carmen came over to join her.

But Darla was not finish with her cutting remarks. "Still haven't given you a duty, eh? Maybe they've realized you're no good for anything?"

Carmen turned to Darla bravely. "Actually, I've just come from working with one of the males…"

"Oh ho! She's got herself a boy friend! That's why she's different."

Carmen sighed in resignation. "Darla," she said with resolve. "I'm not going to let what you say bother me anymore. Life is too short to spend it wasting time hurting because of people like you."

"Ooo brave now aren't we?"

Carmen ignored her, and sitting down ordered her meal from her 'Keeper'.

Curious, Jenna remained to talk, as Carmen ate her lunch.

"Is this guy nice?" she ventured.

Carmen looked up, a glow in her eyes for the first time.

"No one has ever treated me this decent in a long, long time."

Jenna grinned. "I know what you mean. They're very gallant. Tyler, my guy…I find flowers in my room. I know they're from him. Yesterday it was a dozen yellow roses. He understands the colour meanings. Yellow means friendship, you know. Oh, my guy is sooo romantic!"

"Yes. But you do realize these guys are just kids. I wish Marcel was a little older…he's kind of young for me."

"Oh, girl friend! They are not kids!" Jenna objected. "How old does he look?"

Carmen pursed her lips. "About…early thirties, I'd say."

"Okay? That means he's at least sixty."

"Huh? What?" Carmen exclaimed shocked.

"Ya. They are twice the age they look…in human."

"No way!" Carmen's tone went to dreamy. "Really?"

CHAPTER 26

The room filled with the fragrance of ginger.

Ram giggled.

Up to this point, he and Kara had been most attentive as Chrystal taught them advanced mathematics.

"We know you are there," Kara declared with a seriousness beyond her years.

And now her teacher finally realized there was someone invisible in their midst.

I thought they weren't permitted to do that?

"Quit hiding!" Kara growled in annoyance.

A muscular thirteen year old slowly came solid between Kara and Ram. He was seven foot plus at least, his copper-blond hair straight, falling to his shoulders. And even though he had blue eyes with the black vertical slit, they somehow seemed familiar.

There was also something about that scent as well that triggered a memory, yet it remained evasive.

Kara looked up at the new comer. "That's better Unca Shawn. Hi!"

Chrystal was startled by the name.

Shawn? Do I know this teenager?

"Hi yourself, mini-monarch. What's you up to?"

"About four feet tall," Kara returned without missing a beat, her face dead serious.

Shawn grinned in delight. "Still sharp as a tack, aren't we?" He tweaked the little girl's nose fondly, drawing a giggled from her.

"Always! For you!"

The boy chuckled.

"Where you been, Unca Shawn?"

"Oh, serving guard on the perimeter. Why? You miss me?"

"I miss you terrible when you're not here to play with. You're always working since we came back, while we have to take lessons."

"Awww," he sympathized. "Lessons too slow?" She nodded. "Well, guess what? I've got the day off. Want to do something?"

"Yes!" both Ram and Kara yelled in unison.

"Better ask Teach before you get all fired up."

"Can we? Can we?" they pleaded together.

"Well," Chrystal hedged. She was uncertain whether they were aloud to be with this guy. "I think your great-grandmother might have something to say about it. We'll have to ask permission."

"She doesn't 'member you Unca Shawn," Kara observed seriously.

Shawn chuckled. Chrystal frowned.

"Have we met before?"

Her lack of recall seemed to amuse him. "Well, let's see," he mused. "I think you were sitting on a cement barrier wall by a fast flowing river about to fall in. You were kind of emotional, so that might explain your forgetting my presence."

Chrystal felt suddenly uncomfortable warm. She was certain she was blushing, remembering the incident.

"That was you?"

Shawn just grinned mischievously. "Small world isn't it?"

"Oh, Man!" Chrystal felt embarrassed enough she would like nothing better than to be a bug and crawl away beneath the furniture.

Shawn simply laughed, then let it go, turning his attention back to the children. "I was thinking we could go pick raspberries. They are always loaded, and they're easy to pick...good for eating while you do."

"Oh, yes! Yes!" Kara was jumping up and down now in her excitement. "You can come too, Miss Chrystal."

"Come on Teach," coaxed Shawn. "Time for recess."

"But...what about Sonia?"

"Okay," Shawn relented. "You kids go ask your great-gran, and I'll take Chrystal. We'll meet out in the orchard."

"You're pretty sure she'll say yes," Chrystal challenged.

"Of course, she will," Kara declared fervently. "Oh, but Unca Shawn, great-grandpa Sky said we must not teleport from inside. We'll have to walk," she moaned.

"Won't hurt you. You need the exercise. You go see gran and I'm sure she'll rescind that order for the time being."

"We'll have to walk to her quarters?"

"Well, you better make haste then mini-monarch," Shawn suggested. "If you don't hurry, I'll have all the fruit eaten before you get there."

Kara ignored the remark; turned to challenge Ram. "If I get there before you, what do I get for beating you there? And don't let me win like you always do!"

Ram grinned accepting her wager. "I'll have to remain invisible beside Djura outside while you talk to the Lady."

Both young ones took off at a fast walk.

Shawn chuckled. "We'll see you in the berry patch," he called after them.

"Why aren't they running?" Chrystal asked with a frown.

"Sky has also dampened the racing in the halls. That's how they got into trouble in the first place."

Chrystal could not help but laugh.

****

Kara was winning; she suspected Ram was doing that deliberately so he would lose, then she would have to face great-gran alone. *Coward!* His legs were longer; it would have been easy for him to pass her. But, now she was nearly at the chamber Kara didn't care.

As she rounded the last corner, she found a large human in her path.

Darla took up most of the corridor, swaying from side to side her huge rear like the butt of a dumb beast. She was a good foot and a half taller than the young girl, and twice as wide. Kara wondered how to get by without being rude and shoving her.

I'm not aloud to jump. I won't disobey Sky, she reasoned. *Maybe if I slip by invisible, she won't notice me? This human is a mean one. Scary!*

To Kara's eyes, the woman appeared a freak of nature with her spiked black hair streaked a raspberry red, and with her heavy dark eye makeup and the black lipstick. Kara's first thought was of a vampire movie she had once seen. Shivers of dread crawled down her spine. Not since she had been dormant, had she seen a human this ugly.

In fast action mode, Kara darted past as rapidly as possible, near invisible to the naked eye. Just as she reached the buxom beauty, Darla swayed her direction slowing the girl's process. Unable to compensate quickly enough, Kara collided with the human. The child's foot caught against the ankle of the older woman. The human went spinning against the wall, and Kara barely managed to remain upright.

Darla cursed grandly. "You little shit!" She caught the girl's arm, and wrenched her hard, pulling her closer.

Kara winced with the pain of the violent move. She could easily have teleported away, but the obedience ingrained in her made her stop short. This creature was older, and courtesy was required by great-grand's teaching.

"Who do you think you are anyway, squirt?" Darla shook the girl violently.

Just at that moment Ram came around the corner behind. He stopped short in uncertainty, his eyes narrowing in preparation to defend. Fortunate for Darla, Djura came visible just beside the doorway to the "Leader Female's' suite, preventing Kara's guardian from doing what came natural. Ram relinquished the situation to the elder warrior.

Djura rapidly stepped to Darla, threat in his very demeanour.

Darla drew back in shock at his sudden arrival, releasing Kara's arm. The woman quickly regained her equilibrium.

"Weell...big boy!" Darla crooned seductively, her voice now a breathy deep tone. "Where have they been hiding you? Where'd you come from so fast?"

Ram darted past the two protagonists, to stand protectively beside Kara. The two youngsters remained, curious to see what would come about. Darla intent on the giant guardian, gave them no farther notice.

Towering more than three feet taller than she, Djura stared down at Darla, anger in his eyes. He crossed his arms across his chest, and waited. Darla showed no signs of being intimidated.

"I am aware, you men are mostly harmless. Gentle giants, the girls call you."

"You are to cease your harmful behaviour."

"Really? She's the one who tripped me buddy! If anyone needs correction, it's her. The little squirt's got too much freedom."

"That is our concern not yours. Your own freedom will be curtailed if you persist."

Darla laughed derisively. "And are you going to be the one to make me listen, big boy?" Her voice again dropped, dripping with seduction. "Just bring it on. I'd love to tangle with you, and…I'll make it worth your while."

Taken aback at the implication projected, the huge guardian just stood there as if confused.

"I've heard you keep a woman next to your quarters so she can service you. Bet I could satisfy you better than that whore."

Djura dropped his hands to his sides, the only evidence of his shocked anger the clenching of his fists. He said nothing.

"What's the matter? I'm not good enough for the likes of you? I was for you, wasn't I? I know that was the real reason we were picked…"

Horrified, Kara looked up to the guardian warrior. *How can he endure this? The disgusting insinuations are cutting deep. How can she be this heartless?*

"What? Are you a cold fish? I'm not attractive to you? You want a man?"

"Enough! You will cease this!" Djura hissed venomously.

"Awww…I got under its skin…"

"You will never be mean to the females again," he growled, returning to the matter at hand.

Darla stood daring him, her hands on her hips. "I believe you have orders to be non-violent," she sneered.

"Sonia will decide your fate."

"Seems that old lady has a lot of control for such a little person," she challenged. "Big guy like you should make his own decisions, don't need to follow her like a lap dog. Makes you guys look like a bunch of panty-waists."

Djura's eyes narrowed.

"Why don't you leave her, big boy?" Darla's voice was again as sweet as honeyed sugar. "I'll make it worth your while."

The guardian's control was ready to break; he barely held his anger in check. "Be gone with you!" hissed Djura.

Ram caught Kara's hand and fled, escaping to the 'Leader Female's' chambers, as Djura won the face off by transferring the obnoxious woman instantly to her quarters. Then shutting away his seething wrath and humiliation from the younger, more sensitive minds Djura allowed the other men balanced him emotionally.

As they entered Sonia's rooms, both young people heard her unguarded thought.

It is time that woman be placed on a work detail!

****

Chrystal stood looking out over the valley instead of gathering the fruit. Shawn was picking near her; Ram and Kara, a short distance away.

"It is so beautiful out here," Chrystal marvelled. "I would love to paint some of this breathtaking view. The pictures should sell for a good price."

Shawn was unimpressed. "They will prevent any likeness of Sanctuary from being viewed by the outside world," he warned. "Humans must not learn of its existence."

"I am a good artist, Shawn," Chrystal avowed. 'I've been painting all my adult life; even sold a few canvases. I could do it justice. I know I could."

"I'm certain you could, but it would put us all in jeopardy…if you want to paint for your own pleasure, I guess that would be okay. Your 'Keeper' can supply you with supplies…"

Chrystal returned to picking berries. "I guess, I could do that, but it just won't be the same."

They gathered in silence for the next few minutes.

"Where are the kids?" Chrystal asked suddenly. "Aren't we responsible for them?"

"They moved over to the cherries…around the corner. Ram is guardian. He can defend. Stop worrying and enjoy yourself."

"Is that why he's always with her?"

Shawn grinned knowingly, but said nothing more. After a time he decided to put Chrystal straight.

"She doesn't really need teaching you know," he stated bluntly. "We just want you to be her companion. She already knows everything the species knows, and more…she will someday take Sonia's place. Her amethyst eyes means she's a "Leader Female' in waiting, Sonia's successor. Gran holds the records of the race."

Chrystal gave him a blank stare.

"Their memory capacity is phenomenal…"

"Are you saying, the records are in her mind?"

Shawn nodded. "Sonia has already transferred many of the records to Kara; double files so to speak. They were transferred to duplicate in case Sonia is killed suddenly. We hope Kara will be able to separate on time, and continue the race should Sonia be lost quickly…"

Chrystal frowned. "What do you mean…separate?"

When Shawn gave no answer for many minutes, Chrystal knew she would not receive an answer.

Finally, she observed, "You expect a lot of that little girl. She is only six."

"That's eleven in human."

"Even so…she's just a little girl."

"I believe Sonia warned you, she's an exceptional child."

"I'll say she is! Was I supposed to teach her anything?"

"Just…the value of adult friendship."

"Oh, I think she's already got that down pat."

Shawn grinned.

"You guys quit talking about me," Kara interjected from behind a nearby bush. "Or Ram and I will go play tag."

"Why don't you, mini-monarch," Shawn suggested. "You don't have to stay."

"Okay. We'll see you later." Abruptly, both children were gone, leaving Chrystal alone with Shawn.

"You call her mini-monarch," Chrystal observed. "Because of what she is?"

"Yep."

"She's sweet on Ram, isn't she?"

"You noticed." He laughed. "And he is smitten, tongue-tied sometimes…for her."

"Do they need these berries for something?"

"Not really. You can eat them. Let's sit down over there, and see how they taste.'

He led her to a bench she had not noticed until now. As the fruit disappeared, Shawn finally grew brave enough to bring up the real reason he had her out here.

"Say…can I ask a favour of you?"

"Sure. Ask away."

"Will you be my date for the banquet?"

Chrystal turned to look at him, puzzled. "You want me to go with you to the wedding ceremony? Aren't I a little old for you?"

The guardian actually made a rude sound.

"Why is it all you humans think we're just kids?" he exploded.

"Maybe, because you look like a kid?" Chrystal returned bluntly.

"Well, actually, I'm older than you!" he declared indignantly.

"In human?"

"In human…and our years!"

"And, how old is that?" she asked, still doubtful.

"Twenty-eight…in human!"

"You look thirteen!"

"Sometimes this ageless state can be a curse," he grumbled. "Aww…just forget it! I'll just go alone!"

As Shawn stood up to go, Chrystal grabbed his hand.

"Shawn…I'm sorry," Chrystal pleaded in regret. ""I was kinda…giving you a hard time. Course, I'll go with you…if you still want me?"

He turned back and grinned, once more the jovial teen.

"Guess, I had that coming," he admitted. "I've been rather a tease with you. Nice to know, I've got a partner with a sense of humour."

"Partner?"

"Someday…" he grinned. "I might like you for my pair."

"Oh, you would, would you?" Chrystal punched him in his side; she couldn't reach any higher. She was only five foot four.

Shawn laughed, the sound rolling from deep within that big chest.

CHAPTER 27

The apples were coming in by the buckets. Wade and Zane were stacking them manually in one of the far pantries. Shawn had joined them because he liked the physical labour. Also Chrystal, Kara and Ram were in the kitchens indulging in a mid-morning snack, and this way he could be near Chrystal without being too obvious.

It was expected Zane's reasons were much the same, to be near Chantel, as she worked with Jessica being her companion. Both women were busy making apples into sauce, jam, jelly and various baked delicacies.

The men thought, they would always need tasters.

"I need a man's opinion on this apple strudel," Chrystal declared, bringing the large pan to the counter.

It was amazing how easily a guardian became distracted. Zane was the first to rush to her side, followed quickly by Shawn, Ram, and even Wade. Like a mass exodus.

Jessica laughed delighted. "Isn't this fun? We could lead these guys like lambs to the slaughter."

"Best way to a boy's heart, even the biggest of boys," Chrystal agreed. "Just make sure the bread basket is as big as the eyes."

Chantel was transferring slices to plates as fast as the hands were held out to receive them. The four males ignored the remarks, moving to a table to eat sitting down.

"May we have seconds?" Shawn asked.

Behind the counter, Jessica grinned and winked at Chantel. "Do you think my brother put in enough labour to deserve more?"

"I don't know," Chantel teased, scanning Shawn's heavier physique. "He does look a little thin…"

Laughing at the female banter, Shawn's uncle Zane took a huge mouthful which slipped down the wrong way. He began to cough, choking, unable to get his wind.

"Opps," Chantel giggled. "No more for you."

It took a moment, but at last when the guardian had his breath, he fired back with a voice hoarse from the struggle. "I'll get you back later, female."

Giggling, Chantel slipped away to take another pan from the ovens in the next room.

And just at that point Darla chose to make an entrance. The room went from pleasant camaraderie to instant silence, as if cold water had been poured over their heads.

As Darla moved behind the large counter stretching across from wall to wall, she noticed Kara perched behind on a stool. Anticipating trouble, Ram immediately stood from his place with the males at the table, quickly walked to his assigned charge, his eyes going wider in the preparation of defence.

"Well, look who we have here," Darla snidely declared. "If it isn't the little twerp herself."

Jessica looked up in shock; Wade frowned and stood up, his eyes turning defensive.

"So, little pest," Darla challenged. "You better get out of here." She made a shooing motion with her hand. "Go run to your momma."

Jessica bristled. "Kara is my daughter," she defended. "She may stay in the kitchens when ever she wishes. And please refrain from calling her names!"

Darla made a rude sound. "You should reign in your kid, not let her run wild. That's what comes of having babies when you're just out of diapers yourself."

Chrystal, standing on the other side of Kara, gasped with disbelief. But Jessica, choosing her battle, remained silent. Wade walked to her side, catching her hand to give her comfort.

"Oh, and I suppose, this is daddy," Darla added sarcastically.

Zane and Shawn stood to their feet in preparation to intercede.

"Oh, wow!" Darla feigned surprise. "She's got a whole regiment at her disposal. Don't worry fellows. I'm not going to hurt your precious females." She laughed, derision in her tone.

A powerful fragrance of vanilla and cinnamon overpowered the room.

Just behind Darla, unnoticed by her, Sonia appeared with Karine at her side. The subtle scent of gunpowder entered with them, but that owner remained invisible.

Karine having been unprepared for the sudden jump stifled a gasp as the 'Leader Female' released her hand. The human had realized immediately, they had come upon a situation that required her to remain silent.

Behind Darla's back, Sonia moved back against the wall, silently shaking her head at Zane and Shawn. They quietly took their seats. Darla, however, assumed their action meant surrender.

"Well, see." She turned to Kara's parents. "It's all in how you talk to them."

Jessica shook her head, disgusted.

"So who's in charge here anyway? I was told I'm to work in here."

Just at that moment, Chantel returned with a second tray of baking. Sliding the pan on the flat counter surface, she stopped short at sight of the contentious nemesis.

"Don't tell me it's you, cripple?" Darla growled in derision. "What qualifications do you have to work in here?"

Caught off guard, Chantel defended herself. " I am a trained military chef…"

"Ya, right! So these dorks make you boss over the rest of us?"

Jessica finally spoke up. "Actually, I'm in charge of the kitchens."

"Oh…the twerp's juvenile mommy? No way!"

"I asked you not to call Kara names," Jessica returned, ice in her tone.

Suddenly, Chantel realized they were referring to Jessica's daughter, and joined in to defend. "Kara's a delightful little lady! Why would you think other wise?"

"Stay out of this, cripple!" hissed Darla.

Zane's big hands, flat on the table, clenched. Sonia shook her head slightly to ease him.

Jessica had endured enough. "If you came to work, start cutting apples." She pointed beside Kara where a bowl and a paring knife appeared.

Darla scowled.

"Go on!" ordered Jessica.

"Yes, your all mighty majesty!" sneered Darla, saluting just to get another rise out of her, but Jessica would not be bated farther.

Darla moved to the counter; picked up the knife. Kara suddenly fearful decided to move out of the way. Stepping down from the stool, she missed her footing. Chrystal beside Kara reached out to catch her, but was too late to stop the stumble. Kara jarred against the larger woman just as Darla picked up an apple. It went flying in the opposite direction.

Darla raised the knife in anger toward Kara, snarling. "Get the hell out of my way...you pitiful useless creature!" she hissed under her breath.

Ram had heard the comment. His eyes narrowed. He would have done the woman serious harm if not for Sonia's mental command to hold.

Kara turned with tears in her eyes.

"Great-gran, how much longer must we allow this one to remain?" she pleaded. "She's such a...potty mouth!"

Darla spun, suddenly realizing Sonia was present. She lowered her knife; crimson spread across her cheeks.

"So," she hissed to Kara under her breath. "Tattled, did you? Can't fight your own battles, eh?"

Sonia's eyes narrow with annoyance.

"My great granddaughter knows more of battle than you ever will, and she at least knows when to fight them." Then Sonia answered Kara's plea. "Little one," she comforted softly. "We are being tested. She is here as an example... Some are good; others can not be trusted."

"Ah!" Kara smiled with understanding, as if the two of them had a secret only known to them.

Sonia winked at the child.

Darla saw, and that provoked her. "If you think you can scare me old lady, you don't!"

Darla turned to Kara. "See kid, the way I see it. I'm here as an example to show you and everyone else just how far a human can defy your powerless leader. And after I'm through, maybe you won't blindly follow her every whim."

"You show great-gran some respect!" Kara thundered back viciously. "Or I'll show you how powerful we really are!"

"Ka...ara," Sonia warned quietly.

"Sorry, great-gran..." The little girl dropped her eyes, contrite.

"Oh, now...isn't that cute," Darla sneered. "Just like that, she drops to her knees. Why?" she asked, and pointed at Sonia. "What makes her so much better than the rest of you?"

Kara shook her head. "You are very stupid…for a human."

"Kara," Sonia warned again. "Remember? A test…let it teach you self-control."

Darla laughed. Thinking she was winning, she turned to Sonia. Her next words died on her tongue at the look in the 'Leader Female's' eyes. Sonia was not smiling.

In a low, even tone Sonia declared. "If you intend to stay here, from now on you will remain civil, and…obedient!"

Darla finally realized she had pushed too far. Now was the time to back down. She turned, picked up an apple and began coring it for cutting.

Sonia turned to the others. "Leave her here by herself for an hour. Perhaps, her mood will have improved by the time you return from your break."

Jessica wiped her hands on her apron, reached out to Wade. The two disappeared. Zane walked to Chantel; they touched and were gone.

Shawn stood almost defiant, his arms crossed. He remained standing by the table.

"Go grandson," Sonia encouraged softly. "I am not alone."

Shawn beckoned to Chrystal, who ran to him eagerly. The two vanished.

"Go Ram," Sonia ordered.

The boy linked hands with Kara, departing in an instant. That left Karine…and Sonia.

Just before these last two disappeared, Sonia warned, "One more such incident and you will leave this place."

"And when I do," Darla fired back. "I'll tell the whole world about your little endeavour here."

Sonia smiled sadly. "If you can still remember your stay here when you go, you are welcome to try."

Then Sonia took Karine by the hand and vanished. It wasn't until then that Darla saw Djura just as he first came solid, then with an angry glare disappeared again.

"Bitch! Bastard!" Darla exploded wrathfully once she was certain she was alone. "I'll have the last laugh in the end."

Her 'Keeper' appeared hovering above and behind her, where she couldn't see it. A wave of static energy past rapidly out from it, over the ample form of the human, sending her violently to the floor.

A disembodied voice resounded through the cavernous space.

"A derogatory epitaph referring to the 'Leader Female' will result in instant punishment, which can be harmful to your physical well being. First rule of my programming is defence of Sonia."

"Oh, hell!" hissed Darla, rubbing her stinging arms. "Since when?"

The multi-coloured flashing sphere dropped down to eye level in from of her, as Darla sat up.

"I am programmed to no longer disclose information to you, only provide for your needs and administer discipline when you cause distress to other beings."

Darla had not bargained on a mechanical watchdog. Rising from the floor she realized, though she could inflict unmeasured verbal abuse upon her captors, she was powerless to do anything to an automated invisible device programmed to police her every move.

"I thought they were non-violent," she mumbled to herself. "So much for telling the truth."

Darla set about paring and cutting apples, her mood decidedly sullen and vengeful.

The scent of gunpowder grew pungent in the air. Darla spun. Djura stood behind her, his arms crossing his chest.

"You! You did this!" she spat. "You reprogrammed that darn 'Keeper'!"

"We did adjust it," Djura proclaimed calmly. "But you still control it. It all depends upon your behaviour."

He abruptly faded from her presence.

Darla desperately hated that man! She would make him pay! If it was the last thing she ever did!

CHAPTER 28

The man started violently when Morgan stepped out of the bushes by the pond. She put it down to a man thing. Sometimes men went to that nothing box in their heads, just sitting, vegging out, when they were fishing.

"May I join you?" Morgan asked, dropping to the rocks beside him. "I'll try not to scare the fish away."

"Doesn't appear I have much choice," he returned sullenly.

"Well, in that case, if you'll just give me a moment to catch my breath, I'll move along."

"Sorry. Didn't mean it like it sounded. You are welcome to stay."

****

Actually, Lance found he was more annoyed with himself then the female. He had been concentrating so hard watching the perimeter she had actually snuck up on him. Since Darla's last foray out here, they had been extra vigilant.

Got to watch that. My awareness of my surroundings is slipping.

It then occurred to him his mother might have had something to do with that. She was forcing the issue, as he was the last to make contact with his chosen. He was usually quite cognizant of what went on around him.

Mother, you set this up, didn't you?

In his mind, he heard Sonia chuckle. *Go with the flow, son. It's time.*

Thanks! he complained in thought.

****

"You're Lance, aren't you?" Morgan observed. "I remember you now, from the interviews."

"And, you didn't even mix us up," he returned with candour.

"I remember about the scents. Yours is like...basil."

"Obviously you cook? And I guess I need a bath..."

"Oh, no. I like your...ah, anyway...Yes, I like to cook, but I seldom get the chance. Why? What gave me away?"

"You used a cooking herb to describe my personal scent."

Morgan laughed self-consciously. "Sorry if that offends you."

"Doesn't. Okay by me."

"So, are you on a break day or something?'

"No, actually I'm working."

She looked at him with amazement. "You could have fooled me. If this is your job, fishing, you have the most cushy job on the site."

He grinned. "I'm perimeter guardian; fishing is a disguise. Too obvious if I simply strut around on patrol...I am only one of many out here." Somewhat embarrassed, he added, "I get to keep you all safe should the enemy rear its ugly head."

"Humm…you expect this enemy to show up here by the lake?"

"My mind's watching elsewhere…even while we are talking."

"You seemed pretty observant when I walked up to you," she reason with irony. "What if I'd been that enemy?"

"Who says you are not?"

That took her back a step. *Why is he so hostile? Is it me?*

"Why are you out here?" he bluntly asked.

"I've got a lot of free time, and I like the great outdoors. Used to go camping a lot with my boy friend. But…that was a long time ago…" She turned away from his penetrating gaze, remembering the unpleasant circumstances. "Haven't gone since he was killed on his motorcycle."

"When was that?"

"I guess…" The memory of the accident flooded over her like it had happened yesterday. "It must be over fifteen years now…" Grief was still there in her voice even though she made an effort not to show it.

"Still hurts," he observed.

She sighed. "Aww…I think it will always hurt. When your partner dies, you die a bit too…some of us just maintain the shell we live in."

"You don't like it here?"

"Actually, I'm more at peace than I've been in a long while…"

He did not comment on her equanimity, almost like he was sharing a similar experience being outside.

"You didn't really answer my question…"

"What was that?"

"Why did you come out here?"

"Oh! Well…I'm Rhea's companion…and she keeps telling me to take free time… she wants to spend time with this big guy…the one that smells like chocolate."

Lance laughed outright. "You mean our 'Jolly Giant'? That's Ihor."

"Oh. Now I think of it, she did call him that."

"The reason they're so intent on each other is, they are about to be paired. That's why we are preparing for that fancy banquet. Both Jade and Rhea are to be paired."

"But I thought Rhea already had a partner…isn't she Kara's grandmother?"

"Both my sisters were once married…to humans. Their men were both killed in separate car accidents: Jade about ten years ago; Rhea's last fall…and yes, three of the children belong to her."

"Oh, that's sad…"

"That's she's getting paired?" he asked, tongue-in-cheek.

"Oh, no!" She laughed. "That both your sisters lost their husbands in such a violent way."

His eyes went dark, as if the memory hurt somehow. "Ivan's death could have been prevented," he declared coldly. "If a certain one of us had been more vigilant…"

He returned his attention again to his fishing pole.

This guy is not a happy camper! Morgan decided, wondering if there was some way to get him out of his funk.

She sat there for a long time, just thinking. Suddenly, she was struck with the answer. "Why don't you like me, Lance?" she demanded. "Is it because I'm an ex-cop?"

"Don't much like cops," he stated sullenly.

So that was it!

Morgan laughed harshly. "Well, I won't hold that against you. I'm not too keen on them myself at the moment. Had enough shit police work to last me a life time!"

He turned to stare at her; his jaw dropped open in disbelief.

"You sound as if you hated the job."

"Oh, I loved it at first. I thought I could actually keep people safe. But, over the years I did more hurting than helping. I saw so much ugliness…humans preying on the weak, the rich exploiting the poor. It was the kids that finally got to me; gangs who tormented just for pleasure. The young got too violent to my liking…a seven year old killing a five year old. Why? Because, the little one wanted to tag along…and the offender's age gave her protection by law. I finally just wanted to leave the human race behind…

"I wasn't a happy cop by then. They kicked me out…"

Lance studied the fishing pole. "I never quite looked at it from the opposite side before," he finally said, his voice subdued. "I'm sorry. I think I've been rather rude to you."

It's strange how these beings are so quick to accept blame and apologize.

"You've been behind bars, haven't you?" Morgan surmised quietly.

He nodded ever so slightly, without looking at her.

"Never a nice place to be," she admitted. "I was a guard at a women's prison for seven years."

Lance seemed reluctant to confide. Finally, he seemed to win the battle with his trepidation. "They deliberately lost me in the system."

She didn't question the truth of the statement. "For how long?"

"Ten years."

She had not expected that. "How does an alien get locked up in the first place, and for that length of time?"

"When we are dormant we are very human-like...without powers, and...we were all born dormant. During that time we were subject to the human legal system."

"Here on earth?"

He nodded.

"What did you do to get put behind bars?"

"I took the wrong woman to bed."

Morgan wasn't sure she wanted to hear more, but her curiosity overruled.

"Rape? Murder? Which was it?"

"Does a man have to be guilty to go to prison?"

"Usually, I know they all say they've been framed, and everyone of them is innocent, but in my experience, they are not."

Lance said nothing, simply turned away again.

After a long pause, Morgan spoke first.

"So, okay. The women all tell me your kind are incapable of lying…what did they accuse you of?"

"Does it matter?"

"No. I suppose not. I would understand if you had done something. I've been provoked to the end of my limit."

"I slapped a child."

Her jaw dropped with shock. "What? You got ten years for what?"

"Sentence was eight years; the final charge incest. The mother and her child got inventive…and greedy, when they got me in lock up."

"You had property!"

"We had just built this fabulous two-story together: hot tub, Jacuzzi, two car attached garage, lighted, underground sprinklers, beautiful landscaping, the works. I had done it all myself."

Morgan sat back in amazement. "The oldest scam in the book!" She had known the legal system was flawed, but this was beyond comprehension.

"You can't have a fondness for the human race," she observed after a time.

"You got that right! But...I am half human," he stated frankly. " However, cops are still not my favourite people...nor human women. Although...I am learning to be...forgiving."

"Lance. I'm soo sorry. I misjudged you, too." Morgan fervently wished she had not pried into his past. "We are not all beasts like those you've met," she pleaded quietly. "Give me another chance."

His eyes went soft; his smile tentative.

"Well, enough about me! Tell me something about you. What of your family?"

It was Morgan's turn to sigh and look away.

"I have none. When I was three, my father shot my mother. He went to prison, died in the inmate showers. I never knew either of them. I was raised in foster care, grew up with the intense desire to help other children in like circumstance. So, I became a cop..."

"Why were you, ah...let go?"

"Thirty years in law enforcement, and I let a prisoner take my gun. She was just a kid, sixteen; killed a male guard with it...and, I wasn't sorry either."

"You let her steal it?" quizzed Lance.

"Maybe. He was a..." Morgan kept the epitaph on her tongue to herself. "Anyway...he had it coming!"

"Why didn't you report him?"

"I did. No one else would back what I told them."

Lance nodded, as if he had experienced exactly how that worked.

A sudden thought occurred to him. "Say, how did you get this far out here on your own anyway?"

Morgan had to laugh at herself. "I got turned around inside the tunnels, found this door, and it led out to that far rope bridge."

"You walked all that way through the gardens?"

"Yeah, it was a little more than I bargained on for walking distance. I was really exhausted by the time I got to you. Kinda dumb, I guess."

Lance grinned. "Actually, my mom did much the same thing the first time she explored the caverns, came out on that very bridge. So don't feel bad."

"You mean...Sonia?"

"Yes."

"You're kidding me?"

"Tell you what; I'll jump you back."

"I thought you were on duty?"

"Duty's finished. I have a lunch break; care to join me?"

"Suddenly, I'm starving!"

He chuckled. "Now, I wonder why that is?"

****

Karine lay on the bed in the chamber next to Sonia's. Djura was standing guard duty, but it was sleep break for both Sonia and Sky, so Karine could rest instead of being with the Lady.

She could hear the couple talking in quiet tones.

"They were like little children," Sonia giggled.

"Excited by new found treasure," chuckled Sky. "I remember how it feels...when I began falling hard for you, and you desperately kept me at bay, because the timing was all wrong..."

"That was soo hard for me Sky. I was falling too. The last thing I wanted was for you to keep your distance..."

"I know that now, Love..."

"By the way, I think you still have your band turned on."

"Opps! Did we say anything inappropriate?"

Sonia giggled again...and then, there was silence.

CHAPTER 29

It was mid afternoon when Ziva went on lunch break. To her annoyance, she found Darla was the only one working in the kitchens.

Morgan and Carmen were at a middle table, so Ziva chose a different one to their right rather than sit with them. She had a need to be alone.

Ziva did not mind working with Joel. He was actually quite jovial, a quick-witted fellow, coming back with joking phrases when she least expected it. He made time pass rather quickly.

But today he had been exceptionally quiet, intent on that one outside monitor, as if his life depended on his not missing anything. His preoccupation had bordered on rudeness.

Most of the day, he had either not heard her questions, or simply ignored her.

And now he had sent her on break in the middle of the shift, obviously to get rid of her. Ziva felt slighted, mistrusted, rejected, and that made her angry.

Now, Darla was coming over. The woman dropped into the seat opposite, and realizing Ziva was in a bad mood and brooding, she laughed delighted.

"Tough day at the office?" she chided sarcastically.

Ziva merely grunted. She knew better than to share. After ordering her lunch by 'Keeper', she sat toying with the coffee cup, leaving the sandwich sit. She was not really hungry.

"You need something stronger than java," Darla observed. "Have you noticed they never have alcohol available when you need it? Especially not here!"

"Yeah, I've noticed," Ziva returned sullenly.

"I've been dying for a beer ever since I got here," Darla admitted. "Just too bad we can't make some on our own. We could bootleg. It would sure liven things up."

"I was never one to drink, so I really don't miss it."

Darla continued as if she hadn't heard the comment. "I've come to the conclusion, these creeps can't tolerate fermented spirits…"

Morgan cut in from across at the other table. "Actually, it's a personal choice they've all made. Lance and I were talking about that just the other day. He had a problem with substance abuse when he was dormant. They are all empathic; when one drinks, all will feel the effects. The others won't imbibe for his sake."

Darla stared at the other woman, venom in her eyes. "Do you mind?" she hissed scathingly. "We are having a private conversation here."

"Sooo so…rry!" Morgan shot back with equal acidity. "We were just going, anyway. Weren't we Carmen?"

"Then, scat!"

The two arose, but both were casual about it, taking their time just to provoke the cantankerous woman.

"Watch yourself with that one," Darla warned. "She's gotten all cosy with their 'Warrior Leaders'!"

Ziva said nothing, just picked up her sandwich and started eating.

Suddenly, Darla leaned across the table to whisper harshly. "I found the men's quarters…"

"Oh, Darla!" Ziva exclaimed with annoyance. "What are you planning now? Aren't you in enough trouble?"

"Shh! My 'Keeper' will hear you!" Darla hissed. "It's programmed to punish me."

Ziva laughed. "You're kidding me? So that's why you've been so civil of late."

"Shut your…" She looked around worriedly, as if she expected to be zapped by a death ray. When nothing happened, she leaned in again.

"Anyway, I'm not the one going to do it," she whispered. "You are."

"What am I going to do?" Ziva demanded suspiciously.

But Darla wasn't quite ready to tip her hand. "I also found where that big security guy keeps his woman."

"You talking about Karine?"

"Yeah. That's the one. Do you know, she doesn't sleep in the room when he's on duty. Her room is empty…"

"So. Where is she when he works?"

"Who cares? Thing is she has access to his suite…the door between is always open…so he can get into her apartment any time he wants, and vice-versa."

Darla was making it sound like Karine was giving out sexual favours.

"Sonia said she'd stop any hanky-panky."

"Ha! You believe that, then you're more naïve and dumber than I thought."

That ticked Ziva off. If anyone was dumb, it was Darla. But this Jewish woman had not kept her job to near retirement by being careless with her tongue. Even though she would love to tell Darla off, Ziva kept her thoughts to herself.

"Here's what I want you to do…" The large busted woman leaned in closer, her breath fowl and offensive. "See, if you can sneak in when you know Karine's out, and try going through that doorway between…"

"I'll get in trouble…and that'll blow my cover," Ziva hissed back.

"Well, if something happens with you, I'll hear about it. They're sure to make a big fuss about it."

"Do you want me to get kicked out of Technical centre?"

"Well, you ain't doing much good there."

"I'm trying! I sent another message this morning."

But Darla's mind was on one track alone. "You gonna do this?"

"What?"

"Try out that doorway. See if just anyone can get through."

Ziva knew Darla was not about to let this go until she agreed.

"Okay! Okay!"

"Good. Do it next time she's gone out. I'll know it's safe, if I don't hear anything about it."

Jessica appeared in the kitchen just then, and Darla scurried back behind the counter to get back to work.

As Ziva left the lunchroom, she reason to herself. *No way, in this lifetime, am I going into that giant's bedroom. I'm not suicidal!*

CHAPTER 30

The humans called the 'Aopato' common area the 'waterfall room'. When many caught their first sight of it, they stood gaping in awe. The library was so immense; the falls so spectacular, none could do other than be amazed by the accomplishment. And Carmen was not shy at boasting. She knew the architect; her man had done all this!

Today the 'Aopato' women had announced a concert to be held in that very room: Nadia's first ever. Angel felt proud of being her companion. She could hardly believe how far the young girl had come in the few weeks Angel had known her, nor the unusual and fabulous talent Nadia possessed.

The recital was for females only. Nadia was too shy to perform before the males on this her very first try. But the human women had been included. Everyone except Ziva, who was working with Joel, and Darla had shown up. No one knew what had become of Darla, nor did anyone care. Most avoided her; she was just too abrasive. She'd only spoil the performance anyway if she came.

The alien women too were all present. Jade, Nadia's mother, sat proudly with her sister Rhea. Jessica had declared a holiday from kitchen work thereby freeing up Chantel and Darla to attend as well, coming herself to hear her cousin play. Little Kara sat at her mother's feet excitement evident in her every movement. It was obvious, though these people had no musical history; they were not unappreciative of the concept.

Sonia sat centre front, the silenced waterfall at her back, the rainbow from it like a halo on the ceiling above. She too showed great pleasure and anticipation at the coming performance. Her family had gathered closely about her.

The human women were surprised by the diversity of appearance in this one family. It was the first time the six females had put in an appearance all together, and without the presence of guardians yet.

Facial resemblance was apparent, but that was where similarity ended.

Unlike the men who were all from six foot five to eight feet, the females were all under the five foot six mark, Kara being the shortest at four feet tall. Still none of the humans stood as tall as they, save for Ziva who was over six feet.

The beauty of all 'Aopato' women was exquisite. None appeared over forty; most seemed merely in their teens. Sonia, Kara and Jessica were blond, but the 'Leader Female' and young Kara had amethyst eyes, while Jessica had one of blue, the other purple; a decidedly weird phenomena in the opinion of the humans.

Rhea, Jessica's mother and Kara's grandmother, had the same eyes as her daughter, but her hair was a light copper tone, something humans might call 'a ginger'. Her sister Jade, Sonia's other daughter, had eyes the colour of her name, hair of light brown.

It was hard for any human to decide which was more gorgeous, but Nadia got most votes with her caramel skin, long silken spiral curls falling down her back, and her brown-gold eyes. At the moment her strawberry scent was very evident due to her nervousness.

Actually, few but her family and Angel realized that she was anxious, as Nadia placed herself calmly upon a chair direct centre of the circle of women. The humans were spread out behind her and up either side.

They each expected to see instruments, yet there were none in evidence. Nadia simply closed her eyes, and sound filled the spaces around her. After that, rapture brought time to a stand still for all.

The room first was deathly silent, then a faint piccolo escaped with a solo sound, the music surrounding. It seemed to come from everywhere at once; be inside you. The humans moaned with the ecstasy of the sensation. Angel would never get used to that intimate caress, even though she had listened to Nadia practice the piece countless times.

Sonia closed her eyes to enjoy more fully, smiling. The other 'Aopato' women all did like wise, so the humans followed suit.

It was even more pleasurable with your eyes shut; it seemed to transport you to another plane, to ultimate peace, near hypnotically so.

Now a harp joined the piccolo; castanets increased the beat. Excitement crawled your spine.

An oboe, clarinet and bassoon took harmony with the piccolo, while violin and base cello did the same for the strings. The xylophone and tabor joined the castanets.

Pitch was perfect; the beat, melody and harmony so precise you felt as though living in the sound. It gave you a hunger for more, a desire to skip the next pause; it left you waiting with baited breath for another measure. When it came you swayed again to the music.

When Nadia finally came to a quiet stop, two hours had passed. Many of the women were in tears.

How does she do it? This from a child who could barely play a note only weeks before!

"Oh, please don't stop, " begged Carmen, who sat across on Nadia's left.

Morgan, the stalwart cop, wiped away the wet on her cheeks. "Your music makes the bad world go away. Please? More!"

Sonia came to her granddaughter's rescue.

"She is exhausted," she explained in empathy. "Her talent takes a great deal of mental energy. We must let her rest a while. Perhaps for fifteen minutes, okay, Nadia?"

The girl nodded slightly. "Yes...I would love to do more. And I think, after a break, I could do another...hour, perhaps."

"Excellent!" Sonia expressed the thought of all present.

The chamber filled with murmured, excited conversation.

Oh, how much fun this was, Angel marvelled.

****

Karine had worked it so she would not miss the concert. She had rested while Sonia took her sleep break, and because Djura stood watch at the same time, he was now going to his rest period. That left Karine free to enjoy with the others.

When time was up Nadia signalled she was ready, and a new composition began.

Everyone once more closed their eyes to partake jointly.

Suddenly, instead of the pleasure of sound, Karine had the oddest sensation: as if someone naked had just slipped into bed with her. As well, she was aware of the same lustful feeling Djura had allowed her to feel to teach her on that first day. And once again, it seemed like he was uncontrollably angry with her.

Am I reliving that past experience? Why now?

Karine opened her eyes, meeting those of Sonia just as the 'Leader Female' went rigid in shock, and the human companion instantly knew, it was not just her perceptions.

I've just felt my big guardian's feelings, simultaneous with his leader?

That had never happened so powerfully before.

Nadia's serenade stopped abruptly on an ugly discordant note.

Karine looked at the other 'Aopato' women. *Had they all felt it?*

But the alien women only seemed to have sensed something wrong in Sonia. The humans around them opened their eyes in puzzlement at the abrupt ending to the music.

Karine noted, from the looks on the faces of Sonia's daughters, that something very unpleasant was taking place.

Concern for her guardian giant flooded Karine. She was quite certain he had sent her his impressions like a warning...or perhaps as a plea for help.

But, what do I do?

****

Joel and Ziva were both watching the monitors of Technical Centre. Suddenly Joel tensed.

After a second, turning to Ziva, he declared, "We must go into lock-down mode."

"What's that mean?"

"'Keepers' take over!" Joel commanded. Again to Ziva. "I will return you to your sleep quarters. Stay there!"

By the way he gave the order, Ziva realized she had no choice in the matter, but unlike usual, Joel did not get up to walk her to the women's quarters. He simply jumped her there, by willing it.

Upon arriving, as she attempted to slip through her doorway again to investigate, her 'Keeper' prevented it. Ziva found herself unexpectedly confined to her bedroom.

"What's going on here?" she demanded indignantly. "Am I a prisoner?"

But the 'Keeper' would give out no information.

****

Nadia turned to the 'Leader Female'. "Grandma?"

The other 'Aopato' women suddenly became extremely distressed. Nadia rose quickly from her chair and ran to her mother Jade who immediately wrapped her tightly in her arms.

"What do you suppose is wrong?" whispered Carmen. Beside her, Morgan simply shrugged.

Sonia's eyes narrowed.

"Djura!" Sonia ordered forcefully. "Attend me!"

The humans all knew that giant guardian belonged to Karine, so when she started softly sobbing, Angel sitting beside her put her arm around her, thinking Karine upset because Djura was in some sort of trouble.

Karine push Angel away, and stood up, preparing to go to the front.

"No, Karine!" Sonia admonished, disapproval in her tone. "Stay out of this!"

At that, Carmen wondered, *is Karine in trouble too?*

"Djura! Attend me!" Sonia ordered vehemently a second time.

None had ever seen her angry before.

Abruptly, the big guardian appeared, seemingly not by his own volition. He was bare chested; only wearing shorts. His pectoral muscles taunt with the strain, his fingers tangled in her hair, he struggled to control what appeared to be a smaller naked woman.

That's Darla! Carmen gasped. *Man! He's huge!*

Darla weighed over two seventy pounds, but she looked like a midget sumo wrestler next to this man, as she struggled to free herself.

She fought valiantly against his strong hold, but he easily held her at arm's length with one hand. Her painted black nails dug deep at the skin of his wrist, to no effect.

Wrath etched every line of his features. He shook her furiously, fire sparking from his eyes.

Neither seemed to realize where they were, nor that they were physically exposed before others.

Exasperation showing on her face, Sonia waved her hand, and at once both were fully clothed again.

It was that action that made Darla realize Sonia had brought them before her. "It was his idea!" she squeal-screamed at Sonia, the effort to talk through her pain evident. "He said he wanted me!"

"I will kill you," hissed Djura through clenched teeth. "You lying, vile female."

He shook Darla until her teeth chattered. She was like a puppet in his hand.

"Release her, Warrior! Now!" Sonia commanded urgently. But the giant seemed deaf. "Djura! Obey!"

Sonia stood to her feet. "Let her go! Djura! Look at me!"

He snarled like an animal, turned, so angry it seemed he would strike his 'Leader Female'. The witnesses held their collective breath.

"She crawled into my bed as I slept..." The male finally met Sonia's eyes. He moaned with a deep tortured agony.

At last he had come aware. Djura dropped the human woman as if she were hot, sank trembling to one knee, and covered his face with his hands in shame.

"Oh, my Lady. I've lost control," he groaned. "Forgive me."

The colossal warrior began to shudder uncontrollably, his tremors so violent the floor shook around him. A sudden static light in shades of red and blue began to flash through his frame, across shoulders, through his chest.

Sonia moved back a step in trepidation.

"My Lady!" Djura raised his eyes to his leader, genuine panic in his tone. "I can no longer balance!" His voice rose to a wail. "I can not control! I'll go Nova! Help me!"

No one in the room needed to be told what Nova meant.

"Sky! Chi! Attend! Immediately!"

The instant Sonia gave the command the Navajo and the Oriental were beside her. Immediate assessment of the situation had each man quickly at an arm of the Arabian. All three abruptly vanished.

An audible gasp of relief past out from the humans.

But the world had not righted itself just yet.

****

Quietly Karine had sobbed in the background, her spirit devastated with anguish. Angel took her hand to comfort, and Karine clenched it like a lifeline. She was not aware when Angel winced as the pressure became unbearable.

Djura is gone…maybe forever.

Sonia turned enraged eyes to Darla. "Do you realize you nearly killed him! This is why I said no intimacy!" Sonia shouted bitterly.

Darla yelled. "He assaulted me!"

"The male quarters were off limits to all females!"

"Like I said," Darla replied calmly. "He invited me in."

"Is that so?" Sonia hissed venomously. "May I remind you, I can read your every memory, should I choose?"

Darla turned a light shade of green.

"We all know you are lying. We also know of your plans…Until now, I have given most everyone the privilege of privacy within their own thoughts. I will not make that mistake again."

"You think we are some kind of animals you have the right to control? We have a free will. We can do what we want, when we want!"

"Our males are not available for your sexual favours!"

"Why don't you let them think for themselves?"

Sonia's voice took on the ice of dislike. "They hand picked nine of you because they knew those ones would honour our basic rule of abstinence. But it was I who picked you Darla, giving you a chance to change your chosen path…but I knew from the start you would be the one deviant female. I chose you to be a negative example by which the others would steer by…"

"Why?" Darla spat. "You think you're so much better?"

"Some way was needed to show what happens when that basic rule is broken…"

Did Sonia use Djura as bait? Or did she simply suspect Darla would go after some male, and Djura was the unlucky guardian the evil woman had chosen? Did he suspect he would be targeted?

"Here is the one basic rule no one breaks while with us," Sonia reiterated, menace in her voice. "My guardians remain celibate! They and our single females will remain so until each are paired. We expect you humans to honour that, to treat them with due respect. Sexual promiscuity unbalances the individual, and our society, as you have just witnessed…are about to witness farther. If one goes off balance, and…it cannot be corrected…madness ensues. Death is the end result!"

Sonia let the words sink in. Tomb-like silence reigned in the room.

"When one of us stays unbalanced," Sonia continued with slow emphasis. "That distortion carries through the species. An unstable individual can destroy the entire race. We are all connected…and trust me," she added for emphases, warning in her tone. "You do not want to be around us when we all go unstable."

Sonia took a breath to calm herself. "Should you still misunderstand the gravity of what Darla has just accomplished…" The 'leader Female' deliberately left the sentence unfinished.

But giving evidence to her words, Kara made an attempt to rise from the floor. Her legs buckled beneath, her to the horror of those present. Jessica, her mother, reached down to help her, pulling her up into her lap. All 'Aopato' sisters and daughters were suddenly trembling; they joined hands as if in support.

Sonia wiped a sheen of moisture from her own brow.

What is wrong with them? It is like they are getting sick.

"You...Darla."   Sonia gave a soft moan. "You have succeeded in unbalancing us all."

The unpleasant woman gave a contemptuous laugh. "Good!" she snarled. "I meant to hurt you! 'Bout time you got your coming down."

Sonia shook her head in disbelief.

"I never...even imagined," she said regretfully. "That such unmerited hatred could possibly come from human kind...you are very like an 'Opposite'..."

"Well, get this through your thick skull: you won't live long when my people get to you. There are more where I came from."

Karine felt the anger boil within her. She wanted to shout at Darla, to tell Sonia the rest of them did not agree with that woman.

Sonia never harmed any one of us! She has been generous and kind!

As if she'd heard her, Sonia turned her eyes to Karine.

"Human anger and fear hurts us," she rebuked softly, as if reprimanding Karine personally. "Jealousy, hate…it cuts…deep…"

Karine burst into tears at the admonishment.

Darla laughed delightedly, then hissed sarcastically, "Well, I hate you beyond measure…lady!"

Sonia frowned, puzzled.

"Why? Why do you dislike us so?"

"Because, you have everything: looks, power…because you are different!" Darla hissed. "And…you're good!"

Sonia sadly shook her head.

"Always, I hoped…by being among those who were more pleasant…you would change…"

Fury contorted Darla's features. "I don't want your pity," she snarled. "I don't like your mercy!"

Sonia sighed.

"That you can not stop, Darla. I will give it always."

As if her legs would no longer support her, Sonia carefully took the seat behind her. For a second, she scrutinized the wretched creature before her. "It is time to end this. I will pass judgement," the 'Leader Female' proclaimed quietly.

The vertical slit at the centre of those amethyst eyes widened.

"Darla…you will have no memory of your stay here, but if ever we come in contact again, you will have an unexplained fear of us…for your own protection. From now on your mind will be at the level of an infant. You will live long, under expert medical care, the most advanced equipment available used to prolong your life, studied by your scientists...yet never cured nor your condition understood. Your present employers will find you wandering the streets of your home city lost and alone...you will forever be useless to them."

Darla sneered, defiant to the end. "They have ways to bring memories back. Why don't you just kill me?"

"If I took your life...I would be no better than you."

Sonia's image dimmed. Then Darla was gone.

Neither Karine, nor any of the others in the room, doubted that Sonia had just done what she had predicted.

Sonia again made eye contact with Karine. Next she uttered a prophetic word the Irish woman would never forget.

"Often you have jealously desired to be like us, coveting our powers, wanting to know the secrets we hide. You all will soon see what it is really like to live our lives... the down side is coming. And you will not find it so enviable then."

Great tears of remorse slipped from Karine, down her cheeks. She knew she was guiltier than any other, and the reproach was meant mostly for her. Her lip trembled, as she hesitantly enquired.

"Will Djura...be okay?"

"He is the least of our problems right now..."

Sonia made no farther comment. Karine realized: Sonia never lied. She did not know the results of their future. If the answer were negative or unknown, she would say nothing rather than hurt by an untruth.

The 'Leader Female' was trembling visibly; the other 'Aopato' woman had relaxed a bit, but had gone very quiet. It seemed their interlinked hands balanced them.

Why is Sonia seemingly worse?

It dawn on Karine, as she remembered something Chantel had told her about her healing.

Why, Sonia is balancing the females!

That really frightened Karine.

Sonia is in agony! Is she healing someone? Healing Djura...from here?

A tear slipped down Sonia's cheek, and her tone held pain. "Please...do not hurt us...anymore."

Is she speaking to me?

The 'Leader Female' made an attempt to calm herself.

"If any...wish their freedom..." Her speech became slurred, the words seeming to come with great effort. "Now...is your time to escape!"

Stunned, Karine could not believe what she was hearing.

"But, if you do still wish to remain," Sonia hopefully suggested. "For your own safety...return to your quarters." Sonia seemed to rally at this optimistic prospect. "The 'Keepers' will seal you in...when they release you, it means, they have

260

determined we are balancing. But should we go Nova, even Earth will not be saved."

Sonia gasped in pain, doubling over; her female family members went tense; suddenly all were shaking. The 'Leader Female' straightened; the 'Aopato' women relaxed.

"May Lin...." Sonia gasped. "Do not go to the suite beside my chambers...I am...ground zero!"

Ice entered Karine's heart.

Jade reached out a quivering hand to her mother. Karine assumed it was to comfort, but when Sonia took it, the 'Aopato' women, as a group, vanished.

****

It was such emptiness, like a sudden shock of separation. Karine felt like wailing; instead her body went numb.

Have I somehow been connected to Sonia? Is that why I understood what was taking place?

Depression slugged at her gut. On her own she could not deal with this. She needed Sonia, but the female had abandoned her.

Djura is dying; Sonia is suffering unfathomable pain. Sonia is ground zero... Sonia is ground zero!

Horror filled her mind; agony seized her chest. Even tears gave no ease to this affliction.

It's all my fault! Darla got to Djura through my adjoining bedroom...I should have kept him safe! She wouldn't have gotten to him if I'd been there...where I should have been.

Hopelessness took over; Karine stood in the middle of the empty common room, paralysed by indecision. She had not even realized when the other human women left the room.

If Djura lives, will he ever forgive me? Sonia will never want me here...he will not want me! I have nowhere to go...back in that other world no one will care.

Her head felt like it would explode. That intimate connection with Sonia, now gone, drove her near mad. Djura had cried out for her help!

I feel so empty without them!

Karine longed to have Sonia erase her memories also.

There is nowhere to go...Sonia is ground zero!

CHAPTER 31

Karine moved like a numb ghost toward her chambers next to the men's quarters.

Maybe in my room I will hear what they are doing with Djura? Surely that's where they have taken him. Then again maybe they have a special place where they treat the unbalanced, an area where they can safely fight a violent guardian...

The idea brought hot tears again.

Slipping through one of the actual doors, she knew of, beneath the waterfall, Karine was reminded of Sonia's words. 'If any wish their freedom, now is the time to escape.'

Wonder if any of the other women tried to leave...or are they all locked safely in their rooms?

Karine crossed the stone bridge, looking down at the beautiful valley.

Is that 'Keeper' guarded now? Or have they been all brought inside to protect as a last defence? Are the guardians and 'Aopato' women locked away safe?

This valley is so fabulous; who would have it if they are gone? Would the 'Opposites' come and ravish it? These creatures who made it are now unprotected; could their enemy surprise them and annihilate all?

Karine shivered at the thought.

I should go. I'm to blame for this. I should just keep walking.

But where can I go? This is my Sanctuary!

Karine opened the door leading to the second set of caves. She closed it quietly behind her. As she turned, she felt someone beside her.

It was Sonia, leaning weakly against the wall behind her.

"Please…" Sonia pleaded softly. "Will you stay with me, Karine?"

Karine's heart leapt. *She's not mad at me!* Yet, the human still hesitated.

"Please," Sonia begged in an unsteady voice. "I am not certain I can make my quarters."

"I will support you." Karine reached out to slip her arm around the trembling female, but Sonia drew away.

"Best not to touch me, Karine…"

She is angry! Will she ever forgive me?

Sonia uttered a weary sigh. "It would be deadly for you to touch me right now. I do not wish to accidentally kill you."

Karine's heart accelerated to a rapid drum beat. "What do I do, my Lady?"

"Just walk with me…stay with me. Please, do not leave me alone, I beg you."

"I will not leave your side, my Lady."

Together they moved forward slowly, Sonia ahead, her gait unsteady, Karine a few steps behind.

They had not gone far when Sonia stopped, leaned heavily against the wall, slid down, to sit on the stone floor. Her breath came in pants, rapid and uneven.

Tears blinded Karine. *I did this to her.*

Karine dropped down next to Sonia, turning to watch her. The 'Leader Female's' eyes had closed; she seemed in a dead faint.

I did this! I did this!

Karine moaned with anguish.

All at once, the red and blue static lights appeared, zapping across and around Sonia. It appeared to be painful to the one suffering the phenomena, but Karine did not draw from the female. It no longer matter to her if she died along with this gentle lady.

Karine sobbed quietly, as she sat waiting beside her 'Aopato' companion.

****

Suddenly, Djura was standing over them.

"Female! I've been calling you."

Karine turned her eyes from Sonia her vision cloudy. The guardian dropped to one knee.

"How long has the Lady been like this?" Djura asked, his tone turning serious.

"I didn't mean to hurt her," Karine cried out remorsefully.

Djura frowned.

"How did you hurt the 'Leader Female'?" he asked coldly.

Karine swallowed around the phlegm in her throat. He will be so angry!

His voice gentled. "Tell me, female."

"I…I was jealous…and…and angry…afraid…"

Puzzled incomprehension was mirrored in his eyes.

"She…she said those emotions hurt her…I couldn't stop…"

Djura sighed, as if frustrated by the unreasonableness of a nonsensical child.

"Female," he reproached. "Did the Lady not choose you to stay with her just now?"

Karine nodded. Reason probing her fog, she swiped at the tears with the back of her hand.

"She is trusting you with her life," Djura reassured.

"I wouldn't blame her for hating me…"

Djura shook his head again, obviously perplexed at her behaviour.

"It is all my fault…I should have been in my room. None of this would have happened. Sonia said, what we feel and think cuts her deeply."

"Aww…female. What is wrong with you? Sonia was not herself. She was… unstable. She would never blame any human. She knows what it is like to be fallible. She would not have told you this if she had been in her right mind."

Djura studied Karine with concern. "Why are you, a human, like this?"

"I'm evil! She said…if we wanted to leave, now was the time to escape."

He appeared at a total loss for words. At last, he put a question to her, simply to reason away her objections.

"So why did you not flee, female? Surely Sonia explained how dangerous we are when unbalanced."

"I couldn't just leave her...like this? Besides, where would I go?"

"Ahh...dear one..." he muttered softly. "What am I going to do with you?"

Karine looked up at him, saw his eyes were brimming with tears.

"You did not do this, Karine!"

He must have decided, to argue would be pointless. Djura stood to his feet.

"Sky," he queried. "Are you enough recovered to balance another?"

The answering voice was wary, and weak. "Why?"

"You need to join me. Your pair needs you?"

"How bad?"

"She does not look good, Sky. She's still pre-nova stage."

Sky moaned in discouragement.

"I'll need...a little more time, guardian. Watch over her...please."

Djura stood looking down at Karine. His puzzled eyes suddenly change as understanding dawned.

"Female, when this began..."

Karine squeezed her eyes shut; she could not watch the anger she expected. Tears leaked beneath her lids as she began to cry again.

"Female," Djura pleaded softly. "Look at me. Please!"

Her vision swimming, she finally met his gaze.

"You and Sonia were connected.!" he exclaimed in amazement. 'No wonder you are so emotional. Sonia allowed you to feel when she connected with me. Why would she do such a thing?"

"I...thought you did it," Karine said in surprise.

He frowned, uncertain now. "Perhaps, I did...but that can only happen if..."

Karine blinked her swollen eyes trying to clear away the film. "If what?"

Sky chose that moment to materialize beside them. Djura turned quickly to him, allowing him no time to assess his afflicted pair.

"Sky," he demanded anxiously. "Is it possible for a human to pair-connect to us without being blood healed?"

"Why would you ask that?" Sky seemed equally concerned now as well.

Both men turned to Karine as if their minds shared the same thought.

Sky chuckled. "Djura, I have a question to answer your query. How came you to be half human?"

"Huh? What?" It was Djura's turn to frown.

"You and I are both half human. How can that be?" Sky waited a second to give the other man time to consider, then answered his own question. "Our fathers both found a human who was a sensitive!!"

Sky winked at Djura. "Proceed with caution, my friend. Treat her as the treasure she is…"

"Is it safe to touch her?" Djura asked in awe. "To balance her emotionally…"

"Hand touch would be the safest. Now truly, guardian. I must see to my pair."

Djura suddenly realized his thoughtlessness.

"Sir, may I help?"

"There is little to be done. It is not safe to touch either of us. And, it is not far to our suite; I can carry her."

Sky knelt, gently lifting Sonia. He stood to his feet. The static energy engulfed him, zapping over both he and Sonia.

"Are you strong enough, sir?" Djura wondered, concerned.

"We will drain from you should we need it," Sky agreed. "Stay near until I am safely in the chamber."

"I will remain even after…to protect, sir."

Sky nodded, turned, and strode away.

****

Djura slid down to the stone floor beside Karine.

"Female, may I touch you?"

Karine was surprised he had asked permission. "You always take my hand when we jump."

"This is different."

Karine placed her hand trustingly in his. As soon as their palms touched, she felt immediately different, as if a sudden weight was lifted from her shoulders.

"Better now?"

She nodded guiltily, embarrassed now by her crying jag. "What did he mean?"

Djura pursed his lips in an attempt to hide his smile, but delight danced in his eyes none the less.

"Just before our couples pair, an emotional/physical connection develops naturally between them. After that, they are always aware of where and what the other is doing. It's special, usually exclusive to pairing 'Aopato'."

Karine's brow puckered in thought. "You mean...we?"

"...have established such a connection," he finished for her. "That is why you felt what I did, and... that is why you connected with Sonia. I don't think even she realized it ...due to the situation."

"But...when she broke away...I felt hurt, empty."

"That is because you now have become connected to all of us. As a species we need Sonia to survive. You may not be of our kind, but now you will feel a similar want."

Karine suddenly remembered Sonia. Sky had disappeared with her into their chambers.

How can Djura be so calm about this? Sonia is ground zero!

Djura chuckled. "She told you that too?"

Karine nodded soberly.

His shook his head in amusement. "Females are the strangest creatures when they are unbalanced. How long did she remain in the presence of the humans, anyway?"

"A long time," Karine returned uncomfortably.

"She must not have been able to transfer the females, and obviously they were of no help to her..."

"She isn't...ground zero?"

"I suppose you could put it that way. She is 'Pure' and...'Leader Female'. If she went Nova the universe would be no more. She barely prevented Earth's destruction when Myron went Nova."

Karine gasp, horrified. "Is that how he died?"

Djura shook his head. "Another time. This is crisis enough for now."

Karine sat there thinking. "You almost went Nova..."

He agreed, immediately sobering.

"You okay now?"

"Yes, female. I am emotionally and physically balanced, but it was not easy on us. Sky healed me...the males are my balance-normal."

Karine sighed, relieved.

"However," Djura cautioned. "I am actually the only one truly balanced at the moment. The others all have jointly taken my instability upon themselves."

"Is that how you're...healed?"

"Yes. And Sonia being our main healer-stable, is critical…"

"But…you said, I didn't cause this…If that's right, why is this happening to Sonia?"

"She was balancing the female side when Sky was healing me. It took more physical strength on the male side than we were capable of, so it was drained from the females through Sonia. And because we don't have sufficient females…"

Karine frowned, unable to follow.

"We are all joined, female…like one being. Therefore, we all suffer together."

"Oh, my!" Karine gasp, shocked. "Can't you change that?"

"It is the nature of our species…but…more females in the race would help balance us out…"

Karine dropped her eyes, a flush of embarrassment flooding her cheeks.

He grinned at her discomfort. Slowly, with regret, he released her hand.

He stood, reached down to help her up. When they stood together, he said quietly, "I am not yet strong enough to jump you to your quarters. You will have to go alone. I must remain here as protection to the 'Leader Pair'."

"I can go into the joint chamber?" Karine suggested.

He disagreed. "No. Best you go to our other quarters. I would see you safe. Too close to Sonia creates the risk of your linking with her again. That would not be good for you. Once she is well, she will prevent that from happening."

"Is it not good for me to be pair-connected to you?" she asked worriedly.

"That which has begun, we can not change. Only my death could sever than bond."

"Does that mean…we are paired?"

"Not quite yet. Like engaged…if you wish it so…first you must learn more about us…in order to make a wise decision."

Karine took a deep breath. *This is too much to take in.* Suddenly she was so very weary.

"Go to your chambers, female," he suggested softly. "Let the 'Keeper' seal you in."

"You are okay?" she pleaded. "Would you tell me if you were not?"

That made him smile, his face lighting with affection.

CHAPTER 32

Ziva was thinking.

Joel feels more like my protector than my employer; he seems to genuinely care about my welfare.

It was hard for her to believe these guardians were as lethal as everyone said.

Through several different sources, she had pieced together what had happened. Everyone blamed Darla for the violent instability of the head of security, and Ziva knew, the intent of the vengeful woman was purposefully to throw them off kilter.

The other women still appeared to trust the men they were with, but then none were so fearsome as Djura.

Now that he was stable again, Karine did not even fear him. She seemed even more enamoured by Djura since his episode.

Ziva found that hard to comprehend.

Karine should be terrified that male will kill her. Why isn't she?

Though heavier and shorter than the head warrior, Joel appeared less a threat.

Yet, maybe he is as deadly, as well?

No, he seemed too humble to be a risk.

That stupid Darla!

It made Ziva fume that that dominating woman had put her in such a position. She had never asked for this assignment; all Ziva wanted was her pension so she could retire in safety. Now here she was alone, undercover, in over her head.

Just what will the agency require of me now?

It was not as if these women wanted rescue; it wasn't against the law what the aliens were doing. They had all become more like friends to her, both the women and the men. Ziva had never had friends before. In her former work community, it was measure up, don't fail, don't trust the guy at the next desk, or anyone for that matter. Ziva had much to lose by betraying these beings.

I can't afford to go sentimental, she chided herself. *I've got more to lose if I fail. My life will continue in the outside world after I'm finished here, and I'll need my retirement package to survive. It's not like anyone is concern about my future. I only have me to supply my needs.*

Even if I wanted to do differently, I have no choice. They'll send the government heavies after me, and they'll hit me with all they've got if I don't come through.

But in this case, the government was wrong! This was no terrorist organization! These were creatures much like humans, with needs and feelings, doing their best to survive. Yes, they had defences that were formidable, but they weren't the attackers; they would defend themselves only when threatened. Ziva was not at fault that Darla had provoked them. She had not taken part in it.

That idiot, stupid woman got less than she deserved!

But how was she, Ziva, going to get out of the mess Darla had placed her in?

Ziva also realized Darla had tried to set her up as the fall guy. If she had actually done what the woman had wanted, it would be Ziva now who was a vegetable in a scientific sanatorium, the subject of probes and experiments.

The thought crawled panic through her insides.

What if Sonia discovers I was working with Darla?

The other women had told her the females had also gone unstable. That had been why they had all been locked in their rooms for three days. If the males were deadly, what of Sonia at such a time. She was supposedly all powerful.

The last thing Ziva wanted was to get on the 'Leader Female's' wrong side!

I'm caught in the middle between my old superiors and these dangerous lethal beings. What can I do to save myself?

Then there was another side to consider: if Sonia and her kind had not brought the 'Opposites' along with them, there would be no risk to the human race, no threat to be wary of. Who was to say which species was right in this war? They should have kept their battle off the human world.

My responsibility is to my own kind! That's what is important here!

But…if there was only some way to save all: the human race, the 'Aopato' lives, her own skin, even the friendships she'd made, without turning traitor to either side, she'd go for it.

Could I be a go-between, a mediator?

But, if there was anything she knew about the intelligence community and the government officials in charge of them it was this: those in control would always rather choose to misconstrue the motives of an alien race. No matter how Ziva presented the situation or defended the creatures, those trigger-happy, testosterone, brain-dead, military heavies would rather shoot it out in battle, then develop any peaceful interaction. That was humankind; a race of violence.

Sonia's side would be the losers, especially with the knowledge of them Ziva had in her head. And her employers would get that information, even without her consent. Ziva felt it best to side with the potential victors to save her own skin.

But...what if humans were not the champions? What if in the end they become a casualty, as Darla did?

Ziva sighed, overcome by her conundrum.

If her superiors had seen what she had already witnessed, they would quake in their collective boots. The things these creatures could do, without even trying. They could simply blow the human race into non-existence if they chose.

Are the 'Aopato' really peace seeking? If they are so intelligent why did they fall for Darla's ruse? They had chosen the woman from more than fifty others. Why? Was it to bring about a confrontation? What did they really want?

Then again, why did the agency get the brainless idea I would make a good operative, at this time of her life?

Had they all become addled-brained at once? Or had someone...helped them...guided them, to make decisions they would not otherwise have made?

Ziva sat in a far corner of the lunchroom stewing, trying to reason it all out, to fit the puzzle pieces together. Oblivious to what went on around her, it was as if she failed to realize she was no longer confined to her sleep chamber.

When Morgan dropped with a plunk to the seat opposite Ziva, Ziva started violently. The Jewish woman looked up, shocked. She had thought she was alone, but apparently while she had been brooding, the space about her had gained more than one occupant.

"You missing your friend Darla?" Morgan asked sympathetically.

Immediately, Ziva realized the danger in admitting any personally relationship with that unfortunate individual. She made a quick mental choice.

Her mouth made a rude noise. "She was never a real friend; more like a pest than anything. Because we arrived together, she clung to me like a leach."

"Well, there sure is a thunder cloud hanging over your head. What's got you so fired up, if you didn't lose your best friend?"

Ziva made a faced. "You wouldn't understand if I told you."

"Don't be too sure. I was a cop for a long time. I can pick up things. It's hard not to miss when a person's holding something over another's head. Sometimes a gal gets caught in a position between those who hold sway over her and what she really prefer to do."

Ziva frowned. *What does she think she knows?*

"I don't know what you've been asked to do," Morgan offered. "Nor do I want your confidence if you'd rather not. But, I'd like to give you a bit of advice that's always worked for me...if you'll take it."

Morgan did not wait for Ziva's permission, simply continued.

"Go with your gut, girl. It works best every time; the perks never measure up. It's not worth your life."

Morgan rose to her feet. "Oh, and you might consider this: if you're thinking of continuing whatever Darla was up to, Sonia revealed something when she dealt with her..."

Ziva gazed intently at the other woman, suddenly interested.

"She told Darla she knew what she was planning," Morgan warned. "Anyway... if you ever want someone to talk to, I've got a good listening ear."

Morgan then walked away to join Angel at the far side of the room.

I'd be a fool to tell you what I'm about, Ziva thought silently. *You'd spill to that fellow Lance you're so cosy with.*

Without speaking to anyone else Ziva left the lunchroom, making her way to Technical Centre to join Joel, knowing she had already stayed away far too long.

CHAPTER 33

Ziva was watching ten screens at once. On most, all was quiet, needing little or no concentration. She was only vaguely conscious of Joel at her side.

She wasn't sure when she became aware something was wrong. The tremors began with his hands, then travelled up his arms until the whole counter in front of them shook.

Ziva turned alarmed.

His body was shaking like it had a mind of its own, first moving only slightly, then increasing in violence as the vibrations progressed down his thighs to his knees. It was as if he was being zapped by electricity.

Is he playing a joke? If so, this isn't funny!

Ziva gave his chair a shove.

"Stop that! It's annoying!"

The chair moved just enough to turn him facing her. His gaze was fixed, blank, the vertical slit so narrow you could barely see it.

"What the devil's wrong with you?"

When he failed to answer, staring right through her, it sent shivers to her spine.

Surely this isn't how they go Nova? Did I do something to trigger this?

****

Djura and Karine were in the orchard picking cherries. She had been surprised when he first asked, that he would even stoop to harvest the ripe berries. Until now, he had been mostly protection oriented.

Now, she understood. This was his favourite fruit, and more went into his big tummy than reached the container. But his reasoning was, if he gathered them maybe she would want to bake him a cherry cobbler from scratch. She had found his behaviour most delightful.

Karine chuckled. "If you continue to eat them now," she scolded. "This will take us all day."

An embarrassed grin played at the corners of his mouth. "They're good fresh."

"Well, you won't get your cherry cobbler this way."

At first his reaction seemed exaggerated; he went tense, his face turning intense. And as quickly, Karine realized it had not been what she said; he had sensed something wrong in Sanctuary.

"Leave the berries," he ordered abruptly, and reached for her hand.

Karine frowned, set the basket on the ground obediently. She was becoming used to sudden emergency jumps. After all he was head of security.

"It's your off time Djura, " she dared to remind him. "Let someone else handle it."

"Not this time! It involves Technical Centre."

****

Joel was jerking uncontrollably. Ziva did not dare touch him. She had heard all the warnings. The women had told her it was dangerous to touch them if something was wrong.

The giant security chief and Karine materialized beside her, and despite her fear of the huge warrior guardian, Ziva was relieved to see him.

Immediate assessment of the situation brought acute alarm to his features. Karine moved back out of the way, her face a mirror of the security chief's concern.

"How long has he been seizing?" Djura demanded curtly.

"Several minutes."

Djura's eyes narrow with thought. "Why did you not call out for someone?"

"I first thought he was funning. And...whom should I have called?"

His look spoke exasperation. "Did you touch him?"

"No!" Annoyed, she fired back, "I know that much!"

Puzzled, Djura watched the convulsing Joel. He seemed wary as well to approach.

"What about calling Sky?" Karine suggested from behind.

Djura shook his head. "He and Sonia are on sleep break together. They rarely get such a chance, and I will not disturb them unless absolutely necessary." In a puzzled tone, he added, "I am not certain what is causing this. It's not..." He shook his head again, perplexed. "If I touch him, and this spreads to me, call out for Sky. Otherwise do nothing."

"Is it some sort of sickness?" Ziva demanded.

"Do not concern yourself..."

"I think you'd best tell me. If this is something contagious, I work with him you know."

Djura grunted, disgusted. "If it is what I think it is, this will not effect a female... especially not a human."

Ziva frowned, concern coming at last to the surface. "I'd like to know...so maybe next time I can do something for him."

"Next time," Djura retorted brusquely. "Call out for someone!"

"I don't know who to call!"

"Sky! He's the physician!" He glared at her, then suddenly his face softened. "I forget; you were not with the others at the music recital the other day. You are always here with Joel on watch. Forgive my impatience. I should not have expected you to know."

Is this guy for real? He's supposed to be so deadly, and here he is apologizing!

Djura turned again to Joel, and frowned. "If you must know...Joel is our last 'Pure' male...he is dying."

Both Ziva and Karine caught their breath in shock.

"Can nothing be done?" Karine cried out in sympathy.

"He needs a pair...a mate..."

"What?" Ziva yelled without thinking. Caught off guard, this was the last thing she had expected. Her anger exploded at the realization of what this implied. Swallowing hard, she tried to calm herself.

"You're telling me, you guys die if you are… without a mate?"

He stared at her, obviously debating whether to answer. "A 'Pure' dies, yes, " he agreed candidly. "Especially when he has no other 'Pure' male to balance him, as with Joel."

Ziva felt shivers crawl her spine.

"There are lots of men here!" she protested angrily.

"All the rest of us are half human."

Ziva pondered that a few seconds. "Well, why doesn't he take one of your females? Won't they have him?"

Djura grunted, annoyed. "Joel is over sixty in human. Our two youngest are but children. The rest are either paired, or about to be. Besides, they are all immediate relatives."

"Well…obviously you can mate with humans! He should take a human wife!"

Djura surveyed her, his face a passive mask. "Are you volunteering?"

Taken aback, Ziva quickly shot back. "No!"

Djura sighed. "Now I understand…"

Ziva's blood began to boil. *What is this? He's acting like Joel's condition is my fault!*

But rather than argue further, before Ziva could confront the male, the giant guardian stepped to Joel, lifted him to his shoulder, and abruptly vanished with him.

Ziva and Karine were left behind, each holding their breath, one out of fury; the other in concern.

****

Karine was stunned by Djura's revelation. He had avoided a direct answer when Ziva had asked if all guardian males died when not mated, which meant it was quite possibly the end result.

Djura will die without a pair? We have established a pair connection! Does that mean he is safe?

Ziva also seemed preoccupied, no longer concerned with the monitors in her charge.

Sonia came visible beside the women.

"My Lady, I thought you were resting," Karine exclaimed in surprise. "And you are here without guardian protection."

"I have you to guard me..."

Karine understood. Sonia trusted her, a human, with her safety. That could also be construed that Ziva was considered a threat.

"Where is Chi?"

Sonia grinned mischievously. "I think he too needs a rest period. He has not yet noticed only May Lin is in my quarters. I left her sleeping, unaware also that I've left."

Karine raised an eyebrow in reproach.

Sonia chuckled. "I sometimes like to tease my overprotective guardians; they expect it; keeps them on their toes. Off times, when they grow weary, the guardian can grow bored...a little slow. If I slip away unexpectedly it wakes them up."

Karine scolded, "My Lady…"

Sonia laughed, delight at the reaction she was getting. "My bad; I agree."

"Maybe Chi is also affected by this?" Karine reasoned. "Djura took Joel…"

"I know, dear," Sonia interrupted. "He asked me what to do. I woke Sky, and sent him to Joel's chambers. As for it draining on the other guardians…that is quite possible."

Sonia turned to the monitors. Ziva was still preoccupied with her own thoughts.

"Ziva, you are not monitoring," Sonia rebuked quietly.

Looking up in surprise, Ziva seemed to realize for the first time that Sonia was present.

"Oh, I'm sorry." She turned her chair, and sat down to face the screens.

"I will help. Eric is in sleep break. Djura will wake him when he has the chance." Sonia pulled up another chair, and sat. Without turning to look at her, she ordered, "Karine, be comfortable."

Karine moved to the chair on the other side of Ziva.

"'Keeper'?" Sonia demanded. "Wake Angel please."

Karine was used to Sonia speaking orders to things unseen, other beings both mechanical and 'Aopato', but Ziva turned and frowned at the 'Leader Female'.

"You control the 'Keepers'?"

"Among other things," Sonia admitted frankly. She pointed to a larger screen. "This outside view is the most important for now."

Ziva turned to scrutinize it. "Joel usually watches that one."

"Was he watching it when this started?"

"I think so."

Sonia went suddenly quiet.

****

Eric materialized with angel at his side.

"My Lady," he objected in surprise. "I thought you were on sleep break."

"Seems I'm awake now. Besides, I was needed."

Eric and Angel dropped to seats on the other side of the leader.

After giving the screens a cursory glance, he left them in Angel's care, and turned to Sonia.

"Have they discovered Darla yet?" he asked quietly.

"Yes," Sonia acknowledged. "She is safe. They picked her up almost immediately. I made certain, before I became unstable. I placed her conveniently near them."

Ziva frowned. *Sonia was seeing to Darla's welfare, even while indisposed herself? Why? I thought Darla was their enemy.*

"They have her in a special facility," Sonia continued, sadness colouring her tone. "As I predicted, she is viewed more like an experimental lab animal by them…these scientists! They are like the Hitler man!"

"Sometimes, I find my human heritage most regrettable," Eric agreed.

"Guardian." Sonia's voice took on remorseful gentleness. "You have no idea how much I was loathe to do this."

"She wanted this?" he observed horrified. "She trusts her handlers to unlock her memories?"

"Her desire was to live no matter the end condition."

"You went by our justice requirements; mercy according to the choice of the guilty?'

"It usually works for us; why not with a human? Her preference was there in her mind."

He shook his head in discouragement, turning back to the monitors.

Are they saying Darla chose her own punishment?

When she thought about it that seemed very much what Darla would do. It was typical, obnoxious Darla.

****

Karine was observing Ziva, as the woman pretended to watch the monitors like the rest did. The woman was listening with all ears.

Is Sonia deliberately giving her this information? Will Ziva realize Sonia does not wish to hurt anyone?

"Eric?" Sonia pointed to the large screen. "How long has their weapon been completed?"

288

Ziva became alert, searching her own screens.

Eric peered closer. "That must have happened over night!"

Sonia nodded, her manner now contemplative. A moment later, she came to a conclusion.

"I believe...Joel's episode might have been triggered by a back wash from the gun. Has he ever shown signs previously?"

"I know he'd been concern about Ziva, sent her away early one day. I was puzzled by his action, but I never realized..."

"He said nothing about feeling unwell?"

"If he did, it would be to Sky, not me."

Sonia nodded, as if the words confirmed a suspicion.

"My Lady," Eric observed with trepidation. "If the thing is now operational..."

"It is still faulty. They work to correct it."

"We need to increase the shielding; and security, " Eric exclaimed in alarm.

"I have Djura already on it. I also placed a stronger protection around Technical centre."

Agreeing, he peered intently at the screen. Both he and Sonia seemed no longer aware Ziva was listening.

That troubled Karine.

Sonia tapped the bottom of the large monitor. "Notice the human on the far right?"

"Oh, no!" Eric moaned. "As if we don't have enough trouble with the 'Opposites'."

"He's new?"

"Definitely."

"Increase coverage. Split the large screen into two, and keep watch on the human when he leaves."

"He is watching them?"

"Yes. He is still unaware we are here. He can not see Sanctuary."

"Good…for our safety…"

"Safe for the present."

For the first time since she had arrived, Ziva's face mirrored hope. Karine did not understand quite why that should give her a feeling of foreboding. But, Darla and this woman had often been seen together.

Sonia and Eric were intent on the two large screens. While Angel was over on the opposite side carefully monitoring the rest. None saw the look on Ziva's face.

Taking the chance Sonia might be monitoring her thoughts; Karine attempted something with her she only did easily with Djura.

My Lady! Karine warned in thought. *Look at Ziva!*

Sonia turned abruptly, made eye contact with the Jewish woman between them, seemed to study her intently for mere seconds, then spoke.

"Ziva, I don't believe we have need of you further. You may have a free time until Joel recovers. Please, go to your chambers and rest."

For a moment annoyance fluttered through her eyes, then Ziva seemed to realize there was no point arguing. She frowned, looked at Karine as if she suspected she had betrayed her somehow, sent her an ugly look, and rose to her feet.

"Karine?" Sonia seemed apologetic. "Perhaps it would be best if you also would seek your quarters. Djura will be occupied for some time."

Karine realized Sonia was making an attempt to ease the tension between the Jewish woman and herself. It worked. A look of triumphant approval fled across Ziva's face.

The two women vacated the room together.

****

Once out of earshot down the hallway, Ziva turn venomously to Karine.

"You are sure thick with the Queen, aren't you Irish?" she hissed. "Don't think I didn't realize you gave her some sort of signal. I'm not Darla, you know! And I'm not stupid either. Maybe I'm slow to catch on, but that doesn't mean I'll just fall moony-eyed, and give them what they want like the rest of you, either.

Karine made no reply.

Man! She's beginning to act just like an alien! Giving me the silent treatment, are you?

Ziva turned and stalked away, her body taunt she was so livid.

How dare they! I'll not be any man's trophy human! If I want a man, I'll pick my own! No one's playing matchmaker with me as the bait!

Her very step was wrathful, her mind malevolent, and her spirit one of total rebellion.

I don't care if Joel is dying! He is the enemy!

CHAPTER 34

"Oh, where am I going to find a formal gown in this place?" mourned Chantel to Morgan and Carmen as they sat at a lunch table. She had just found out the banquet was formal. "I haven't worn a dress for years. I've been in a wheelchair most of my adult life. Nobody takes a cripple to a wedding, you know."

"I'm in the same boat," Morgan agreed. "I've been in uniform most of my life. Never thought there'd be a need for a fancy ball gown when I applied here."

"Who's getting married?" asked Ziva from across at another table. "And do we all have to go?"

"Well, we've all got partners already, girl," Jenna challenged. "If no one's asked you, you'd better do the asking. Try your work partner."

Ziva dropped her eyes in embarrassment.

Jessica approached Chantel's table; stood wiping her hands on her apron. She laughed. "You guys don't realize, do you?"

"Realize what?" Chantel and Morgan asked in unison.

"That you can use your 'Keeper' to design your own gown. And Ziva; yes, it is required that everyone attend. Joel would be your escort. And the answer to the third question: the pairing ceremony is a double. My mom and Jade are both taking a new partner. The affair is the reason we returned to Earth, at great risk to all, I might add. We wanted to make it special for them. This is where they met, and we were all born here." Her voice took on a scolding timbre. "If anyone misses this, I will order your 'Keepers' to give you nothing but bread and water."

"Aww, Jessica, you couldn't be that mean," Chantel chided.

"Don't test me then," Jessica returned in all seriousness. "The event is in three hours. Get out of here, and start dressing."

"What about the kitchen work?" Chantel wondered.

"We are done here," Jessica declared. "Oh yes, Ziva, Joel says, he forgot to ask you. He wants to know, can he come pick you up fifteen minutes before the banquet?"

Ziva's head came up in shock. "He still wants me?"

"Why wouldn't he? And," Jessica warned. "If you don't agree, you'll have me to deal with. Great Uncle Joel is special today. He's the last 'Pure' male. He has a place of honour, and it's a great privilege to be his companion. Don't let him down. So, what is your answer?"

"I'll do my best to be ready," Ziva agreed meekly.

"Good. Now the rest of you, shoo. Get out of here! I want to get ready myself."

"Oh, I've just got to tell the rest of the girls first," Morgan decided. "About the 'Keepers', I mean...don't know that I'll be any good at designing..."

"Ask the 'Keeper' what looks best on you," Jessica suggested. "Now git! When I leave here, I want this room empty. No more loitering!"

The women fled en masse.

Jessica chuckled. "Never knew humans could move that fast." She did a little private dance. "Ohh! This is going to be such fun!"

At that, she disappeared...and the kitchens were truly empty.

****

"May Lin will please to come to the hallway outside," her 'Keeper' ordered in Mandarin.

May Lin obediently shuffled to the corridor outside her suite. She was surprised to find Chi waiting there.

"Honourable sir?"

"We go to ceremony in short time," he declared. "I wish you to know, it will not dishonour me if you sit with me in public. I wish you to eat with me, not attend me," he decided. "Here, this is the custom. I will be embarrassed should you stand beside me like a servant, for no one else is required to do so. Do you understand me? You are not my servant! We are equal."

May Lin politely dropped her head in acceptance.

"I wish you to act as the other women during this public ceremony. Watch how they treat their escorts."

"Yes, honourable sir."

His voice took on a note of tenderness. "Remember...you are to be...my future pair."

295

May Lin raised her eyes, blushed like a young school girl, but smiled ever so slightly.

"And now that you have finally looked at me, I desire one more thing…"

May Lin dared a hesitant query. "Yes?"

"I wish for you to wear the Cheongsam, one with the bright colours of our people …with your hair done up…and a flower in it."

The heat in her flesh grew uncomfortable, and she shyly dropped her eyes.

"I will come for you fifteen minutes before the event is to begin."

When he had left, May Lin almost shouted aloud for joy. *He had said they were equal!*

****

"Oh, Kara," Chrystal bemoaned, as she stood before a mirror in a gown she was designing for herself. "I am so slow at this. My mouth won't describe what I want. It would be so much quicker, if I could do it by thought as you do."

"Some day you will have such abilities too…"

Chrystal spun. "What do you mean? I'm not 'Aopato'."

"If Unca Shawn has his way, and pairs to you, they would 'blood heal' you. Then you would gain powers like ours."

"What's 'blood healed'?"

"Great-gran makes you half 'Pure'…like the males. She increased my blood balance when I changed. I was only an eighth 'Aopato'; now I am half. She did it with my father also. He was fully human, and he wanted so badly to remain with my mother and I, he willingly underwent the change. Great-gran wouldn't let it hurt him, he said."

"It hurts?"

"As you change, it would hurt each one of us…just a little bit. But I would gladly endure the discomfort to make you one of us."

"It has to be done?"

"Great-gran wouldn't allow a pairing unless the human is willing for this to be done. If not, Shawn would watch you die of old age…so would your children…"

"But sometimes that happens even in human lives.'

"You fail to understand…we live very much longer." Kara frowned. "Maybe I shouldn't tell you this, but…if Shawn pairs to you and you remain human, he will also die much younger…soon after you do. He won't be able to live without you."

Chrystal stared at her puzzled. "Why?"

"The pair bond is so strong in us, that even a 'pair connection' already means that 'Aopato' male will perish if the female is killed."

"Have any of the males developed such a 'pair connection'?"

"Only one has it with a human at present. My dad never knew this when he chose to become like us, but if he had not, my mom and I would both have died when he did. Our species also would have ended, if father had not been changed."

"Would that happen now, if the human that the male is 'pair connected' to refuses to go through with a change?"

Kara nodded soberly.

Chrystal stared at the young girl in disbelief.

"Then why are all the guardians courting human females?"

"Because they will also die early without mates."

"The survival of your species rests with us, either way?" Chrystal observed appalled.

"Yes." Kara turned away, a certain attitude of defeat in her posture. She pretended interest in her own gown. After a moment of introspection, she reassured. "Great-gran would never make any of you 'blood heal'. Your love must be real, willingly sacrificial, and without fear, or she will not permit it. We would all rather die then hurt you...we just hope you each have the courage...the regard for us...to step willingly into the unknown with us."

Chrystal found the revelation more than she could comprehend.

"But, you said, one of the guardians is already 'pair connected'?" Chrystal fearfully objected. "It is already in motion..."

Kara smoothed the folds of her gown. "It happened by accident...to the one we least expected to bond."

"Which one?" whispered Chrystal.

Kara lifted her eyes and smiled gently. "She already loves enough...do not fear."

****

"Sonia," Karine queried tentatively in thought, as she dressed in her room.

"Yes, dear," Sonia's voice answered inside her head.

"You heard me!"

"Of course, dear. I am always available to you anytime you wish. What is your desire?"

"Aw…may I wear my hair up for the banquet?"

Sonia chuckled. "Oh, yes! It will look lovely the way you have planned it."

The 'Leader Female' had even visualized how Karine wanted to wear it. *It is so wonderful to just call out to her in thought.*

"Ask your 'Keeper' to do it for you, dear," Sonia suggested. "I think Djura will like it. I will prevent him from seeing it until the right moment. It shall be our little secret."

Karine laughed in delight.

****

Djura gazed wonderingly at her, saw the form fitting shape beneath the sheer overdress of teal chiffon. Then his eyes went to her hair beneath the transparent veil. At sight of the braided coils circling her crown, the material attached to the back and draping only slightly over it, barely hiding the entwined tresses, his eyes went wide in surprise, as if at that moment, Sonia had allowed him full vision.

Karine held her breath. *Will he be angry?*

But he said nothing, did nothing. His face mirrored awe. That meant he approved!

Djura reached for her hand.

****

From her place across from Marcel, Carmen watched them file in. The women both 'Aopato' and human were breathtakingly arrayed. Each entered on the arm of a tuxedoed male, every dress perfectly suited to the wearer, skirts sweeping the marble floor as they walked. It was like a fashion show; as if flowers from the magnificent scenery on the walls had come alive, transforming into these grand beauties.

It brought the world to a stand still.

****

When all were present, and every male did likewise, Djura proudly seated Karine. As he took his own seat, he could not help but note her sever tension. He frowned.

"Do we have to sit in this spot?" she whispered apprehensively.

Their position was at the edge of the smaller, straight table by the entrance door: his guardian position. Her back was to the room.

"I don't much like crowds, especially at my back," she explained nervously. "Sorry, I guess, I'd rather be seated against the wall."

Djura probed her feelings deeper. *Why she's litterly terrified!*

He stepped into her memories to see why.

"I never realized before," he observed with trepidation. "You are very claustrophobic, female."

"I'll be okay…"

"Give me your hand, female," he ordered. "You will not suffer on my watch!"

****

Karine could not stop her trembling as she offered her hand to the guardian. The human women had been in Sanctuary now for three months, and though they had all been together with the 'Aopato' women, they had never been collectively in one room with all the giant warriors. Also, when with the females they had been strewn out in a row beside each other, none behind Karine. Then, she could see everyone else; now, all females were in the centre, surrounded by males.

She had always been careful not to let a man place her in a position where she could not slip away. It was a matter of survival. Only one time had she been cornered; that had nearly cost her life.

Karine had been his property; his income had been threatened, but he dare not disfigure her. He had approached from behind, slipped a plastic bag over her head, drawn it tight. He kept her in that position, body taunt, head back, gasping for air, until she went limp and stopped struggling.

Karine wanted to scream for the fear in her memory, then Djura was in her mind with her. He was comfort, the one to turn to, her protector, the conqueror. She watched him battle her adversary. And the agony, the fright disappeared.

Warmth caressed up her arms; a feeling of relaxed contentment flooded her person. Karine sighed.

It no longer mattered that others were behind her. She was safe. Djura watched her back.

"Better?" he asked quietly.

She nodded. He released her hand.

"You just healed me," she marvelled. "Again."

He grinned, pleased.

He looks so gentle when he smiles, Karine thought dreamily.

CHAPTER 35

Silence abruptly filled the room, as if someone had flipped a switch to turn off the sound. The time had come. Everyone knew it without been told.

Six seats remained vacant in the centre of the horseshoe shaped larger table: three on the female side; three directly opposite across on the male side against the wall. The three remaining 'Aopato' women sat, seemingly abandoned by family, looking lost: Nadia on the left, Kara and Jessica to the right of the vacant seats.

As if by a signal, they rose now, pivoting to face the empty inner centre. When the guardians stood as well, so did the human companions, each turning to face in.

Mere seconds passed. Then Sky Hawk with Sonia on his arm slowly became solid at the immediate heart of the empty circle. The room burst with a rare perfume: the essence of a rain-washed meadow with the ozone awareness of impending lightning. It seemed to emanate from the 'Leader Pair' together, as if they were one individual. The sense was of peace, of this couple's ultimate protection, and the watchers felt blessed by their presence.

Their scents change when they are together, Karine mused silently.

Djura answered her unspoken observation. *The fragrance is their scent. It only happens when they unify. Take note later, as the new ones are paired.*

Sonia wore a shimmering sliver, floor length gown; Sky was in white buckskin, Navajo apparel.

He pivoted full circle slowly, one step at a time, turning the pair as if presenting his partner proudly to the assembly. Until once more they faced the empty space.

He left Sonia beside the centre-most seat standing facing in, moved to her right, walked to circle the end of the long table, crossed along the sunset wall behind, stopped and stood, at that centre seat directly opposite his pair.

Those gathered waited with bated breath for the next revelation.

To Sonia's right, at the space between the two tables, Ryan his arm linked with Jade's gradually became solidly present.

The olive skinned guardian was dressed in a white tux, his darkly tanned Italian features more prominent because of what he wore. He was slight of build, handsome even at a distance.

Jade's green eyes shown, enhanced by the jade-green form-fitting gown. It dropped to her knees where a ruffle of a darker shade flared out in pleats. Her feet were shod in flat sandals of silver.

Ryan moved with his partner in a measured beat until they stood facing Sonia.

The silence of anticipation was palpable.

Sonia raised her hands to either side waist high. Jade crossed over to take her mother's right hand; Ryan moved to Sonia's left. As their hands touched simultaneously, a rainbow of light appeared in the 'Leader Female' travelling from her both ways, up the arms of the waiting pair, through their bodies, rising upward until it formed an umbrella effect over the heads of the trio as they came together as one.

An awed collective sigh escaped the human women. The pairing couple simply waited.

The two on either side moved slightly forward joining hands with each other forming a circle, their backs as before to the shorter entry table.

As Sonia released their hands, the rainbow vanished, and the room filled with the intense aroma of exotic incense.

Sonia laughed with delighted pleasure.

The guardians suddenly moved as one, raising their right arms horizontal, palms down, toward the new pair in the centre as a salute.

A hesitant, shy smile fled across the faces of the two; they linked arms and Ryan moved Jade the few paces to the empty place beside her daughter Nadia; then following the path Sky had taken, took his place to the right of the Leader's pair partner.

Once more the audience went into waiting. Seconds passed.

Ihor with Rhea on his arm appeared at the joining of the tables to Sonia's left. The guardian everyone dubbed the 'Jolly Giant' wore a tux of sky blue; his blond crew-cut had been allowed to grow to short-wave's length, and the sturdy individual seemed to have sobered at the prospect of pairing to the copper-haired beauty, Sonia's second daughter.

Rhea's auburn curls were gathered like a crown atop her head, and she wore a short knee-length dress of pale yellow edged in rust, the skirt full with a hemline of varying length.

Having witnessed the first pairing ceremony the humans fully expected a repeat performance, but never let it be said Rhea was a carbon copy of her sister. Today, the opposite was evident in every way.

No one notice or gave a thought to Nadia as she unobtrusively shut her eyes to begin the solo: the melody of serenading guitars entered on discreet wings over the hushed audience. The sound was so peaceful and tender it appeared both a part of the pairing couple as they walked, and appropriately amorous. No one felt inclined to search for the source of the sensual tones, to turn away their gaze from the most important subjects to find the musician. Those listening simply accepted.

When the couple stood before Sonia, she once more extended hands to her sides, but unlike with the former duo, these two did not cross over. Each remained in place, turning to face forward before linking hands with the matriarch.

This time the static light was first green, turning only to rainbow as it ascended to an umbrella of light over the heads of the three.

Next, rather than form the circle with their hands, Sonia simply let go. The couple reached across in front of Sonia to link together.

A static spark of green zapped between the two, and the room exploded with the scent of cherry blossoms.

Rhea gave a quick, almost inaudible embarrassed giggle.

Sonia smiled indulgently. The guardians beamed as they once more raised their hands in salute.

And the pairing ceremonies were over.

****

Yet the 'Aopato' all remained standing facing the inner circle, even after Rhea and Ihor gained their places.

What are they waiting for now? wondered Ziva.

Sonia stood very still, her eyes downcast. Her lids lowered.

In the hushed space all "Aopato' moved silently as one; male and female alike raised their hands horizontal palms down toward their leader, also closing their eyes.

In unity, including Sonia, each turned their palm upward, then raised the arms vertically toward the ceiling, and once more turned palms in toward the circle. It appeared as if they were reaching for something as the palms twisted up again.

All this was done in utmost quiet, and as each could not see, they must have been doing it by sensing each other's movements. The witnesses were spellbound waiting for the next action, in wonderment at what it all meant.

Suddenly each figure began glowing, their essence so brilliant one must squint to screen out the glare. For many minutes they remained thus, then abruptly all vanished.

Karine and May Lin released a simultaneous gasp of comprehension. These two were in the inner know of the "Leader Pair', more privy to the ways of the species.

What are they doing? Where did they go?

Ziva waited with the other women for the two to explain.

It was May Lin in her broken English who finally dared speak aloud.

"They worship," she explained in a hushed tone. "They worship their Almighty Creator!"

No way! These powerful creatures believed in a supreme being!

Cold shivers ascended her spine.

Only a second after the words were spoken, each of the human women closed their eyes, and in perfect imitation of their hosts, proceeded to do as the 'Aopato' had done.

Just because they do it, Ziva complained to herself. *Don't see why we have to.*

Stubbornly, Ziva stood there, rebellious to the very idea. She would not take part. Nor did she. No one could see her; all eyes were closed.

For five minutes the humans stood so, then the room was abruptly plunged into darkness.

Ziva held her breath with wonder, half fearful, yet plagued by anticipation.

Once more, gradually, the 'Aopato' became visible, and even though their eyes had been closed, the human women were in sync. When their hosts dropped their hands and opened their eyes they did likewise. It was as if during the worship human and 'Aopato' had become one.

Everyone sat as if an unspoken order had been given.

Ziva shivered visibly. Then scrambled to seat herself, feeling uncertain, out of place...excluded.

Why didn't I join them? Is my pride so enormous?

Shamed, Ziva fervently wished she had followed the example of the others. No one appeared to have noticed her misdemeanour. The food began to appear, was passed around, and the room filled with the buzz of conversation.

****

All were enjoying the meal immensely. Joel loved the feelings he felt coming off the females when they were so excited; especially young Kara was so exuberant. She was so happy and filled with energy as she stood behind Rhea and Sonia. She had moved over to them to tell a funny story to her great-gran, and all three were giggling with amusement.

Kara's always been my sister's pride and joy, her special treasure, Joel mused to himself.

He felt Sonia tense. Fear and shock entered his awareness as it flooded through his sister's consciousness. At once he shared with her the vision she saw, just a second of pictures cascading as they flashed rapidly through her mind.

So this is what her flash-forwards are like. Most unpleasant! No wonder it makes her cringe. At least she handles them better than before.

He could not help but react to the horrors he was seeing, then Sonia cut the connection for his ease. The sudden pain of separation always hurt, bringing with it the memory of past isolation. But he knew for the moment it was best, even if it left him gasping. It was less desirable then to see the sequence of future events, as they would enfold.

****

The room seemed suddenly charged with negative energy. Even Ziva was aware of it. What once was a place of laughter, unexpectedly turned to a room of terrified beings.

For an unexplained reason Ziva's eyes immediately tracked to Sonia.

She always seems the source of anything unexpected. Surely she is responsible for this new phenomenon.

Sonia sat frozen, a look of horrified concentration on her features.

What is happening now? They all look frightened by their own shadows.

Kara seemed the least effected. She dropped to one knee and tentatively touched the 'Leader Female's' hand in concern.

What occurred next sent rivers of hot dread through Ziva's system.

In God's name, what are these creatures?

As she watched in disbelief, when the two females touched, a static blue light passed between them. It travelled through them like hot lightning across the nearby females to either side.

Ziva looked to Karine for an explanation, but her face was as puzzle-shocked as everyone else.

Looking back again, Ziva saw the static energy jump to Sky, zap across the males sitting against the back wall to either side of him. The light turned white when it reached both outer edges, jumping to the smaller table from Lance to Djura on one side, Tyler to Chi on the other.

It's coming my way! Ziva realized in panic.

But never once did it touch a single human being.

Ziva wheeled around just in time to see both static light beams end at Joel. It stopped. He seemed to absorb them. And the room returned to normal, busy conversation, laughter, as if nothing had happened.

Ziva was still terrified.

"What just happened?" she demanded of Joel.

****

Joel's eyes filled with tears of gladness.

"I was part of it this time!" he exclaimed jubilantly. "I am no longer separate! It feels so good to be whole, a part of the one."

Next to him, Eric reach out and clasp his hand reassuringly, then returned to his conversation with Angel.

He read her, as Ziva thought in surprise *this isn't a bad thing?*

She frowned, and asked again in uncertainty, "What was that?"

Joel grinned. "Kara's comfort-beam…a balance correction. When we have a sudden overbalance of negative emotion in the species the two 'Leader Females' correct us while in junction. The serving female and her successor connect to instantaneously balance us. Kara discovered how to do this by accident the first time it happened."

"What caused the imbalance?"

"My sister received a vision of the future." Joel shook his head, marvelling. "It always seems to happen when we are all together in this room."

He sighed in sympathy for Sonia. "She always finds it difficult when she is warned of the future. Very hard on her. Usually means trouble is ahead."

"Who warns her?'

"The Almighty Creator."

Ziva frowned, disbelief mirrored in her eyes, but she let it go.

"You aren't afraid?"

Joel shrugged. "For a second, we were all terrified, hence the need for Kara's comfort beam."

"Were you safe the other times?"

"The Almighty Creator always has a plan worked out for us. My sister is warned in order to prepare us. She will be shown the solution when the time is right. It always comes out okay in the end. And if it doesn't..."

"You place a lot of blind faith in Sonia."

"No. We all know the answer and the results ultimately rest with our Maker. The Almighty Creator is the one who prepares our way..."

"You believe such nonsense!" Ziva retorted disapprovingly. "Powerful creatures such as yourselves have a need to believe there is someone in charge of you?"

Joel simply grinned sympathetically. "If you don't," he returned gently. "Then you are the fool."

Ziva was taken aback.

Who is he to judge me? Joel heard her think.

It chastened him.

I once was where she is, he reminded himself.

"More than once the Almighty Creator has come through for us, brought us back from the brink of extinction," he revealed. "I have experienced...seen with my own eyes. I had to learn the hard way...in the most terrible of circumstances...all of my own making. I warn you female, do not play with destiny. Don't follow in my footsteps. It is never pleasant to learn things that way."

CHAPTER 36

They had mostly finished eating. The dishes still floated over the tables, half empty. Some of the males were still munching.

"I think," Ziva observed. "As long as there is food available a male of any species will eat until it's gone."

Angel beside her, chuckled. "I'm inclined to agree with you on that. These men must have hollow legs."

Eric grinned sheepishly. "I should quit," he decided, pushing his plate away. "If you are right and we do have bottomless pits, we are in a whole heap of trouble because these platters will simply keep filling until we stop."

Joel eased back in his chair, his substantial weight causing it to creak ominously.

Behind at the entry, a 'Keeper' appeared. Ziva watched it float into the room, and hover over Joel's head.

"I never noticed before, the 'Keepers' are visible in here," commented Ziva.

Joel glanced up. "Ahh, no. That's not good. That's one from Tech Centre."

They watched as the sphere glided across to where Sonia sat. The 'Leader Female' turned toward it.

All guardians had tensed, on alert.

"Why the intrusion "Keeper'?" she asked evenly.

"Does the Lady wish communication to be private?" the machine inquired.

"Speak for all to hear. It will alleviate uncertainty in those present."

"A sentry drone on perimeter has been rendered useless…was fixed…"

"And?" Sonia prompted.

"An 'Opposite' is now in Sanctuary."

"Only one?"

"Yes, Lady. It is headed here."

"I see it now. Return to your posting."

The 'Keeper' abruptly vanished.

For a moment Sonia sat considering. The rest waited instructions. She looked to Djura.

"My Lady?" he queried, ready and willing to do whatever requested.

"It carries a full compliment of weapons plus a miniature of the prototype to test on us."

Djura grimaced. "We've been expecting such a move. Too bad they picked this day."

"No matter. This is where we will challenge it."

He nodded compliance. "What of the humans? The weapon will not harm them, but still, they are susceptible to mind control."

Sonia sighed, regretful. "I would see them somewhere else, but they are safer with us."

Djura stood. "Your orders then, my Lady?"

"One moment. Guardians who are unaware, this weapon is meant to drain our energy…only ours!"

A groan from the males was the only reaction.

"How do we fight it?" Lance questioned.

"I do not know...yet. Until they use it on us, we do not know its full effect. See that this adversary does not get to use it. We need the weapon for examination."

Heads nodded consent. The warriors rose as one.

Sonia turned to Djura. "Centre circle the humans, next our females; males outer, the same as in battle."

"And you, my Lady?"

"I will remain to the side. It will expect me to be centre core; we will do the unanticipated."

Djura's eyes narrowed in disapproval. "That puts you in a vulnerable position."

"Should it use this new weapon on me, we will certainly see the effect on the entire species. All or nothing. It is doubtful the ray gun is of sufficient power to incapacitate all concerned."

She's acting as decoy? Ziva thought in surprise.

"As you will be imperceptible, it will not be aware of the rest of you," Sonia pointed out.

"Understood." Djura made no farther challenge.

"Sky, you will remain beside me. Djura forward to my right. Chi takes rear flank. All three non-visual. Rest of the warriors form the circle. Prepare!"

The tables, food, and all non-essentials disappeared from the room. The human women were herded to the direct centre of the chamber.

Five remaining 'Aopato' females interspaced themselves around them, and the leftover guardians placed themselves beyond that. Suddenly, it was like all were in this light bubble. They could see out, but around the edges all was distorted and fuzzy.

Sonia seated herself on a chair to the side. One would assume, one young female all alone in an empty room. Her eyes turned from amethyst to a light shade of blue.

And Ziva wondered why.

****

Inside the inner circle, Ziva felt sudden dread. She began to tremble uncontrollably. She had never even been on a battlefield, let alone one such as this, an Alien war zone.

She had watched on the monitor screens, as this vicious enemy punished its own with death for insubordination. They were nearly as big as guardians, but put next to the empathy of the 'Aopato', these creatures were far more aggressive, brutal, and merciless.

They terrified Ziva like no other enemy.

Why do they insist we humans remain in the room? I already know how vicious these monsters can be.

Jade stepped back from the second circle into the humans. She slipped her arm about Ziva in comfort.

"Do not be so fearful Ziva. My mother will vanquish easily; you will see."

Everyone thinks Sonia invincible, that she can do anything. What if they kill her?

"You can be a help or a hindrance. The 'Opposite' will sense your fear. They are very adept at detecting negative emotions," Jade cautioned. "Please calm before it shows up or it will find you."

Ziva tried to swallow her panic, but instead the memory of what Sonia had done to Darla surfaced harshly only adding to her alarm.

I am at the mercy of both species; caught in the middle, she reasoned irrationally. *No matter which one gets me, I'll be killed.*

Reassurance, soothing warmth spread from Jade up Ziva's shoulders to her mind. Her turmoil immediately dissipated.

It's Jade wedding day! Ziva suddenly realized. *What a horrible way for it to end.*

"Better now?" Jade asked gently.

Ziva nodded. Jade stepped back to her place, and incomprehensibly Ziva felt lonely and lost without her.

****

The air filled with a nauseating stench. A lizard-like being stood framed in the doorway. The belt criss-crossing its chest and also the one at his waist were filled with obvious weaponry. It appeared to be smaller than normal, very young.

It hissed angrily when it caught sight of Sonia.

"Welcome to our humble abode," the 'Leader Female' said pleasantly. "Your commander sends you alone, on a suicide mission."

It ignored the last comment, firing back a challenge of its own. "Ha! Female! They leave you to bait me. I'll just take you as hostage; trade you for the 'Leader Female'. It is known she will always sacrifice herself for her subjects."

It stepped into the room, nearer, gazing around apprehensively, noticed the paintings still gracing the walls. "Typical! A memory collage. Don't like the sunset," it hissed. "Too harsh!"

Sonia said nothing, only sat calmly, her hands in her lap.

The creature wheeled, towering over her. She did not cringe.

"Who are you, female?"

"I am Sonia."

"Where is your 'Leader Female'...Sonia? I have something for her...a gift, a delightful promise." It waved the ray pistol it carried at her.

"What name do you go by, 'Opposite'? You know mine, only fair I should have yours."

"I am Yt," he hissed in disapproval.

"That is 'Opposite' for Ty..." Sonia observed. "Ahh...I see your future. Someday you will no longer be 'Opposite'; you will return to our side."

He growled. "Never! I was born 'Opposite'. We can not return to what we never were."

"It does not mean change can not happen.

Yt was silent, thinking it over, observing her with narrowed yellow/black slit eyes. "I can never be your kind," he repeated almost wistfully.

"That is what you have been told?"

"I will kill you all!" Yt hissed, ignoring her.

"How old are you in human?"

Yt spat. "Human! Human! Why would I gage my age in human? I am six plus half in our years!"

"That makes you thirteen in human. I have a great-granddaughter only two human years younger."

"Why should I care? I will take pleasure in torturing her."

"You will never enjoy barbarism again, Ty."

"Do not call me that! And you will not stop my nature."

Sonia smiled knowingly. "You will stop yourself."

"Where is your 'Leader Female'!" Yt shouted.

Sonia's eyes turned from blue to purple. "This conversation has been very enlightening, Ty, but it is time for you to depart. Remember me when we meet again."

The 'Opposite' boy vanished. And the ray gun from his atrophied paw clattered to the stone floor.

****

When the room returned to normal, Kara turned to her great-gran.

"He was my age! Only my age! And they send him on a mission of suicide."

Sonia half smiled, as if she knew a special secret.

Ziva turned to Jade. "What did she do with it?"

That female's eyes were sparkling with tears. "She saved this one! Sent him away to learn a more peaceful way."

"Is that possible?"

"If mother says it is his future, it will be so."

Again with their confident yet misguided faith in Sonia! She can't always be right!

Ziva would never understand them.

CHAPTER 37

No one wanted the day to end now that the danger was averted. None wanted to head for bed just yet, so they all stood around in the banquet hall conversing in clusters.

"Sky..." Sonia reached out for her pair's hand, seeking his attention, but his mind was on the subject he was discussing with Joel, and he did not notice.

As if the wind had just been knocked out of him, Djura abruptly dropped with a gasp to one knee. Shock mirrored in his eyes.

Karine turned frowning, searching for the reason of his discomfort, aware immediately it must connect to Sonia.

"Sky!" Djura gasped hoarsely, pointing.

The Navajo wheeled just in time to catch the 'Leader Female' as she crumpled like a rag doll. "Whoops!"

Sky smiled, shifted his pair to his arms, and tenderly kissed her on the forehead. It appeared as if she had simply fallen asleep instantly.

The 'Leader Couple' vanished.

Djura exhaled as if a weight had been lifted from his shoulders, then went into instant command mode. The other guardians had come immediately alert, tensely awaiting a command or some action.

There is something wrong, Karine surmised. *This isn't usual, is it?*

"Chi take post outside 'Leader Quarters'. Take May Lin with you," Djura commanded.

Those two gradually faded.

"Boys, get your females to quarters before they also go down. Don't forget their companions. The humans will stay the night within the bedchamber. You take post; sleep state, half alert."

Ram obediently took Kara and Chrystal by the hand. All three vanished. Chad followed suit with Nadia and Jenna, then they were gone as well.

"Wade stay on guard. Leave the companion inside with your pair."

Jessica, Wade and Chantel disappeared.

Djura turned to the two newly paired couples. "I know tonight you hoped to go 'pair intimate', but under the circumstances I doubt that will be safe.'

The two males nodded soberly, not questioning, as if it were a most reasonable and acceptable statement.

"Our treasures will go down shortly anyway," Ihor agreed compliantly.

"Sorry, dear," both Rhea and Jade as one murmured regretfully.

"It's not your fault," excused Ryan.

"Again, as with the others, companions in their rooms for safety," Djura cautioned. "And you stand guard outside."

On their wedding night? Karine thought that unreasonable. *Why is it necessary?*

Djura ignored her thought.

"Carmen, come." Ryan held out his hand for the human, taking Jade's hand as well.

"Morgan." She joined Rhea at Ihor's suggestion.

In unquestioning obedience, all four were gone that instant.

It was obvious to Karine there was something taking place here she did not understand. By now, she knew better than to question farther, or interfere. She stepped away to wait.

Djura turned last to Joel and Eric. "'Technical Centre' will have to remain on 'Keeper' watch tonight. Take your females to their quarters and each of you stand watch at the entrance to the human's chambers until I give you leave. Half alert."

They nodded. Joel linked with Ziva, Eric with angel. No explanation was given. By now, even these humans two realized there was some unknown danger about. All four vanished.

Karine alone now stood with the remaining men. There were six left; Marcel, Lance, Zane, Tyler, Shawn, and Djura.

"Go take rest, but be prepared," the security chief warned them. "I should get any warning first should they mount an attack. Stay half alert."

****

May Lin found herself in the 'Leader' sleep chamber. Chi had simply transferred her there, while he remained on the outside doorway.

Sky was gently placing Sonia on the bed. He remained standing over her, gazing fondly at his beloved.

"Honourable sir," May Lin ventured timidly. "Why did this happen? Is she ill again?"

"Not ill..." Sky sat down beside his partner, turned to meet the Oriental's eyes. "Tonight this happened because the day was too long and draining on her energy. Be seated, female." Sky motioned to a nearby seat. "I will try to explain from the beginning."

May Lin sat obediently.

"Last year we all almost lost our lives. The females have never been the same since. They have a deadly weakness. Because they are all interlinked, when Sonia becomes too exhausted she drops into instant sleep, and the others so intimately connected as they are go down shortly after. We have done our best to hide this malady, to guard against the joint reaction happening when in public, but this day they had three strikes against them."

"This can not be cured?" May Lin wondered.

Sky shook his head ruefully. "Our females are too few..." He hesitated unsure he should continue to confide. "When the females heal, even when doing it in junction, they are slowly killing each other. Even though it depletes the group energy, the female need, their compunction to mend others, must be satisfied or they go mad."

May Lin frowned. "You are saying...the must heal to stay sane?"

"Precisely. And because our 'Leader Female' is our core energy, and we all are mutually supported, if the females die, so will the males." His voice took on a soft regret. "Our species is dying. We returned to Earth for a two fold reason. First: we hoped by pairing two more couples it would strengthen the female side. And second: if each male took a pair it would make both sides equal. If not, then we are prepared to die where we began."

Tears filled May Lin's eyes.

"Ah, do not cry, human," Sky reassured. "The Almighty had a plan from the beginning. There is always an answer, and soon the solution will present itself. Sonia has already seen it. She holds it private, even from me, but that usually means the remedy will not be easy or pleasant."

He sat thinking. May Lin wiped at the tears that had wet her cheeks.

"But the future is not our concern tonight," Sky decided. "When the females go down like this the males are left without their female balance. They are somewhat handicapped because of it. It is best for all to rest. They will still awaken if needed, but it is best at a time such as this to rely on 'Keeper' protection. You humans will be an added alarm system. I wish you to remain in our sleep area, beside the bed. If Sonia begins to fade, even in the least, you must wake me."

"How am I to do that, sir?" May Lin asked appalled. "Is it safe to touch you? Could I hurt you?"

"To touch me would be deadly to you," Sky admitted. "Shout out; make a noise; anything. Only make sure that I wake up...and quickly."

"What can you do then, sir?"

"I can give her my life energy."

May Lin's eyes flooded again.

"You must be loud and aggressive, human!" Sky reproved. "It is not the time to be soft hearted. Your nature may be timid, but do not think of not doing this! Our lives depend on you tonight."

"Yes, honourable sir," May Lin whispered.

"The females must regenerate. Until then we are defenceless."

****

Karine and Djura stood alone in the empty banquet hall. He turned his scowling gaze her way.

"You expect the 'Opposites' will attack?" Karine asked tentatively.

"No," he admitted. "They do not realize we are vulnerable, though it is they who have put us in this position. They can not know of our present weakness. Sonia returned the boy to them in a semi-catatonic state. He could not tell them, and they assumed because he returned unharmed, the mission was a success. But…on the other hand, we never under estimate the enemy if we can help it."

"But…it never tried the weapon, did it?"

"As far as we are aware, this weakness is due to an over exertion by the species. The multiple events drained too much from Sonia. Until she heals back we are vulnerable."

"Wouldn't it be wiser to have the men on guard?"

"Yes," Djura admitted. "If we had the energy. But with all females down, they drain the male energy for heal-back. We must conserve our strength…until the species is again balanced."

He took her hand and immediately jumped them to her quarters.

Isn't this forbidden?

"I am sorry to intrude into your private chambers," Djura apologized. "But tonight I can not make the long way…" He sighed wearily. "Sonia drains from me the most. I am strongest male…"

That's why he went down first!

Karine suddenly noticed how he trembled.

Djura moved toward his room, stumbling into the bedside table like an unsteady drunken sailor. Karine reached out to offer assistance.

"No female!" he objected. "It will cause the ultimate connection. You will then suffer this with us. I don't want that. I will make it on my own."

He staggered to the door between, but as he reached it, his image began to fade. When he vanished from her sight, she called out worriedly, "Djura?"

"I am in…my quarters, female." His voice sounded unbelievably weak. "I am simply unable to maintain the headband any longer. Go to sleep…do not worry."

His voice faded at the last syllable like a man falling asleep in mid sentence, and with its absence Karine felt an emptiness she could not explain.

She began to shiver, not from cold, but with a premonition of dread. She once more felt lost…unprotected…severed.

Is this what it will be like without him?

I am his protection now! Think it's better I stay awake.

CHAPTER 38

Sonia sat assessing the situation. She realized what had happened was irreversible, not that she wished to erase the results. The humans would have found out eventually.

Sky sat across from her, waiting, the giant chessboard between them, but it was obvious to him the 'Leader Female' did not have her mind on the game.

Sonia admitted, the human women now all knew their reasons for coming back to Earth, the 'Aopato' condition. There had been no recourse but to tell some, how vulnerable they were the night of the banquet. And none of the women to whom they had given confidence had failed them. Each watched over them when the species was down.

The companions had watched with diligence, faithful and concerned over beings who were now powerless, yet never thought to harm, only to serve, as their charges healed back in the days that followed.

All had been considerate; none had used the advantage to slip away. None had even considered fleeing.

Even Ziva had taken her turn, maintaining Technical Centre on her own.

That one merely needs time! Sonia decided.

The pairing of her daughters had been successful. The males were attaching.

Now the waiting game begins: to see if these human women 'Pair connect'.

It was time to allow the new females to join the 'Aopato' community in earnest, to let them see what the species was about, what it had become.

But... Sonia reasoned. *We still need to be extremely cautious. Circumstances are such; they have the potential to go amiss very easily.*

****

Sonia looked up when she heard Eric enter the Common Room. She knew immediately something needed her attention.

"Yes, guardian?"

"My Lady, humans are in trouble," he disclosed. "There has been a nine point seven earthquake in Peru. Millions are trapped, injured or dead. The big cities have already moved to rescue their own but...up in the mountain villages they will never reach them on time."

"It is your suggestion, it is time for intercession?"

"You did say to watch for such an opportunity."

Sonia nodded. "Where was the epicentre?"

"A small remote village up in the Andes. They are completely cut off from any form of help."

"Can we get to them...unobserved?"

"Yes, my Lady. And, we are their only hope of survival."

Sonia spoke aloud, but also delivered the order by thought. "Come, Djura. Bring Karine."

The two came visible within seconds. Karine stepped away as she often did, knowing this matter must be important.

"We have a situation in the human world to which we can give assistance," Sonia told her security chief. "We will include the humans in this rescue effort."

"Your orders then, my Lady?"

"Put Sanctuary on 'Keeper' alert. Have all guardians meet us in the meeting room with their females…say in fifteen? Joel with Ziva will remain to man Technical Centre."

"And the human women?"

"Couple each with a male guardian for easier protection, should there be any danger to them."

Djura agreed.

****

When the two guardians and Karine had gone, Sky raised an inquiring eyebrow.

"You are beginning inclusion before complete pairing? Is that wise?"

"It should prove interesting," Sonia admitted. "We'll try it."

Sky grinned. He reached to the chessboard, moving his queen. He had been as patient as a cat with a mouse.

"Check mate!" he declared jubilantly.

Sonia wrinkled her nose in displeasure.

"You've been waiting to do that for a long time, haven't you?" she rebuked. "Think you can only win if I'm distracted."

He laughed good-naturedly. "I know you seldom let me win. Besides…you have important matters to plot."

"Funny today, aren't we?"

Sky chuckled. *She knows me too well.*

"Let's go save some humans, shall we?"

****

When all were gathered in the meeting room, Sonia began.

"Each human has been paired with a guardian male; he is your protection. Today you are not companions. As with our females, your purpose is to rescue and comfort humans in need."

A murmur of surprise escaped those listening.

"We enter an unstable area, the scene of a major earthquake, which has levelled all structures. There will be after shocks, many injured and frightened individuals, and a language barrier. Humans let your guardian do the talking." Sonia continued. "The males will be disguised, human-like and dressed in ethnic apparel. So also will our females. This is to prevent alarm in the victims; they need no extra trauma."

They put themselves at risk, yet worry about giving hurt to humans? Jenna thought in amazement.

She had assumed from things Tyler had told her, that the 'Aopato' viewed humans as enemies.

"Guardians, your duty is to dig out those beneath the rubble," Sonia pointed out. "At no time are you to heal. Bring those needing it to the healing pairs."

A nod of acceptance came from more than one.

"Great-gran, may I be permitted to heal?" Kara pleaded. "I am a 'Leader Female'. I could use Unca Shawn or Tyler for support...or even Great Unca Joel."

"No, little one, not this time," Sonia gently disagreed. "You are still too young. There will be small children; babies. You and Nadia will see to them; comfort and hold them."

"Oh, goody!" Kara squealed. "Real babies?"

"Yes dear."

Beside her, her cousin Nadia giggled.

"Real babies, Nadia!" Kara exclaimed in awe.

"They may be injured," Sonia cautioned. "You must control yourself. No healing! Only comfort, Kara."

Kara bobbed her head. "I'll be good great-gran. I know it's not safe."

It suddenly dawn on Jenna why this was such a big deal.

The 'Aopato' have no children! Kara is their youngest.

Sonia added,

"We now have four healing pairs: Jade and Ryan; Rhea and Ihor; Jessica and Wade..."

She sought the eyes of her security chief. "Djura, you along with your human partner, will act guardian sentry for the group. Chi you will be with the 'Pair Ultimate'."

"What is the 'Pair Ultimate'?" whispered Jenna.

Nadia turned in surprise. "Why Grandma and Sky, of course! They are the fourth healer pair, our 'Ultimate Healers'."

Jenna frowned, still not fully understanding.

"Their healing power is the strongest," Nadia supplied.

"One last thing..." Sonia was speaking again. "We heal only those near point of death today. There will be too many casualties to do otherwise. Dress the other wounds by the human method; no repair either. Darkness comes on this region shortly, and we can not safely stay long."

"Are you afraid the 'Opposites' will show up?" Jenna wondered.

"No," Tyler at her side answered. "But our healing energy will deplete quickly after sunset. We don't wish to be stranded...unable to teleport. That would be deadly."

"Shall we go then?" Sonia suggested. "Guardians circle the females, please."

****

They were suddenly in the midst of chaos. All the human women were now wearing long hooded cloaks, making it harder to see their faces, and surprisingly Karine found the garment cool, as if somehow it was insulated to keep out the intolerable heat of the region. The guardians were disguised as young human versions of themselves, but even so, they were larger than the Peruvian norm.

Horrified by the devastation around them the human women stood indecisive, until each male took his partner in hand and led her off to his designated search area. Each seemed to know what was required of him without being told. Obviously the 'Aopato' no longer communicated aloud.

Djura headed to the outer limits of the ravished stone village, up a slight incline over looking the site. Here he had a vantage point that put the fields around and every inch of rubbled space within his view.

After explaining to Karine that she was to watch the fields at his back, warn him should anyone approach, Djura dropped to one knee, and closed his eyes.

"Do not touch me," he warned quietly. "Simply think my name should you need to get my attention."

Then he went still as a statue; his muscles tensed; his breathing slowed. Karine could feel his mind go…different, and she knew he was now listening and watching distantly.

What a strange way to stand guard, Karine thought.

She herself turned to watch the distant slopes behind them. After a time, Karine grew tired of standing, and sat down on a large rock.

I'm here to watch his back! I'm his protection! she reminded herself. *He trusts me with his life.*

The hours passed slowly for Karine, but then she was used to waiting.

****

"The 'Leader Pair' are going to heal?" questioned May Lin as she and Chi followed the couple.

"Together. Yes. It is less dangerous as a pair."

"But…will it not harm…make your lives shorten?" May Lin demanded.

"Our purpose in life is to heal," Chi told her. "We lose nothing that is not already in jeopardy, and these humans will surely lose their lives if we do not do this."

May Lin marvelled at their bravery.

To be so selfless is indeed honourable. If only I could be so.

****

Morgan looked up at Lance as they strode to their station. "Your mother helps humans?" she observed in disbelief. "After what they've done to you…"

He reached out and gently ran a finger down her cheek, smiled fondly. "It is our way. 'Be kind to your enemy'."

"How do you feel about that?" Morgan challenged.

"These were not the ones who hurt me," he responded generously. "It is amazing how it eases the wound when you offer love in return."

Morgan shook her head. "That's an extraordinary concept. So…what's our duty here?"

"We are to guard the new healing pair, Rhea and Ihor. Whatever you do, do not touch either while they are healing."

"If I did, what would happen?"

"It would kill them both…but before you could do that, I would be forced to eliminate you."

Morgan assumed it was a joke, and laughed.

"It was not a jest," Lance declared soberly. "They are my first priority today. You come second…I'm sorry."

Morgan caught her breath sharply, finally realizing he was indeed serious.

He would really kill me?

****

The two males were working in tandem, like machines set in perfect sync. First Eric seemed to sense where each victim was buried alive, then Marcel and he would lift the huge rock slabs together.

Carmel could feel Marcel's pectoral muscles contract each time he pulled up another gigantic stone. It almost made her own chest ache.

"Pull him out!" Eric shouted as he strained to hold up his end of the huge block. Carmel and Angel both jumped to grab the legs of the smaller man beneath. With great effort, they pulled the unconscious man from his prison. He was elderly, and set up a mournful lament as he regained awareness.

"He's not hurt that bad," Eric surmised. "Merely frightened. We can leave him to recover on his own."

As they moved toward another spot, Carmen leaned in to whisper softly to Marcel. "I could feel inside you back there," she said sympathetically. "Lifting the rocks hurts you."

Marcel's reaction was unexpected. He looked at her with apparent delight, and chuckled, but before he could comment, Eric spoke instead.

"Guardian! You two have 'pair connected'! Congratulations."

Then he and Angel moved ahead, giving them privacy.

"What did he mean by that?" Carmen demanded.

Marcel stopped short. When he turned to her, his hand came up to gently stoke her cheek. "I will explain later...when we are alone," he softly whispered. "At the moment, the duties we perform are more important then our private occasions..."

****

"Helicopters come, Sonia!"

Djura's warning was non-verbal, but even Karine had heard it in her mind.

Where are they? I can't even hear them, leave alone see them.

Karine peered into the darkening sky. The sun was just beginning to set behind the distant shadowed peaks. She had not realized how quickly dusk set in and night descended in the valley.

Sonia's thought voice was heard by all. "Depart immediately! We have done all we can here. Everyone is on their own; don't forget your human."

Djura waited to the last; he made certain all others were away safely first. Karine could now see the choppers on the far horizon. Then Djura took her hand, and they were instantly back at Sanctuary.

****

"Oh, great-gran!" exclaimed Kara eagerly. "Can we do that again sometime?"

Those around her smiled at her exuberance.

"You know, it makes it even better," Jessica agreed. "That if they told someone what we did, they would not be believed. To outsiders, they will seem only confused, traumatized..."

"Those we healed will be told they only imagined it," Jade chuckled. "And the ones who do listen, will make legends of us."

"Enough girls," Sonia reproved. "I know it was heady, but...reality check? You are all exhausted. We will all take a rest period...it is necessary! You are in the lull before going down again. Away with you! Everyone!"

****

Sleep was a long time in coming to most of the human women. In their wildest dreams they had never imagined the 'Aopato' would do anything like this.

CHAPTER 39

A few days later Shawn caught up to Chrystal in the passageway leading to her quarters.

"We are having another party," he breathlessly exclaimed. "Will you go with me? Everyone's invited."

"Where? In the banquet room again? Is it formal?"

He chuckled. "No. It's a roller skating party."

"Oh, yes! That sounds like fun!"

****

When she entered the room, Karine was amazed the human women had not known of its existence; there hadn't even been an inkling, yet it was there big as life.

The space resembled an open-air roller-coaster pathway minus tracks, its rising and descending course meandering all around the circular centre court, where a revolving carousel of benches turned. Overhead lights blinked in multi-colours causing star-like images to pulsate in flashes upon the skaters below.

Karine and May Lin walked hurriedly across the floor to take seats in the middle where it seemed safer. They intended only to watch.

Most of the younger ones were coupled, already on the smooth polished floor. What surprised Karine was, there was Sonia, guided expertly by Sky, in the very middle of all the youngsters. As she watched, they traded partners; Sky took Kara, while

Sonia went for Ram. There seemed no social order here, not that Sonia had ever encouraged such veneration at any point. Perhaps that was why all 'Aopato' showed her such respect.

Every guardian is present. Even Joel and Eric.

Who is manning Technical Centre? Is it on 'Keeper' again?

Sonia's two daughters were having as much fun as anyone, enjoying the exercise with their new 'pair' partners. Jessica and Wade from the kitchens were racing Nadia and Jenna. And even though they were over sixty, Ziva and Carmen were out there with Joel and Marcel.

What has gotten into them all? Karine wondered.

With Chi following close behind him, Djura rolled up to where Karine and May Lin sat.

"Come," Djura suggested to Karine, holding out his hand. "Skate with me."

"Oh! No way!" she objected, pulling back. "I'm seventy-eight. You'll give me a heart attack, or I'll fall and break every bone in my body."

"Wouldn't you like to have some fun?" he grinned mischievously.

"It would probably be fabulous, but I am much too old!"

"May Lin," Chi interjected. "Do you trust me? Will you join me?"

"Honourable sir?" May Lin gasp in shock. "I am even older; eighty! Never in my life, I do this."

The males looked at each other, chuckled.

"If we ask a couple of our females to help," Djura suggested. "We could do this."

"Oh! No way! No way!" Karine shivered in dread. "I am not crazy. No way!"

May Lin kept shaking her head, quite beside herself.

Sky and Sonia rolled to a stop beside them. Then Jade and Ryan came from another angle, stopping abruptly beside those by the bench.

"Need some help guys?" quizzed Sonia.

"These two are party poops. They won't trust us to keep them safe as we help them skate," Djura teasingly complained.

Karine sent him a scathing look that should have burned the conscience of a lesser man. Djura only laughed with pure pleasure at her reaction.

"We need two females, one at each end," he suggested nonplused.

"Oh, that sounds like fun," Sonia exclaimed. "I'll do it!"

Karine had expected Sonia to come to her rescue.

Even the 'Leader Female' betrays me!

Sonia chuckled, as she obviously read the thought.

"I'm in, too," Jade agreed.

"No way. No way." Karine was near to tears. Who knew what these beings had in mind?

Chi reached for May Lin's hand.

"No!" She turned desperate eyes to the 'Leader Female's' pair. "Oh, Master, sir! Help us, please!" May Lin plead of Sky.

He only laughed. "I would try it," the Navajo suggested. "If any can make this an experience, these four can. You never know what you've missed until you've tried it."

"I too am in my late seventies," Sonia cajoled. "Why should the fun be only for the young?"

"But you, my Lady, are 'Aopato'," Karine objected. "We are only human."

"True. But we will be shielding your feelings and your bodies. You will only experience the thrill of it."

I would really like to try, admitted Karine in herself.

"You're sure?" she insisted, caving in under all the pressure.

"If we are able to heal, don't you think we can prevent, as well?"

"Only if May Lin does, too."

The gentle Asian whined plaintively.

"I was once a cripple...in a wheelchair, May Lin." Jade added her voice to the urging. "I would never let you be injured."

Finally defeated, May Lin reluctantly agreed.

As they were pulled to their feet, the two women found they were shod in roller skates. May Lin let out a frightened squeal as her legs slid out, each a different direction, until the slip was corrected, when Chi on one side, and Jade on the other, took her hands. The tiny human's cry became one of immediate pleasure, as all took to the smooth circular court.

Djura and Sonia had been just as swift to take Karine in hand, with equal results.

****

As Sky rose to meet his pair, Karine sank exhausted to the circling carousel bench. Djura slid to a stop beside her.

"How long have we been skating?" Karine gasped breathlessly.

"Over an hour."

"Really? I'll sure feel it tomorrow."

"You will have no after effect," Djura reassured. "We've absorbed any shock to your system."

"That was...out of this world!" Karine declared exuberantly, when she had her breath back. "I'd forgotten how great it feels to move like that."

He chuckled, please with himself for pulling it off, and giving her such delight.

Out on the roller court, Sonia clapped her hands for attention. "I am sorry, but our workout must come to an end. A scrumptious lunch has been prepared to end the festivities. We will meet you all in the kitchens."

****

They stood around talking even after all had eaten. As always, none wanted things to end.

Karine was standing next to Djura when she felt him drain of energy. He gasped, sinking heavily to one knee. In concern, without thinking, she made to reach for him.

"Don't touch, human," he croaked painfully. "Remember? I am strongest male, Sonia's strength balance. Never touch when this happens."

Horrified, all human eyes went to Sonia. It was early in the afternoon, why was this happening now?

"Sky!" yelled Zane. "Watch your pair!"

Sky whirled, catching Sonia just as she folded in a dead faint.

"Watch the other females!" warned Sky, dropping violently to one knee, as if it effected him as well. "Humans! Do not touch us!"

The puzzled women moved away.

Ihor caught Rhea, Ryan Jade, as both sisters went down simultaneously. What was happening here? This wasn't normal.

"What the devil's going on?" muttered a perplexed Lance.

"There's a weapon drone in here!" gasped Djura. "Find it before it kills us all!"

As Jessica went down, Wade barely catching her on time, Nadia too folded into Tyler's arms.

"Kara!" yelled Sky. "Zane get her!"

Zane stepping to Kara just on time, catching the child just as she collapsed, was enveloped in static shock, visible as a crackling band of light that zapped from point to point with their bodies.

"Aw, ouch! Geeze, Mini Monarch. You bite!" moaned Zane. "Where is the darn thing? Find it before Kara kills me with her defence reflex!"

"Hurry! Locate it!" Djura plead painfully. "Before it succeeds in bringing the males down as well."

"There!" Lance pointed. "Upper left; near the ceiling!"

"Don't destroy it! Neutralize, so we can examine it," ordered Sky. "It contains a miniature of the newest 'Opposite' weapon."

"Man! That thing's deadly," Lance said in annoyance. From the direct centre of his eyes a beam of blue light discharged to the tiny pyramid above, now very evident to all.

The disabled machine dropped into his waiting hand.

The human women who had listen with bated breath to the rapid fire comments, gave a sigh of relief. Even Lance's use of his personal weapon had been taken in stride.

Sonia moaned, and sat up, holding her head in her hands. "I guess we now know, they have perfected the weapon," she declared acerbically. "And what it can do..."

The other 'Aopato' women were beginning to revive, as well. Djura rose to his feet.

"Give me their stupid toy!" he ordered tersely. "I will see it personally to Tech Centre. Come Eric, let us see what makes this thing tick."

As Lance tossed it to him, Djura caught the object, and vanished with Eric.

Zane stepped back from Kara. "Mini Monarch, you have a terrible bite when unconscious," he rebuked. "Remind me not to get on your wrong side."

Kara smiled uncertainly, regret mirrored in her eyes.

Chrystal asked the question on everyone's mind. "What was that thing meant to do?"

Zane willingly explained. "It is programmed to drain the energy of a particular being. It won't harm a human. It was meant exclusively for us. It is target specific, first to our females, because they are the weaker physically. Its main aim is to drop the 'Leader Female' because she holds us. That would be my mother Sonia, as you well know."

"Don't much like that little beastie," muttered Shawn coldly. "If ever they turn the larger weapon on us, we'll all go down at once."

"Let's hope that never happens," Ihor warned ominously. "As of the moment, we have no defence against it."

From where she was seated on the floor, leaning resting against Sky's shoulder, Sonia stated the obvious. "Well, we'll have to do something about that, won't we?"

"How about going inside their compound and destroying the larger weapon?" suggested Lance.

"It is protected by a force field of a similar draining quality as the weapon itself," Sonia disclosed. "Keeps us out just as effectively as our shields work against them."

"So, as before," Joel reiterated. "We just wait for the final blow."

"We will find a means of defence," Sonia assured them. "We are not in this position by chance."

CHAPTER 40

The humans were once again summoned to a meeting, in what they now labelled the 'Jump room', because it was from here they were transported out, when they went on planned missions. Today only Angel was excused, as it was her shift in Technical Centre with Eric.

Ziva had decided to join in, to see what this was all about. She had heard the other women talking, and though they described in detail, she found what they said hard to believe.

The others were extremely excited, hoping this was going to be another mission like the last.

"Please, make yourselves comfortable," Sonia suggested.

Chairs appeared at their backs. The large males moved to the rear against the wall.

"I'll get right to the point," Sonia continued. "Ihor, how is our supply of fruit? Do we have extra to share?"

"Always have a surplus, my Lady," answered the big blond male, who had just been paired to Sonia's daughter Rhea. "And an excellent idea to share."

"Good. And Jessica, how are our bread supplies?"

"Whatever you require, I can supply. How much and how fast?"

Sonia chuckled. "Seems we are all eager to go out again."

"Yes! Yes! Yes!" Kara bounced on each word, her excitement infectious.

Many giggled. The guardians merely showed fond indulgence.

"Shh, dear! Kara, be still." Sonia's eyes twinkled with amusement, though she tried to retain a sober countenance and reprimand her great granddaughter. The 'Leader Female' returned to the matter of discussion. "We have been monitoring the many catastrophic weather events and related disasters about the globe. I see a need here... Many go hungry in refugee camps..."

A murmur of approval passed through those present.

"Today it has been decided, we will enter a flooded area near Pakistan, to a tent city above where a mud slide buried most homes. We will do much as we did last excursion, but this time we will do no healing. We will pass out bread, fruit and bottled water, to the children and women first. They are the ones being neglected, because most old and the very young have no one to care for their needs.

"The human women and our females will be veiled, so that they draw less attention and will blend in. There seem to be few men in the camp, but it is always best to err on the side of caution."

"Won't white women be quite noticeable?" Morgan asked. "This is an ethnic area."

"True, dear," Sonia agreed. "That is why many of us will appear to have skin and hair of a darker colouring that our norm."

"And how are you going to do that?" Chrystal blurted out without thinking. She was fair complexioned, and didn't relish the thought of dyeing hair, let alone skin.

"Still always viewing things the hard human way, young lady," Sonia reproved gently. "If we can change garments at will, why not exterior appearance?"

"Oh, my Lady, I'm sorry," Chrystal returned in mortification. "I didn't even think of that."

Sonia simply smiled. "No problem. It will take time to think non-human. Now," she continued without missing a beat. "The females of both species will hand out the supplies. Kara, Nadia and Jessica will keep you supplied with the food articles. Just ask in your mind; do not speak aloud. There is once again the language barrier, and your difference of tongue will draw attention to you."

The 'Leader Female' made eye contact with her security chief. "Djura, you will again act as main sentry guardian, but because the area is more hazardous to us, Chi and Marcel will take watch with you. A triangle formation around the area, close in, not outside camp…walk the site. We do not need personal casualties because we do this."

The three males nodded.

Sonia's eyes narrowed with warning. "Keep your human charge intimately close guardians. You do not want them to come to harm either."

She turned to Joel standing at Ziva's side. "Will my brother offer his services as extra guardian to the 'Leader Pair'?"

Joel gave an amenable silent nod.

"And Lance, you and Ihor. Will you also remain with us?"

"Affirmative," both males agreed in unison.

"Jade, you will do best with the other females. The rest of the guardians are our inner protection shield for the younger females. See none are approached by a local male."

Why is Sonia acting so possessive? You'd think these helpless refugees were about to kill them. Man! She's controlling! thought Ziva.

"I believe that will suffice," Sonia finished. "Shall we proceed? Guardians circle the females."

****

Ziva realized as soon as they appeared in the village, all 'Aopato' now appeared not only human, but very native to the region. It was also extremely weird to see Chrystal, Chantel and even Jenna with dark brown skin under the silk veils. May Lin and Chi Cho were no longer Oriental but Pakistani. Djura was the closest to his actual image though smaller and human-like. Ram, Chad and Nadia had changed little. But all males now wore the white Moslem attire: loose fitting pants and over shirt that hung past the knees. Even Sky Hawk had replaced his usual buckskins.

****

All about them was obvious misery. The people stared vacant eyed and lethargic, sitting in numb acceptance of their plight: bleak, vulnerable, disheartened. There was mud everywhere: soggy grey soil, clinging clay mud, reeking humus peat. The air was stifling; humid and blistering. Makeshift tents, which had been formed from colourful silks or worn blankets, were now soggy from the rain, steaming in the sun, yet dripping on the occupants.

Viewing all the wretchedness, Ziva thought, *one meal is not going to make a difference. These people need more.*

She fully expected to have to tramp through the mud for the fruit, bread and bottled water, but each time her hands were empty, Joel handed her what was needed. Ziva knew he was using thought transference.

Wow! she marvelled. *Wouldn't he be handy in the real world!*

Between the giving, Ziva was aware of Sonia nearby. By her face, she got the impression the female would like to do more, but something was preventing her. Perhaps the needs here were just too overwhelming?

Then something the other women had told her came to mind. When unbalanced Sonia had mentioned the feelings of humans hurt the 'Aopato'. The creatures were empathic.

Perhaps that's what I'm seeing mirrored in all their faces.

If they are as affected as they claim, this venture must be excruciating to them, litterly tearing them apart. Why would you do this at all, when you feel the suffering around you with such perception?

Is this some sort of sadistic training exercise? An implement to familiarize the younger ones with pain and agony? What a sick way to teach!

****

Later, as they moved through a deserted empty space, Sonia suddenly stopped. She dropped carefully to her knees in the mud.

Ziva moved up beside her to see what had caught her attention. There, half buried in the saturated ground was what appeared to be a bunch of rags. Sonia carefully unbound the filthy bundle. Inside was a shrivelled infant of approximately six weeks old.

The baby barely fit in the 'Leader Female's' hands. The tiny girl was naked, her lower limps malformed; her face had been badly burned. The child lay gasping for breath, each intake a supreme effort. It was obvious she was fading fast.

A collective moan escaped those around Sonia. Rhea and Morgan had appeared as if from nowhere. The males too closed in about them, as though protection was needed.

It began to rain, and the baby, as if suckling, sought the moisture, gulping at each drop pitifully.

"Sis," warned Joel, at Sonia's elbow, as he became aware of the thoughts running through her mind. "You said, no healing on this mission."

Ziva looked to Sonia. Great monster tears had formed in her eyes, sliding down her cheeks; her compassion mirrored in her eyes.

Sonia groaned. "Oh Joel! I cannot leave this poor infant like this. She is barely alive, yet she still struggles for life. She is a fighter; not one to give up! They have tossed her away as if she were nothing," she sobbed. "She deserves to live."

"You will put the whole species at risk," Lance stated almost coldly, moving to stand over his mother.

From over to their left, Sky's voice joined in. "Female compulsion. If Sonia must heal," he defended. "She will; you know that son. The question is whether we support her or not. Our lives mean little, if we come upon something like this and do nothing."

Lance gave a curt nod. "Do it mother," he encouraged without hesitation. "We are in agreement. I was merely stating the risk factor."

Morgan looked up at him in surprise, as if she had expected him to challenge. Lance said nothing in his defence.

****

Sonia lifted the trembling child to her bosom. Her eyes turned to the purple hue that was her norm. Rhea crouched down in the mud beside her. The four males: Joel, Sky Hawk, Ihor and Lance, formed a circle around the two 'Aopato' women, enclosing Ziva and Morgan with them. Just before the men turned their backs to the females, Sonia spoke to her brother. "Joel will you be male support?"

Joel caught his breath, as if he had not expected the request. "You will trust me... even though I failed you the last time?"

"Always, brother," Sonia declared fervently.

"You have matured brother-in-law," Sky reassured, placing a hand gently on his shoulder. "And we are a people of second chances."

Joel stepped back into the inner centre, dropped to one knee. "I will not fail you this time, sister!"

Then the other males turned their backs to the women, standing guard over those inside.

Sky came back with one last order. "Human. Touch none of us during this procedure, especially not Sonia. She is the primary healer."

"What will happen if I do?" Ziva asked.

"It will kill the entire species."

****

Morgan narrowed her eyes in warning at Ziva.

Does she realize these creatures trust her with their lives, just by allowing her to remain within the healing circle?

Is Sonia testing Ziva or were they careless because Sonia is desperate to heal?

Ziva could choose sides against them. She has the perfect opportunity to destroy the 'Aopato'. She was Darla's friend. Is she dangerous?

Sonia seemed to trust the Jewish woman, but that didn't mean Morgan would let her guard down. Morgan realized they had left her, as the first defence should Ziva make a move. And she was prepared to stop her; to do whatever it took.

If push comes to shove, I can always throw myself over her.

Morgan hoped Sonia was right. The last thing she wanted was to hurt Ziva, but if the lives of the 'Aopato' were at stake, she would protect even at the cost of her own.

Lance is worth it!

****

Why is that cop watching me like a hawk? Ziva fumed. *It's like she expects me to touch Sonia.*

Is this a test? Are the humans in on it?

Well, so what? Even if my employer wants me to turn traitor, I would not kill these beings deliberately!

I am not Darla! Ziva seethed at the injustice of her situation. *How dare they put me in this position! Can't trust my human bosses! And now the 'Aopato' can't be trusted either! To top it off, I've got a cop bodyguard staring me down.*

****

Ziva's attention was caught by Sonia's next actions. She closed her eyes. The broken child in her arms seemed to transform as Ziva watched: the raw burned skin became a healthy brown sheen; the twisted limbs appeared rubber-like as they straightened; the breathing became less laboured. With a comfortable sigh, the infant dropped into a light sleep, going limp in relaxation.

Ziva looked fully at Sonia, and backed away in horror, right up against Morgan.

"Stay put!" hissed the other woman.

Ziva hardly heard; she was too petrified as she watched what was happening to Sonia.

The 'Leader Female' was changing: her face took on the raw ugly burn that had once been on the face of the baby; her legs became the twisted, misshapen limbs of the small one.

Sonia sat down hard in the mud.

This is how they heal? They take the injury upon themselves! Hell!

Ziva heard Joel's voice inside her mind.

Don't feel bad. The first time I saw her do this, I ran.

Ziva wondered. *Did I really hear him say that, or am I hallucinating?*

Ya, I said it, Joel answered. *Watch!*

Ziva once again turned her attention to Sonia's gruesome person. The face was altering rapidly, the damaged limbs straightening visibly.

Sonia sighed, and opened her eyes.

"Give me a moment to catch my breath," she pleaded weakly. "Rhea, you okay?"

From behind her, the copper haired beauty replied, "Right as rain, mom. You hardly needed my help. She was such a little thing."

"True," Sonia agreed. "Too bad we can not keep her with us. She would have a better chance."

"It does seem a shame to leave her in this squalor," Rhea admitted.

"Gentlemen. You may relax," Sonia told her guardians.

Joel got to his feet. His sister sent him a thankful smile. The other males turned as one.

And suddenly it seemed, the ugliness of the world beyond closed back in.

****

Sonia rose gracefully to her feet, lifting the child with her. Across the way an old Pakistani grandmother sat dejectedly.

"She has lost her grandson," Sonia disclosed softly.

A blanket appeared from nowhere. Sonia wrapped the infant in it, transferring it to lie against her shoulder. Then she made her way to elder woman, while the rest held back. They did not wish to seem threatening.

Gently, in the old woman's own rapid-tongue dialect, Sonia pleaded with the wrinkled senior. After a moment, the woman held out her arms.

Sonia cuddled the baby close on last time, kissed her on the forehead, and released her to the arms of the other. The aged lady never noticed when the 'Aopato' stepped away. She was cooing pleasantly to the little one in her arms.

Quietly Sonia moved to Sky, and spoke in a low tone.

"Time to return…"

****

By the time all had returned to the 'Jump Room', every 'Aopato' female was in tears. Ziva wondered what was the matter with them all.

"Oh, great-gran," Kara wept. "They live such ugly lives. It is so…dark in their world. What good did we even accomplish?"

Sonia shook her head, equally sad. "One moment of love can make an immense difference in a life. These people live for the moment; pleasure is seldom something they experience."

"Are we just going to leave them like that?" Nadia demanded. "What of that baby?"

"She will live and die in that squalor…"

"Then why did we even save her?" Rhea joined in with rancour.

"Perhaps, I was…selfish." Sonia dropped to her knees, hiding her face in her hands.

What is wrong with these women?

She gave the child a chance to live longer…a better place in life.

"Could we go back and change their conditions?" pleaded Jessica.

Sonia lifted her head, tears flooding her eyes. "I could dry out the land, give them all beautiful homes, a better food supply, but…the governing authorities would only take it from them. It is a dictatorship."

"You could hide them…" suggested Jade.

"Should I do it for only a few, the whole region," Sonia probed. "What of the rest of the world? All the third world nations live in similar conditions."

Kara began to sob softly. "What…good…did we do?" she repeated.

They are serious! They expected to relieve all the suffering!

Ziva couldn't believe the irrational view of these people.

Sky shook his head. "Females," Sky rebuked softly. "Your emotions have gone unbalanced again. To be exposed to such pain and suffering is a shock to any system; for you it is beyond endurance. You did extremely well..."

"You made a small dent; did all that you were able," Lance agreed.

"It wasn't half enough! It doesn't change a thing, Sky" Sonia declared almost angrily. "We must face the fact, there will always be those we can not help... They must first fight against their own darkness..."

"Time to rest. All of you," Sky admonished. "See to them guardians; watch over them. Humans...will you please stay in your rooms? Give comfort if you dare, but be warned...their depression is spreading to you. Sleep will ease the shock...for all."

Karine caught Sonia by the hand. The other women also began to slip away with their companions and their appointed guardians.

But Joel remained. "Even after rest, what we have witnessed will never be erased. The neglect and lack of concern for their own people..." he declared bluntly. "The loathsome condition displayed by the human race is appalling. Darkness, the females spoke of, sensed, is self-absorption, self-gratification...there is no hope that the affluent will ever indulge in self-denial, giving all for others...ever. It wounds me also, for I feel by proxy, I am part this race."

Ziva felt as if Joel was including her, like it was meant for her personally.

Sky looked at Joel and frowned.

"I believe you also are unbalanced, guardian," Sky reproved, gently.

Sky reached out just in time to catch Joel, as he collapsed against the Navajo's shoulder.

"Help me get him to his quarters."

Chi took one side; Sky the other, and all three were gone.

As Ziva stood in the chamber alone, she felt chastised. Joel's harsh assessment of human kind had hit close to home. She had judged the 'Aopato' for their inadequate measures, thought Sonia only toying with lives, but in all her life, when had she even given a small amount for someone else? The reality of Joel's view had been more enlightening then the muddy fields of Pakistan.

****

"Sir!" Neil approached his superior at his desk in Central Intelligence.

The burly man in uniform looked up. "Did you find her yet," he asked without preamble.

"We just picked up her homing signal in Pakistan, of all places. We watched it for hours, then it seemed like it just jumped to another location, and we lost it."

"So she's gone rogue; joined the terrorists?" assumed the superior. "That's why we've heard nothing from her all this time. Where did you lose her?"

"Very near to where we discovered the Alien base. What's our next move, sir?"

"It's not the first time we've lost an agent like this," the director stated. "She was too green. Without Darla she probably caved to pressure. When we found Darla in such a condition, I knew

Ziva would be no help. Seems we're pretty much on our own now."

"Why would she still be wearing the tag device, sir? Maybe, she's a prisoner… forced to comply against her will?"

"Not likely. But, they do prefer thorough brainwashing…"

"Let me go in…I can get her."

"Fine. Start at where you last saw her."

"Yes, sir!"

CHAPTER 41

Joel had been despondent and withdrawn ever since the night they returned from the excursion into Pakistan. It was like he'd given up hope, and was just going through the motions of his life.

Ziva wondered if she was the cause; if perhaps he had finally realized she would have no part in their mating games.

His sullen and defeatist behaviour made her angry. She preferred him to fight and argue it out. It would help them both feel better.

Why do I let it bother me, anyway? Who cares if his feelings are hurt? These beings have a lot to learn about individual choice, and the rights of others. They don't have the patent on how to live life!

As if she had spoken aloud, Joel finally defended himself. "In our world your thoughts are not yours alone. You learn to school them, or the others will withdraw from you...and for our species, separation, going solo, is excruciating."

It dawned on her, he'd been listening in. "You're not suppose to read my thoughts!"

"Sometimes, it can't be helped. It just happens; the thoughts are out there...yours are big as life!"

She didn't know quite what to do with that, so rather than think on it, she chose to change the subject. She let the silence drag a bit, until his guard was down, his attention returned to the monitors.

"Why do you all allow Sonia to control like she does?" Ziva suddenly blurted out angrily. "You're like a bunch of puppets!"

Joel looked away from his screen in surprise.

"That bothers you, doesn't it?" he observed. "Because you've been controlled by a heavy hand."

She made a rude noise, but did not comment.

"If you must know, we are unified with my sister," he stated calmly.

"For what!" Ziva hissed. "What power does she hold over you?"

He gave a dry laugh. "Humans always think there must be an ulterior motive."

"Isn't there?"

He sighed in resignation. "To us, Sonia is like your energy is to you. She supplies a force, the mental power, our physical strength, and she maintains the species' emotional balance."

"Yes, I can see that," Ziva observed sarcastically. "She's real good at that!"

A flash of displeasure lit his eyes, then it was gone. "It is not her fault she can not stay balanced; there are not enough females!" He shook his head, annoyed. "As a human, you can not understand."

"Why don't you try me? Explain it!"

"We are all inter-connected, symbiotic; living together as one entity, yet each separate physically."

"You're what!" squealed Ziva, caught off guard. "Symbiotic? One entity? You're joking!"

He almost smiled. His face poker straight, Joel continued: "We are inter-connected and we cannot separate on our own. Sonia holds us all together. She is the heart, the females are the soul. Together they give us life. Were Sonia to die, should the female side be lost, all males would perish as well. Our condition is exclusive to our species; the only way we can exist. To not be what we are, creates a madness in us."

The very idea of living in such a state, willingly, shocked Ziva to the core; filled her with a dread she could not shake. She became aware she had been holding her breath from the beginning of his disclosure, and finally exhaled hard.

Just to add more drama to his revelation, Joel added, "Until Kara reaches maturity, and can replace her should something happen to Sonia, without an equal balance of females, we teeter on the brink of extinction."

Ziva stared at him, incredulous. "You actually believe that?"

"Oh, I have experienced it first hand."

She wanted to reason against it.

"Sonia's not strong enough!"

"No," he disagreed. "You've almost got it though. The female side will always be too weak. It would balance out if we had the exact number of females as the male side."

'So that's why you each are so set on pairing with a human," Ziva declared scathingly. "You want to use us like power generators so you can stay alive!"

"No...it's not like that! Yes..." he admitted abashed, being honest with himself. "We do need you to survive."

"We are not even the same species!"

"A human can be blood-healed, integrated into the genus, made to be half 'Aopato', but...it must be of your own free will."

Ziva was steaming. "Instead of using us like guinea pigs, find a male to take Sonia's place, to do what she does!"

"It doesn't work that way! A male can't do it! Only a 'Leader Female' has been found able: only she is mentally strong enough to support and hold so many together."

"Use two then...or go separate! Human beings do it all the time!"

"That doesn't work for our species. Division causes mental breakdown."

"Oh, come on! You've been pre-programmed. Sonia's got you all so brainwashed ...it's her way to dominate!"

Joel abruptly ended the discussion, by turning back to his monitor.

And Ziva finally had time to digest all that he had said. Now that she could sort it out, she realized this explained why they did the things they did. Still, she wanted no part of being their liberator.

After she had sat for some time, Ziva decided to change tactics, to again prod Joel to debate.

"So, does this mean, you just let your leader make all your decisions? She's even picked your partners for you. Do you realize that?"

"So?" Joel returned with unconcern.

"It doesn't bother you?"

"No. I know she's wiser than I."

"Oh, hog wash! What's the matter with you? Any man who follows a woman that blindly is a fool!"

"I used to think that way also, until...I learned the hard way."

"And just how was that? She punish you?" Ziva laughed at such an idea. Joel was at least three times Sonia's size.

When he remained uncommunicative, she tried to taunt him farther. "Explain to me. What happened?"

"Through my pride and desertion, I very nearly destroyed the entire species. Sonia is like she is now because of me."

Ziva was getting very tired of hearing these people were on the brink of a fatal incident. "I suppose you drained all her energy," she chided.

Joel glared at her, then abruptly switched topics.

"And, for your information, Sonia never picked any of you. We each picked our own partners."

That brought Ziva up short.

Why would he pick me?

Her nasty attitude had finally transferred to Joel. His reply was curt, sarcastic and acerbic. "I can't for the life of me remember why I did," he replied vituperatively, and Ziva realized once again, he had heard her thought.

And that made her angry enough to shout.

"Who do you guys think you are? Earth isn't your private breeding farm!"

"We had no other recourse…" he excused, suddenly chastened. "Sonia said we could try… We could come back where we were born, and try to find human women who would care for us…" His temper abruptly flared again. "You don't realize what you do to us! Sonia permitted you into our society from the goodness of her heart. She said, it was up to us to do the rest; to woo you; to win you, but again, I have failed so miserably… Your heart is so hard…"

"You could have asked me before you brought me here…"

"I tried a gentle approach; your mind always says, no."

"A woman's heart is what you appeal to; change her mind!" Then Ziva realized what she was saying, and added quickly, "I don't need a man!"

"I know…that's what you think." Joel sighed and went back to the surveillance screens.

"You kidnap us, hold us virtually prisoners! Do you really think that's the way to win me?"

"You've been free to go at any time."

"Really?" Ziva spat back hotly. "Each time there was a crisis, each time you went down, I've been ordered to my room! If not there, I've been stuck in this hole watching your monitors for god knows what!"

He seemed to see her point. "First time was for your safety," Joel excused. "And you could have fled anytime you weren't in your chambers..."

"But the second time, you stood guard outside my doorway."

Joel shook his head with exasperation. "We were quite powerless. You could have hit me over the head and easily killed me...or just walked by. I was in sleep stupor. It would have taken a shout from you even to arouse me!"

"You were that powerless?" Ziva asked shocked. "And how was I to know this?"

"If I had told you...would you have finished me off?"

Tears sprang to her eyes. "No! I'm not Darla! I'm not a killer...Why would they trust us like that?"

"Back then...I trusted even you."

"I...couldn't kill you...ever."

He sighed. "Then why Ziva, do you still wear your medallion?"

Startled, her hand went to the chain at her throat. She had not thought of the necklace since Darla had been sent away.

Joel's eyes were filled with reproach. "You betray our trust...and your employer has located us."

Ziva angrily yanked at the chain, forcefully breaking it free. "Here!" She held it toward him. "Why didn't you take it from me when I came in?"

Joel was silent. She dropped the medal on the console.

"Testing me, right? You know," Ziva said mournfully, tears filling her eyes. "I never wanted this assignment in the first place; I was given no alternative. I was just following orders."

His eyes narrowed in speculation. "We know, Ziva, but you do have a choice…"

"Ya, right! How would you like to be caught in the middle?"

"Just what have they offered you that could replace what you have here?"

"Oh, so you think you can offer me a future?" Her venomous spirit was back again. "You are dying Joel! What good would it do me to pair with you?"

He nodded soberly. "I'm beginning to see… From your point of view the outside world has more to offer than you think I do. We…my people and I, don't have a chance."

"That's the way it looks from here."

"Is that all that counts?" His penetrating gaze seemed to cut right to her core. "Okay. If I was entirely straight with you, would that make a difference?"

"Maybe."

"Very well. Ask me anything…that will ease your mind."

"Anything?"

He nodded.

It took her a minute, then she remembered something that had been egging the back of her mind.

"You never really answered my original question."

"Which question was that?"

"How did you learn the hard way? Just what did you do?"

Not expecting her to go there, he sucked in a shocked breath, as if she had punched him in the gut. But he was bound; he had promised, and she knew it.

After a long moment, he replied softly, "I betrayed my sister…"

"How?"

He sighed dejectedly. "Remember the other day, in that muddy field, Sonia gave me a second chance?"

Ziva thought back to the healing of the baby, and suddenly realized there was much more to the story.

"How did you betray her?" she asked quietly.

"The first time she asked me for support…she was dying after healing an injured guardian…one, by the way, who got hurt because I was prideful and refused her protection. I was in the way, and that meant, she couldn't protect him either. Anyway, when she asked to use my energy I would not give her my strength so she could heal back. At that moment, she could only use a 'Pure' male to balance herself. And I am…the only 'Pure' male."

He looked at her with soulful eyes, regret and shame so evident, Ziva wanted nothing more than to hug and comfort him.

"I ran," he continued woefully. "And my sister died that day...so did every other person in the species...except for me. And when alone, I...went mad."

Ziva stared at him unable to comprehend, unwilling to believe what he was saying. "But Sonia lives! You all are very much alive."

"That is because of Sky. He was the last to fall; the last energy and he might have survived alone, being half human, but he sacrificed his life for my sister. And in death they paired. This repaired her energy balance, ensuing she could restore them all. But because I rebelliously remained separate then...I slowly die now."

She shook her head to clear it, trying to wrap her mind around the complications of this species.

"I wanted to rule in her place." His voice had dropped to a hushed whisper. "I wanted my sister to die. I litterly hated her that much, for what she was, and couldn't help being. I intended to start the race over, but when Sonia's life force, for that small space of time, ceased to be evident...I could not exist on my own. I went into madness... mutilating myself. I began to go...'Opposite'!"

"What do you mean?" Ziva cried, horrified. "You can become 'Opposite'?"

"Only when we are separate. They are the...depraved side of our nature."

"Oh my God! Oh my God!" It was as if he had suddenly grown horns. "You can become 'Opposite'!"

Tears flooded his eyes. "I do not want to be 'Opposite'," he moaned in shame, pleading with her to understand, to not reject him. "That is why I must...always...why we all, must stay with Sonia. It is better to die...than turn 'Opposite'."

"Oh...Joel."

Ziva's anger could no longer sustain itself, not in the face of his honest and demeaning admission. He could have withheld some of the more damning circumstances, even refused to confess at all, as he had done previously, but he had not. How could she be less charitable?

"I still don't understand how all this is possible, but I have seen enough evidence to believe what you say happened..."

But he seemed not to hear her. Still caught in horrific memory, he sighed heavily.

"If Sky had been unwilling to give to the point of death that day..." Joel closed his eyes in humiliation; still, a tear slipped from beneath the lid. "He bought us a year. Now if we don't all successfully 'pair connect', my deed will have completed our destruction."

"You mean?" Her voice dropped to serious concern. "It's not just you...who will die?"

He shook his head. "Even one fails...all will die together. We are joint. But the burden of guilt weighs heaviest on my shoulders...and once again, I am the one... unsuccessful."

"You mean...all because, I...won't have you?" Ziva whispered.

"I do not intend to force you. It will not work if I do."

"Why can't you chose someone else?" she cried with anguish. "It's too much to ask of me. Surely, another would have you."

"I can not. It is now too late...I have 'pair connected' to you, and...the bond can not be severed."

Tossing her head angrily, tears spilling unchecked down her cheeks, Ziva desperately hated her weakness.

"I don't want you!" she moaned pathetically. "You can't have me!"

"I know." He turned back to the monitor. "You are as stubborn as I ever was. We would have made the perfect pair."

Sobbing brokenly, she watched him through water-blinded eyes, wondering why she was crying so hard when she didn't even want him.

****

Joel watched the screen stoically, doing his best to show no feeling, ignoring her tears. Inside, he was failing miserably. He set his jaw, so his inner core would harden.

It seemed ironic that he was spending his last days watching for danger to the human race. His species expended energy and the time left, to go to the aid of mankind, yet those like Darla would as easily terminate any one of them, simply because they were different.

Ziva had been a traitor in their midst, had already done her damage by exposing them, yet here he was, expecting her to somehow save him.

Yes. Perhaps, it is asking too much?

****

What am I going to do now? Ziva wondered.

One thing she knew, she couldn't be the blow that finished them.

But, what good will it do him, or them, if I pair with him? For the life of her, she couldn't see the reasoning. *Unless, it happened like with Sky and Sonia?*

But it inevitably boiled down to living with each other, however long that was.

"Why would you still want me, when you know that I'm a spy?" Ziva wiped away the last remaining wetness on her cheeks. "Do you realize what they want me to do?"

Without turning, with a faith in his tone she herself did not possess, he answered. "I know there is more to you than being a pawn for them..."

He sees potential in me?

"But...I've already done the damage..."

Joel finally turned to look at her; he could not hide the hope that had leap into his eyes.

"Do you really think the human race can best us?"

"When you are at you're weakest..."

"But suppose we were strong, each guardian paired and whole. Which side would you rather be on then?"

Ziva felt shame, could not meet his eyes. She looked away.

He's right! I have nothing, really, to go back to. There is no comparison! All the money in the world would never erase the guilt I'd carry, if I went against them.

"I'm afraid, Joel. So afraid."

"Come here." He opened his big arms wide, and resistance seemed futile. Their chairs rolled together. Somehow she was on his lap, those strong arms holding her close.

Until this moment, he had never touched her, except to hold her hand. She felt so protected, safe, as if their problems were so trivial.

She thrilled to the touch of his skin, and she felt he could conquer anything in the universe. Then the devil's advocate popped a suggestion into her mind.

What if he were to turn 'Opposite'? Where will that leave me?

She drew back from him, was once more on her own seat.

And the world went wrong again. It was like that first forbidden kiss with an unsavoury boyfriend of whom your parents disapproved. But again she felt remorse, began to reason against herself.

If he were a drunk or a drug addict trying to recover, would I cast him away like this? Is this any different?

I'm so afraid...Oh, Joel, I'm so afraid.

Ziva began to tremble violently.

And patiently, Joel waited.

"I don't know if I can do this, Joel," she whimpered.

"I know," he reassured softly. "One step at a time. Let me be your guide…I've been there before you. We'll help each other."

Ziva looked up and met his eyes. A shiver past through her.

What am I doing? she thought in panic.

Joel broke the contact first, looked away, turning back to his monitor. Ziva felt sudden abandonment.

Dutifully following his example, she drew in a sharp breath, and turned to her own screens…

As if nothing had happened between them.

What did happen between us? Ziva wondered.

Joel merely smiled to himself.

CHAPTER 42

When they assembled in the 'Jump Room' in answer to the summons, all human women knew they were going out again. This time, even Ziva was excited.

It had been weeks since their last excursion.

"Do you know where we are going?" Morgan asked of Angel.

"Somewhere in Greenland," Angel revealed. "The air force has been looking for a downed military plane. For some reason the humans can't see it with their radar, but we can."

"What was that you said?" demanded Morgan astounded. "Did I just hear you say 'the humans' as if you weren't one of them?"

"Oh, sorry," Angel apologized, laughing. "I'm so used to listening to Eric, I'm beginning to talk like I'm 'Aopato'."

Morgan grinned good-naturedly. "I know what you mean. I'm with Lance or Rhea so much I forget I have to talk aloud to the other women."

"You don't talk out aloud to the aliens?" Ziva asked with surprise. "How do you do it then?"

"Why, I just think in my head, and they read me. Lance taught me that right from the first."

"You let them read your mind?"

"Why not?" Morgan demanded. "Lance and I are 'pair connected'."

"Most of us do," Angel agreed. "It's so much easier."

"How many of the other women are 'pair connected'?" Ziva enquired.

"Why most everyone," Morgan admitted.

I'm the only one not 'pair connected'? Ziva realized. *Joel said he was to me.*

"How do you tell when you're 'pair connected'?"

Angel giggled. "You can feel him, and…you always know what he's doing."

"You can talk to him, even when he's somewhere else," Karine added from behind them.

"That's distracting them when they're on duty!" Ziva reproved.

"A little diversion never hurt anyone," laughed Morgan. "Especially if you're boringly watching the Sanctuary perimeter."

"Do you realize, you could get them killed?" Ziva scolded.

"You're one to talk," Angel chided. "You've got Joel so distracted he's missed things on the screens."

"No…I…I mean…" Ziva felt warmth creeping into her cheeks.

The other three giggled, highly amused at her expense.

"Time to 'pair connect' girl," Angel teased. "Try to feel him sometime, or… talk to him non-verbal."

"Anyway," Morgan broke in, effectively dismissing the subject. "Why are we going out?"

Angel willingly filled them in. "The downed aircraft is in an ice crack. Their locator beam can't be read because of electromagnetic disturbance from the erupting volcano. The ash cloud from that caused whiteout conditions; the pilot lost his horizon and they've crashed into this huge ice crater in the glacier…"

"Whoa. Back up, girl," Morgan interrupted. "Why don't they just let the humans go after them?"

"Oh," Ziva broken in. "Because they were way off course when it happened. The rescue search hasn't a clue where to look, and they'll all be dead by the time they get a fix on them."

"They are searching half the globe away," Angel added.

"So…we are their only chance at survival?"

"'Peers so."

By now, all the women had gathered around them, listening to the conversation.

Carmen asked, "Won't this expose the 'Aopato', reveal their presence to those who mean them harm?"

"They don't seem worried about that," Ziva marvelled. "Besides, if anyone knows how to protect themselves, it the 'Aopato'."

At just that moment, the alien women appeared en masse. Each hefty guardian came visible one by one along the walls. Only Sonia was still missing.

Suddenly, Ziva had the feeling Joel wanted her. She turned to go to him.

"I thought she wasn't 'pair connected'?" Morgan remarked behind her.

Angel answered her. "That couple has a funny way of relating."

"Well, you don't sense like that unless you are 'pair connected'!" Morgan declared astounded.

I'm not 'pair connected'! Ziva challenged in her mind. *He is to me! I just knew he was looking for me.*

There was an unexplained twinkle his eyes, when Joel met her in the middle. He was trying very hard not to show it though, and Ziva felt him tense to steel his exterior expression.

You heard what the other women said? Ziva observed. *Didn't you, guardian?*

He laughed. "Sometimes it happens by touch."

"What does?"

"'Pair connection'."

Ziva swallowed what felt like an obstruction in her throat; her belly suddenly felt hot. "Aw…"

"Never mind…you don't want me," he teased.

"Joel! Quit it!" she hissed.

"Anyway…" Joel held up the medallion Ziva had been wearing for so long. "We want you to wear this when we go out."

Ziva felt mortified. "Ah, Joel…don't be like this. Don't rub it in."

"It is to make certain your government knows you are with us when we execute this rescue, so the stories of the victims are collaborated."

"But...won't they track me back here again?"

"We want them to. They are already near our location. We are hoping to force a confrontation. Please wear it? Trust us."

Then he added as an extra incentive. "Sometimes, when we least expect it, two enemies may cancel each other out."

Ziva stared at him appalled.

They are hoping the humans will fight the 'Opposites' for them?

Joel grinned, and she realized he was doing it again. He was there in her thoughts.

Ziva frowned, then hissed at him. "Stay out of my mind!"

Joel turned away then, hiding a soft chuckle, but she heard it in his mind. She wanted to scold farther, but just then, Sonia appeared at the front.

Ziva moved back to be with the other human women, absently slipping the repaired medallion over her head as she went.

The room had gone silent with expectation.

"I see there is no need to explain," Sonia observed quietly. " So I'll simply proceed with instructions. Same partners as always, also the usual guardians for the healing pairs. We will not need outer sentries as these men would be the ones to fear, and the 'Opposites' would never follow us into the cold."

Sonia met the eyes of her security chief. "Djura you will be in charge of the expedition. I want to seem just another female. They don't need to know we are female ruled. It might bruise the collective male ego. Their military has a certain mindset."

Djura nodded.

Why let the men lead? Ziva wondered.

Following the human example, to present less threat, Joel answered in her mind.

Ziva frowned. *Why must he do that, when he knows I don't like it?*

Sonia continued. "Those we are rescuing today are hostile to us. Expect no quarter, even from the humans among us."

A collective gasp rose from the humans present; they had thought they had reached an understanding of trust.

Sonia ignored them. "These men have been trained to be suspicious. When they realize what we are they will not trust us. Therefore, we should not trust them. This is a potentially deadly position we place ourselves in, so guardians, your first priority is to guard your female. Secondly, those who are healer protectors, be especially vigilant. If the occasion merits, it use force." Sonia's voice lowered with the seriousness of the matter. "Remember, these are merely human males, plus they will be confused from injury and the temperature. Treat them gentle. Your defence beam need not be strong."

Ziva remembered the lethal effect of Lance's beam when he had rendered the deadly drone ineffective.

Is their power stronger than that?

"If these men use their weapons, your natural shield protects you, but...a stray bullet will harm the vulnerable healer, or...one of your human companions. Do not let the soldiers get to their weapons!"

Sonia finally addressed the human women. "You are also their early warning system. Should the male need to fire his beam, you will notice his shield dim around him moments before he releases the energy burst. For that second he is exposed. Should a gun be fired at him, or a knife finds its mark, he can be injured like any human. My hope, our hope, is that we have progressed beyond friendship, and you will warn or protect your male, if you are able."

She let that sink in; it put a whole new light on her previous statement. They were all placing their lives in their hands, but were prepared for betrayal, even expected it. They were dealing with emotional human nature with all its frailty. Bravery was not in everyone's character.

The 'Leader Female' went back to the lost soldiers. "These men have been without warmth for two days. Most will be suffering from some form of injury or weakness; they will all be disoriented and dehydrated. A few may still be trapped under wreckage. As with our earthquake victims, the guardians are responsible to free them. Your partner will provide blankets and nourishment. Girls, simply think of what you need. I will see it is supplied."

Sonia looked to her daughters. "Sky and I will refrain from operating as a healer pair. It is too risky under the circumstances. We will use only one healing pair: Jessica and Wade, with Jade and Ryan as back up. At all costs, protect them! And…we only heal the near death casualties. For the rest, use the human technique."

Sonia sought the eyes of the humans. "Any questions ladies?"

"Ah, my Lady," Chrystal ventured timidly. "Isn't it going to be rather cold on a glacier?"

"Most definitely," Sonia agreed. "And that matter does need to be addressed. As with the earthquake, we could simply issue each appropriate apparel, but you will still get hypothermia very quickly. Also at that elevation there is the likelihood of altitude sickness. You don't need either. Sky will explain what we have prepared."

The Navajo, Sonia's pair, moved up beside her, and continued the conversation without missing a beat. "Our species is equipped with the ability to adjust our surroundings to a comfortable level; we call it our outer shield. For example: if the weather is too hot or cold the area just around our bodies remains at an agreeable temperature to our need…which I might point out, would not be comfortable for you. When you touch us, we must carefully and quickly adjust so we don't harm you. Once 'pair connected' that problem is alleviated; spontaneous touch will no longer cause friction.

Is that why the males always ask first if they may touch you? Ziva wondered.

Sky continued. "Rather than have you follow so closely to your companion as to be included in his protection shield, I had Eric develop a headband for you which duplicates what we do naturally. Wearing this, you will not need heavy gear to keep you warm, and will be able to move about unencumbered. The band will also prevent altitude sickness."

Ziva felt the band circle her forehead, as if at Sky's admission, it became her possession. Unexpectedly, each of the other women found they were wearing like instruments, as well.

"For now you will notice little difference, but when we reach the site, they will adjust to your needs. Should any band be faulty, and you feel the cold, simply tell your partner through mind talk, and he will adjust it immediately. From now on you will wear them; it will save us adjusting the environment of Sanctuary to suit you."

Ziva hadn't realized they'd been doing that.

Sky stepped back to his place against the wall.

Sonia smiled. "Shall we go rescue some hostile broken soldiers then?"

"One question, my Lady," Djura interrupted. "Just to clarify…injured and bodies sent to their nearest base when we are finished?"

"Yes."

"And all memories erased?"

Sonia pondered a moment. "Considering, some humans already know about 'Opposites', let us test them. Permit three to retain full memory of their encounter with us, in vivid detail, so nothing is misconstrued. We make certain they see us clearly, and understand our intentions, so we are not mistakenly identified as 'Opposite'. So they realize there are two distinct breeds."

"And, which ones should sustain recall?"

"The leader, the pilot and…one private. Surely, when they debrief them, they will not dispute or twist the facts, if the source is from more than one rank."

Wouldn't bet on that, Ziva disagreed.

****

They jumped into freezing darkness, and none felt cold. It was snowing heavily.

Their 'Aopato' companions had not bothered with disguise.

A small fire burned to their left, and as a group they made for it. Sonia remained at the centre, Joel to one side, with Ziva between him and the 'Leader Female; May Lin on Sonia's opposite side, and Chi kept even with them. Up ahead, Djura lead; Karine behind, almost hidden in his shadow.

"Who goes there?" The sentry at the blaze stood to his feet, raised his semi-automatic threateningly, pointing in their direction. The group came to a standstill. Djura kept them just far enough away so the man could not make out fine detail.

"We are a rescue party," the guardian answered quietly, his tone one of tranquility for the mighty warrior.

"About time! Come into the light where I can see you."

"Lower your weapon, or we proceed no nearer."

"Sorry. Can't do that," the soldier returned evenly.

"Do you want help or not?"

"Identify your self! Or I shoot!"

Djura made no effort to comply. Instead, the man's weapon suddenly went spinning through the air, landing with a thud far out in the pitch blackness of the night.

A malicious curse split the arctic surroundings, and their foe went for the glock at his hip. Once in his hand, that became too hot to hold, and he dropped the weapon in the snow at his feet, clutching at his burning glove, trying desperately to remove it and ease the pain in his hand, all the while, his mouth spouting irate expletives.

When things quieted down, as if nothing serious had transpired, Djura calmly reasoned with the man. "I warned you, we can not help with weapons pointed at us." Abruptly, the pistol joined the rifle far out beyond the fire.

"What the devil? How the hell you do that?"

Djura stepped into his line of sight: a giant near eight feet tall, with the powerful build of a wrestler, dressed only in casual jeans and a white tank top, his skin a glowing caramel against the brilliance of the garment. The only other evidence he was nonhuman were his eyes, which was hardly visible as he was backlit by darkness, and of course, the gold band around his forehead. His sheer size was enough to cause the soldier to step back, rethinking his position.

He raised his hands in the position of surrender.

"Do you need help?" Djura asked again.

"What are you? Doesn't the cold effect you?"

Djura answered with a question of his own. "Where is your superior?"

"I'm in charge...the captain's...indisposed," the man returned sullenly. "What are you?" he repeated.

"Does it matter?" Djura enquired indulgently. "We have come to your aid."

He moved past the man, deliberately turning his back. The rest of the group knew to remain in the shadows where they were.

His deferent attitude having been ignored, the soldier dropped his hands. Deciding it was in his best interest to trust, he turned to follow. "Cap's trapped under some wreckage; most of the guys are too hurt to lift the piece off..."

Djura entered the sheered off tail section, stood taking in the scene: the injured men huddled together, some lying down, all shivering. He whirled on the soldier sentry.

"We will help you, but...under our conditions." He stared coldly down at the man.

"Guess we can't be choosy right now," the human grumbled.

"We have healers with us." Djura gave the thought command. "Come." And the rest of his party entered the confines of the plane.

"Two dead," Djura stated to Sky. "Another near death; the captain trapped under wreckage over there." He inclined his head toward the far corner. Sky nodded.

"What the hell are you guys?" the soldier asked for the third time, at last seeing the party in better light.

"If it will ease your mind," Djura finally revealed. "We are from away; not of your kind; nonhuman. Now, be quiet and let us work."

****

All went smoothly until near the end. Most of the fifty human men were now bandaged, legs or arms in splints; their captain had been freed and administered to. As a group they were huddled under blankets together, drinking coffee.

A soldier lying on his side, suddenly reached out and grabbed May Lin as she bent to him pulling up his blanket. It startled her; she had thought him sleeping.

One swift movement, and he had her in a choke hold.

Chi whirled. For a second, he had dropped his guard as he couched beside the injured captain, ministering to him.

May Lin's fear made Chi narrow his eyes in anger. He stood to his full height towering over the man.

"Come closer," warned the aggressor. "And she buys it." He held a knife at May Lin's chest. "Back off!" he hissed again. "Nobody takes me prisoner."

Behind him, Joel asked quietly, "What gave you the idea you were prisoners? Have we harmed you?"

Their females close beside them, the other guardians moved up silently into a circle about the injured men.

"I don't know what you creeps did to me, but I'm not no experiment."

"You were near death, sir," Sonia remarked, astounded. "We made you well... and for this, you threaten us?"

"This chink dies, any one of you comes closer!"

May Lin trembled visibly. Ziva expected the Oriental senior to succumb to a heart attack at any moment, if they did not stop the stand off shortly.

Chi's vertical slit widened; his imaged dimmed. And Ziva knew he was about to strike.

Karine stepped away from her partner's side, as if she sensed her man intended to do the same. Djura's imaged dimmed.

Almost simultaneously, two beams of blue light shot toward the antagonist. Chi's beam hit dead centre in the forehead of the man who held the knife. In reflex, the hand dropped, point down, toward May Lin's breast. The second beam, from Djura, melted the weapon. The assailant rolled away, limp.

That's when, from the corner of her eye, Ziva saw the movement. A second soldier pulled a glock from beneath him, where he had hidden it.

"Look out!" Ziva yelled instinctively, not considering the repercussions. "He's got a gun!"

The pistol was aimed toward Djura, who's image had dimmed for a second warning beam, but he had not time to turn toward the threat. Without hesitation, Karine stepped between the weapon and her male.

"No Karine!" Sonia quickly warned. "They kill you, he also dies!"

It all seemed happening in slow motion. Rapid thoughts went through Ziva's mind: *Karine dies; Djura dies; the whole species goes with it...Joel dies!*

If someone doesn't get that gun...

As Karine had done before her, Ziva moved to intercept. Fortunately for her, Joel standing behind her was larger and taller than she. As she moved, his imaged dimmed. At the same time, Djura swivelled.

The soldier with the weapon, sensing danger from behind, turned toward Ziva. He fired.

A red-hot beam stopped the bullet in midair, dissolving it. Joel's aim was perfect.

Djura's beam melted the gun, and the errant soldier yelped in pain.

The ensuing silence was pregnant with the shock of the soldiers. The anger of the 'Aopato' was palpable; you could feel it emanating from them.

"We help you, heal you, and this is what you do!" Sonia hissed. "Enough of this!"

She turned toward the captain, her purple eyes clearly visible; no longer hiding.

"We expected you could be a potential enemy, and now it is obvious, you are!"

Sonia turned to her pair. "Are they all accounted for?"

Sky nodded. "These are all the living. The two dead are back farther in the tail section."

Sonia turned to the soldier from the fire. "Tell your superiors, we came to rescue when you had no hope of survival. We could have left you here to die! But we did not! And...we would not have done you any harm. You chose to use weapons against us!" She let that sink in a moment. "The unconscious man will awaken with a headache, and no memory of what transpired here. See that you report truthfully."

The human soldiers abruptly vanished.

"Chi," Sonia asked turning to the Oriental male. "How is May Lin?"

"She...still frightened," he admitted, obviously shaken. His arm held his frail partner securely, as he knelt at her side. "It...my fault. I look away, but...she face with honour."

May Lin looked up at him, as if he'd given her the greatest gift imaginable.

"Jade." Sonia looked to her daughter. "She needs physical balance. The heart rate is too rapid."

Jade knelt down and took May Lin by the hand. After a moment, Jade asked, "Feeling better?" The senior nodded.

"Ladies," Sonia ordered. "Centre, please."

The human women obediently flocked to the middle, and instantly, they were back at Sanctuary.

CHAPTER 43

Recreation had always released their pent up frustrations, so the 'Aopato' decided to spend the next day outside. Sanctuary and Technical Centre were placed on 'Keeper' control, so everyone might have the day off.

No matter the age, they all came to take part in a baseball game; whether to play or cheer the others on, they each had a part.

The field lay beside the great waterfall, only yards from the pond beneath it. Though the day itself was beautiful, it actually made no difference because, those playing and those watching, each now constantly wore their new environmental-controlling headbands everywhere they went.

Sonia sat on the sidelines between her two human companions May Lin and Karine. Chi and Djura stood serving double sentry duty, on either end of the bench, like two book ends, because their 'Leader Female' was out in the open.

Those watching were especially excited over the match, yet unquestionably torn as to which side to cheer for. The teams were each a mixture of human and 'Aopato', both male and female, but they had divided by age, oldest against the youngest.

Each guardian had chosen his favoured female to help him best the opposing team. Sky was the only one without such a partner, but he had agreed to pitch for both sides.

Lance lead the older team consisting of Morgan, Ryan and Jade, Ihor and Rhea, Eric and Angel,

Marcel and Carmen, and Joel with Ziva, making it a total of twelve.

The younger generation, captained by Zane, was composed of Chantel who, considering she could walk again, found thorough enjoyment in the phenomenal speed with which she could run bases. They also had Kara and Ram, Nadia and Chad, Jessica and Wade, Shawn and Chrystal, and last but not least, Tyler with Jenna. All were young, fit and competent players.

It seemed an unfair advantage, as the older human players were definitely less agile. The 'Aopato' players also had added benefit, so it was agreed to handicap those players to make things more equal. The nonhumans would take on their former aged human form, with all its fragilities and limitations.

Had any outsider come upon the game, it would appear, save for those sitting at the sidelines, this was merely a game of elderly humans making a feeble attempt to best their younger offspring. To say it was amusing was an understatement.

The game had already reached the third inning, with Tyler on second, when Shawn came to bat. He hit a punt, and just when it appeared the ball was heading to the sidelines, it gained altitude and took off for the outfield.

"Fowl!" Djura yelled angrily, making Karine jump with his sudden furious outburst. She looked up at him in shock; surprised he was so involved in such a trivial game.

May Lin was also amazed, when a second later, the normally complacent Chi indignantly bellowed, "He used his powers!"

Shawn made for first base; Tyler for third.

"Time!" called Sonia, as the obedient referee.

The two human women almost laughed at how serious everyone had become. It was as if a crime with a lethal weapon had been committed. As far as the 'Aopato' were concerned, it had.

Every player on the diamond froze.

Quite by accident, the human companions were now introduced into the internal justice system of the 'Aopato': the discipline of the young, and how seriously viewed was honour in the breaking of a promise. What would have normally been a silent exchange became public, because each of the species, to ensure audible communication, had activated their headband for the game.

"Sky, in your opinion, was that ball normal?" inquired Sonia.

Sky frowned, and turned to the teenager in the guise of a human of twenty-seven.

"Shawn? Did you use your powers?"

Shawn looked sheepish, then dropped his gaze to his toes in shame. "Aww... I did it without thinking!" he declared in self-rebuke. "Old habits die hard, grandpa."

Unsympathetic, Sonia broke in. "Games are for physical release, you know that!" she scolded. "When powers are used to manipulate the outcome, that is cheating!"

Shawn raise unhappy eyes. "Ah, grandma, I know...I'm sorry."

Sonia softened. "You must choose your punishment. That's the rule."

Shawn gave a visual shudder. "Ah…geepers," he moaned. "Before all these females?"

"Was your offence not in public?"

"Ahh…I guess so. Punishment to suit the crime. I deserve that…" Shawn sighed; stood thinking a moment. "I guess the thing that would bother me most today…Jessica has made my favourite…I'll give up dessert tonight."

Shawn loved sweets, and grandmother knew this. Also, on the other hand, he could always indulge the next day.

"Only for this one time?" she prompted.

"Ah gran…" he pleaded, near to tears. Then realizing he had a moral responsibility to designate a correction that was undeniably uncomfortable, he steeled himself, and agreed with a nod. "I will miss two days in a row."

"So it will stand," Sonia allowed. "You are on the honour system. No one will be enforcing your sentence."

"I know, grandma. I will take punishment as I've promised."

"And now," Sonia said quietly, dismissing that matter. "What of the second transgression?"

Silence fell over the ball field.

Djura frowned. "I missed that one."

Shawn held up his hands palms outward, as if to ward off the anger of the group.

"I only moved the ball!" he defended hastily.

All eyes moved as one to the only other player on the base.

"Tyler?" Sonia rebuked softly. "Still hiding your infractions behind your brother's, and hoping not to be noticed?"

"I was caught inches away from the base when you yelled 'time'," the second brother excused.

"Oh, goodness!" Rhea exclaimed indignantly. "Both my sons cutting up at the same time. Haven't you learned anything? I know I taught you better, but it seems when you transformed back to human likeness, your old bad habits resurfaced. You are not dormant!"

Both boys dutifully studied the ground in their shame.

"Well, Tyler," Sonia demanded. "Do I reveal what you did, or will you admit to your offence on your own?"

"I will own up," agreed Tyler. "I manipulated the base until it was under my foot."

"Man!" Zane exclaimed with exasperation. "Twice powers used! That means we forfeit the game! The elders win! You bum!"

"Enough, Zane!" Sonia admonish. "Be a good sportsman!"

"Ah, yeah. I know." Zane sighed. "It's only a game."

"We will deal with one matter at a time," Sonia offered. "So, Tyler," she reasoned. "That leaves your punishment. What is it to be?"

"If I were still dormant!" Rhea exploded. "I'd do you a paddle!"

Kara giggled. "That would be funny, Unca Tyler. A big guy like you."

The human women were finding it hard to keep a straight face. Rhea glared at them, then at her son, who dropped his eyes, trying unsuccessfully to hide the smile that played at his lips. There was no doubt in anyone's mind that Rhea was displeased.

"Remember," Sonia cautioned. "Violence is not the answer."

Rhea sobered. "You are soo fortunate your grandmother is 'Leader Female' and not I," she said with narrowed eyes, then stepped back conceding to her mother's resolution.

"What shall it be, Tyler?" Sonia repeated.

The gravity of the situation came back into the young male's face. "When I used my powers, it was willingly. Not a mistake! Therefore I am more guilty than Shawn. I should have a harsher punishment…"

His human 'pair connect', Jenna, appeared shocked by this admission. But Tyler, with past training in law enforcement, was no less hard on himself than another. He stood suddenly straighter with the resolve. "My greatest hurt at this moment…would be to be separated from Jenna." He dropped his eyes, so as not to see her reaction; continued. "But that would harm her as well, and she has done nothing…is innocent of wrong doing." He lifted pleading eyes to his grandmother for mercy. "I don't know what to say," he implored. "I appeal to the guardians for judgement."

Sonia nodded. "Djura, what do the warriors suggest?"

For a moment silence reign, as if the former were debating soundlessly together. At last the security chief spoke in a quiet voice filled with forgiveness.

"We recommend, he muck out the pig barns...manually...twice."

"Oh! Yuck!" Tyler exploded in disgust. Then once more, he squared his shoulders. "I accept my punishment."

But Djura wasn't finished. "Because we as guardians have failed to mentor you properly, we will join you."

A gasp of disbelief went up from the humans, but Sonia seemed unfazed.

"As this would double Shawn's punishment, he is excluded."

"Grandma...I wish to be included," Shawn contradicted hastily.

Sonia waited a moment, but no one else had an objection.

"Then Shawn's original punishment is rescinded."

A common nod of approval came from the males.

"Is this to your satisfaction, Rhea?"

"Most fair, my Lady," Sonia's daughter agreed.

"Sorry, mother." As one, Shawn and Tyler turned remorsefully to Rhea. "We have shamed you."

"I've already forgotten it," Rhea gently absolved.

"Well," Sonia sighed in relief. "That leaves just one matter. Chi, what was the game score when we got so rudely sidetracked?"

"The 'youngers' were winning by one point," the Oriental admitted.

"Very well," Sonia decided. "What say we call it a tie, and go enjoy that lunch Jessica has prepared?"

That judgement seemed the fairest of all to everyone on the field, and as each jumped to the lunchroom with their guardian partner, many were marvelling at the exemplary example the 'Aopato' had just displayed.

CHAPTER 44

When they entered the lunchroom, Ziva felt a strong sense of foreboding.

Is it just the memory of what happened here the last time we were gathered together? Or have I acquired the 'Aopato' sixth sense? The air seems pregnant with apprehension.

Joel slipped his arm about her shoulders, and she looked up with a frown. Usually, he still asked if he could touch before doing such a thing.

Why are you touching with familiarity in public?

"What's wrong Joel?" she asked bluntly.

It seemed as if after the pleasant game, they had all been doused in cold water.

"We are each feeling the warning as you do," he confessed. "Sonia has allowed us to feel what she senses. Something not good is about to happen."

"Oh, there's not another drone in the room, is there?" Ziva cringed at the thought.

"I don't think it's that," he mused quietly. "Djura has been most vigilant since the last one slipped in, but...we were only on 'Keeper'. They can be blinded..."

Ziva shivered.

As if he'd been given a silent command, Joel removed his arm. "I dare not touch you from now on. I don't want you to be hurt also. Go to the table; I will bring the food."

He moved to join the other males, most of which had made the same suggestion to their partners. Even the paired 'Aopato' were being cautious, leaving their females behind as they went for nourishment.

The platters of fruit, bread, cheese and meat appeared on the counter. By this time, each guardian knew what pleased the palette of his chosen, and the women trusted to their choices.

Near the entrance to the lunchroom, Sonia and the other 'Aopato' women remained clustered in a group, as if reluctant to join the humans.

Ziva took a seat near the back, against the wall. She and Karine both took such seats. They had this thing about facing room centre, as if guarding their backs was important, but Ziva suspected Karine was afraid someone might sneak up behind her.

Ziva was thinking about that, why Karine might be afraid when Djura wasn't with her, when suddenly Ziva realized, every guardian had vanished from the room.

Did Sonia send them out to scout the valley?

Ziva tried to feel Joel, but the connection was gone. There was that sudden emptiness, like he had gone to sleep.

Where is he? Are the males deliberately hiding their whereabouts, so the enemy won't know they are here?

The other human women were looking lost as well, as if they had been disconnected from their guardian companions.

Something is very wrong here.

The humans sought the 'Aopato' females with a questioning gaze. Surely, Sonia had an answer.

Sonia was tensed, as if with sudden pain, but her look was not like when she had a vision. No, this ache seemed more in the physical, then of the mind. Now that she noted them, Ziva had the distinct feeling the females about Sonia also felt disconnected from the males. They all had that same look as just before Sonia went into instant slumber: strained, lost, as if each one had gone separate, and had no clue what to do as a being apart. The fear of the loss of protection flooded across their faces.

Panic spread to Ziva as well. *Where are the guardians?*

Suddenly, the 'Aopato' females joined hands.

Oh, Ziva knew now there was definitely something wrong! Joel had explained to her, this was how the females balanced each other when the males were unable to help them. It usually gave them extra power and energy. But it didn't seem to be working this time.

This is not good!

When it finally happened, it was like every 'Aopato' female was a rag doll. Simultaneously, still joined by their hands, all sank to the floor, as if the air had gone out of their bodies.

Ziva knew they must be alive; they were still visible.

A unified gasp escaped the humans, and many, without thinking, rose to their feet to go to the aid of the beings.

Rising herself, Karine warned: "Don't touch them. Remember, if we touch we might kill them all."

Near beside herself with anguish, Chrystal began to cry softly. "Then what can we do?"

"They are not dead," Ziva declared brusquely. "We wouldn't see them if they were."

"That's right,' agreed Karine. "But Djura once went invisible when his energy was too low. Not seeing them doesn't mean they're dead."

Ziva began to tremble in fear.

Where are the guardians? Are they...invisible?

Angel voiced the thought from a different perspective. "Are the males still in the room then?"

"I can't feel Marcel," wailed Carmen in alarm. "It's like he's asleep, but...he seems hurting."

And then as they watched, the 'Aopato' females just blinked out. The lunch room seemed suddenly empty, except for nine humans.

Next they were abruptly plunged into darkness. Many of the younger women began to cry softly.

****

Neil and his fellow soldiers watched silently from the bushes. He couldn't understand the language, for they seemed to converse in hisses and guttural noise that made no sense. But he had seen enough to make his hair stand on end.

These creatures could shape-shift and teleport with the aid of belts they wore. At one point, they had taken on human likeness to get closer to the barrier, but they seemed to prefer this reptilian form rather than the smaller man shape.

With a laser beam shot from the glove it wore, one of the reptiles fired at a point on the edge of the shimmering barrier shield. A section vanished, disclosing a view of a fertile valley beyond. Then four of the creatures wheeled a huge laser gun across.

No telling what they can do to mankind with that thing, Neil surmised. *We need to destroy that weapon.*

His superior must have had the same thought, for he made motions for the men to follow inside. The unit moved cautiously, automatic rifles pointed and ready, going one at a time, the one behind watching out for his comrade, covering his back, until all were on the other side. They gathered again in a group, behind low-lying bushes, on their bellies, ready for anything.

Is this the enemy's hidden stronghold? Neil wondered. *But then, why don't they put the barrier back up?*

The aliens were busy with the huge gun, shifting the trajectory of its aim. They seemed unaware of the humans on their trail.

They aren't very observant.

For some reason, the reptiles were aiming the enormous weapon toward a distant waterfall, up high above it at the cliffs. They moved dials and flipped switches adjusting the instrument until it began to give off a high oscillating hum.

Is it some sort of protection so they can't be attacked from above?

Through the downed barrier section, other reptilian soldiers began pouring in. They obviously had been hiding in the big barn-like structure on the outside of the barricade.

The humans pressed closer to the ground, doing their level best to gain invisibility, but the aliens passed by them, completely unaware, intent on something they considered much more of a threat than tiny little men.

When the beings were all gone, the commander motioned one of his men to come to his side. Though the conversation was low, Neil heard every word.

"The weapon has been left unguarded."

The other soldier nodded. "Careless of them, sir," he agreed, grinning.

"The rest of us are going to follow them." The commander's eyes narrowed in warning, as he spoke in an undertone. "See they can never use that thing again."

"Yes, sir!" the private hissed in return.

As Neil followed after the others, the man began to unpack his C4.

****

"What could have caused this?" Morgan worried. "They've never all gone down together like this before. At least some or one remained conscious."

Angel looked to Ziva in the dim light of the kitchens. Something like a back-up generator had kicked in after a few minutes, giving them a muted light to see by.

"It's the weapon!" Angel exclaimed in horror. "The 'Opposites' have perfected that energy-drain thing. It's siphoned away their life force. That's the only thing that could do this."

"Even if we could see them," Ziva reasoned. "I doubt it would be good to touch them."

Angel shook her head in consternation. "Sonia knew about the weapon. They examined the prototype. I can't see her not preparing for this moment. Do you suppose she might have left orders with the 'Keepers'?"

"Joel mentioned just before this happened," Ziva remembered. " That the 'Keepers' can be blinded."

"Oh, wonderful!" Morgan muttered. "Are we supposed to do something then? If the 'Keepers' are unreliable, is it up to us?"

Ziva just shrugged. How was she to know? She'd been mostly kept out of the loop until just recently.

"What's the main 'Keeper' called? Maybe it knows?"

"'Keeper Sentry'," Karine supplied. "I once heard Djura address it."

"Okay," Angel decided. "Let's try that. 'Keeper Sentry' if you're present, will you answer me? This is an emergency."

A hallow mechanical voice spoke, as the flashing orb became visible. "I may answer only to Karine, if none of my makers are available. It is then my function to communicate instructions to her."

Karine appeared hesitant.

"That makes sense, Karine," Angel reassured. "Djura was security head, and you are his 'pair connect'. And... Sonia trusted you."

"Djura is head of security! Not was!" Karine corrected, fighting tears. "He is not dead!"

"I know that," Angel reassured calmly. "But it's obvious he's incapacitated. The machine will take your orders..."

"What should I ask it?" Karine whispered hesitantly.

Ziva wasn't as patient. "Get your head on straight, girl!" she hissed. "Ask it what we do? Think! Or they will all be dead."

But Karine chose to find solutions in her own way; wanted answers to her own questions first. Her eyes huge with dread and uncertainty, she addressed the mechanical. "'Keeper Sentry', where are the guardians?"

Good first question, Ziva thought admiringly.

"They are all in this room."

"Then, they are down...invisible?"

"Yes."

"Has Sonia programmed you with an answer to this dilemma? Can we help them?"

"I have answers. At present I am holding perimeter. We guard and defend; there are intruders."

"But...will the guardians wake up?"

"That is an unknown."

The stupid thing is sidetracking her, Ziva realized.

"There must be a key to getting the information we need," she whispered.

The other women nodded agreement.

"Is there something we can do to help the males recover?" Karine asked.

"Sonia will bring them back."

"How do we wake Sonia?"

"Joel is the key."

"What?" Ziva enquired in surprise. "Why Joel?"

But the machine refused to answer her.

Ziva thought for a moment. *Maybe at some point he gave me a clue?*

"Joel is the only other 'Pure'!" she exclaimed. And then suddenly, she knew exactly what the 'Aopato' wanted. "Oh, no way!" she exploded vehemently. "No way!"

All along they had it planned! My life for theirs!

She could hear Joel saying it, warning: 'Don't do things the hard way.'

And his way, this way, isn't hard? For whom? I will end up dead!

Karine was asking another question.

"Can we wake Sonia?"

"Humans are unable."

"Please. Tell me! What must be done?"

"Sonia is dieing. Nothing can be done."

"That means they are all dieing!" Karine cried desperately. "Tell us what to do?" she pleaded. "I'll give my life, if that's what it takes."

Not me! Ziva thought rebelliously. *How dare they put me in that position!*

But, Karine's altruistic compliance seemed to be the lock-key to the 'Keeper's' knowledge.

"You would sacrifice your life for the one Djura?" clarified the mechanical.

"If that's what is needed," Karine declared stoically. "Just tell me what to do, and how."

She's either stupid...or gone mad!

"It is essential, the guardian 'Pure' must receive the final essence...his female must do it last."

Ziva had no intention of doing that!

"You brainless, insensitive machine!" screamed Ziva in horror. "There must be another way!"

Karine turned to stare at her. "You know what must be done?"

"Yeah, I know!" Ziva hissed venomously. "My life for theirs! I'm the spy in your midst!"

"That is inaccurate, female," the machine interrupted. "All humans must give of their essence, you merely need to go last."

"I won't do this! I won't!" Ziva cried forcefully. "I know the sacrifice! Joel told me! Sky had to give his life!" Tears welled in her eyes, as she continued brokenly. "Sky is only half human...she could bring him back..."

"What on Earth are you talking about?" asked Karine, puzzled.

"The last time this happened..." Impervious, obdurate Ziva was sobbing. "The last time they all died like this...Sky brought them back, restored the energy balance by ...by giving his life to Sonia. That's how they became 'paired'!"

"Holy…" gasped Morgan. "That's the reason they were 'pair connected'?"

"That's how you can save their lives," Ziva moaned. "But, we are fully human…"

But the others did not hear her forewarning; they only saw the benefit toward the ones they loved.

"They trust we love them enough to give our last breath…" Carmen marvelled. "So we can all live."

"But will we?" Ziva reasoned.

The women went silent, each weighing the cost.

"Chi has given me untold joy," May Lin stated. "If this doesn't work, I have lived a long life, and if it does, I will gain much. It is not too much to ask."

With resolve, Karine spun toward the 'Keeper'. "How is this done?"

But Ziva had to remind them one more time. "We are human…"

"Sky lived," argued Angel. "Sonia must have a way!"

"We are human!" Ziva repeated. "Not any part 'Aopato'! How? How can she bring us back?"

"She has a way…if anyone knows how, it would be Sonia," Karine decided. "And she has always said, the Almighty works behind the scenes."

Ziva thought about that. *Am I ready to put faith in an unseen higher power?*

And what of Joel? Does he believe this will work?

Ziva knew the answer to that. She shook her head dejectedly. "I don't think I can do this."

"Yes, you can," Angel reassured. "The 'Aopato' have always had faith that you'll come through in the end."

"If you do not trust them…trust their Almighty Creator," suggested May Lin.

And therein lay the problem. *Is there really a Creator? Does it orchestrate our paths? Was that the 'Aopato's' final hope? Or are we all just fools with a crutch?*

"How is this done?" Karine demanded a second time of the 'Keeper'.

This time they all waited with bated breath for the answer.

"Each must willingly give its life energy to its chosen male. This will result in a bond, which then makes you his pair. The female Ziva is to be last to do this."

"And how is this energy given?"

"By touch and will."

May Lin was first to move. "I find my male by scent," she declared boldly.

"All must do it," the 'Keeper' cautioned. "None may hold back, or this will not work."

Ziva went cold. *If I don't do it, I'll be murdering them all!*

Oh, Joel, why ever would you pick a coward like me? I don't think I have the courage to do this.

May Lin had found Chi. She eased to her knees beside the invisible form. When she reached out and touched him, there was a spark of static, and the

Oriental fell against the counter wall, as if someone had struck her.

Karine walked along the barrier searching. Minutes later, she too dropped to her knees. She touched, and with a sigh, slid softly to the floor.

Morgan bravely went next, followed by Carmen, then Chantel. One by one, each of the women found their beloved, touched, and went to oblivion. Everyone, seemed to die, there before the Jewish woman's very eyes.

Ziva sobbed quietly.

Now that its dastardly duty had been performed, the 'Keeper' had gone to invisibility once more.

Ziva stood for long moments, debating. She seemed undeniably alone; the room as silent as a tomb.

And suddenly she heard them: the staccato rapid-fire of automatic weapons in the distance; the yells of frantic human men, and screams of violent death. They and the 'Opposites' were battling it out not far away.

Ziva turned, and fled toward the sounds.

CHAPTER 45

As she escaped the lunchroom, her thoughts were not on freedom. Ziva realized, if any of the combatants found the fallen behind her, they could easily touch one of the women, or stumble over an invisible 'Aopato'; then these lives would be as easily lost, as if she herself had failed to do her part, and had left them to die.

It was one thing to refuse to connect to Joel, but to weigh the fact the other women had given their all, perhaps for nothing, did not sit well with Ziva. She had both brought about this means of destruction, the possible annihilation of all as they recovered, and had the means to protect them, not to mention she was still the missing trigger to their revitalization. She knew, if she left things as they were, she could never live with the guilt.

I can undo what I began. I have to undo it! Ziva reasoned. *I have to convince the advancing men that the place is empty, keep them from coming into the kitchens...then they won't find them. We will have time to recover...*

She caught herself as she realized, like Angel, she was now thinking as if she was no longer human.

What will it be like to be 'Aopato'? To be Joel's pair?

Why did I wait so long? Will it be too late, if there's a delay?

Now that she was away from the scene behind, she wanted nothing more than to be whole with Joel. Her life meant nothing away from here.

Maybe, I should just turn around and do what they asked of me?

Yet her feet carried her around the corner, and then it was too late.

At the other end a soldier in camouflage gear turned into the tunnel up ahead. In one hand he held a tracker, the other a glock.

Ziva suddenly remembered the medallion around her neck. Joel had insisted she keep wearing it.

Too late, was her last rational thought.

"So, there you are," hissed Neil. "I've been tracking you since I came into this place."

I should have destroyed that stupid medallion when I had the chance. If I'd taken it off, they would never have gotten this far.

Her hand went to her throat, ripping away the chain in one violent wrench. Ziva tossed it to the stone floor, and ground it under her heel.

"I never wanted this stupid assignment!" she yelled furiously. "Tell your superiors they were wrong. These creatures aren't the terrorists they think. They've done nothing but help the human race."

Neil chortled. "They really have you brainwashed, don't they? If you come with me quietly, we'll counteract the drugs in your system. We'll see you don't remember a thing."

"They never drugged me!" Ziva defended forcefully. "And I'd like to keep my memories; I'd rather stay here. You go back where you came from, and leave them alone."

"You've got to be kidding me!" Neil exclaimed in amazement. "You prefer living with these lizards?"

"There are two species! The lizard beings are malevolent, the 'Opposite' to the benevolent race, and you are helping them destroy the 'Aopato'. The 'Opposites' invaded their stronghold, the 'Aopato' Sanctuary. They want to annihilate the compassionate individuals. These are the good guys!"

"Really?" Neil laughed. "I don't see any good guys; only one kind. And why should I listen to you, a traitor? They reported what you did on the glacier, you know. You betrayed your own kind!"

Ziva had no argument with that, neither about the missing visual presence of the 'Aopato', nor that she had betrayed the men in the artic. She had gone for the gun, but it had been to save lives. He would never believe that, she knew, even if she tried to explain.

Neil dropped the tracking device to the stone floor, its rattle resounding through the empty tunnel. In one swift motion, he switched the glock to his right hand.

"I have my orders," he warned. "If you refuse to come with me…"

At those words, Ziva realized she was running out of time.

"If you want to see the others…" Ziva made an attempt to stall him. "They'd go outside…"

It wasn't really a lie; the 'Aopato' would hide in the sun…if they'd been able right now.

"So…" His eyes narrowed speculatively. "You were going to meet them?"

Ziva made no reply. If there was one thing she had learned from Joel, it was how to avoid giving the wrong answer.

"Why would they go outside?"

"Because they can't be seen in the light."

He laughed sarcastically. "Yeah, right! You expect me to believe that? We see them just fine. My platoon has already eliminated most of them, and…we've blown up that big laser gun of theirs, in case you're interested."

Good! Ziva thought. *At least that is one threat eliminated. So, Joel's idea is working.*

She sighed in relief.

But Neil mistook her delight for regret. "That doesn't get you off the hook, even though we've quelled this threat. You're still an agent gone rogue…and I have orders."

Ziva thought of Morgan's words: 'the perks are never worth your life', she had said. It seemed to Ziva, her life would be forfeited either way.

But if I had my choice, I'd rather lose it to Joel.

Ziva turned her back to walk away. It was no use running; he would only fire sooner.

Neil was like Darla; he'd sold his soul to the highest bidder. He was prejudiced, even having evidence to the contrary. He had closed his mind to any sort of reason, because this was the way he wanted it. Being an agent who obeyed blindly without an ounce of compassion, a seasoned veteran who could kill without qualms, he would actually enjoy executing her.

As she walked away, she expected the shot, waited for it, yet was unprepared when it came. Nor did she anticipate the point of impact.

The first bullet blew away her right kneecap.

A scream escaped her, as she was slammed against the stone wall behind. Agony ignited, bolted up her thigh, and her leg gave way beneath her. Ziva went sliding down the rigid barrier, moaning. Then mercifully, her leg went numb.

"That is so you can't run from me, traitor," Neil spat out coldly. "This is what we do to spies that turn. Their death is slow and painful."

A few steps, and he was standing over her, the gun aimed at her head.

Tears sprang to her eyes. Her greatest regret was, this death would have no benefit to Joel.

Oh, God! If there is a maker, help me, please?

"I could just plug a hole through that empty brain of yours, but I think it would serve a better purpose if I let you watch your own life ebb away." He dropped the barrel a few inches, pointing at her belly. "One in the gut for good measure…"

He fired at close range, from the hip, without a glimmer of sympathy in his eyes. The second blow impacted with her abdomen, but Ziva never felt a thing. The numbness from her knee had spread up, and frozen all sensation.

Neil lifted the weapon a little higher. "And another in the lung, so you can't breath…or call out."

Once again, he fired callously, his eyes hard as cold steel.

This time Ziva did feel it; the slug penetrating just above her right breast; the hot pain of intrusion, the air escaping in a sudden explosive rush.

Neil stood over her, watching, enjoying, as she began to struggle for breath. He seemed to observe her with a morbid curiosity, as her garment became soiled with her own red blood, and the crimson pool spread across the granite floor beneath her.

To Ziva, it all felt disconnected, like watching herself in a dream.

Even when an 'Opposite' appeared out of nowhere behind Neil, it took a minute to register. She raised her eyes, tried to warn him, but he was laughing at her effort, until he felt the being standing behind.

Neil spun toward it, firing rapidly as he turned. The creature got off one red laser beam of light from its gloved hand, just as the soldier's shot found its mark in its temple. Neil disintegrated, was no more…and time stood still.

The 'Opposite' appeared about to topple forward across Ziva, but at the last moment, the creature pressed a button at its belt; a reflex of a dieing already brain-dead entity, but never-the-less effective. It also vanished, like a spirit from a vision.

Ziva had no thought as to where it went, nor was she concerned there might be others like it near by. The marble hall about her began to waver and blur at the edges; air proved too difficult to pull in, then near impossible. Gagging on blood that filled her mouth, gasping for life with every movement, Ziva struggled to rise. Yet fate was against her, and the world, as she knew it faded to oblivion.

****

Ziva moaned, opened her eyes, breathing roughly. She heard yelling in the distance, sounds of the battle still raging. Then the excruciating pain hit full force. She retched, spewing all over herself. And somehow, it lessened the agony.

I've got to get to Joel, was her first conscious thought. *Why did I wait? Now it's probably too late.*

But if she had to die, she wanted to be with them, with Sonia…and Joel…and all her friends.

Impossibly, the world stayed in focus. Carefully, Ziva rolled to her side, but things started spinning again. Resting her cheek on the cold granite floor, she waited, her breathing laboured, rasping.

Slowly, she began to drag her throbbing, useless body down the corridor. Inch by laborious inch, with only the use of her left arm, Ziva made it to the corner…and turned it. When the world went black around the edges, Ziva rested her cheek against the cold stone beneath her. As her vision clear, she began a mantra.

I must get to Joel! I must get to Joel!

And so it went: pull, pull, rest. Pull, pull…rest.

I must get to Joel! I must get to Joel!

It seemed like such a long way. She didn't remember she had gone this far.

How much further is it?

Ziva coughed achingly, tasted the metallic tang of blood.

Pull, rest. Cold stone a comfort.

If only she could stay where she was, with her cheek pressed against the floor.

She thought she heard Joel calling, encouraging: *Don't give up! Don't give up!*

A sobbing breath later, she found the doorway.

Where is Joel? Where are the bodies of the other women?

She couldn't see them.

I can't see!

And there it was, ever so faint...the scent of chilli.

Joel! I must get to Joel!

Ziva found his hand. She remembered...the touch of his skin had sent a tingle of energy between them.

He had been good to her...better than any human man ever was.

If I must die, Joel...I will die with you.

Ziva placed her head against his chest. With great effort, she pulled his arm over her. Then with all the energy left in her, she yearned to be a part of him.

And the rebellious, shattered spirit finally joined the fold. Ziva knew no more.

CHAPTER 46

Joel came alert with a gasp. His first thought was: Ziva came through!

He had known she would, and it humbled him yet again.

But when he recognized what lay in his arms, he cried out with the torment of reality.

So broken! She came with such difficulty. Just as stubborn as I am. We always have to do things the hard way.

Joel enclosed her body in strong arms and for long moments held her, as if he could shield and shelter take away what had happened. He moaned in despair; he wept. At last, he gently, lovingly eased her body to the floor beside him.

When he stood, he saw the crimson trail leading all the way out to the hall, looked down to find the front of his garment saturated in her blood. He cried out with a deep guttural, animal sound of anger, at the injustice done to her, while imagined images flashed though his mind.

Only a human could be capable of this cruelty! An 'Opposite' would have taken her body with him as food.

Sonia lying near the entrance, stirred. And somehow, at the last minute, Sky must have shifted, for now he lay next to his beloved. The Navajo reached for her hand, as he too awoke.

Joel stood numb, watching as the pair arose. Near by, Djura got to his feet. The security chief looked down at Karine, a worried expression on his face, then he made his way to the 'Leader Pair', abandoning his love, for duty.

Sonia noticed Ziva. "Oh, Joel! She came so hard...I am soo sorry."

The tears threatened, but stoically, Joel held them at bay. "Will you be able to fix her?" he pleaded brokenly. "Or is it too late?"

"We have greater strength now," his sister assured. "The band she wears holds her life essence. It is an excellent hope...that we have all awakened."

About them 'Aopato', both female and guardian, were rising. Each hopeful pair of male eyes sought his chosen. All had the same question in their thoughts:

Can the life force be retrieved? Or is it too late?

Sonia turned to the guardians, at once assuming the roll she was born to: the 'Leader Female' in command.

"Go," she ordered softly. "End the battle that rages outside. Send them all back where they came from, bodies included. One of the border 'Keepers' was destroyed; repair it."

The men appeared to hesitate, their delay bordering on disobedience. They each agonized over the fate of their chosen companion. But loyalty won out; they would trust the Lady.

"Leave your loved ones to us," Sonia reassured quietly. "Remove the 'Opposites' from our compound, so this can be done safely," she instructed. "And...allow no human record of what transpired here."

The mighty warriors vanished willingly, all save Sky and Joel.

"Go my brother," Sonia encouraged. "Your female has done honourably; she did not disgrace herself. She fought for us!"

Relief spread across the 'Pure' male's face. He sighed, then half smiled, content.

"Leave us now," his sister insisted. "Go do battle, while we fix this. You too Sky."

Sky lifted his eyebrow questioningly.

Sonia answered his unspoken question. "Things can be done differently now that we are stronger. Our females are complete. Your balance may be taken from a distance. Besides..." she added. "This should be in private...a womanly endeavour."

Sky chuckled. Then he and Joel disappeared together.

****

Sonia turned to her female relatives. Along the counter, lay the human women, still and seemingly lifeless.

"Form their bodies in a circle with Ziva in the middle."

The deceased appeared to glide across the marble floor of their own volition. They placed a human beside each 'Aopato' female, two on each side of Sonia: fourteen women in a circle with Ziva lying on her side in the very centre.

"Link hands with them."

As they obeyed, a band of light spread across and around the circle, bonding them all. The standing figures took on a glow, brightened rapidly, growing in intensity until the space around all the women exploded with a flash as bright as the sun.

Abruptly the light dimmed; the room returned to normal. And those conscious lowered their hands. Dropping easily in one fluid motion to their knees, the 'Aopato' sat back quietly, resting on their heels.

And they waited.

One by one, those beside them stirred. First May Lin, then Karine, and so on, in the order they had given of their essence, as if by age they were counting backwards. And each had been transformed: Carmen; Angel and Morgan; Chantel...and lastly, the two youngest, Jenna and Chrystal. They had become 'Aopato', invisible to the world, no longer evident to human eye; each younger by half, taller and incredibly beautiful: blonds and copper crowned; jet black and mocha brown, with skin so smooth it seemed it could melt, in tones and shades, ranging from delicate peach to silken caramel.

Sonia marvelled at the variety; her flower garden.

What a species we will be when they increase!

And Sonia waited, giving them all time to assimilate; to feel the union with the others, see the joint knowledge supplied.

To be one unit will take adjustment. They are no longer, nor ever will be, separate again.

Tears of wonder flooded the eyes of the new ones, as they realized their new potential, felt the combined love offered, knew the balance available.

As one they raised their arms to the Almighty Creator in praise, sighing at the pleasure of wholeness.

Still Sonia waited…for them to be ready.

She knew they needed more time before they experienced the unified healing force, but she could not afford to wait much longer. Death lingered too close. They needed to act!

One remained to restore. A task that would prove far more difficult.

At last, all female eyes turned toward her. Sonia gave the order.

"Now…Ziva!"

As one, in unity, they obeyed, circling the body in the middle, joining hands in resolve.

"Be prepared to experience severe discomfort; her injuries are mortal. And even though we are now many strong," Sonia warned the new ones. "Even though each will feel a mere fraction of the whole, it will seem excruciating for the first time. I will keep us balanced emotionally."

The room became a Nova once again, bursting forth in warming bright waves, washing over the lifeless form. As once more the space dimmed, each female was suffering, and healing back slowly. The figure at the centre was whole.

Some around the circle laboured to draw breath, while others panted with the agony of the internal abdominal wound. Another had the visibly shattered knee.

As the women took time to heal back they were encouraged, watching the one laying between them begin to transform. Truly 'Aopato' in every way, Ziva was a beauty beyond compare: raven dark hair, olive tanned skin, sweeping long lashes and full crimson lips. Younger and taller, she was over seven feet tall, stretching supple limbs as if asleep.

Joel will absolutely adore you! Sonia marvelled.

The new creature lay, breast rising and falling evenly. The bloody trail leading across the floor to the doorway, that announced her desperate struggle, vanished. Replacing the crimson, blood saturated garments Ziva wore, Sonia gave her clean cream-coloured silk, the skirts flowing around her sleeping form.

She shifted, awakening gradually; raised her hand to her temple, and sighed a deep blissful groan.

"Do not move quite yet, Ziva," Sonia cautioned. "The others have not fully recovered."

The eyes that opened, and looked her way were unusual, different from any recent 'Aopato' to date. They were brown with a vertical slit of silver.

A paired warrior female! She's perfect for Joel!

Tears formed in the distinctive eyes.

"I'm soo sorry," Ziva regretfully moaned. "I've been so…self-willed."

Sonia chuckled. "We are in need of those with fortitude," she admitted acceptingly. "The ones who challenge the entrenched, inflexible habits of others are a necessity for growth. It will teach us all not to be so hasty…dragging heels keep out feet to the right path."

The 'Leader Female' gazed about her. All were relaxed now, eased of their pain.

"Is everyone normal again?"

They answered in one voice. "We are complete."

Ziva sat up.

Suddenly Karine was beside her, enfolding her in a affable embrace. "Welcome, sister," she proclaimed for all.

Morgan came from the opposite side. "Forgive me for being so hard on you. I am sorry I ever doubted you. I was…only human."

Sonia laughed with the others. *How easy to see now.*

"There's no need for forgiveness," Ziva objected to Morgan. "I was the stubborn …inflexible one. So stupid! I can't imagine now, why I was so fearful. Sonia does make all the difference; she balances everything."

"Not everything," Sonia disagreed. "The unknowns are maintained by the Almighty Creator."

CHAPTER 47

The 'Leader Female' had ordered them to 'Go to battle', but the guardians knew she had not meant for them to litterly fight. What she required of them was to secure Sanctuary, and make all within the enclosure right again.

Not many 'Opposites' had survived. Those they had saved were instantly returned to the nearby farmyard that was their base, just outside the barrier boundary. Their memories had been adjusted, and they no longer had knowledge of the hide-away behind the barrier.

As well, very few human soldiers remained alive, but the ones the guardians encountered were healed, and then teleported immediately to the nearest army base camp. They also would have no memory of the incident.

It was amusing to consider their superiors puzzling over the mystery, wondering what had become of the other men sent off on a mission cloaked in secrecy, of which there now seemed no reason nor record. The 'Aopato' males had by mere thought and will expertly destroyed any written or recorded data of the valley or the species that peopled it. Even the 'Opposite' base had been erased from memory and record, but if those beings continued as before, the humans would soon once again discover they were out there.

As of now, Sanctuary was hidden, quiet at last, the valley serene…and the outer barrier back up and sentry patrolled.

In a group, the weary warriors jumped to the lunchroom, wondering: *Have the females been successful? Sonia had hidden the results from them.*

The males were still all living, but did that mean their human females had been revived? And if not, how many had been saved?

Joel wondered: *Do I have a pair? Or is our species still hanging balanced over a precipice?*

When they materialized, the brightness behind his six female relatives concealed from all males what lay beyond.

And to add to their apprehension, Sonia was extraordinarily secretive. "Sit down," she ordered. "Each male separate."

Every individual heart beating in a guardian's breast picked up rapidly with alarm. Each anticipated the worst.

Was this good or bad news?

"None of us have had our lunch," Sonia stated matter-of-factly. "We will serve you."

The sigh of relief escaped as if the males were one being.

****

Sonia moved aside.

May Lin stepped out from behind her, and Chi's eyes lit with pleasure. Though much smaller than he, she would fit just nicely beneath his arm. Lithe and well formed, shrouded in a white cotton shapeless dress, she walked with the same carefully measured steps as always. Younger, about forty, her eyes down caste in submission, the jet-black braid swaying with her movement, oriental heredity

431

evident in the features, his bride carried a platter of his choice favourites.

Chi's stoic demeanour near gave way. He was exceedingly enamoured by this beauty. As May Lin reach his table, he rose to honour her.

"I will not partake alone," he declared, testing her.

Without missing a beat, nor giving a word of objection, she offered him the plate, permitted him to move out her chair, and sat opposite. A second platter appeared at her setting.

Chi hurriedly sat also.

Life, in his opinion, had just been perfected.

****

Contentious Djura had refused to be seated; his image before others more important, a mate was secondary. He stood resolutely beside his table.

But when he saw Karine, all thoughts of duty fled. There was no disguising the satisfaction in his eyes; it infected the rest of his features until his face bloomed. The gigantic security chief stood there grinning like a mesmerized teenager.

His chosen female had decreased in age to just under forty. Her feet now seemed tiny, the full-figured form slimed, because she had gained near two feet in height. Her hair flowed across her shoulders and down her back to her hips, golden-auburn waves curling at the ends, fanning out like a cape.

But it was her eyes that held him, swallowing him whole, their green velvet depth arresting all thoughts of the food she carried.

He no longer cared that her head was uncovered, nor that the dress accentuated her curves. Let the other guardians notice. He had the most beautiful female ever known, and he wished the universe to know it.

Somewhere, through all that had happened, he had lost his stringent ideas. His desire was for her alone, to be alone with her.

I will run my hands through your sunshine tresses, he thought boldly. *And pleasure you as never before. You are mine...forever!*

Karine blushed to the roots of her hair.

And Djura laughed aloud, amused by her embarrassment. She raised her arms, and fled to him. Somehow, in the time it took to step to him, the plate of food had vanished. Both forgot there were others in the room.

The pair disappeared...perhaps planning to eat in the gardens?

Sonia chuckled. *Such a duty bounded male...wrapped around the tiny finger of a female.*

Nothing could please her more.

****

Unable to be patient any longer, Carmen and Angel came at the same time.

Angel: fair, blue eyed, short-bodied and no taller than six feet, but then, she was only twenty-eight now. To Eric she was just perfect; he was shorter than most 'Aopato' males. They would fit just right together as a couple.

Carmen had short brown hair that curled around her face like a cap, blue eyes, delicate features and figure, and had become thirty once more. Marcel knew from that moment, she would always be the love of his life.

****

Next Morgan and Chantel put in an appearance. To Zane, Chantel had been perfect from the moment Jade had healed her, but now she was more his age and size, twenty-five and at least six foot four.

Lance would have taken Morgan however she came. She was still on the chunky side, ample where it counted, just the way he liked her. A foot taller now, she was younger by half, an even twenty-seven.

****

Jenna and Chrystal giggled openly when they were presented, each holding the favoured dessert of the teenage grandson of choice. All past sins were forgotten; all judgements and failings erased; punishments rescinded, in view of what had just transpired.

Though by 'Aopato' standards they were considered young, the pairing was complete been these four, and none could, nor would, reverse it. Beyond doubt, thirteen year old Jenna belonged to fourteen year old Tyler; and Chrystal, though only twelve, would always be for thirteen year old Shawn.

Let no one dispute it! After all, they had all lived the equivalent of older…in human.

****

With some trepidation Joel had waited and watched as each female was presented. Now, it was his turn; only Ziva remained hidden.

He stood to his feet, holding his breath in anticipation.

The Jewish woman appeared, stepping from a rainbow of bright light. Sonia had dressed her as a bride, the flowing skirt floor length, fluid in motion as she walked toward him. From beneath the garment peeked perfectly formed toes; they were naked.

His breath caught in his throat; his belly ignited at the sight of her: over seven feet tall, a powerful, muscular Amazon, a Warrior Female!

Such a one had not been seen since the days of the first 'Pures'. She was 'Pure'! Sonia had given her not merely half, but 'Pure' blood.

How did she accomplish that?

The raven dark hair; the olive skin; the sweeping lashes, and full lips, these came from human heritage. But the brown, silver slit eyes were pure 'Aopato'.

Joel stood spellbound, rooted to the spot, doubting reality. Humbly he thought: *I am unworthy.*

Ziva reached him…and, she was incredibly, undeniably real.

****

"Well, my love," Sky said at Sonia's side. "With all that work, you must be hungry. Shall we have lunch?"

Sonia sighed blissfully. "Oh, Sky. After the look on my brother's face, I doubt I will ever need nourishment again. I think, at last, he will be happy."

"Feels good, doesn't it?" he agreed. "Was it your idea to make her 'Pure'?"

Sonia chuckled. "Now why would I do that? It gives him exclusively, the 'pure' bloodline. I never even considered that it might happen. No, that was an accidental bonus provided by the Almighty Creator. It seems we must be tested continually."

"Makes you wonder what next is in store for us?" Sky mused. "Our Almighty One does have a sense of humour. Perhaps, because so many have difficulty believing in Its existence, every so often, It needs to show us who is really in command."

EPILOGUE:

The number in the cluster of light trails was larger this time, thirty strong, as they fled Earth's atmosphere.

"Well," Kara commented as they streaked away. "That was an educating place to visit, but I certainly wouldn't want to remain surface-bound there for my life time. It would be like living in hell."

Beside the young girl, Chrystal chuckled. "True. Life there is not always pleasant; they are forever experiencing trials. But that is how they mature…the hard way. I am glad to be non-human. Our new world will be better…right?"

"It is as dissimilar as darkness and sunlight. These exist in a sorrow land…our world is peaceful, exquisite, and secure. There we have no predators."

****

On the planet below, one lone 'Opposite' watched a monitor. He saw the meteorite-like trails above, but was not deceived. He knew exactly what they were.

Night now, was Yt's most favourite shift, for he could search and ponder many thingts, when left alone like this in the observation tower of the old barn.

Why should I call Superior? The others will only make fun…no matter what I do.ter

His comrades had called him coward, said if it had been them, they would have quickly snuffed out the essence of the purple-eyed monster. Then there

437

would no longer exist two kinds…only the reptilian conquers. And they would rule the universe!

But the boy knew something they did not. The one he had encountered was not vengeful; she would harm no one. And her kind would win out in the end…because they were benevolent.

He wondered why the 'better ones' took off for space? Why they abandoned the fight?

With all his heart he longed to follow them. *Maybe I could find peace with them?*

Morning was suddenly there. The screen was blank again. His relief came to take his place.

But Yt told him nothing of what he had seen.

###

About the Author:

Margaret Afseth, a Canadian novelist, lives in Saskatoon, Saskatchewan. She is a widow with four grown children, and five grandchildren

An avid reader and clandestine writer since her late teens, she only recently stepped to the publishing stage. Though she has training in both art and as a freelance writer, she is self-taught, her expertise gained mostly from observation and life experience.

From an error in judgement early on, she learned a hard lesson. A narrow-minded counsellor burned the only copy of her first novel. Perhaps this man did Margaret a service, as when one of the manuscripts destroyed was later rewritten, a single novel became the trilogy she now offers for your enjoyment.

Discover other titles by Margaret Afseth at
Amazon.com
Aopato
Turn Back

If you enjoyed this book here is a sample of the third in the series:
Turn Back
By Margaret Afseth

Prologue:

Like naughty children, they were playing just beyond the edge of the protective planetary barrier out in outer space. As a guardian, he should have known better, but she was so delightful, and he so enamoured watching her play like a sunbeam against the obsidian backdrop, he had allowed her to move farther and farther away from safety, not realizing the distance.

And then, it was too late.

He did not even sense the diminutive four-passenger space vehicle. That region of space had been unoccupied by others for so long, he had become too confident, lax.

She saw it first, attempting a rapid shape-correction, but the transport beam caught her mid-change. She vanished so abruptly it took him a moment to realize what had just happened. In that instance of hesitation, he also was caught in a similar ray, and transported to the small craft. Unlike her, he had no time for a form change, though for him that mattered little. He was but a warrior, and a male.

The energy drain of the transport beam was not enough to kill him, but was sufficient in strength to render him powerless and senseless. When he awoke, they had separated them.

****

The guardian male struggled valiantly against the chains. The others planned to keep him alive for sport, but Yt found their pleasure at taunting and torment revolting. The 'Better One' was much younger than past captives, and this one was half human, or the drain ray would have killed him right off. Redro and Wollof liked nothing better than to toy with humankind.

The laser-like weapon of Redro's glove spat a red-hot beam at the victim, cutting a second deeper, hideous slash where an old one was still raw and festering.

Yt hissed in sympathy, and turned away.

"Leaving so soon?" laughed Wollof. "He'll need your tending when we're done."

"You can call me when he is no longer conscious. I am bored, and have better things to do."

"What's better than torturing a half-one?"

"The animals need to be let out to pasture…"

"Go then, enjoy your menial labour." Redro sent another hot missive toward the helpless prisoner.

****

Something furry crawled beneath her to hide.

She was lying on bare boards covered in dirty straw in what smelled like a cattle shed. The ammonia odour of urine, and the pungent stench of manure caused her eyes to water even while still closed. The lids seemed frozen, or at the very least glued shut by dried sleep goober. Though she made a tremendous effort, she could not open them.

Someone is standing nearby.

She heard the wooden bar gate slid across the front of the stall; laboured rasping breathing, as if through a facemask or someone blowing through a metal pipe.

What is that?

She remained motionless, feigning unconsciousness.

A claw-like hand passed beneath her body, moving the sack dress slightly. Something small, quick, and warm squeaked when caught. And she knew the rodent was gone.

"What are you doing in the prisoner's cell, Wollof?"

"My lunch got away from me," the creature near her responded in annoyance. "I'm hungry! Couldn't let it get away, could I? So I chased it in here. Never meant to go near the female...just after my lunch!"

Redro laughed derisively. "Well, it's not like you could have her in that condition anyway. Silly thing is caught half dormant; neither human nor Light being."

"What do you mean?" Wollof asked, approaching the door.

"Don't you see how she looks human? We know she's Light; we caught her. She was trying to disguise when we hit her with the transfer beam. Look at her eyes."

"They're half closed. I can't see them."

"Exactly. Her eyes are blue with no slit. I checked when we brought her back. What I don't get is why this one and the warrior were so far out in space when their base is somewhere here beside our installation."

"They are both very young; suppose they were playing out there? I didn't know they had them that immature."

"The male is an adolescent, but yes, the female is definitely below puberty. Puzzling. That's probably why she made such a mess of going dormant."

Redro laughed mockingly. "Can't be as old as Yt, and you know what he's like. Stupid; slow."

"So, what's wrong with her eyes?"

"Must have figured if she changed her eyes we wouldn't know what she was. Made herself blind in the process."

Wollof hissed with excitement. "Let me be the first to have a go at her. If she can't see me coming…"

"Better not. She may be dormant, but I hear, when awake if they sense you, they have this painful reflex that shocks the hell out of you."

"Did she shock you when you looked at her eyes?"

"She was out cold, and drained of her energy…"

The voices drifted away as they moved off. But they had forgotten to close the barrier slider, and her prison was left open.

Yet, she could still feel another nearby.

Why is it hiding?

****

Yt stepped from concealment when he was certain the other two had gone. They had left the gate to the cell unlocked, open wide. If he took her away at this moment, they would think she had escaped on her own. But they believed her too injured to get far, and he knew that was indeed the case.

Where can I take her?

Maybe humans might help?

He bent, lifted her, throwing her across one shoulder, then pressed the teleport button on his belt. An instant later he materialized in the shadow of a hospital. A man was just exiting the doors at the lighted front of the building.

I cannot stay to make sure she is cared for.

Yt dropped the female, pressed his belt again, and vanished.

****

Redro was growling angrily when Yt appeared back at the stall.

"Where'd you hide it?" he hissed venomously. "Tell me! Or I'll make you pay!"

"I put her where the humans will take care of her…"

"You stupid imbecile!" snarled Redro. "We can't go into their units. We can't get her back now! Your infantile behaviour needs correction! Don't you understand yet, we inflict, not mend? You act like one of the arrogant 'Better Ones'. Are you Healer like they, that you bleed for their offspring?" He dug his claw mercilessly into Yt's shoulder, and hissed. "You'll come with me now to the torture platform where I will teach you the meaning of cruelty; what is expected of you."

Dragging the young male by his arm, Redro stormed from the stables, not stopping until he reached the captive boy warrior.

"Now!" thundered the superior. "You will torture this one until he shrieks for mercy; till you hear his squeals in your head!"

"Master, please, I'll do anything else…"

"You will not! Idiot newborn!" Redro was so livid spittle flew as he yelled. He picked up the glove weapon on a nearby table, and viciously tossed it to Yt. "Coward! Weakling! Slacker! Put that on! I will stand here to watch you. Make him scream!"

****

An hour later the 'Better One' boy hung from the wall, sagging in the shackles. He was covered in angry open gashes, raw and bleeding; his eyes were swollen shut, blood seeping from beneath the edges of the lashes that swept his cheeks. He appeared not as a living male, but as a hammered meat carcass.

Yet, he had uttered not a sound through it all, never cried out in mind or verbally.

Yt abhorred what he had done; loathed Redro for forcing his hand. He felt like an animal; wanted somewhere to scream and lash out at his world. For that matter, he'd like to take on anyone who might challenge him, or get in his way.

Redro laughed, elated. "Now you get it! Doesn't it bring the pleasure? Makes the ire come to the surface; gets the blood boiling so you make a good predator. You'll learn yet!"

Yt hissed, and spat at him. Redro raised his fist and struck the younger male across the face. Yt staggered back.

"Let the anger come," Redro encouraged. "Then you will finally be one of us!"

Wollof came from behind and cuffed him across the back of the head, adding his form of challenge, as well. A sense of a presence watching made Yt turn toward the prisoner.

The boy had regained consciousness. His eyes half open, he watched Yt's humiliation. Yet, what was mirrored there was not condemnation nor agreement, but sympathy. It was as if, though one was chained and the other not, they were comrades, prisoners each, in a different form.

Yt heard the words inside his head: Don't let them win. You are better than that.

As if the effort to project the thought had drained him of what little energy he had left, the guardian boy went limp.

Yt shivered visibly, grappling for control over the negative emotions, as if the encouragement of his victim meant more than life itself. The effort made him gag. Then as he righted in his own mind, the stench of blood and the appalling sight of what he had done made him retch, spewing all over Wollof.

Shame shot to the surface within Yt. Wollof cursed. Redro laughed.

"Sissy!" he hissed. "Worthless Healer!"

Yt turned and fled.

Wollof made to pursue, but Redro held him fast.

"Let him go," he decided. "He's nothing but a half-wit; useless to us. Out there, he'll go dormant; I've seen it happen with others. They can't rationalize how they were born, so they revert back to the in-between. He won't last long among humans. They will teach him the same as we, to be violent just like us."

****

Yt took flight, running with all his might, fleeing from the barn, down the long driveway between arching trees on either side. He reached the railed double gate at the end of the roadway, pushed it open, and plunged headlong into a field of corn; running, running until he reached the pasture, then through it; never stopping, always fleeing, as if somehow he could escape reality. When he felt he was far enough away, was certain they had not followed, he hit the teleport button on his belt, thinking wildly of the big city where he'd left the unfortunate female.

But nothing happened. They had already rendered the instrument inoperable.

He wrenched it angrily from his waist, tossed it fiercely to one side, and took off running again, toward the distant mountains, and the city that lay beyond them.

Yt would rather be anywhere else than where he had been born.

When he was too exhausted to proceed, he stopped to catch his breath.

Somewhere around here is the Healer base. But...probably they will not even let me inside. And...they are likely not even here.

He felt utterly hopeless. Despaired.

My only other recourse is the humans.

But, if they saw him, his life would be nothing. They would end it.

There is nowhere to go. I am not going back! I'm not!

I wish I could be dormant; in the in-between state they would think me human. But...I don't know how...I don't know how...to become human-like.

Having rested enough to have his second wind, he turned toward the nearby highway, took off at a walk, going parallel to it.

His longing to be different was so strong in his spirit he could near taste it.

When a beat up pickup truck came over a rise, he quickly hid in the ditch. The old farmer pulled to a stop almost even with Yt, and his heart pounded in his throat, but the old man merely needed to relieve himself. When he got out to take care of nature, Yt climbed into the back and hid among the straw bales.

In the night, the boy awoke feeling cold. He tried to burrow deeper into the straw, but found his claws were now hands, the scales had become smooth skin, and the reason he was freezing was that he was naked. Yt shivered, realizing he had become an in-between.

****

The emergency room was crowded, the staff rushed. When the young girl was rolled in, the attending physician merely made a cursory evaluation. He quickly noted the child was blind.

Her breathing seemed normal; pulse rate a bit fast, but there was no obvious reason for her to be unconscious.

Probably faking it. She's most likely a street imp wanting a bed.

As he listened to the heartbeat, it abruptly arrested.

"Heart's stopped!" he yelled. "Crash cart!"

The white sack dress was brutally ripped away, exposing a budding adolescent beneath. A cart rolled to position; the paddles trust into his hands.

"Charge!" he ordered frantically.

The machine whined, quickly rising to peak.

"Clear!"

One second the young girl lay still as death; next her body jerked violently with the impact from the electrical charge.

He looked away to the monitor for only a moment, then back again, ready to order the renewal of the charge.

But the child had vanished from the gurney.

****

She had purposely tricked him, deafened him to the heart sounds, just long enough to fool him into reacting. The energy was sufficient to enable her to teleport.

But…it was not enough to get her home.

Result: destination unknown.

And with the artificial energy jolt…memories of the life she once had, vanished as completely as she did.

TO CONTINUE READING PLEASE GO TO AMAZON.COM TO PURCHAR

www.ingramcontent.com/pod-product-compliance
Lightning Source LLC
Chambersburg PA
CBHW021244050726
47498CB00003BB/696